MW01451853

Mike Black

The Merry Pranksters

Normal is an illusion. What is normal to the spider is chaos to the fly.

-Morticia Addams

Chapter I

It's impossible to say with any shred of certainty, but it can't be that much past midnight. I'm ambling around this deserted, pathetic shell of a gravel road in East St. Louis with burnt ashes fluttering around like dejected snowflakes. The air is thick with a summer's worth of humidity festering around idly and threatening to unload a biblical downpour of infested rain at any moment, flooding all that has built up and washing away any trace of existence. I pause, take three steps off the industrial soot covered road to a small patch off to the side where the weeds have even ceased growing, kick a rusted Colt 45 tall boy out of the way with the toe of my brown leather flip-flops and carefully set down the Macho Mug I just stole from the strip club on to the dark grey, cracked dirt. Warrant's *Cherry Pie* is still banging around in my head with no real way of escaping.

I stand up straight, crack my neck and, taking a glance around, notice the sign that reads in bright neon yellow: *Cheeks* with a hot pink arrow pointing to an ominous two-story brick building. Silhouettes of dilapidated factories with broken windows, cracked foundations and rusting steel paint a bleak landscape on the dark horizon. Closer in peripheral are unseasonably dressed crackheads sharing glass pipes and malt liquor bottles and hookers with half of their teeth and even less of their Lee Press-On nails. *The Devil's playground* is spray painted in blood red letters across an enflamed dumpster.

I pull a pack of Marlboro Reds out of my faded Levi jeans pocket and light one with a white Bic lighter, hoping I'm not sending some unknown signal to the homeless community around me. I inhale, put the pack of cigarettes back in my pocket, pull my dirty blonde hair back off my face with my hand then take the cigarette out of my mouth and exhale up into the heavens. Looking up to the vast, angelic expanse I notice that the night sky is crisp and as clear as an opal. The moon is high and winking suggestively at me.

I pivot around when I hear a car approaching. The headlights of my 1995, pearl white Cadillac DeVille are shining bright spotlights, slashing through the darkness, the tires are kicking up massive dirt clouds before skidding to a stop right before my feet. I cover the top of my Macho Mug with my left hand and let the storm of sawdust filled, malignant air blow past. As the dust settles, my Caddy idling before me, I take a double gulp of beer and a drag off my smoke before curiously squinting at a spec of mud on the silver hood ornament. I pause, take the hem of my black Danzig T-shirt and wipe it off before stepping around to the passenger's side of the car and pulling on the handle. It's locked.

The tinted window rolls down with a snore and Curt leans over on my elbow rest from the driver's seat and laughs, "You need a ride, Pone?"

I reach in and open the door from the inside, sabotaging the game of cat and mouse that losers like to play when they're driving your car. I sit down in my passenger side's plush, beige leather seat and give my car a quick inspection as Curt peels off again down the dusty gravel path. I eject Sublime's *40 oz to Freedom* CD that Curt has replaced my *Vulgar Display of Power* CD with and toss it out the still opened window as we speed down the road, away from Cheeks and all the rest of the strip clubs on the East side.

"What the heck took you so long?" I ask, looking around the car for my CD case.

"Dude, you're fuckin' lucky I don't make you get out and go find that." Curt says sternly, ignoring my question. Without looking over at me he tosses the CD case on my lap.

"Is there an age?" I ask, dismissing his threat, fanning myself from the oppressive August heat with my hand as I turn the Caddy's AC up to full blast.

"An age for…" He starts fiercely, then gaining some composure, asks, "An age for what, Schultz?" He glances over at me briefly, then back on the road.

"Oh, I don't know Dog, maybe an age in which you see yourself, us really, just a little bit too old for this whole charade?" I ask, flipping through the CD case.

"Oh, come on Dude, we haven't gotten kicked out of Cheeks in like…at least a year." He laughs.

"*We* didn't get kicked out of Cheeks." I start. "*We* have never gotten kicked out of Cheeks. *You* however have gotten kicked out so many times I'm surprised they don't have your picture on the wall with a big red X through it."

"Well those bitches are nothin' but little fuckin' cock teases, Dude." He laughs, "You should have heard that bitch…"

"I know, I know." I say, cutting him off. "Let me guess, she told you she wanted to suck on your dick, she was sticking her pone in your face and rubbing her tits all over your balls… Am I in the ballpark?" I ask still flipping through my wide verity of CDs. "2Pac's *All Eyez on Me*? No." I'm mumbling to myself. "*The White Album*? No…"

We pull off the gravel road and onto a paved one with lines and everything that leads us to highway 70 West, into downtown St. Louis. I decide on Cake's *Fashion Nugget* CD and turn the volume up.

"Well you're always just sitting at the bar." He shouts over the music. "Why don't you ever sit where the strippers are, ya fag?" He asks, grabbing his *Ride the Lightning* concert Tee from behind the collar and pulling it off over his freshly shaven head. He's wearing torn blue jeans, black leather, steel-toed boots and of course, his signature one-armed shades even though it's pitch black out.

"Hey man, true pimp niggas spend no dough on the booty." I say, flicking my cigarette out the window and pushing the button to roll it up.

"Whatever Homie." He says trying to throw up a gang sign, failing.

"Dude, I've said this a thousand times, strip clubs are the worst place to hook up with chicks. The last thing those girls wanna do is mess around with customers." I explain.

"Why?" He scoffs, though I'm sure I've broken this down for him at least a baker's dozen times.

"They think all the guys who come in those places are total losers." I say taking a hit off of my newest Macho Mug. "Unless you've got mountains of blow or you're the fricking Sultan of Brunei or something, chances are you're going home and beating off."

"You used to bang a stripper." He argues. Then, grabbing at my Macho Mug, "Let me hit that."

"Yeah, and I didn't meet her at a strip club." I say, carefully passing him my beer. "I met her at Cooper's. She was there with some nerd who she met at work and when she met me, she ditched him like a crack-whore ditches a baby."

"She was fucking smoking hot." He says, laughing. "What ever happened to her?"

"She was way fricking ate up, Dude." I say, "Strippers are strippers for a reason. The whole myth of the *honest stripper*, putting herself through med school or whatever is total bullcrap."

"Yeah, but she was hot." He reminds me unnecessarily, doing a real number on my Macho Mug.

"Yes Curtis, she was hot." I say, snapping at him to pass my beer back immediately. "It didn't take hooking up with her to realize how lame strip clubs are though. I've never understood why chicks don't want their boyfriends or whatever to go to strip clubs. They're like the safest place for a dude to go."

"Well obviously they don't want their man having some hot, young stripper rub her tits in his face all night and spending a shitload of money." He says, thinking he's made a valid point.

We're on the highway now, the city lights shining on the St. Louis Arch twinkle from where we are. The Poplar Street Bridge, crossing the Mississippi River from East St. Louis into the Lou should be right around the bend up here. The air gets cleaner the farther we get from the East side. I roll the window back down and let the humidity from the river's air mix with the AC of the Caddy and let the two forces wrestle around with each other.

"The spending a shit…*a crap* load of money is the only rational part of that equation." I say, looking out the window, letting the moist air blow in my face. I'm starting to drift off. "Any dude has a much better chance of actually cheating on his chick at any local dive bar than he ever

would traveling all the way to East St. Louis and going to a strip club." Then add, "That's a statistically proven fact."

"Well most people don't think as rationally as you do Schultz." Curt reminds me for the seventh time today.

"So you've said." I say, then admit, "I've never been able to understand that."

As we cross the bridge over the Mississippi River, I look down at it, completely zoned out at this point. The water's rough, sharp waves contrasting with long, smooth patches send my mind into a tailspin. Warped back in time, I'm sitting backwards in my mom's old station wagon, staring at the river for as long as I could until the city swallowed every last drop. I thought it was majestic, a beautifully crafted paradox of where we were, where we are and where we are headed. I didn't need to know why some parts were white with choppy rapids and then it would smooth out and look like a mirror. I get it now, still water runs deep. What I can't stop going back and forth about now is, whether that adds to or takes away from the beauty and awe of the Mighty Mississippi.

We're passing over the river from the Illinois side to the Missouri side rapidly but whenever I zone out, time seems to move in slow motion if not stopping all together. At some point I look down and can see the reflection of the St. Louis Arch in the water's vastness. I look at the riverfront on the Missouri side and all the steamboats that are a throwback to the old days when St. Louis was the gateway to the wild west. The last stop that the brave settlers made before taking one of a few trails off to settle the American frontier.

"Did you ever hear about the big fire of 1849?" I ask, snapping out of my daze momentarily, still idly gazing out the window as we drive over the river.

"Wasn't that in Chicago?" Curt asks, rubbing his tattoo covered pecs.

"There was that, but that was like 30 years later." I say, re-engaging. "But up until 1849, the biggest fire in American history was the *St. Louis* fire."

"No shit. I didn't know that." Curt says, giving me a dismissive *I'm driving* tone.

"Can you imagine what this town was like back then?" I ask, mostly to myself.

"Pretty fucking moin." I think I hear him say distantly.

"Well no kidding, Man, think about it." I say. I light another cigarette but just let it burn. "Right here, where we are right now was the frickin' hub of, not the world, there was other stuff going on, but it was blowing up here like never before. Think about that year, 1849. The 49ers, right? That was the year of the California gold rush, that's why the San Francisco 49ers are named that right?"

"Yeah, I fucking got that." He says sarcastically without looking over.

"Well by that time, the East coast was pretty settled. I don't know how many states were states then or how many were still territories, but we had done the Louisiana Purchase from, I think France and the U.S. government was in charge of everything west of the Mississippi up to like, the Rocky Mountains."

I take the last gulp off of my Macho Mug and, without looking over, Curt, reading my mind and disregarding his anger management coping mechanisms shouts, "Schultz, don't you fucking dare throw that Macho Mug out the window!" Pause. "Dude…" He's counting backwards from 10 out loud now before calmly stating, "Schultz, I will fucking sket you with my thumbs if you throw another Macho Mug out the window."

There's a pause. I let an audible sigh escape and toss the Macho Mug in the general direction of the backseat. Another pause. I think of something profound then quickly forget what it was. Annoyed, I reach behind the seat and fish through a red, Colman's cooler and pull out two Budweiser cans. I toss one on Curt's lap. He swerves, shouts obscenities, regains composure of the car and his one-armed shades and drives on.

After sucking the foam from the can I continue. "So anyway, then gold gets discovered in some far-off land that Mexico owned, California, right? Way over the Rocky's, and people were like, "Eff it, let's go get rich!"

"Yeah, that's pretty hard core." Curt says, opening his Budweiser can with one hand.

"Yeah, well those people had rambling in their genes, Dog. I mean, they left Europe for one reason or another, sailed across the Atlantic fricking ocean in wooden ships with a, I don't know, maybe a 50/50 chance of making it across alive. Then one or two generations later, they're like, "Hey, this place is cool, but I hear the grass is even greener on the other side of those mountains. Who's with me?"

"Motherfuckers were tough back then." Curt says, packing a one hit from a wooden dugout with a scull engraved in it.

"Right? Well, you know, we all played The Oregon Trail back in elementary school, right? Where did they start out at? Fricking St. Louis, Man. That's why they call the Arch the 'Gateway Arch', it was the gateway to the wild west, Man. You had to stop here to stock up on everything you were going to need to make it the whole rest of the way out there; new horses, clothes, food, fricking wagon wheels, whatever man. This was basically the last gas station until you got over the Rocky Mountains."

"Alright, so the place was booming." He says, holding in the one-hit.

"Yeah, the place was booming. That's literally what they called them, *Boom Towns*, only St. Louis was like the king of the Boom Towns. These cats came from Europe, left everything they knew, they risked death, complete chaos man. They risked everything to come to the new world. Then they got established, fought a fricking revolution against the greatest empire the world had ever known to gain their sovereignty…"

"Hold up Schultz, isn't sovereignty just like, a code word for freedom?" He asks, passing me the dugout full of decent weed.

"No, not really." I say, packing myself a onie. "I mean, Britain had freedom. A lot of places had *freedom,* I mean, it depends on what you mean by freedom. What we fought for was *sovereignty,* like from Britain and like, from the state to the people. Ya' know, We the *People*, replaced, We the *State*. That's what sets our revolution apart from other revolutions.

"Like what other revolutions." He asks curiously, not a dusting of aggression.

"Like, oh, say France's revolution. That wasn't really about freedom, it was more about the government giving the people more crap. That's what France has always been about." I'm explaining, lighting the metal one-hitter. "In our revolution we wanted the government out of our lives. France has always wanted the government to be *more* involved in their lives. The shepherd becomes the wolf, ya know. They *love* them some government, that's one of the reasons we never really see eye to eye. Anyway, those settlers, Man, they were no stranger to ramblin'. Chaos was in their DNA, it's in our DNA."

There's a pause, a moment of reflection.

"Anyway," I say, shaking off that rabbit hole. "St. Louis was doing pretty well. It was established and the people here were just starting to get settled, finally getting some roads paved, planting some crops, laying down some roots, you know, starting fire departments and stuff."

"Yeah, so…" Curt says, taking the dug-out from me and snapping for another Budweiser.

"So…" I continue, "everything was going fine until one night, *one* little steamboat caught on fire. The fire burned the rope tying it to the dock, so it started floating down the river catching *all* the boats on fire along the way. Before they knew it, the fire jumped onto the landing, right here, right where we are right now, and it started catching all the buildings on fire. The flippin' fire burnt everything from Olive Street Rd. all the way down to Market Street. It was the worst fire in St. Louis history. And another little fact, it was the first time a fire fighter died in the line of duty in the whole country."

"No shit?" Curt asks, holding in a hit.

"No crap, Dude." I assure him. "Everyone had to start all over, from scratch. They had to redo everything. After the fire, that's when we started using bricks and stones to build with. That's when we started the water system and sewage system that we have. We still use that stuff today. If not for that fire, we'd still be living in straw huts and crapping in outhouses."

"So, it was good that there was this huge fuckin' fire that killed a firefighter?" Curt asks, a whiff of aggression is sparked.

"You could look at it like that I guess." I say softly, gazing out the window. The hum of the freeway and the reflective decals that are evenly spaced on the median start to hypnotize me again. Although I'm somewhat mesmerized by them, I can feel an ebb and flow of panic in my stomach with each passing. Though I can rationalize that the decals are evenly spaced along the median, somewhere in my subconscious mind I fear that the Caddy won't fit in between the markers as we speed past them.

"Change is painful." I whisper, letting each syllable fog the window.

When the low humming of Curt's voice first becomes vaguely audible, like an alarm clock weaving itself into a dream before finally breaking a blissful stream of Zen into the cruel reality that pillages the imagination, it's crudeness jettisoning any sense of nirvana you were within a winter's breath away from. His rantings about some unknown threat that I know nothing about, want nothing to do with, it takes much more than a polite, *Ahem* to break my gaze.

But like that stubborn alarm clock, like that of the annoying buzz of a protruding tattoo gun that stretches and pulls at the most vulnerable and transparent parts of your flesh, it gets the better of you in the end. It simply wears you down, breaks you, until your will to stay tuned out, the intoxication of the unconscious folds to cruel reality.

"Dude, *Dude!* Do you fucking hear me?" Curt is shouting as we pass Grand Blvd.

"What? What the freak, Man?" I ask, shaking my head in disbelief that we're suddenly all the way to Delmar Rd., wondering how much time I've lost.

"Dude, I'm trying to tell you, those bitches are fucking nuts." He says for the… I don't know how many times, the first, maybe fifth time today, talking about some *bitches*.

Confused, I turn down the *Cake* CD a little. *Sad Songs and Waltzes* is playing, then I take the cell phone out of my pocket and check it for any missed calls or messages. My heart skips a beat when I see that there is one new message from Valerie.

Hi Baby,
What R U doing tonight? I wanna C U!
-Val
xoxo

I read it two more times, flip the phone closed and shove it deep into my pocket. My brain is racing.

Pause.

"What bitches?" I finally get around to asking. "Are we still talking about the strippers? I think I went to school with one of those girls."

I turn down the Cake in the CD player all the way to zero, smell my fingers, look at the Slimey's Auto Sales that ripped me off on a car once, not the Caddy, I got a great deal on the Caddy, but a crappy Ford Tempo I had in high school that Slimey pulled a bait and switch on me before I knew what a bait and switch was. I give them the finger. "Mother Effers." I say, "He can go and suck..." There's a brief pause, I need to choose my words carefully. "on my knob."

Curt snaps at me, "Who the fuck are you talking to now?"

"Who the Eff are you talking about?" I ask again, genuinely lost.

"What?" He asks frantically, glancing over at me, then at the road, then back at me.

"Fricking pones." I say to myself, indirectly answering his question. Then wonder if I shouldn't change my *middle finger* stance from my current, lazy, fist with a halfcocked middle finger to something more aggressive and militant like when Maverick flips off the MIG while in a 180 inverted...whatever that was in the opening scene of Top Gun.

"Hey!" Curt barks. "Focus, don't zone out on me again."

"Hey yourself, B-word." I say finishing my beer and fishing around the icy waters of my cooler for another one. "I'm here. I-I am focused, and I clearly have my hands full. You made a statement. You made a statement in a very accusing manner and I asked you a qualifying question." I'm waving my hands around rapidly, splashing cooler water all over everything. "You Sir, you have not answered my question. The ball is in your court gosh dangit!"

Curt, without answering my question, tells me to roll a joint so I grab one of the Disc Golf frisbees from the back seat, dump what little weed is left in the dugout onto it and grab a Zig-Zag. Not a whole lot of weed to work with here, just shake of off brand Missouri dirt weed.

"Motherfucker, you know what the fuck I'm talking about. You're not that fucking ate up yet." He shouts with no appreciation for all the things I've got on my disk right now. With the weed I have in front of me, this is going to be a pinner amongst pinners.

"I can't believe you two. Those bitches are nothing but trouble." He continues, sounding sincerely disappointed. I notice my head sinking down in shame before remembering how incredibly jejune this conversation is. I manage to get the lion's share of the weed in this rolling paper and I carefully twist it up. Pitiful as it is, my impeccable rolling skills have led to another success.

Then I finally say, "Dude, you're uh...you're simply going to have to narrow this all down for me."

Curt finishes a Budweiser and tosses it in the back seat in a clear act of aggression. I can tell by this unwarranted reaction that he's lashing out, not just at me but against the Caddy as well.

Clearly, he thinks he has acquired some kind of social capital over me. How far will he take this? The question is not if, but *how* much is he going to milk this thing, whatever this *thing* is.

"Brewski." He demands, snapping his fingers like some kind of gay, Russian Czar or something.

"Oh, for Eff's sake, Dog." I say, not under my breath, as I reach for a beer from the cooler. I manage to find a Bud Light bottle and hand it to him, then flick the ice water in his face. "What, you're incapable of getting your own beers now? You want me to drink it for you too?"

"No Schultz." He says somberly, opening the bottle with his teeth. "Those fucking bitches know where we live now. Whatever happens with this shit, it's on you."

This does little to jog my memory.

The Distance comes on the Cake CD and Curt can't resist turning the volume up and singing along to the *"... Churning and burning, they yearn for the cup..."* part. I lick my forefinger to even out a run in the joint, hit it again and then pass it.

Out of nowhere, a rust colored, late 80's Chevet eases over into our lane right in front of us doing, of all things, the speed limit, causing Curt to slam on the breaks. I cover my beer and brace for the worst.

"This motherfucker." He whispers under his breath. He doesn't shout. He doesn't speed around him and cut him off, doesn't ram him from behind; running him off the road to his assured demise. No, he simply gets into the right lane, speeds up and passes him, using the blinker to boot.

"You must be getting soft man." I say, puffing on the hooter to get it started again. I thought that guy and his crappy Chevet would be a fireball in the ditch by now. You would have totally taken that a couple years ago. You must be getting old."

"My P. O. says I need to work on my anger issues. And I wouldn't want to scratch your precious Caddy, Puddin'." He says, stealing the joint from my mouth and hitting it. Is this his way of apologizing for throwing the beer in the backseat. Have amends been made? I hate playing these gay mind games with Curt. I swear, he thinks we're dating or something.

"That's mighty big of you." I say, blowing out a hit.

"Dude, those bitches know where we live now and everything." He repeats, then hits a nerve with, "And anyway, what's up with Valerie, aren't you like, making some progress with her?"

"First of all, Dog, I don't know what the heck you're talking about. Let's just start there, I feel like you have a point floating around somewhere and I don't doubt your sincerity, but we have to start with some kind of common ground here."

"Those fucking bitches." He repeats to himself passive/aggressively.

"You can keep rambling on about nameless, faceless bitches Curtis, but like, that's not going to make me remember who the in the balls you're talking about." I say, then, "And don't flippin' talk to me about Valerie." I take my phone out of my pocket again and reread her message for a fourth time. I consider replying, then decide against it, easing the phone back in my pocket carefully this time.

"You and Dicky do way too much day drinking." He says without a single hint of irony in his tone whatsoever.

"*Excuse me?*" I gasp, clutching my imaginary pearls. "Um, I beg your fricking pardon man, but like, we're in a band."

"Yeah, I'm supposed to be the, what, the manager or the drummer? You two don't even have a name, remember?" He laughs. "You don't see me getting so hammered that I don't remember bringing two hookers home in the middle of the day though, do you?"

"Hookers?" I think, possibly out loud. My mind is buffering. "Dude, seriously, who in the mother eff are you talking about?!" I finally shout, my patience worn thin.

"Those two bitches that you and Dicky brought home the other day from the bar." The simmering begins. "The crazy ass, red headed bitch and her runaway looking friend. That shit ain't cool, Motherfucker!" He's shouting now, his anger brimming to a boil. "You know how much fucking dope I run out of that house?" He yells, blood rushing to and fro, veins pulsating, eyes bulging. My brain starts to spiral out of control.

Images start flashing in and out of my mind's field of vision. I'm warped to a foggy memory of me in the passenger's seat of Dicky's red Dodge Durango, fumbling around with the radio, a cigarette dangling from my lips, a beer spilling in my lap. Then we're stumbling into the Rusty Hook. I'm squinting at a clock that reads 10:37 a.m. as drinks are poured and quickly drank. A graver image of falling off of bar stools, giant sunglasses in the pouring rain. Goliath mountains of cocaine being cut up into short little lines and snorted with rolled up dollar bills. Pills of all varieties being bitten in half and passed around.

Bartenders. I can almost put a face to the bartenders. All I see is a faceless girl with fiery red hair and a prescription for madness moving from my peripheral vision into the foreground. The wicked witch of the West tattooed on her left bicep and a black spider web crawling up her neck. This is no *rose on the small of her back* kind of girl. This must be what the Madonna girls from 10 years ago are doing now. I look down, a dragon is etched into the wooden bar with a knife, breathing fire that is far mightier than the sword.

The faceless bartender licks her lips, flips her passion colored hair aside and sets down a bottle of Jose Cuervo Gold next to two empty glasses. She spins the cap off with her thumb and then takes a pull off the raw bottle that makes Dicky's liver cringe. Her tongue flips like a snake. I rub my sweaty palms on the thigh of my Levi's and realize that the General is harder than a Hungarian tongue twister.

She splashes the glasses full, pours the liquor strong, tosses a handful of ice at them that miss both glasses. No words are exchanged. We're running on reptilian instinct. Anything can happen here, complete chaos. Drinks are poured. Vomit is spewed. Xanax pills are smashed on the counter and snorted. Deliberately long stares are exchanged. The shepherd is becoming the wolf.

A brunette with pouty lips, dark eyeshadow and fuck me eyes that shoot fire scream some unknown verses at me. Dicky pulls out a rock of cocaine and crushes it with his fist on the bar and breaks out four lines with his pinky finger. He leans down and snorts a small mound off the bar top with no straw. I bury my face in it and so do the two faceless bartenders.

As I'm shaking off that railroad, having gone through quite enough of that horrific scene in my head, the faceless red head's hair starts to blow back, a face emerges. The low resolution comes into focus, Hot Kryptonite colored eyes that are having a superhuman effect on me. The *Brothers and Sisters* album by The Allman Brothers Band plays in the background. The bar is decorated like a Whistler painting, dull and four generations too old, yet here we are, early 21st Century foxes.

The tip of the red-head's tongue is touching the front of her teeth seductively. I take the lot of my drink and then crunch the ice left in the glass while I'm staring at her confidently but then her tongue turns thin, green and split at the end like a serpent straight from hell. I take this in stride and, somehow unfazed, I set my drink down. She fills it up again without breaking her gaze on me and goes back to seducing me with her emerald eyes. After *Hotel California* plays on the Jukebox, she takes the sunglasses from my face, puts them on her and calls me a cunt.

The brunette, who is hotter than two hot things, maybe 15-and-a-half and something behind those brown eyes reveal to me that she is more than likely some kind of runaway. She takes Dicky's shades off of his face, puts them on her own and pours him a tall glass of Jack Daniels. She drops a cube of ice in the glass and then slowly slides the drink over to him. Her playful demeanor exposing a wild side that is coming out, ready or not. Now, both wearing our gigantic sunglasses, words start to form.

"Now we're invisible." The brunette runaway says in a voice that makes the General about a quarter hard. "So, are you guys like, in a band or something?"

"Yeah." We both say in unison.

Ramblin' Man by the Allman Brothers plays in the background.

Lord I was born a ramblin' man.
Tryin' to make a livin' and doin' the best I can.
When it's time for leavin', I hope you'll understand.
'Cause I was born a ramblin' man.

"We're not famous or anything." Dicky admits. "But we have a fucking huge gig coming up soon."

"Yeah, we're trying to make a living, ya know, we're doing the best we can." I say leaning back in my barstool, almost losing my balance.

"We have a hard time writing songs though." Dicky confesses. "That shit ain't easy."

"Yeah," I say, laughing, "We would write more songs, ya know, but we're not ramblin' men. Ramblers get up way too early, they're always off ramblin' by the time the sun comes up."

"Right!" Dicky agrees, "You can get a lot of shit done when you get up that early. We're lazy and drink too much to do shit like ramble around and write songs so, ya know, we gotta live the life first, then we can write about it. Ya know what I mean?"

"Yeah, ramblers have to leave their families and stuff too." I say, stirring the ice in my drink with my forefinger. "I can't get down with that."

The images sort of take a turn for the bizarre from there, my brain racing to catch up: Ice being tossed around, Singapore Slings with shots of Jägermeister, midgets, there was at least one midget, more cocaine, one hits of weed, Kolonopin being crushed and snorted, putting drops of Vodka in each other's eyeballs, glasses being broken, drinks being spilled. An evil round of Truth or Dare where I think me and Dicky may have reached second base. I remember pissing in the toilet...maybe it was a pint glass, could have been the ice bin, either way, a vision of the General getting whipped out. And then...Black. Nothingness. The dark Nihilism, the dragon.

"Dude. *Dude!!* Schultz!!" Curt is shouting as we pass the Rock Road exit.

I come to, shake off those dastardly images and ask no one in particular, "Steak n' Shake?"

“Schultz! Wake the fuck up.” Curt shouts at me.

“Huh? Where the hell is this supposed to be?” I ask. “This is no G. D. Steak ’n Shake! This is all wrong, it’s wrong 5 Ways, Man.”

“Dude, you were in one of your trances, you ate up motherfucker. Here, smoke on this hooter and chill the fuck out.” He says shoving a skinny joint in my face.

“Nothing. Get that rotten stuff out of my face, I want nothing!” I say pushing his hand away. Then, “Well, on second thought.” I say, taking the joint which is nothing but a measly roach by now. I toss it out the open window and then hit the button to roll it up.

“It’s starting to feel like ghetto out.” I say wiping what I hope is spilt beer off of my Levi’s. I sniff. I got nothing.

Chapter II

"Dude, we're getting off at Goodfellow." Curt says, speeding the Caddy up to north of 85 mph.

"I'm not trying to go to Duck's." I say in protest. "It's too late to start smoking crack now."

"Dude, it's only fucking 1 a.m." He argues vehemently.

"Fair enough." I concede. "But put that freakin' window up man, it smells like burnt Brillo out here already." I say, soaking up the ghetto scenery from behind my tinted window.

"Phut, I ain't scared of these shines." He says, looking around at the people roaming idly around the sidewalks. He rolls up the window anyway.

"Shines?" I ask. "What are you, David Duke? That's so racist."

We get off on the Goodfellow exit and take a painful right. Curt hits the headlights when we pull onto Duck's dreary street where, despite all the good faith efforts to turn things around, is still an absolute and utter S-hole. Even the trees look as piss poor as they did that first time I came here, desolate and pathetic as ever. There are still rusted out cars with no tires leaning on cinder blocks and empty 40 oz bottles dressed shabbily in paper bags scattered all about the streets off of Goodfellow, and Duck and his homies are all still crack dealers supporting their crack habits.

Now me and the boys, we still get moin every now and again, like tonight, coming home from the East side, but we're all gainfully employed and don't mooch off of other people or steal crap anymore. I work like three different part time jobs; I wait tables at Steak 'n Shake, that's where I get most of my food, I haul sheet rock at Hackman Lumber, and I substitute teach during the school year when I am also a full time student at Lindenwood University. Curt's a painter, like industrial painting, not like Picasso or anything, and Dicky does concrete work and foundations

or something. That's what he says anyway, I have no idea what that means in any kind of real way though.

We don't smoke crack that much anymore is what I'm getting at. We're only doing it tonight because me and Curt got off work early, went to a bar and couldn't score any coke, which obviously led to us deciding to go the strip clubs in East St. Louis and start an early weekend.

We don't really even steal bottles of whiskey anymore. Not unless it's past 1:30 a.m. and too late to buy booze due to those fascist, draconian laws that they have here in Missouri, and we're in a pinch. What I'm getting at is, five years or so ago, I was a scared shitless, 15-year-old kid, reluctantly coming down here with the boys in the back seat of Dicky's crappy Buick Regal to get moin. We've sort of grown up since then, but this whole part of town and everyone in it seems like they've smoked their way into a time capsule. A state of being frozen in time that future generations of Yale undergraduate anthropologists will study and dissect. This is *homocrackheadious.*

Even Curt was scared to come down here back then. He won't admit it now, but he was. You could tell by the way he would always wear a shirt, meaning he would consciously put on a shirt. Very un-Dog. You don't see that business now. We also used to feel obligated to delve into the depths of Duck's filthy basement and blast away half of a bill with him, even though we probably left him with a nice sack of rocks, just for middle manning the whole deal.

These days though, like tonight, we just roll up to the dilapidated house and Curt, shirtless, shouts out of the window of the Caddy to all the homies on the porch, "Yo, where Duck at?"

Before I can finish my brewski, Duck runs up to the window like a bellhop and asks, "Yo, Curtis, what up? What up Schultz?"

"What up Duck?" Curt says dryly.

"Hey man." I say, fumbling around with a cigarette. "How's yo mama?"

"Oh, she cool. She cool, my man." He says enthusiastically, all smiles. "So, what can I do for you gentlemen this Herr evening? Wha'chu need?"

"A bill." Curt says, snapping his fingers at me again.

Pause.

"Schultz, give me the fucking money." Curt hisses, annoyed.

"Huh?" I ask, finally lighting the cigarette in my mouth.

"Give him the fucking money." He barks, snapping at me some more.

"I don't have any money." I say blowing out a drag. "I mean, I've got like $20 bucks. I thought you had this one."

"Why the fuck would I have this one? I just paid the fucking rent, Motherfucker." He says, ignoring Duck who is idling in the Caddy's driver side window, eager for that first blast of crack yet not expressing any kind of sense of urgency whatsoever.

"Well I gave you my share of it didn't I?" I say, taking a drag and blowing it out. I don't want to get caught in one of Curt's web of mistruths. "It's not like you paid the whole freaking rent by yourself, is it? That was all the money I had. I am just a poor boy man, my story seldom told." I sing.

"You got money, Puddin', don't try and Jew your way out of this." He says playing the Jew card again.

"I got nothing, man. I'm trying to put myself through college." I say, thinking that is a solid argument, airtight, impenetrable.

"Oh, *wah wah. I'm in college. I'm poor. wah, wah!"* He mocks. "I'm so sick of you playing the broke, college boy card. Cry me a fucking river Schultz, you work too, Motherfucker."

"I work…" I pause for effect. "to pay for college." I explain for the, I don't know, seven thousandth time this week, "It's an investment man, like in my future. Why is that so hard for you to understand? I'm not trying to wait tables at Steak 'n Shake for the rest of my life."

"Dude, I fly, you buy. That's the rule, Bitch." He states with absolute authority, as if that had been established long, long ago and etched in stone and marched down Mount Sinai by Moses himself.

"It's my effing car, D-bag!" I say, not falling for it.

There's a pause while Curt gathers his thoughts, how to move forward without losing his crap. Something is telling him that he is going to have to conjure some kind of reason, some hidden logic if he is going to win this battle.

Curt finally declares, "Well all of my money is wrapped up in the three pounds of weed I just got. You got money Motherfucker. This one's on you."

Defeated, I finally concede, "Alright Dog, freakin'…whatever. Let's go to an ATM."

Duck chimes in, seemingly out of nowhere, "Yo, me and my bother need some Berrs, if you niggas," He calls us the "N" word in a plural tense, "is goin' to the sto', we goin' wit'chu." He sniffs.

"Oh, what in the ever-loving, mother grabbing Eff." I think to myself, slapping my forehead as I pull up the passenger seat to let Duck and his "brother" into the back seat of the Caddy.

We drive to the Shell station off Goodfellow. The KOOLS that Duck and his "brother" are smoking are really starting to stink up the Caddy something fierce. Now, I don't know if they are real brothers, like blood related, or if that's just a black thing, but regardless of the nature of their actual relationship, this whole scenario is not in the best interest of the Caddy.

They're also getting grease all over my seats. I don't mean like, Jerry Curl grease, like in *Coming to America* where the black dudes leave *Soul Glow* marks on the couch, but like real grease, like car grease. They are both wearing mechanic's overalls, keeping up the cover that they work as actual auto mechanics in an effort to throw Duck's mama off the scent that they are really just crack heads. This has been going on since the first time I came here when I was like 15-years-old.

When we get to the Shell Station off of Goodfellow and Victory which, by the way, is one of the most ironically named streets in the history of ironically named streets, things go from bad to worse when I get out of the passenger side of the Caddy, walk over the decaying parking lot full of KOOL cigarette butts, empty 40s of Malt liquor and used needles, up to the ATM and the brothers Duck get out and follow me up to the cash machine, closer than dudes at an ATM etiquette dictates.

A terrible panic starts to brew from somewhere down deep, way down in the bowls of subconsciousness, not because I'm worried about Duck and his crack-head homeboy ganking me, but because I know Curt is watching and I can see where this is headed. He knows that I keep a tire iron under the driver's seat of the Caddy and when I see him slip out of the car from the corner of my eye, I can hear it drag briefly against the concrete.

I'm clearly going to need to take matters into my own hands if bloodshed is to be spared. I'm not trying to see anyone get killed tonight, we also haven't gotten the $100 in crack that we came for in the first place. Curt doesn't think things through that far in the future. If he murders the Duck Brothers, he thinks he's doing his duty, as if the situation couldn't have gone any other way. The Duck Bros. are crack heads, sometimes you have to save crack heads from themselves. The wolf must become the shepherd.

I crack my neck and catch a glimpse of Curt positioning himself around the back of the Caddy, stupid-ass grin on his face. He's flipping the tire iron around amongst his fingers while I'm queuing up for the ATM. The crackhead brothers are right behind me, close enough that I can feel the poor rubbing off on me. I have to do something fast or we are going to be the headline on the St. Louis Post Dispatch in the morning, above the fold. I can see the misleading headlines now: *Two white LU students arrested in hate crime.*

My brain is racing but I feel like, in situations like this, for Curt at least, time sort of slows down for him. It must be some kind of a prison thing, in highly intense situations, he has this sort of hyper-vigilance which, I'm sure in prison made him King of the Yard. He is able to stay cool and can assess all aspects of what's going on with a lot more composure than normal people, like me, who just go on instinct.

I glance back and he's got the tire iron behind his back, maintaining a keen eye on the Crackhead brothers, the other people coming and going from the gas station, a lookout for the cops, all the while keeping a watchful eye out for me, for what, acceptance?

"No Dog," I'm thinking to myself. "I don't want you to murder these two cats with a tire iron here at this crappy Shell station parking lot at one in the effing morning." I don't want to get ganked here in a gas station parking lot either. While Curt has a calm yet, *ready to kill* assessment of this situation, I'm all instinct. I have no control over my actions.

I take the bank card from my wallet that is chained to my Levi's and, before putting it in the ATM, I bend down and pick up a brick that's laying on the ground, I throw it as far as I can and yell out, "Kill whitey!"

The brick lands on the windshield of some S-box old Ford pick-up truck, making a loud crashing sound that gets everyone's attention. I quickly turn around, insert my card and enter my PIN. The cash comes before anyone realizes what is going on. In an about, oh, I'd say a level three-and-a-half Jedi mind trick, I take the cash out without incident. Not bad, not bad at all. We get the cash, drop Duck and his *brother* off, grab the crack and head home. No one had to die.

Chapter III

As we're flying down the Highway 70, headed west back to St. Charles, I feel the need to bring something up that should otherwise go without saying.

"Dude," I start hesitantly, not knowing exactly how to move forward in a way that will make my point with the proper amount of tact. "you know that I can't go to jail right?" I say, wondering how that would sound to a sane person.

"Why the fuck would either of us go to jail?" Curt asks, confused. Anger brimming.

"Well Curtis," I start, wishing this conversation was not necessary, "if you kill someone, especially a couple of brothers, we would go to jail. There's no real question about that, right?" I'm pleading at this point. "We'll spend the rest of our lives in prison. I can't go to prison man, it's just not in me. I ain't the one."

"Well I didn't kill anyone because they didn't make me." He says, offering a satisfied chuckle, "If they would've fucking robbed you, Schultz, I would have been totally justified. It's called self-defense Dude."

"Still, that would have, at the very least, completely ruined our night. Surely you can see how killing two brothers would have fundamentally effed up our night." I argue, then offer a compromise, "At least a little bit?"

"I see your point Schultz." He admits blankly, "But still Dude, I didn't kill anyone."

"That's not how they would tell it on the news." I say, shaking my head. "The headline would read, 'Two white college students murder two homeless African American boys in a hate crime.'"

"Dude," Curt demands, looking frantically back and forth between me and the five-lane highway in front of us. "What the fuck are you talking about?" He's asking, becoming frustrated. "First of all Schultz, I'm not in fucking college." Now he's pointing at me without looking at me. "And second, they aren't *boys.* They're grown ass men who have been crack dealers for the last

decade and a half." Now he's pointing *and* shouting, ranting at no one in particular, not looking at the road. "Now pack that shooter and don't be a fucking Jew about it."

"Hang on." I say, tapping out all the weed that's on the frisbee out the window to cleanse it, baptize it. I take one of the five plastic baggies of crack that is the size of a PEZ candy and drop it onto the frisbee. I carefully break it into pieces with my fingers onto the frisbee and, ever so gently, let it crumble like a cookie. I take the shooter that is a glass stem with a piece of Brillo stuffed in it out of the 2Pac CD case in the driver's side arm rest. It's ready to be blasted. I lick my finger, put a nice chunk on the tip, hold it straight up and take the "starter hit" to hold it in place, singeing the crack in place on the Brillo. I blow out that hit, chomp on my teeth a couple times, then take the real blast. I take it all in, it enters my bloodstream like a phantom. The wiring of my brain instantly becoming a slave to this feeling of euphoria that I'm experiencing right now. Inhale, exhale. Yen, yang.

Now I can cognitively acknowledge that we will be taking somewhere in the ballpark of 200 blasts tonight, all very similar to this one blast that I am taking now, but somewhere…somewhere way down deep, I know that they will never be as good as this first blast. And this blast, as it goes, will never be as good as that first blast that I took all those years ago, back in Stamm's garage. We're all just chasing the Dragon, man, the Dragon of chaos. I drop a chunk on the shooter and hand it to Curt.

"Take the wheel Schultz." He says, grabbing the shooter out of my hand, as gently as possible.

"I don't know, Man," The jawing is starting to take hold, the rambling is never far behind. "it's just that the news has a way of twisting things I've noticed. They're not always out for the truth and they seem to have this story, this narrative that's sort of ongoing about how everything is racist." I continue, trying to steer my Caddy with some sort of stability. "It's seems kind of Orwellian"

"What the fuck does that even mean?" He asks, blowing out the blast, handing me the shooter. "You say it all the time."

"George Orwell, he wrote the book *1984* which is basically a nightmare future where the government has way too much power and everything goes to crap. It's the opposite of utopia, it's called a *dystopian* future." I say.

"But 1984 already happened, Dude." He says, already jonesing for his next blast.

"Seriously?" I ask with a straight face. "The book was written in the 40's…ya know, where 1984 was the future."

"Yeah college boy, I got that." He says. "I'm just saying, it still didn't come true."

"It's fiction, not a prediction, Nostradamus." I say, not amused. "And if you think we're that far away from the bull crap in that book…well you obviously haven't read it, my point is, we're not that far off from it."

"In what way?" He asks.

"I don't know exactly, it just seems like the really big industries that have the most influence on all of us like the news, schools and T.V. and movies have become really political or something." I'm saying. "I'm still trying to work through this, I haven't really put my finger on it yet."

We take blast after blast speeding down Highway 70, headed west back to St. Charles and we manage to cross the Missouri River, into St. Charles without going to jail for any of the numerous felonies we've managed to rack up on this little excursion of ours.

I finally snap out of a small, crack induced daze and, after lighting a cigarette, I say, "So anyway, can you just *not* get us arrested again and keep my freaking name out of the news?"

"Whatever Dude, don't be such a drama queen." He says getting off at the First Capital exit.

We pull up in front of our duplex and park the Caddy in the gravel driveway but don't park in the garage. The garage is a dark and dreary, dungeon's prison and is only used to store things that we have made our peace with never seeing again. We pull ourselves together as best we can but there is no stopping the jawing that ten or so giant crack blasts instigates.

The street is quiet and only dimly lit by two streetlamps that are not burnt out, the moon is as high as we are and looks like an eyelash that has fallen from the heavens and landed softly amongst the stars. The park adjacent to our house is pitch black but I can make out where the playground is, the pavilion, the bald patches of grassless orbs where we aim our golf balls while chipping them back and forth.

All the lights on all the other duplexes that line the north side of the street are sleeping except for ours. Luckily, all the duplexes on our street are on higher ground than the street and sidewalk so all you can see is the lights glowing from the windows. If the general public were able to just look in on us from the sidewalk, we would have spray painted the windows black and nailed half-inch particle board up on the inside and out to keep prying eyes away.

As we walk along the three-foot-tall, stone wall that keeps the erosion at bay we can hear music coming from inside the house, but we can't see in until we walk up the seven steps to our front porch. When we get to the front door, we pause, look at each other, take a deep breath, then turn the knob and walk in.

Sitting on the old brown sofa in his underwear, Dicky is wearing mirrored shades and playing Sublime's *Santaria* on the guitar. Two girls that look vaguely familiar are comfortably sitting on the opposite sofas, both wearing cut off jean shorts. The red head, who is wearing a black lace bra, looks at me like I may have fucked her mother and the brunette, wearing a white cut-off wife-beater, no bra, drinking Jim Beam from the bottle smiles mischievously at us.

It hits me like a blast of crack. I turn to Curt and say, "Oh, *those* bitches."

"The fuck did I tell you Motherfucker." Curt says, taking off his one-armed shades, "Not fuckin' cool."

"Hey boys! How was your date?" The ginger haired girl slurs. Then they all break out into laughter.

Dicky stops playing for a second and says, "Hey motherfuckers!" There's a pause, then a small, contained belch, then, "Where the fuck have you two been?"

He squints, shakes his head quickly, erasing that train of thought like an etch-a-sketch then, "I'm joking, hey you remember…" He closes his eyes tightly and snaps his fingers. "Fuck girls, I'm sorry. What'd you say your names were again?"

"We didn't." They laugh, falling over themselves in a drunken, slutty kind of way that makes my dork start to pulse. The ginger's hand touches the brunette's firm tit, they laugh some more, then start making out.

"Oh boy." Curt says, turning around and walking out the door.

This wasn't exactly the vibe I was looking for either. We got a pocket full of stones after all, so I follow Curt back down to the sidewalk and we take refuge in the cemetery that is just east of the park, across the street. We find a nice big gravestone, sit down and blast away at the crack

until our lighters run out. Equally inevitably, at some point, the morning's eternal battle with the night, the heavenly Yen and the Yang begin to shine victorious. "Until we meet again, Sunshine." Our collective darkness concedes, "Until we meet again."

Chapter IV

Dicky and I are sitting on the crappy, old brown couches in our living room, *Houses of the Holy* quietly playing on the hand-me-down CD shuffle system. The 40-year-old, cheap wooden flooring is giving a real sauna feel due to the summer heat that is still lingering and peeling the last bits of paint from the smoke-stained walls. The sun is being held back by the faded red bed-sheets that cover the windows facing the street, but nothing can keep that heat from seeping in like a snake in the grass.

It's so hot that I'm only wearing a pair of faded red and blue checkered shorts from Goodwill and a hemp neckless that Valerie made me for my 20th birthday, my dirty blond hair is still wild from last night's restlessness. Dicky, who, I'm noticing looks a lot buffer than me with no shirt on and bears a slight resemblance to Richard Gere, whose wild, curly brown hair is bursting out of a backwards St. Louis Cardinal's Cap, is wearing Baby Blue Adidas shorts from Target. We're smoking a joint of some fair to midland weed and trying to write songs for our upcoming gig at Coopers.

Coopers is an Irish style pub whose owner is a crazy Japanese cat named Hiro, a youngish dude with a Japanese Jew-fro, a wide smile and always wearing a version of Cooper's Polo style shirts. Cooper's has been open for well over a year and has sort of turned into our home away from home, but he's just getting around to having a Grand Opening bash on September 10th

which is a little more than a week away. He asked us to play a few songs and we said *Sure* though we had been drinking at the time.

"How about this?" I ask, putting down the red notebook and black Bic pen carefully on the old wooden, badly scarred coffee table. My confidence waning and ebbing the closer I am to revealing this new masterpiece.

"Hit me." Dicky says, stopping the lick he was working out on his Starburst colored, 1978 Epiphone Les Paul guitar with a white pick guard.

"It's called *Heart Burn.*" I say strumming an A minor, D minor, G to the F progression on my blood red Kramer Striker I got for Christmas when I was seven.

"Whoa! Hold it right there. No Dude, sorry, that sucks." Dicky says, holding in a hit off a pinner of St. Louis dirt weed and doing the 'cut' gesture with his hand to his neck.

"You haven't even heard it yet, what the freak!" I exclaim, throwing up my hands.

"We get to have veto power over shit we think sucks, right? No questions asked. That's your rule." He says, passing me the little joint.

"Yeah, well you have to hear me out first." I say, my confidence fading. I'm almost pleading. "This could be the best song you've ever heard."

"Alright, sorry Dude, you're right, shoot." He concedes, waving his hands in surrender. "Let's hear it."

"2, 3, 4… (Guitar strumming) *Baby I got heart burn…*"

"Stop, stop. Cut." There's a pause while he puts a cigarette in the black, plastic ashtray on the table and waves his hands around in the air. "Just stop. Don't say another word."

"What's your beef, D-bag?" I shout, confused. I'm wondering if it's too early for a beer.

"Dude, c'mon. Be fuckin' realistic." He begs, "That sucks, and you know it sucks."

"Well what do you have?" I ask, deciding it's not. I walk into the kitchen that has never been redecorated since the house was built in the 40's; off-white tile floor that is heavily stained and flaking, yellowish refrigerator that hums like a wounded moose, old dusty pictures of flowers that would be worthless even if they were originals. A simple wooden dinner table with a stack of assorted coasters from various bars, a warped deck of Confederate Flag playing cards with one Joker and no Queen of hearts, three matching wooden chairs with faded blue cushions and one green lawn chair.

I peel open the sticky door to the fridge and take a look inside. There's an open 12 pack of Bud Light bottles, a butter compartment with a dozen or so ketchup packets from Burger King, empty jars of various condiments, a half drunken box of Franzia Sunset Blush wine that we keep in there for the ladies, and both crispers filled with onion skins and random, off brand beers that people have left behind. I take four Buds out and shut the door.

"I do the music; you do the lyrics. You know that shit." Dicky says opening a Budweiser and drinking it casually in one deep gulp.

"Whatever Dude. *What-ev.*" I say, shaking my head in disappointment.

"Alright, well let's write a song about this flat." He says, looking around. Then in his best attempt at a posh, British accent, he starts, "We've got this wee flat."

"What are you doing?" I ask dryly. Confusion mixed with a dash of panic start to simmer.

"Nice humble living room with holiday lights up all year round." He continues, "…two couches on either side, broke in as fuck, I think the white bedsheets cover the cigarette burns

quite nicely. A bad ass *Abby Road* poster on the wall with The Beatles in the background and Paul, dead as a fucking doorknob, smoking a fag from his right hand and barefoot as a bloody leper. The black and white poster of the New York Skyline at night that looks like the dog's bollocks, all smoky and what not, proper fucking smashing…"

He continues, the accent fading, "The front porch with two garden chairs from Home Depot, perfect for sitting and playing guitars and singing, overlooking the park. The cracked cement, the rusty steel rail, the dying tree, the brown, dying grass, the cigarette butts, the BBQ pit and all the ashes really make this house a home." He's looking at me enthusiastically. I give a look of general acceptance, so he continues. "Ghetto ass neighbors that don't talk shit and are cool as fuck to hang out with. The bad ass park across the street that, even though the disc golf course we petitioned hasn't come through, is still a great place to chip golf balls back and forth and do some brewin'. Even the playground is bad ass and a great place to bring your bird or whatever…"

"But there are roaches." I interrupt. I wasn't trying to shit on his point but we both know that I did. The pause that follows slithers in and out of our collective conscious.

"Yeah, well there is a snake in every garden." He finally says dismissively.

"Oh, don't forget about the Graveyard!" I chime in. "Great place to chill or get moin or whatever."

"Get moin, Schultz? At the Graveyard?" He interrupts solemnly.

"Can we just focus?" I ask, trying to scribble this all down in the notebook.

"Alright Dude, write it." Dicky says, practicing the intro to *Lonely Stranger* from Eric Clapton's MTV Unplugged. "This is a pretty tight fucking crib."

"You start thinking of a good name for us." I say, still writing, possibly onto something.

"What about The Sex Beatles?" He suggests.

"We're not playing this gig as The Sex Beatles." I say. "That was a joke! I just made that up that morning we were playing at The Rusty Hook and you ran with it. Let's just figure out a solid name and stick with it."

"I fuckin' like The Sex Beatles." He says and I can't tell if he's lying or not. It's become impossible to gauge the truthfulness of anything he says. "It works on a couple different levels, ya know?"

"Oh, I get it." I assure him. "It's too risky though. I think I heard that somewhere anyway."

"What about The Pink Tacos?" He asks.

"No. No fricking way." I say definitively.

"The Cherry Poppin' Daddies?" He suggests optimistically.

"No. Already a band actually."

"The Brown Holes?"

"N…" I start to say.

"I mean The Brown Eyes. The Brown *Eyes*." He corrects himself.

"Dude, seriously." I'm ready to move on but I can see that he has one more in the chamber.

"The Wet T-Shirts." He says, full of hope.

"Shut the…" Pause. Then, "*Please* shut the eff up!"

I flip my guitar over, grab the notebook and start writing the first verse of the song I've titled: *Shangri la* when Curt comes out of his room scratching his nuts through his blue Fruit of the Loom boxer shorts.

"Dude, those bitches." He starts up again, straightening out a cigarette butt from out of the black plastic ashtray from a forgotten bar on the sticky wooden coffee table and lighting it. "You two motherfuckers." Another three worded statement that is more like the worst political campaign slogan of all time. He takes a drag and shakes his head in disapproval.

"Yeah, Schultz. What the fuck." Dicky says, finishing his third beer of the morning.

"Wait, why the heck is this my fault?" I ask, opening another beer of my own. "I'm the only one to hook up with some strange on a Tuesday afternoon. You were there too ya drunk bastard. You banged that young brunette, runaway looking b-word, what's-her-name, Lolita?"

"Was that her name?" Dicky asks. "I thought you were calling her that to be ironic."

"Well what was the red heads name?" I ask.

"Huh, I thought it was Ginger, but maybe that was just something ironic we made up too." He says. Now both of us are completely dumbfounded. Looking around, we both notice a cockroach crawling across the floor that we both take turns trying to step on. Curt tries to burn it with a Zippo and a can of Aquanet but he singes the edge of the couch instead. Failing, it scampers away under the dust and darkness of the couch.

"Yeah, I think we just started calling them that and then it kind of stuck." I say, now stoned and slightly beer buzzed.

"You two motherfuckers." Curt says, shaking his head some more. I wonder if he thinks this shaming is working on anyone.

"Hey eff you, butt plug. You screw around with Christy Drapper, and she's married to Jake." I say to Curt, gathering the courage to stand up to him.

"Yeah, and I'll fuck him up too if he wants to start some shit." Curt says flexing in the broken $10 mirror from Wal-Mart that leans against the paint-chipped wall.

"Dude, you're having sex with his wife, like, on a regular basis. I like that guy." I'm saying with all the compassion my wake and bake can muster. "What has he ever done to you?"

"He's cool I guess." Curt says, checking out his back muscles now.

"Well that just makes you a total prick. You see that, right?" I say.

"Whatever Pones." He says, annoyed that we interrupted his body inspection. "I didn't bring her back here. You two motherfuckers brought those bitches back here and fucked them."

"Whoa, negative Jackson! *Ne-ga-tory*!!" Dicky interrupts, strumming an E chord. "I did not have sex with that woman." He says in a convincing Bill Clinton voice, pointing a stern finger and biting his lower lip.

"No seriously, what were their names?" I ask sincerely, racking my brain, fading into a song.

"I don't know, Dude." Dicky says slowly. "I just don't fucking know." He says even slower.

"I don't know if they ever said them." I say.

"Dude, whatever the fuck their names are, those bitches are nothing but trouble." Curt says stepping on a roach and killing it. "You let those bitches in our house like snakes in the garden. Snakes in the garden of fucking Eden, Dude."

Dicky slurs, "Hey, easy with the bitch talk. Those are nice girls."

"We gotta come up with some songs for the show, Dude." I say to Dicky.

"Yeah, right. Let's do this." Dicky says shaking his head, focusing.

"Alright, I just wrote this. It's called *Shangri la.* It's in G."

I don't care if I'm lonely,
I don't mind if I'm broke
I got a funky little pad with Christmas lights and marijuana smoke
Dicky's got a guitar, he plays a song for me
There's bitches in my bed and zip-locks full of broccoli
It's paradise but the serpents slither in

It snows here all year-round singing fa la la la la
It's where the girlies get there blow here
Here at Shangri la

"What do you think?" I ask optimistically.

"I hate it." Curt says picking up his one-armed shades from the wooden coffee table from the Goodwill, blowing some ashes off the lenses and then putting them on.

"Me too, come on man." Dicky adds. "Try harder."

"Cunts!" I shout. "The lot of you!'

"Did he just cuss, Curt?" Dicky laughs.

"I don't think *cunt* counts, Dude. Tell us what you really think Schultzy baby." Curt says picking up the bongos and beating them rhythmlessly, then tossing them on the cigarette burned couch.

"Eff both of you monkey savaging knaves." I say, deflated.

Chapter V

Curt Fick is the son of Bert and Sandra Fick. Bert Fick grew up in a small town just outside of Des Moines, Iowa called Edensville. Bert was from a medium sized family for the mid 1940's, his father, Norman was a Goliath of a man who fought the Germans in France in the second World War. He then went on to make a handsome living selling typewriter parts door to door.

His sales territory stretched as far west as Bloomington, Illinois and as far east as Scottsbluff, Nebraska. If you owned a typewriter in the early part of the 20th Century, it's said that there is a 78% chance that you got your repairs from Norman Fick. Bert was the middle son of the Fick clan, he had two older brothers, Robbie and Bradly and a baby sister named Cynthia.

Bert was a strapping young man; tall, handsome and a very fast runner. They say he could out-run a horse on his bare feet in the summertime. He held the Edensville High school record for running the 100-meter dash, a record that they say still hasn't been beaten to this day. Bert also lettered in baseball as a shortstop and he was the captain of the football team as the Quarterback. He led the Edensville Serpents to the State Championship his Junior and Senior year.

The only athletic endeavor that Bert was not successful at was swimming. He had never learned to swim because when he was young, he accidentally fell in the Upton Lake and almost

drowned. Bert was a polite and well-read young man who loved his mother and father, Norman. He loved his brothers and his sister, he feared God and he loved America too.

Bert wanted to go into the military as soon he finished high school to help fight the Nazis and then hoped to go into sales like his father. All that changed though when, in his sophomore year of high school, he met a beautiful young blond headed girl with emerald green eyes and the most beautiful smile Bert had ever seen in his red-blooded American life named Sandra Davenport.

The first time Bert set eyes on Sandra was at the Edensville county fair. Sandra and her family, mother June and father Jeremy had just moved to town from nearby Mason City during the summer because Jeremy accepted a teaching position at the Community College heading the English department. The minute Bert saw Sandra standing in line for the Thunder Canyon water ride, it was love at first sight. He walked away from his baseball teammates and told them that he had to go get a waffle cone and ran off to join the queue for Thunder Canyon even though he was deathly afraid of the water. He stood three people behind Sandra and was determined to talk to her before it was her turn to get on the ride.

Fate had been shining down on Bert that hot July afternoon because a strong gust of mid-western wind blew Sandra's bonnet right off her head. All the young boys standing in line, most of whom probably had the same plan as Bert, ran to fetch it for her but Bert, being so fast, was the first one to reach it. He snatched up the bonnet and, as calmly and coolly as he could, walked it back to her.

"Here's your bonnet, Miss." He said, handing Sandra her hat back with a hint of bashfulness.

"Oh, why thank you so much." She said with a little blush in her cheeks, giving Bert a quick once-over.

"May I join you?" Bert asked politely yet with just the right amount of confidence.

"Well sure. It looks like all the other boys have changed their minds about riding this ride." She said as half the line walked away defeated.

"My name's Bert, what's your name?" He asked, keeping an appropriate level of eye contact.

"It's Sandra." She said smiling yet composed. In total control of the situation.

"Ah, and I'm Bert." He repeated, blowing any chance of coming off as cooly as he'd hoped to.

"Yeah, you said that." She laughed.

"D'oh." He said slapping his face.

She was right, after Bert had beaten everyone else to the bonnet, they all just gave up and walked away. There was no use riding the ride now that Bert had beat them all to the prize. Bert's luck was about to run out though because now, with no one else in the line, it was already their turn to get into the logs and brave Thunder Canyon. Bert tried to keep his composure, but his nerves were getting the best of him. Sandra couldn't help but notice that Bert was shaking like a leaf on an October Oak tree.

"Are you alright?" Sandra asked tactfully.

"Oh, it's just that swimming isn't exactly my strong suit." Bert replied, rubbing his sweaty palms on the legs of his black trousers. Exposing himself vulnerably for the second time in as many minutes.

"Don't be silly." Sandra said, "It's just a little county fair ride. I'll be there with you in case you fall overboard." She smiled, touching his hand gently.

That was all Bert needed to hear. They both got into the ride together. As nervous as Bert was, Sandra told him stories about her life in Mason City before her family moved to Edensville two months prior and she asked Bert about Edensville High, where they would both be Juniors in the fall. Before they knew it, the Thunder Canyon's big finale had come and gone without Bert and Sandra hardly noticing at all and their log came to a sudden stop with a muffled thud.

As they departed the ride, Bert saw his father, Norman standing just past the exit with his arms folded and a stern look on his face. The Midwest summer's cumulous clouds were flashing with lightning in the sky behind him.

"Oh, there's my father. I wonder what he's doing waiting for me here." Bert said, slightly confused. "I'll introduce you to him if you like."

But before Bert could introduce Sandra to his father, Norman shouted, "Bert, what do you mean running off like that without telling me or your mother? Get over here right this minute."

"Ye-yes sir." Bert shouted back. He turned to Sandra and said, "I don't know what he is so cross for but maybe now isn't the best time for introductions. I tell you what," Then he whispered cooly, "At seven o'clock, meet me by the Death Balloon. Make sure you're not followed."

"Alright." Sandra said, looking deeply into his eyes. "I'll be there."

When Bert ran up to where his father was still standing like an old Elm tree, Bert apologized for running off though he wasn't really sorry. He was sixteen after all, practically a grown man but Norman wasn't treating Bert like a man at that time. He grabbed him by the ear and said, "I don't like you running off to meet easy girls that aren't accompanied. I don't want you to ever see that girl again, do you hear me?"

"Yes Sir. I-I won't. I promise." Bert stammered, lying.

Bert had no intention of keeping that promise though. As soon as the bright orange harvest moon hid behind a sheet of thin, scattered clouds and The Lonesome Drifters started playing their Bluegrass music to the town of Edensville, Bert snuck off again to meet Sandra. Not many words were spoken but certain understandings were made between their souls.

When school started in the fall, Bert and Sandra started "going steady" and Bert desperately wanted to share his love of Sandra with his family but every time he would start to bring it up, his father would get angry, as if he knew what Bert was going to say and would stop him before he could say it. "I don't want you associating with that tart!" He would shout.

One night, Bert and Sandra were alone when she started crying and turned to him and said, "Why? Why does your father hate me so?"

"I don't know. I really have no idea. He's never acted this way about anyone before. Even little Cinthia plays with other little boys and he doesn't seem to care. I think that maybe, if he could only meet you, surely, he'd see the beauty within you that I see. Sandra, I love you, I want to marry you. Sandra, will you marry me?"

"Oh Bert, I would love to be your wife but not without your father's blessing." She said with tears in her eyes.

"He's a good man, he really is." Bert said, and then, "I know, why don't we go to him right now and tell him that we are engaged to be married. He'll have no choice but to love you then."

"Are you sure that's a good idea?" She asked wiping her tear stained eyes on his shoulder.

"Well it's worth a shot. I-I can't keep sneaking around like this anymore. It doesn't make any sense. And this is not the kind of man I want to be. Sneaking around like we're some kind of

criminals. I want to be the kind of man that you deserve, a proud man who can look anybody in the eye."

So, Bert summoned up all the courage he could muster, took Sandra by the hand and marched into the family's front door. Norman was at his desk going over his typewriter paperwork and smoking his pipe. His mother was in the kitchen and his brothers and sister were doing a jigsaw puzzle on the floor. As soon as the front door shut the whole house stopped what it was collectively doing, sensing a disturbance. Noticing the quiet, his mother came out of the kitchen drying off a wooden bowl with her apron. Norman slowly took the pipe out of his mouth, exhaled a puff of tobacco smoke and postured firmly, eyes squinted, chest out like he'd never lost a war.

"Mother, Father, I have something to tell you." Bert started nervously, looking back and forth between the two of them. "Sandra and I, we uh, we want to get married."

Norman stood up slowly, took one, two steps forward then, pointing with his pipe said, "Young lady, I think you'd better be getting home now."

"But Father, it's just..." Bert started but was cut off.

"Get the hell out of here, now!" Norman bellowed, throwing his pipe against the wall, shattering it into pieces.

Sandra started to cry and turned to leave when Bert got a sudden charge of courage, grabbed her by the wrist and said, "No Father. She's not going. We are in love and we are going to get married. I don't see why you don't approve of her Father. You've never even given her a chance!"

Norman took another long, slow step towards the young couple and before his boot landed heavy on the floor, his right backhand hit Bert so hard that it instantly split his lip wide open.

"I told you to stay away from her! No son of mine will disobey me so blatantly, now get the hell out! Get out and take this little hussy with you." Norman shouted angrily.

Bert and Sandra ran out of the house and sped off in his old Ford pickup truck. They spent the night under the stars in the bed of the truck without saying a word to one another. The next day they went back to Bert's house, snuck in his bedroom window and packed everything he could fit into an old suitcase, crept back out then jumped in his pick-up truck and drove it as far as they could, as fast as they could. They stopped only for gas and after two long days on the road, they made it to a small town in Illinois called Effingham. They went right to the city hall and were married by a justice of the peace. The couple got their marriage certificates and then moved on before stopping in St. Louis, Missouri.

Once settled, Bert got a job on a construction site and Sandra became a schoolteacher. They bought a farmhouse in St. Peters where they grew corn and tobacco and raised chickens, hogs and sheep. Within a year, Sandra was pregnant with Curtis. He was born a strapping, brown eyed boy. A year later she was with child again. In the winter she gave birth to her second child, a green-eyed ginger called Aaron.

As the boys, Curtis and Aaron grew, it became evident that the two boys, though bore of the same parents, raised in the same home, could not have been more different. Curt took to working in the fields, but Aaron was more interested in working with the animals. Curtis was more mischievous than his brother and trouble seemed to follow him everywhere he went. Aaron seemed to be successful in all his sheep tending endeavors. One of his sheep would get pregnant and she would give birth successfully to a whole flock of healthy lambs. Curtis on the other hand,

couldn't catch a break when it came to his farming. He would plant a field of corn and half of it would sprout dead.

Curtis seemed to be constantly out of favor with his father as opposed to Aaron who was usually in his favor. One year for Christmas, Curtis took great pains to tan a pig's skin and stitch together a fine leather wallet with the family name *Fick* branded on it for his father's gift. Aaron gathered some flowers from the garden, put them in a glass and filled it with water. Come Christmas morning, Curtis very proudly presented his chain wallet to his father. His father looked at it and promptly set it aside. Aaron handed his father his simple bouquets of weedy flowers and his father's eyes lit up like the illumination on the Christmas tree. This angered Curtis to no end. Why did his father favor Aaron's crappy flowers over Curtis' cool wallet with the family name on it? He couldn't let this go.

Curtis carried this burden around for a long time. Months past and the tension between the two boys grew thicker and thicker. One day Curtis took Aaron to an underground fort that he had dug out near Spencer's Creek and would go to be alone from time to time. Curt led him down into the dark underground tunnels he had dug until they came to a small room with bench-like seats carved out and three indentions in the wall where three candles were lit.

Curt started digging a new hole while Aaron, who sat down only after placing his handkerchief down on the dirt first looked around and casually wondered how his brother could have made such a place with his own hands. After about three Mississippi's he came to a conclusion that satisfied his curiosity: he must have had help from those Neanderthal friends of his. They must have been the ones who carved *Boug Boys* and *SPMC* on the walls like the cavemen that they were. After what seemed like a lifetime to Aaron, Curtis jabbed the shovel in the wall and asked, "Why does our father love you more than he loves me?"

"I don't fucking know, Bro. Why don't you ask him?" Aaron answered bluntly.

Curtis stopped digging, wiped his brow with his forearm and threw down the shovel, piercing the ground with a striking clang. His heart raced with rage, his face, blood red. *I don't fucking know, Bro.* my ass! How could he be so cavalier about this? Like he didn't even realize, *didn't know* that there was any favoritism between them. That's absurd! And now look at him just sitting there looking bored, amongst all this brilliance! This fucking kid sits there biting his nails.

The nerve of that kid! What kind of world is this, what kind of existence allows someone like that to be favored so heavily, by our father, by our society, hell, even by nature itself! All the while so quick to just dismiss me and all my contributions? I was the first born, I was supposed to be the one who inherited favor. This world is so fucked up! It's fucked up beyond repair. If that's the way they all feel, if they are so ass backwards that they think that this little piss-ant is God's gift to humanity and I'm just some loser to be discarded, then fuck them. Fuck all of them! Fuck God for making such a stupid ass world! None of them deserve to breath the same air that I breath. I'll show them, I'll show them all!

Curt picked up the shovel, walked calmly over to Aaron and stood over him. The shepherd becoming the wolf.

Aaron said, "Dude, could you not stand so close to me, you kind of stink."

Curt turned away, his back to his brother, then let a smirk emerge from his lips. He paused for a moment and considered one more time if there was any other way to get past this, to come to some kind of an understanding that would explain all of this. *I don't fucking know, Bro.* That

phrase kept repeating itself over and over again in Curt's mind. It started as a low-resolution whisper, then it grew. It grew in volume, it grew in speed, it grew in tone, and it grew in intensity until Curt could hear nothing else but an irritating, repetitious chant. *I don't fucking know, Bro.*

Curt gripped the shovel tightly, took a deep breath, then spun around and whacked his brother across the face causing a satisfying look of confusion on Aaron's face. He tried to stand up but couldn't find the energy, the breath. He dropped to his knees and, still in a state of shock looked up at Curt with pathetic eyes and held his trembling hands out in front of him.

Curt was numb and already growing tired of how dramatically his brother was handling all of this. He was ready to move on with his life and was in no mood for any groveling or any kind of a Q and A session. Curt raised the tip of the spade up to Aaron's throat as Aaron gasped for air, for words, for answers. Curt closed his eyes and took a deep breath, deep enough for both of them, then raised his steel-toed boot to the foot of the shovel and slowly stepped down until the tip of the spade reached the dirt behind Aaron's neck and could go no further.

Aaron's body lay slumped over with blood streaming from his neck and mouth, his eyeball had popped clear out of its socket. Curt had never seen a dead body before. He looked it over curiously as he removed the shovel head from his brother's throat. He was surprised at how little emotion or panic he felt, he just sort of took note of it as if it were an albino dwarf that he could now tick off the box as having had seen and could now move on.

Curtis left Aaron's body in the fort and covered the entrance hole with dirt and leaves and went home practicing his cover story that he hadn't seen Aaron all day. When he walked in the front door of the Fick family home, his father asked, "Where's your brother?"

"How should I know, what am I, his keeper or something?" Curtis replied.

Days turned to weeks, weeks to months as police, investigators and media searched for Aaron. Had he thought it through, Curt probably could have foreseen the amount of attention his missing brother would have gotten, and he could have written some *Dear Father* letter in his handwriting but thinking things through was not Curt's forte. Eventually the investigators gave up looking, the media all moved on and Bert and Sandra made their peace with losing their son.

Bert never found out for sure that Curt had killed his brother but he, nevertheless, never forgave him. Curt left home with a duffle bag full of Metallica T-shirts, a pair of steel-toed boots and one-armed shades never to return again.

Chapter VI

Fooky comes over in his new-to-him, poor man's Cadillac, a 14-year-old black Lincoln Town Car that doesn't even have leather seats. He's wearing oversized, even for him, jean shorts from the Big and Tall store and a white, off brand Polo shirt, sunglasses that look like they're kids size compared to his giant head and a knock-off beige Kangol hat.

"Curt, I need an ounce." He says, walking in the door without knocking. "And make it fat, I need to pinch at least a dime out of it."

"Motherfucker!" Curt shouts. "How many times do I have to tell your fat ass not to just walk in here without knocking, huh? You know how much shit I move outta this place every day? You're lucky I don't shoot your ass!"

"Alright Dog, Jesus!" Fook says with his hands up in a faux surrender. "I don't want any trouble, *Tony Montana*, can you just give me a giant ounce that I pinch out of?"

"They're already weighed out, Dude." Curt says, lowering his tone down to about an 8 1/2. "You know that shit."

"Quit being such a fuckin' Jew. Sorry Schultz." Fooky says, plopping his fat ass down on the dusty brown couch. "Just put a little something extra in there for me."

"No way Julio, I sell them cheap because of portion control." He explains in a somewhat calm manner. "Give it to them for $90.00 and keep 10 bucks. That's the best I can do."

"Whatever you fucking Heeb." He says, then, "Oh look, that's that bitch!"

"Not you too with the bitches!" I say, wondering who else knows about them. "What the flippin' balls? Dude, this is not that big of a deal!" I'm exasperating to no one.

"No! I mean…wait, what?" Fooky asks, doing a double take, confusion setting in. "No Dude, the bitch on T.V. Have you seen this shit? It's that Jew broad that went missing, Shandra Levy. She was working in Washington D. C. for some congressman and she's been missing for like, I don't know, a couple of weeks or something. People are saying all kinds of crazy shit."

"Saying shit like what?" Curt asks, the spark of curiosity elevating his core temperature.

"That this is some kind of political hit job or something!" Fook says picking up the empty 6-inch, green plastic bong and hitting the resin in the bowl.

"No way!" Curt says. I'm still listening but passive/aggressively staying quiet. No one notices.

"Dude, maybe she knew something she shouldn't know, saw something that she shouldn't have seen…" Fooky is explaining.

"She could have just run away or gotten killed by a stranger." I say, still pouting.

"Maybe, but people are saying a lot of shit, like maybe she got a little too close to the Congressman or something." Fook speculates, then asks, "You guys haven't been following this?"

"No dude, I don't give a fuck about politics." Dicky chimes in dismissively, twisting the cap off of a Budwieser bottle.

"Dude," Fooky starts, walking over to the mirror and adjusting his gay hat. "this is starting to get really juicy. It has all the elements of a great news story; corruption, power, sex, coverups, ya' know? This is good shit!"

"Fook, she could just be on a long weekend with some dude she met." Dicky says picking up a bottle from the table, goes to take a drink, then realizes it's just an empty, sets it down, picks up his beer and proceeds to drink it.

"Maybe, but this could be the story of the century." Fook says standing up straight, checking out his teeth, then walking over and sitting back down on the couch.

"Dude, the century is like five minutes old." I say taking a drag off a Marlboro and then sticking it under the low E string of my guitar.

"No shit?" Curt says, ignoring me, somewhat interested in Fooky's conspiracy theory.

"Yeah, no shit. Just watch this." Fooky says, staring at the T.V.

"Alright, whatever man, let's go hit some balls." Dicky says, standing up and stretching his arms above his head.

"Yeah, I could take a break." I say. "Dicky, bring the 12-pack of Buds, not the Lights."

"Where are the clubs and bucket of balls?" Fooky asks actually offering to chip in a helping hand for once.

"Right there." I say, pointing at the assorted golf clubs we keep in the corner by the front door.

The park directly adjacent to our duplex is perfect for an array of things. There's a big pavilion with BBQ pits for Q'ing, there's a playground, of course, which is actually a good *bringing it in* spot. Not like, bringing in little kids or anything, I mean, if you've got a lady friend, our pad is not the most romantic place in the world, so you can bring her to the park and it's a nice change of scenery. You can sit on the swings, play a little grab-ass on the animal spinny thing and have a great time.

Valerie digs it, she says that it reminds her of her childhood, the happy parts anyway. I don't know what she meant by that last bit but, I hear what she's saying. It's innocent fun, it takes you back to a simpler time. A time when getting high meant swinging up into the stratosphere until you thought you'd fly away up to heaven.

Where the road curves through, opposite that is a cemetery, which is a cool place to burn a few and reflect on life, death, the afterlife, and the balance between order and chaos. How close we all are to falling through the thin ice of life that we're all skating mercifully on. The rest of it is just a big field, perfect for chipping golf balls back and forth, drinking beer, and tossing the disc around. We've petitioned the city to put up a proper, full Disc Golf course there, we even mapped out where the holes would go but thus far, it's fallen on the deaf ears of the city's bureaucratic red tape.

It's a steamy August afternoon but there are hints that the worst of the excruciating Missouri summer is behind us, the sun is shining down but it's not as an oppressive heat as it was even yesterday. The clouds that are scattered across the blue mid-western sky are enough to make it either sweater weather or jeans and a T-Shirt weather, depending on how much cocaine you've done that day. That's a real factor, look it up. The only real question is, do you need to put socks on.

"Nobody ever mentions the weather, can make or break your day." I'm singing as we walk down the green hill to the park.

"Schultz!" Curt shouts, chipping a ball with the 7 Iron from the far pitch. "Tell me again why it's cool to be a snitch." He's wearing a black *Samurai Blues* T-shirt from Spencer's Gifts, a chain wallet from the Harley Davidson store and the same steel-toed boots he's been pimping since before I met him.

"Nice shot Dude." Fooky says, shaking his ginormous ass before taking a *Happy Gilmore* style shot.

"Alright, so here's the thing." I start. "If you get busted with another dude, you always want to snitch on the dude before he snitches on you." I say. I'm wearing a forest green, Earth Day T-Shirt from Target, Levi jeans and a pair of brown, leather sandals from Wal-Mart, obviously no socks.

"Snitches get stitches, Dude." Dicky says. He's wearing a pink Polo shirt, a pair of American Eagle, jean shorts and no shoes. "Don't fuckin' forget where you come from Schultzy."

"Yeah, well in prison you get raped so, ya know, there's that." I say, looking at Curt, wondering if I've gone too far, said too much.

"It's best for both of you to keep your fucking mouths shut." Curt says, squaring up for his shot.

"Yeah, you're right." I say, then, "It's like…" I'm thinking how to put this philosophical point in the plainest possible language. "It's called The Prisoner's Delima. Think of every episode of Law and Order you've ever seen. The theory goes like this: Two guys get busted and are in separate interrogation rooms at the cop shop. The cops offer both guys the same deal: Rat on your friend and you can walk out of here right now and your friend gets 10 years. But the deal only goes to the first one to rat. So, you have two choices; You can rat on your friend or keep your mouth shut and hope he doesn't narc on you. If you both keep your mouths shut, you both go free.

"Sounds reasonable, why doesn't everyone just do that?" Curt asks.

"Damn, you sound as naive as the simpletons who sit around thinking this crap up. You know how it goes down; stuff happens." I say.

"So, what happens next?" Dicky asks.

"Well now there are three different scenarios." I'm twirling my 3 Iron around with my fingers. "You can keep your mouth shut and hope your friend does the same. That's the best scenario, obviously."

"Yeah, but shit happens, right?" Curt redundantly reminds me.

"Yeah, well so alright," I'm explaining. "if you take the deal first, your friend goes to jail for 10 years and you get to go home. That's the second-best scenario." I say, then finish, "The worst scenario is your friend takes the deal and you do the 10 years."

"You just have to have a pack with your boy and make sure you both don't talk; you both go free." Dicky says, as we walk to get our balls, mine is clearly the closest to the dirt circle we were aiming for.

"Well that's where the theory comes in. Are you willing to bet 10 years of your life that your boy is going to keep his word and *not* rat you out?" I ask, making my point. "That's why it's always best to take the deal."

"Well..." Curt starts but I just do not have the patience to continue explaining this for the 100th time.

"Think about it this way," I say, unable to hide my distain. "you're going to sell a pound of weed to someone."

"Yeah." He says, at least listening and not just wanting to make a point that I will then destroy.

"The best scenario is that you bring the weed," I say, looking at everyone individually to assure that they are paying enough attention. Fooky is unapologetically not. "And he brings the money. You swap and then you both go home; everyone is happy and you can go on to have future drug deals."

"Yeah." Dicky and Curt say at the same time, then share an awkward glance, then quickly look away in random directions.

"O.K., well what if he brings a gun and ganks you?" I ask. "He walks away with all the weed and all the money."

"That would never happen, Schultz." Curt says without emotion. Golf club in hand, he's shaking it at me.

"Or the other way around." I offer in an attempt to stop the swinging. "You could bring the gun and gank him, taking home the weed *and* the money."

"OK, closer." He says taking off his T-shirt by pulling it from the back, revealing the 6-pack abs we all know so well. Every time is an event with him. The wind chill factor has to be in the double-digit negatives for it to be too cold for the Dog to *not* go bare back.

"The point is," I say with emphasis. "the best thing to do is to bring a gun, just in case."

"So, the point is that you can't trust anyone?" Fooky asks, finally engaging in the conversation.

There's a significant pause while try to think of a reason to say *No*, then finally, "That's one way to look at it."

"Well look, the Chuck D. concert is Sunday." Fooky brings up, changing the subject completely. "We're all going right?"

"Hell to the yeah." I say enthusiastically.

"Love me some Charlie Daniels." Dicky says, eyeballing his next shot.

"Well how's this gonna go down?" Fooky asks. "Are we bringing dates?"

"I think Valerie and Blair are going?" I say trying to hide the "look" on my face that everyone says I get when Val comes up.

"Cool, so I can hook up with Valerie? 'Cause we all know you ain't fucking her." Fooky says, only half joking. Dicky offers a bland chuckle then starts to walk up to the house. Curt is distant, unengaged.

"Yeah, you're funny...looking." I say. "You can have Blair."

“Goddamn Dude, is there anything you’re not a fucking Jew about?” Fooky asks, not joking at all. “You’re even stingy with bitches? You’re a fucking little bitch.”

“Get your own bitches, you fat tub of donkey crap.” I say in frustration.

“Good one, Nerd.” Fooky says, then changes the subject again. “So, I’ll drive the Caddy.”

“Shotgun.” I say instinctively.

“No dork.” Fooky fires back. “You sit in back with Valerie and have Blair ride shotgun. I’ll give you the full chauffeur treatment. Don’t fuck it up, maybe she’ll let you touch her elbow.”

“There’s no more beers.” Dicky shouts down at us from the front porch, then, “Fook, you got any Coke?”

Chapter VII

Waiting for me to get home by herself, Valerie is at our crib, sitting on the old, dusty brown sofa, making hemp necklaces that she sells at LU and various hippie festivals that come through town. It's around 9 o'clock and I'm just getting home from a five-hour shift at Steak 'n Shake. I walk in the front door armed with a bag full of food; two orders of Chili 5-way with oyster crackers, four double cheese steak burgers with everything on them plus lettuce and tomato and two large orders of cheese fries with the cheese sauce, obviously on the side. I wasn't raised by a pack of wolves after all.

"I'm home." I say, walking in the door still wearing black Dickies trousers, a white, short-sleeved work shirt and the standard issued, black Steak 'n Shake apron folded down at the waist.

"Hi Baby." Valerie says, glowing angelically, smiling in a low, scratchy voice, coming out of a brief nod. She picks up the half made hemp necklace she was braiding from her lap, sets it on the wooden coffee table and stubs out a cigarette that she lit maybe 3 1/2 minutes before, took one drag off of, then allowed it to burn down to the butt in the ashtray, filling the house with smoke like a funeral pyre.

"I brought food." I say in a sing-songy voice as I set down the bag on the kitchen counter. The TV was obviously left on from *Jeopardy!* because Oprah is on and Valerie hates that show. They're discussing that congressman, Gary Condit that Fooky was talking about who, it's looking more and more like he probably had an affair with his intern, Chandra Levy. She went missing like three months ago and now they're starting to put the puzzle pieces together. First, she went missing, then we find out that she was "close" to the congressman, now we're finding out he was most likely banging her in what is quickly becoming the scandal of the century, though the century is only a year and a half old.

Valerie is wearing an old school, baby blue, long sleeve Cardinal's jersey, jean cut-off shorts, the white scarf she always wears, and tan, leather sandals. A matching white bandana is holding back her wild brown hair which is resting gently on her bronze shoulders. Her pupils are as small as pin heads and generally glossed over which takes away from their divinity but adds a sultry aura of chaos.

On the wooden coffee table is the latest issue of US Weekly, the black, plastic ashtray from a nameless bar with two fully smoked Marlboro Light cigarette butts, the tips of the cigarettes that Val always tears off before lighting them, one half-smoked KOOL cigarette butt and a roach. The one-foot, green plastic bong is put away on the side of the couch with a packed bowl that has only been hit once. There is a little less than a nickel bag of weed on the table which would usually be kept in the metal Jack Daniels box that we keep all of our paraphernalia in, only I don't see the box anywhere.

"Yay!" She says cheerfully, walking into the kitchen and hugging me from behind seductively and rubbing my semi-firm abs. "What'd you bring me?"

"Just the usual." I say, trying to flex my abs as much as I can without it being obvious. "Some burgers, some noodles and cheese, you know the routine."

"Sounds yummy." She purrs, pressing her lips against the back of my neck, sending chills down my spine. Her hands making their way up to my chest.

"Did you bring any cheese sauce?" She asks suggestively, fingers tickling my toned pecs.

"You know I got some cheese sauce, Baby." I say, choosing to forget about the dilated pupils, the long-sleeved shirt in the summer, the missing drug box, and the half-smoked KOOL in the ashtray. I choose to let her seduction distract me. If there is one thing Val is good at, it's distracting me.

"*Mmmm.*" She hums, kissing my neck. "I *love* cheese sauce."

Her hands are now flirting with my belt line. I suck in my stomach, inviting her hands to go as low as they please. She presses her body aggressively against mine when suddenly there is a banging on the front door and familiar voices from the other side demand, "Open up! We've got beers!"

"Oh, Sarai's here!" She says, snapping out of her almost pre-orgasm. She bounces over and unlocks the front door and lets Josh White and Sarai in who quickly make themselves at home in the living room.

"I like what you've done with the place." Josh says sarcastically. "You know, if you threw some paint on the walls, got some new furniture and replaced the bedsheets with real curtains...This place could be a real shithole."

"Is that how you turned your mom's basement into the posh bachelor pad it is today?" I ask.

"Bite me, Fag. I hope you have a hamburger in there for me." He says, lighting the fat bowl that is already in the bong.

"They're *Steak*burgers." I say, putting the 12 pack that they brought in the fridge, next to the other 12 pack, and taking out four for all of us.

"Whatever Nerd." Josh says coughing out a bong hit. "Where's Dicky and Curt?"

"I don't know, out? I just got home." I say, taking off my apron and throwing it towards my bedroom door.

Josh is wearing beige Docker shorts, a Tie-Dye Allman Brothers Band T-shirt with white tennis shoes and ankle high socks, his hair is heavily gelled and spikey. Josh is tallish and thin, not un-hot and loves to argue. He passes the bong to Sarai who is wearing faded bellbottom jeans from the Goodwill and a blue Dave Mathews T-Shirt with brown leather sandals and rim wired glasses. Sarai is also tallish but has a stout frame and a big booty that have all the brothers lining up.

"Sarai, come in here, I need to talk to you." Valerie calls from my bedroom. Sarai blows out the bong hit, tries to make smoke rings, fails, puts the cashed bowl back in the bong and disappears into my bedroom without saying a word, locking the pale white, paint-chipped door behind her.

"Dude, are you hitting that?" I ask, tossing a burger to Josh and finally packing a bowl for myself.

"No." he answers flatly, "Are you hitting *that*?" He asks nodding toward the bedroom door.

"Uh, you know, I don't like to kiss and tell." I say, holding in a gigantic bong rip.

"Shut the fuck up, she still won't let you fuck her?" He presses. I give him a look that is intentionally neutral.

"Damn!" He says, shaking his head, then jives, "She suck on yo dick?"

I pause, teeth gritted, screaming for him to shut his filthy mouth with my eyes, pushing around the ashes in the cashed bowl and then hitting it again.

"Has she ever even *seen* your dick?" Josh asks, amazed with each of his questions he's answering. "You two are fucking nuts, I'll never get you two. You've been like, *together,"* he says doing air quotes, "for like four years and she still won't let you hit it? Dude, you're in some bizarre friend zone that I've never even heard of before. It's never even been invented before because it's so fucking stupid!"

"Alright, alright, calm down." I say, motioning with my hands to keep it down, looking around. "We…have…ya know, done…stuff."

"Yeah right." Josh says unconvinced. "You probably ain't even seen her titties, have you?"

Before I have a chance to address these charges, Valerie and Sarai slowly roll out of the bedroom, both visibly high and itching lazily around their arm and shoulder regions. Val sits down without saying anything, picks up the hemp necklace she was working on and continues braiding it where she left off. Sarai plops down next to Josh on the couch and starts looking aimlessly around the room for some unknown entity. Josh just stares at both of them curiously. Bubbling.

"Where's that…channel changer thingy at?" Sarai asks with absolute sincerity.

Josh looks at Sarai hoping to make eye contact, then down at her plump ass, then back at her eyes, squints accusingly at her, then, still unable to make eye contact, looks to Valerie who is lost in her hemp necklace, then back at Sarai, pauses, then looks at me before announcing to the room as a whole, "You're fucking sitting on it!"

There's an anti-climactic pause, then, "Oh, no shit." Sarai says dismissively, leaning over and grabbing the remote. She looks at it curiously, gives it a brief sniff, then goes about trying in vain to figure out how to turn on the used Zenith 12-inch television.

"Chill out Josh." Valerie says slowly, without looking up from her necklace, "You're too high strung."

I'm busy pretending to look at my grey, flip up, Motorola cell phone. I want absolutely nothing to do with this.

"No shit, Dude." Sarai says, tapping the remote control with her hand, then pointing it at the T. V. before hitting more random buttons. "You need to like, mellow out or something." Then she and Valeri look at each other and start laughing.

Josh pauses, gives the room another once over before asking redundantly, "So you two are just shooting heroin now? What the fuck is wrong with you?"

"Jesus Josh." Sarai says, looking up and slapping her hands on her lap "Be a dick why don't you."

"*I'm* being a dick?" Josh asks no one in particular, eyes bulging. "Do we not have enough dead friends already, enough junkie friends already?" He stops to take a breath, looks around again, pauses, looks at me still pretending to be on my phone then, "Are you doing this shit too?"

"Me?" I ask innocently. "I uh, no man. I'm cool."

"You're cool?" He asks, cocking his heavily gelled head to the side in faux confusion. "You're cool with this? You're cool if she fucking ODs and dies?"

"Na…I …I uh…" I'm stammering.

"I…I…I what, Motherfucker?" Josh mockingly insists. "You guys fucking kill me I swear."

"Whatever *Dad*, like you don't ever get high." Val says.

"No shit dude," Sarai jumps in, "don't be such a, like…a two facer, Dude."

"Hypocrite." I sigh reluctantly without looking up from my phone.

"Yeah, hypocrite." Sarai says, trailing off. "Or whatever."

"Don't we like…call cocaine *Josh*, like because you, Josh, like…never *don't* have cocaine?" Valerie asks.

"First of all, no one has called it *Josh* in years. Secondly, like, name one person we know or have ever heard of that died from doing coke or taking ludes or whatever." Josh argues vehemently with his hands flaring around in full preacher mode.

The pause that follows brings a tension that explodes in the room like a buzz killing atomic bomb. Valerie tries to concentrate on her hemp weaving, Sarai continues to let the remote control completely baffle her as I try desperately to look like I am too preoccupied with my cell phone to be paying attention but the blood that is boiling inside of me, turning my face from its usual Caucasian Pink to blood red and then all the way to a pulsating, dickhead purplish color gives me away.

I take what feels like a final look around the room. Suddenly nothing feels the same in this house, the walls are crumbling down around me, bridges are collapsing. My world is crashing in on me. This dragon's name is Chaos. I'm fuming. I'm furious at Josh for calling out the elephant in the room. Furious at Valerie for being so selfish and weak, but most of all, I'm furious at myself. I'm ashamed that I've been so greedy that I'm willing to let this girl that I like, I mean, I do actually like her kind of a lot and I'm going to let her become a junkie right in front of my eyes because I like the way she treats me when she's high? That's pretty lame.

"Long sleeves in August?" Josh continues accusingly, breaking my chain of thought. "You two shoot so much dope that you have to wear long sleeves all the time now, in the summer?"

"O.K. Josh." Val finally says, shooting me a look and hoping I'll jump in to defend her. "You made your point. Can you please go and fuck off now?"

“No, I won’t fuck off.” Josh says defensively, “If Schultz is too blind or too chicken shit to say anything then I will. I’m not just going to sit by and watch you guys kill yourself.”

“Uhhhggg!” Valerie says slumping back in the sofa, defeated, buzz slipping away. I’m looking up from my phone now, sweat pouring form my forehead.

“Is that why you're always wearing that scarf around your neck? In August?” Josh continues without hesitation. “Are you shooting it right into your neck? Have you been doing this all along? What the fuck?”

“Alright Josh, that’s enough!” I finally shout firmly, slamming my phone down on the table and leaning forward.

“Sarai, let’s get out of here.” Val says, standing up and grabbing Sarai by the hand.

The two girls go into my bedroom and lock the door, then come out thirty seconds later and, without saying a word or looking at us, walk out of the front door.

After the door slams shut, I look at Josh and say, “Dude, you’re a gigantic prick.” picking up the remote control, turning on the T.V. and changing the channel to CNN, “You know that, right?”

“Well what the fuck, Dude,” Josh says, reaching in his pocket and pulling out a gram of decent cocaine, emptying it onto the small mirror on the wooden table and cutting out four fatties with a credit card. “Someone had to say it.”

“Have you been following this story?” I ask, pointing to the T.V.

“Yeah, that guy’s secretary died.” He says.

“I don’t think she just died; it looks like someone killed her.” I say. “Now they’re saying that she may have been banging that politician she was working for.”

“No way.” He says arrogantly. “You don’t have any evidence of that.”

“Dude, that’s what they’re talking about right now.” I say, pointing to the screen.

“I don’t give a shit what they say. I do my own research.” He says, waving off the T.V.

“You don’t have to believe them blindly, but you can’t just dismiss everything that they say. That’s just ignorance. That's being willfully blind.” I say.

“Oh, I’m the one who’s being blind now?” He says, changing the story to justify his logical fallacy.

“Shooting it in her neck? Really? You had to bring up the scarf?” I say, rolling up a twenty-dollar bill and snorting a line.

“Well what’s the fucking deal with that thing anyway?” Josh asks, taking the rolled up twenty and snorting a line himself, then rubbing some coke on his gums with his index finger.

“Don’t ask.” I say, turning off the T.V. and lighting a cigarette. I pocket the rolled up 20.

Chapter VIII

"Schultz, don't you have any Chuck D. in here?" Fooky asks, flipping through my CD case while driving the Caddy down Highway 70, headed toward Earth City where Riverport Ampitheater is located. Riverport is one of the greatest outdoor concert venues in the United States, arguably better for summertime gigs than The Hollywood Bowl. Riverport was the home of the legendary Guns 'n Roses riot of '91 where Axl Rose jumped into the crowd and beat a fan with his microphone stand for taking his photo then walked off the stage leaving the crowd with a void that could only be filled with chaos.

Today is a great day for an outdoor concert, it's smoldering now but when the sun goes down, it'll cool off nicely for late August. There's a refreshing breeze, not a cloud in the vast blue sky. I've been drinking Popov Vodka on the rocks since I woke up today and Valerie is clearly high on heroin. She's been very sultry towards me all day and it's catapulting me absolutely over the moon.

"No Fook, I don't think I do. I think there's some David Allen Coe in there though." I say from the back seat, Valerie rubbing my leg, glowing. Val is wearing faded bell bottoms from the Marshalls, a white wife beater, no bra, and a red bandana holding her curly brown hair back, her white velvet scarf and a matching Daisy ring on her forefinger.

"Ugh!" Fooky is still pouting about the CD situation.

"Why is that not good enough?" I ask, arms waving aimlessly.

"We gotta listen to Charlie Daniels, we're going to see *Charlie Daniels*." He insists, adjusting the rearview mirror so I'll see the depth of the disappointment in his eyes.

"Right, we're about to listen to him for like two hours, why do we have to listen to him now? Do we need to like, brush up on the songs so we don't look like posers when we want to sing along?"

"No Schultz," Fooky looks at me with un-amusement in his eyes. "we don't need to study him before the exam, it's just to get us in the mood."

"Well, David Allen Coe should get us there." I say. "Wine is fine, Man, but whiskey's quicker."

"Val, how you doing back there?" Fooky asks, looking at her in the rearview mirror he's still playing with.

"I'm good Fooky, thank you for asking." She says, tearing the tip of a cigarette off, throwing it out the window then lighting it.

"Why do you always do that to your cigarettes?" Fooky asks.

"I don't know, I don't like the first part." She says casually, then remembering something, "Oh," she blows out an unremarkable drag, then, "I knew I was mad at you. You missed my birthday last week you dick!"

"I know, I'm sorry. I had to work the next day." He says, semi convincingly.

"Yeah right." She says, "You had to work my ass, you're such a lier! You promised me that you were gonna bring a *ton* of coke."

"I'm sorry Baby Girl, did it mess up your party?" He asks hitting a joint and coughing out the hit.

It's only now that I'm realizing something; she likes the way he talks to her. She loves it! I always thought it sounded so cheesy, the way Fooky talked to girls. Somehow, I feel like that whole faggy, 'Oh, I'm just one of the girls, it's O.K. to try on clothes around me. It's cool girlfriend.' routine actually works on chicks. If Fooky wasn't such a butt ugly, fat bastard, I'd be popping mad but right now, he seems to be keeping Valerie in a very pleasant mood so, whatever man…let the good times roll.

"Fuck no, we got ripped anyway." Valerie says, opening a beer. The foam that she splashes off of her delicate fingers snaps me out of a brief daze.

"Well happy late birthday anyway, Darlin." Fooky says, looking at her in the rearview mirror, exposing his badly browned and disfigured teeth. "How does it feel to be 20 anyway?"

"I don't feel any different, ya' know." She says, twirling her wild brunette hair lazily, "It's just another day, I guess. I don't feel like a grown-up or anything."

"You thought you'd feel more like a grown up by now?" He asks, as enchanted by her as I am.

"I don't know," She says, wistfully. "I guess I do feel younger than…" There's a pause. "… You know, then I thought I would by now."

"Well you're only 20." Fooky says, laughing.

"I don't want to live forever or anything, and I *really* don't want to grow old." She says, looking out of the window of the Caddy blankly, still twirling her hair. Growing weary.

"Well I'll try to score you some coke tonight." Fooky says cheerfully.

"Ok Fooky, whatever." She barely says, sinking back into the comforts of the Caddy. Her eyes fluttering back in her head. Her white scarf pulled tightly around her neck.

Fooky tries to say something resembling romantic to Blair who is sitting shotgun. She's not really buying it though and when he puts his hand on her thigh, she quickly brushes it away.

Fooky is the perfect fit for the Caddy's driver seat. Cadillacs are suited for 300-pound dudes over 6 feet tall. He does look a lot like a chauffeur too, with his beige Kangol hat and Terminator shades. He's wearing a red Aloha shirt and Calvin Klein jean shorts. I could totally see him and Blair as a couple although I don't think either of them would feel comfortable with that notion.

Blair and Martin are the best example of a "couple" that I think our current generation is prepared to commit to. I think they sort of love each other but it's pretty unrealistic to expect any kind of faithfulness when you're in a constant state of chaotic ravery. They hook up every time it's convenient, but you can't always control who you end up with when the music stops at the end of the night. Blair is pretty but has a way of coming off like one of the boys, even with her giant cans that turn any sized T-shirt into an XX small. She has shoulder length blond hair that is pulled to the side with a decorative hair clip that looks like an antique. She's wearing a white T-shirt that reads, *"My eyes are up here."* and a tight satin floral sun dress with big Gucci sunglasses.

Val comes out of her nod briefly and asks no one in particular if we're there yet. She leans over and kisses me on the mouth which is something she wouldn't have done a month ago and I'm a little embarrassed by it. She whispers in my ear, "I love kissing you. I can't imagine ever seeing you and not kissing you." And is holding my hand in the garden of her lap.

"I've always felt that way about you." I say, then stop myself from saying anything further. That's the closest thing to, "Good, let's run away together, elope in some small town out west and never look back." that I feel I can say without sounding like a stalker and sending her running for the hills.

We pull in the parking lot of Riverport Amphitheater and smoke as many one-hits as we can before we have to park and get out. We find Curt and Dicky who took Curt's red, Chevy F-150 and they tell us to follow them to where we're going to meet up with everyone else. Standing around Too Brewed Rick Tellshrewd's old Chevy Truck, drinking Natural Light from a keg is; Ryan Barnes and M. B., Josh White and Derik Smith, Too Brewed, Ryan's brother, Jon and Bad Bob, Dan Carlos, Conely, Quillman and Hollimaer. Mort and Aaron Dorhoff are walking up looking like they just committed arson somewhere dry. Everyone is shirtless wearing off brand blue jeans, work boots from Payless and all heavily tatted up.

They're talking about construction work like it was the coolest thing in the world to do. I swear, those guys are going to be the happiest dudes in the world, they talk about work like it was a party. I guess if I could drink beer at work, I'd think it was cool too. I can get drunk at Hackmann Lumber but something about making minimum wage gives a degenerate, pathetic aura to it.

Amy Stewart and Katie Barret are there, looking hot. The Bugler sisters, Jenny and Julie, are talking to some other girls who are hot enough, I suppose, but I don't know who they are and not one of them holds a candle to Valerie's radiance, so my brain quickly dismisses them as irrelevant. The parking lot is a vast expanse of crappy old trucks sporting Rebel Flags and oversized, muddy tires. Dudes and chicks with worn out concert T-shirts and cowboy hats, no shortage of stretched out, and misspelled prison tats. Lots of leather, turquoise and silver jewelry, not so much on the deodorant and dental floss.

Fooky says jokingly as we walk up to everyone, "Well, the trailer parks are empty tonight." Jon Barnes and his missus are not amused.

Martin and Daffy finally show up so we should be able to start making our way into the gig but there has to be drama first. Martin, who's wearing a crisp white wife-beater, a silver beaded necklace and a blue St. Louis Rams hat backwards tries to kiss Blair on the cheek, but she pulls away and mumbles something passive/aggressively and lights a cigarette.

Daffy, who is like the Kato Kaylin of St. Charles, a lovable couch surfer who has done time on everyone's sofa in a seemingly random rotation is wearing an oversized, red Cardinals jersey that is lazily schlepping off his chubby frame, a red Cardinals cap pulled down snug, black socks pulled up tight with white Nike tennis shoes. The last time it he did time with us, Fooky was already crashing on the couch so we let him set up all his stuff in our basement that we never use.

The last time I went down there, all his crap; the garage sale sofa, crappy wooden coffee table, old school, two-ton Zenith television set from the 80's when all the highest tech stuff was giant, black and weighed a kajillion pounds. There were eight pairs of women's panties nailed around the perimeter that he claims were left behind by various *bitches* that he hooked up with but I'm not at all convinced that he didn't just swipe them from his step-sister's undies drawer while knicker sniffing one drunken evening.

After we make it through the turnstile, we follow the path to the left, past all the stands selling Charlie Daniels T-shirts and various paraphernalia with no shortage of Rebel Flags on them. We finally make it to the front where we all buy two $8.00 beers and then make our way up the hill to where the lawn seating and standing is. We walk through the sea of people, careful not to step on any group's blanket or tarp they're sitting on, until we find an open place where we can stake a claim and get down to business. This is what Woodstock would have looked like had the South won the civil war.

The air smells like redneck B.O. and cheap weed with a hint of vomit and stale Miller Light. Bad prison tats, Harley Davidson bandanas, black, leather biker vests that are bordering on an aggressive version of *Village People* kind of gay, silver skull rings, and chain wallets seem to be the unofficial dress code. I can hear crisp colors coming to life, greens and yellows that remind me of the Dead Farm and my childhood. Valerie is wearing patchouli and it's driving me crazy; I'm trying to be cool but I'm tempted to sweep her off her feet and fly her away, off to the moon and all around the sun.

We find a decent place all the way at the top of the hill, right by the fence, in front of a bunch of cowboys and their chicks. When you look out west, past the fence and the parking lot you can see the sun setting, causing a starburst of oranges, hot pinks and blues, then pivot 180 degrees and gaze on the sea of salt of the Earth folks, the stage and the anticipation of the modern-day Jefferson Davis hits you like a rebel musket to the gut.

One of the dudes in the group of cowboys in front of us is a brother, but like, Blazing Saddles kind of brother, still pimping a cowboy hat, one of those Western shirts that is button down but the buttons are shiny and clasp shut, you know the type, tucked into his dark blue Wranglers, big ass silver belt buckle, and cowboy boots just like all his buddies. I'm sort of fascinated with the group and I take a moment to sort everyone out, in my head at least.

I consult Fooky and as far as we can judge, we have; Blazing Saddles, who I just broke down, Toothless Jimmy, who's a younger fella with overgrown peach fuzz, stained wife-beater, and chunks of hair cut off like he's used to falling asleep with gum in his mouth and then has to cut it out of his hair in the morning fairly regularly. There's Fat Tom, who is built like a top, I'm won-

dering how he manages to keep himself upright. He's like one of those bodybuilders who consistently skips "leg day", only he isn't buff, not by any stretch of the imagination.

There are a couple of girls in the group, some of them not too shabby, not at all, and obviously easy as hell to bring in. Shoot, the whole *first cousin* taboo is not a deal breaker for these folks, the thing is, they're either like 13-and-a-half and smoking hot or 31 going on 52 and haggard as all get out. Not a lot of middle ground in the trailer park spectrum. I guess when you look that good at 13 and everyone and their uncle, literally, is trying to get into your knickers, you start crapping out kids pretty early and then boom, there goes your youthful beauty. Chain smoking Pall Malls and Jim Beam by the 5th are not great skin moisturizers either.

We're all double fisted with $8.00 beers, but this is clearly not going to be a sustainable scenario being so far away from the beer and food stands. Thank God Dicky snuck in a bottle of Jack Daniels and Martin and Daffy somehow snuck in a gallon of Early Times that they are passing around quite freely. It's also cool to burn joints out here on the lawn and everyone is pretty libertarian about weed but we are living in a Tennessee whiskey world and I am a Tennessee whiskey kind of girl.

After the sun goes down, they hit the lights and the show starts with *The South's Gonna Do It Again* and immediately, Dan Carlos, Jay Conley, Curt and Too Brewed start jumping around, throwing elbows, hoping to start the first ever mosh pit in country music history. The Good Ol' Boys in front of us, who look like they're here to have a good time, they're sort of dancing around in a square dance kind of way. The way that black people make fun of white people for dancing, even Blazing Saddles, he is busting a serious move. They're all kicking up their boots and knee slapping and do-si-do-ing but for some reason when the black dude does it...well, you can imagine.

Long Haired Country Boy starts, and the boys start moshing more aggressively. The music is loud, and the whiskey is flowing. Being outside, on the wide lawn with all these rednecks create a dangerous concoction of hot summer nights under the stars, the anonymity of all the other dudes that all fit the same general profile and party atmosphere that brings out the dog in a lot of us. We are howling at the moon and the moon is howling back.

The moshing starts to spread like a cancer that is becoming malignant. Curt pushes Dan Carlos into the Good Ol' Boys in front of us. He smashes into Fat Tom and he stumbles back but magically is able to stay on his feet. Sufferin' succotash, he really is like one of those Weeble Wobbles. That gets brushed off as an accident and they go back to moshing. Then Dan Carlos shoves Curt into the group and he levels Toothless Jimmy to the ground. They posture briefly but, not wanting any trouble, they let it go. But when Martin is pushed into Scrawny Cliff, sending the dude flying and ultimately lying on his back well, it seems some sort of Mason/Dixon line has been crossed.

After about five other incidents, the patience of The Good Ol' Boys, including Blazing Saddles, starts to run thin. Words are exchanged, threats are implied, things you can't take back. A funny thing about red necks is that they get oddly formal the more pissed off they get. The redder their face gets, the more; *Misters* and *Sirs* you're bound to hear.

"What? You pussies got a fucking problem?" Martin asks with outstretched arms.

Finally, they've had enough. Oh, dear Christ, this is about to get biblical for these rednecks. Tales of the ass-whopping these hillbillies are about to get are sure to become the thing of lore in their trailer parks and job sites for generations to come. I almost feel like warning them.

"Hey fellas, can you just knock it off already, gosh dang-it!" Blazing Saddles asks sternly.

"Hey Motherfucker, if you can't hang then go the fuck home, you fucking Uncle Tom." Curt shouts.

Miraculously, this wildly offensive literary reference seems to go directly over their Ten Gallon hats.

"Hey Mister, we're all just here to have a good time." Fat Tom says, trying to keep the peace. "You know, drink some beers and listen to some good Country music. You know what I'm talkin' about, Partner?" He finishes, slapping his fat Papst Blue Ribbon beer belly. Nice try, *Partner*. Maybe you'll get knocked out last.

"Yeah Motherfucker, we are too." Dan Carlos says, cracking his neck.

"If you can't hang why don't you take your bitches and your niggers back to the Wentzville trailer parks." M.B. shouts just as a pause in the music hits, amplifying the insult he just shot for more people to hear than he had intended.

"Mister, you…you boys are…" Toothless Jimmy starts but is cut off.

Well, that was as good as a consent form as needed to be said, and the first punch is thrown. It's the punch heard around the world. It doesn't matter who threw it, it's like the first shot from the Revolutionary War where no one knows who shot it but I suspect it was Sam Addams. Just like I can't prove it now, but I'm sure that it was Curt who threw it. In any case, The Dog knocks someone out straight away, maybe Blazing Saddles in the cowboy hat, maybe Jeb the Retard, but the cowboy hats start piling up on the lawn.

Chaos ensues, immediately the dust starts to stir. It's like an old Loony Toons cartoon where all you can see is a big cloud of dust with the random fists coming out swinging, an occasional head will pop up to catch a breath, blood is squirting out from all over like a frickin' Gallagher concert, only more amusing to watch. I look around for Valerie and see that she is safely off to the side with Blair smoking a joint and casually watching the action.

Suddenly I see a dude emerge, this dude has to be the biggest dude that is not employed by the WWF on planet Earth. He steps up and has his arm cocked and ready to take out M. B. from behind. The gods of brawling must have whispered in his ear because before the dude can connect, M. B. turns around and punches him square in the nose. He stops, dazed, M. B. punches him one more time in the nose making a noise like a softball hitting a windshield. He fishtails and falls to his knees, he starts to seize and drops on the ground squirming around like a Japanese octopus, blood squirting out of his nose like confetti and when he finally comes up, his eyeball has popped out of the socket.

"Now the last thing I wanted was to get in a fight in Jackson Mississippi on a Saturday night." Chuck D. is singing while playing the fiddle.

Chubby Cliff hits Mort in the head from behind with a brick but he doesn't go down. Mort just stands up straight and turns around slowly, touching the back of his head with his fingers and then, inspecting the blood eerily, touches his blood stained fingers to his tongue like I imagine he's probably done with soiled tampons at some point, just 'cause he's always struck me as that kind of cat.

Chubby Cliff is left standing there, possibly thinking the same thing, doubtful, but possible. More than likely there's just a dim patio light with moths swarming around up there that just blew its last fuse. His bravery is evaporating as a mischievous grin grows on Mort's face. Chubby Cliff's fists turn to waves of surrender, a terrified look overtakes his face as Mort licks the blood from his fingers. He reaches around for more and this time blood is dripping from his hand, he smears it onto his tongue and then laughs like a madman. He lunges at Chubby Cliff, grabs his face and head butts him in the nose with an uncomfortable amount of intimacy, breaking it instantly and then Mort licks C.C.'s face, smearing it with his blood. The guy is screaming like some kind of banshee and when Mort finally let's go of his head, Cliffy scampers away on his hands and knees, crying for his mother slash sister.

Martin has a dude, maybe Toothless Jimmy, maybe one of their bitches, and is just hockey jabbing him in the mouth, teeth flying, blood squirting. I'm even hitting a couple of Rebs so I don't have to hear about it later from the boys, mostly to protect Val though.

Dicky is squared up against an unnamed Confederate, they trade a couple of punches before he gets the dude in a headlock. The dude panics, or I don't know, maybe it's the pone's M.O. or whatever, but he bites Dicky's friggin hand…hard. He lets go of his neck and the dude runs off and spits out a mouthful of Dicky blood. Good luck getting that taste out of your mouth, Jethro.

Fooky has a handheld cooler with bricks in it just swinging away in a figure eight motion. He hits one dude right in the mouth that knocks him to the ground and at first, I thought he was throwing up, maybe a *chunky faucet,* maybe a *master of ceremonies,* but then I see that it's blood and teeth that is spewing from his mouth. Katie Barrett has a bitch by the hair and is throwing punches like a dude, beating the bejesus out of her.

The whole thing turns into a not so insignificant riot and, like a swarm of bees all work together to accomplish a shared yet unknown goal that they cannot see, this whole dust up sort of moves toward the exit. We're a long way from the exit though. We fight our way through the lawn, people either get sucked up in the swarm and throw down or they get the fudge out of the way, taking their tarps and blankets with them. We make our way down the hill; throwing blows all the way along the path.

Now that we're on solid ground, cops and security guards inevitably become involved. I hit a couple more people, I think they're dudes. I'm trying to keep an eye out for Valerie and Blair, but the scene is absolute chaos. I find them, grab Valerie by the hand and try to fight our way out of the madness. Absolutely anything could happen at this point.

By the time we get to the main path that heads towards the exits we are carefully, yet briskly making our way through the punches and kicks, just trying to get out of this alive. I see Dan Carlos kick someone in the face with his bare foot and it sounds like an M-80 going off in a mailbox. I feel like I've seen him do this before somewhere, but I can't quite put my finger on when or where that would have been. I guess it could have been anywhere. A cop grabs Jon Barnes by the shoulder in mid-punch, Barnes turns around and socks him in the jaw.

This whole ruckus overflows out into the parking lot but by that time it's so spread out and there are so many cops involved that everyone is just trying to find a friendly car and get the hell out of Dodge. I finally make it to the Caddy, still holding Val's hand who is still holding Blair's hand. The three of us dive in the back and Fooky hops in the driver's seat and fires her up. M. B. gets in shotgun and starts having an asthma attack. He's bleeding from his nose and knuckles and

I'm not in any way joking when I tell Fooky, Blair and Val to take their shirts off so blood doesn't get on my leather upholstery.

"Damn it!" I shout, looking around in a panic.

"What?" Fooky asks, looking over his shoulder. Frantic.

"We missed *Uneasy Rider*." I say, reaching for Val's thigh. Her buzz must have worn off because she brushes my hand away. I'm devastated.

Chapter IX

I'm kneeling on the passenger's side floorboard of the Caddy, headed down Hwy 70 eastbound, burning some serious calories trying to scrub out the blood stains from the leather interior after last night's debacle. Fooky is driving and Curt and Dicky are in the backseat drinking tall boys of Miller Lite for some reason. We're headed to White Birch Park to shoot a round of frisbee golf which I'm already not up for.

"Look at this bloody mess!" I say holding up a blood-stained rag. "This is like in *Pulp Fiction* where they shoot that black kid in the face and then have to clean it all up and it's all his brains and blood and crap all over the back seat."

"Marvin." Curt says.

"I saw you get it wet Motherfucker, when I dried my hands it didn't look like no motha fuckin' tampon." Fooky quotes the movie, laughing.

"It's not funny ya chubby cunt." I seethe. "This blood may not ever come out."

"I can't believe that motherfucker bit me?" Dicky says from the back, looking at this hand. There are teeth marks on his right hand that may or may not heal at some point. "Who the fuck bites a motherfucker?"

"Anything can happen in a fight, Dude." Curt says relatively calmly.

"Dude," Dicky starts, inspecting his hand. "how many fights have you been in?"

"All together?" Curt asks, deep in contemplation.

"How about just this century." Dicky clarifies.

"Let's see, it's 2001 now…" He starts counting on his hands but quickly runs out of fingers.

"How many times has anyone bit you, Motherfucker?" Dicky asks. "That's the point."

"Yeah well, never." Curt admits. "I'm just saying, Dude, fights are fucked up. It's crazy, anything can happen. You roll the dice every time, a dude could have a knife, a gun, a fucking tire iron, you never know. I've been stabbed, shot at, had bottles broken over my dome, kicked in the

face, ya know…" He trails off, clearly triggered in some unknowable way but maintaining some composure.

"It's just a fuckin' ponish move." Dicky says, now he's shaking his hand as if the teeth marks will disappear like an etch-a-sketch. "The motherfucker bit my hand; I don't know if these fuckin' teeth marks are ever going away."

"You can use them to identify the dude, you could press charges." I say, still scrubbing away at my seats.

"Yeah," Fooky finally pipes up after driving uncharacteristically quietly. "well it could be a lot fucking worse, alright." He says, touching his left ear.

"Oh yeah, no shit!" Dicky starts to laugh.

"Fuck Dude," Curt chuckles, "I totally forgot about that."

"Yeah, well, quit crying about your stupid hand, Pussy." Fooky says, rubbing longfully at what's left his scarred right ear lobe that got bit off in a fight in Lesterville back in the day.

Suddenly, as we get off the highway and are driving down Lindbergh Blvd. a horrible smell fills the car. Lindbergh is not exactly known for its pleasant smells; it gets pretty ghetto the deeper north into North County you get. It smells like piss when you roll through the white trash part of town, and then starts to smell like puked up Malt Liquor once you pass there and get more into the 'hood but this is a smell like I've never smelled before. This is like what a rotting corpse in a musty trash heap covered in a hot, steamy pile of crap in July with spoiled gravy ladled on top inside a Texan construction site's Johnny-on-the-Spot must smell like after the lunch trucks leave.

"Fuckin' hell, Fooky!" Dicky exclaims. "Did you shit your pants?" We all pull our shirts up over our noses. "Roll the windows up, Dude." He's shouting through his FZS Class of '94 T-shirt.

"Is that what a dead body smells like?" I ask, puking into a plastic bag I use for trash.

"What the fuck was that?" Dicky asks, gagging into the collar of his casually unbuttoned shirt.

"That might be a dead body." Curt says, a little too matter-of-factly for my personal comfort level.

After we drive through the stench and we all can finally take deep a breath of fresh air, we burn a joint silently amongst each other. There's a pause that lasts different amounts of time depending on who in the car you ask. For me, it was an eon. For Fooky, maybe an episode of *Jeopardy!* that he allowed to bleed into *Oprah* while on the nod one afternoon on the couch at his mom's house. For Curt, perhaps just the flutter of a butterfly's wing. Dicky finally breaks the ice and asks, smelling his shirt that still reeks of rotting flesh, "Schultz, what is smell, Dude? I mean, why do things stink?"

"I don't know Dicky, why do I sometimes have to piss right after I take a shit?" Fooky mocks. "Things just stink."

"Fuck you Fooky." Dicky says as we all roll the windows back down. "I mean, it seems real, like that smell is still on our clothes, like cologne."

"No, that's a good question." I say, giving this some serious thought. I'm on pause, then I press play. "I guess things stink, or we as animals consider things to stink, that are bad for us. I mean, like 12 million years ago or whatever, it was a way to tell the cavemen to stay away from something, not to eat it. If they didn't learn to separate the safe foods from the rotting food by the

smell of it, you know, they died and the people that could recognize the stench of rotting flesh, well, they went on to have babies and reproduce."

"And here we are." Curt announces, arms held out majestically.

"Here we are indeed." I nod. "So, after millions of years, the people that recognized to stay away from things that stank, they went on to reproduce and people that ate rotten, stinky crap died out."

"Oh shit, Dude, that makes sense." Dicky says passing me a decent sized joint.

"Well, what another question is; How *real* is smell?" I put out there.

There's a pause before Curt asks, "What do you mean?" then he takes the joint from me by force.

"Well like, how material is it?" I ask, wiping away an ash. It's extremely hot out so I roll up all the windows and turn up the AC. "Like, how real is it, how material?" I ask, half in a zone. "I mean, when the smell hit the car, we all pulled our shirts up over our noses… Pause. But should we have covered our beers? I mean, can the odor, I know we can't see it, but is it a real thing? We cover our noses, but should we be breathing it in through our mouths? I mean, can it like, contaminate our brewskis too?"

"Good question." Curt says, passing the joint up to Fook from the back seat, then balking, hitting it again and then finally passing it.

"What's the answer?" Dicky asks, looking at me.

"I don't know." I say, wishing I had an answer.

Chapter X

We pull into the small parking lot of White Birch Park and Curt, wearing his steeled toed boots, chain wallet, obviously shirtless, and his one-armed shades gets out of the car and runs into the woods to tee off the first hole. Even though it's almost September, it's still as hot as Hiroshima in August and being amongst all the greenery just makes the humidity pulsate causing it to feel like an actual atomic bomb went off. Five Mississippi's after emerging from the cool air conditioning of the Caddy and I'm shvitzing through my Guns n Roses T-shirt. I'm wearing Levi's blue jeans, no shoes and a hemp necklace. While it *is* nice to get out amongst nature but for Eff's sake, we do have a park right across the street from our house.

Curt is already yelling at us to, "Come the fuck on!" I'm really not in any mood to be rushed, let alone run to keep up with Curt through this whole course barefoot. Frisbee golf is one of many things that I'm not good at and I'm even worse under pressure. When I walk up to the first hole, Curt has already thrown and is off, running to putt it in. Fooky, who's wearing red Nike *Air Force One* tennis shoes, khaki shorts from The Gap and a green Polo shirt, tomahawks *The Dokken* disk and it goes pretty straight.

Dicky, who's wearing a pink and baby blue, Tommy Hilfiger button down shirt, jean shorts and brown Sketchers, casually tosses his *Cherokee* disk and it floats three quarters of the way to the bucket. I square up, give a couple of practice pumps, take careful aim and then let her rip. My

Masked Marauder hooks right into the creek. I shout out *"Balls!"* and listen to it echo through the forest as the blood returns from my face to the rest of my extremities.

By now, there's another group of dudes waiting to tee off behind me, so I have to run down the cliffs barefoot, through the rocks, over the wet logs, and fish around in the filth and the mucky creek water to find my orange *Marauder.* Good thing my feet are as tough and callused as leather. I toss it from where I stand, which barely puts it back on the fairway, run back up the muddy cliffs, clinging to dirty roots, grasping at straws and when I make it up to the grass, disks are whizzing by my head from the dirty hippies behind us.

I skip my third shot and run ahead to catch up with the boys who have already shot from the second hole which is a massive Par 4 that goes straight uphill. I'm completely out of breath and I'm sweating like Anne Frank on German Unity Day. "Why does anyone like this stupid-ass "sport"?" I'm asking myself out loud.

Besides the obvious super stoner element, being stoned only hurts me. Although I'm miserable, I can appreciate that everyone else always looks like they are having a great time. Are they just as miserable as I am? I've shot some rounds where there weren't any other people around and Curt wasn't being a complete spaz that have actually been halfway enjoyable… the way that this round is not.

I want to get better at this; I just cannot seem to control where that little bastard goes. I haven't been at this that long and God knows that I don't have as much time to make it out here as these losers, but I'm trying to get better. I keep coming out here anyway, I could be sitting in the back seat of the Caddy, cry wanking over Valerie not letting me bang her but I'm not. I'm out here trying, sweating my balls off and putting in the effort.

On the 9th hole I notice, possibly out loud, "You know, for being such a hippy 'sport', this is not freakin' easy by any stretch of the imagination."

"Yeah, a lot of shit is like that." Curt says, confirming my suspicion that I did in fact say that out loud. "People think industrial painting is easy, like it's painting a living room but it's way more hard-core than people think."

"What else is like that?" Fooky asks, cracking a Budweiser tall boy from his shoulder cooler.

"Yeah, like breaking a nail." Dicky says, finishing off his 9th brewski in as many holes.

"Awe, did she bweak a wittle nail?" Fooky whines, mockingly.

"That's exactly what I mean, Dickhead." Dicky says. "You ever break a fuckin' nail off halfway down? It hurts like a motherfucker."

"Yeah Dude, that shit does fucking hurt." Curt agrees. "He ain't lying."

"Or like weightlifting." I say casually, immediately regretting it.

"What the fuck do you know about weightlifting, Stilts?" Dicky asks with a little more aggression than is called for.

"I took a weightlifting class at Lindenwood last year." I say, giving him a quick middle finger. "People think weightlifters are stupid and it's easy, but to do it right, efficiently, there's a lot of crap that goes into it. It's technical as heck."

"Right?" Curt says enthusiastically, "That's what I'm talking about."

"Schultz, watch out for the dogleg around that tree." Fooky says, hooking his disc around the stout, wise old tree.

"Mother eff-word that dogleg." I say, aiming straight for the hole. Falling desperately shy.

On the 11th hole, I slice it into the woods and after I catch back up with everyone, Curt says, "Dude, you fucking suck. You've been slowing us down all day."

"Dude," I say, confused, "we're not some platoon in Nam, knee deep in rice patties, on the lookout for Charlie. Take one of your "chill" pills or find a bag to breath in and out of."

"You pussy, that kind of attitude is why you still suck, you fuckin' Jew." He snaps, characteristically rude and aggressive.

"That's more than a little bit out of line." I think to myself. I hesitate for a beat or two, you know, pause, then I decide, "Eff this crap." and I peel back and slap him on the back of the head with my Marauder as hard as I can. Blood instantly starts spewing from the gash it leaves.

"Fook and Dicky do a, *"Daaamn!"* In unison.

Then, "Dude, are you gonna let him get away with that shit, Dog?" Dicky asks, laughing.

Curt turns around slowly, touches his head, smells the blood, gives a chuckle, and then says after a long uncomfortable pause, "Dude, after all these years, you pick now to start sticking up for yourself?"

Another pause.

"Maybe." I say, then reluctantly raise my trembling arms and, "What's up, Dog?" Comes from out of nowhere.

Long pause.

"Good for you." He finally says. He takes his shot.

Curt finishes four under par, Dicky is par for the course, Fooky is three over and I stopped counting after the 3rd hole.

Chapter XI

I'm sitting on the cigarette burned, worn out brown couch with Dicky waiting for the wake 'n bake to wain so we can get to work writing songs for our gig at Cooper's. Right now, however, I'm mesmerized by a single ray of sunlight that is piercing through the crappy brown blinds on our window, shooting through the living room and landing on the fake wooden paneling on the far wall. Weaving in and out of that one beam of sunlight are plumes of marijuana smoke and a billion dust particles all dancing about, creating the most brilliant patterns right before my eyes. I'm blown away by the notion that the room, all rooms everywhere are filled with infinite dust stars like these, we just don't see them but they're there, all around us all the time.

"Schultz, Schultz!" I start to hear Dicky saying.

"Yeah, Man. I'm right here." I finally say, waving my hand through the light beam, disturbing the beautiful waltz dancing before me.

"Dude snap out of it." He's saying in between drinks.

"Alright, alright. I hear you, you sleaze." I say.

After we've successfully gone through *Alison* by Elvis Costello once, Dicky says, "Dude, we gotta come up with a name."

"What about The Shakes." I offer.

"I dig it." He says with an *I dig it* look on his face. "It works on a couple levels."

"Yeah, like, you get the shakes." I say shaking my hand. "And then, just like a verb. *The Shakes*." I say doing a Twist type dance.

"Right on." He says.

"Well how about this song I just wrote. It's called *Chu-Hi.* Ya know, like the drink. It's an A, E, D thing. You take lead.

I spilt my Chu-Hi, don't you ask why,
I wanna tongue you upside down.

Gauging the reaction on Dicky's face, I keep going.

I look through smoke screens, break guitar strings
Knock birds up all over town.

I'm waiting at the station
I think I missed my train
The red light was my baby
The blackout was my brain...

"Alright Schultzy," Dicky is saying, nodding along, setting a cashed roach in the black, plastic ashtray. "That's not too fucking bad. I think we can work with that."

"Thanks. I just threw that together, ya know." I say, shaking a Tic-Tac case with three Xanays in it.

"Yeah well, write another verse or two and we'll be on to something." He says snapping his fingers at me to hand over a Xanax.

"Yo Curt, you need to get in here!" Dicky yells, snorting the pill whole.

Curt, who is in his bedroom weighing and bagging up ounces of weed shouts back, "What? I'm busy."

"'Cause you're in on this shit too." Dicky hollers back. "You gotta play drums."

"What the fuck!" Curt is raving, storming into the living room with a large Zip-Lock full of weed hanging from a small hand scale. "What the fuck are you talking about? I can't play the..."

"Dude, you'll be fine." Dicky says, cutting him off and motioning tactfully with his hands to remain calm. "There's nothing to it."

"What the fuck..." He starts shouting again but with less momentum.

"Stop *what the fucking* me, Dog." Dicky says, cutting him off again with a stern look on his face, a look that demands obedience. "The first time you drove a car, did someone have to teach you how?"

"No." He says, distracted, eyeballing the scale attached to the Zip-Lock bag.

"Why?" Dicky presses while I offer the last Xanax to Curt. When he waves me off, I empty it onto the small hand mirror on the wooden coffee table and methodically crush it under a dollar bill. I then roll up the bill and snort the powder.

There's a neutral pause that lingers in the living room like the bitter aftertaste of the Xanax in my throat.

"Because I'm not a fucking retard." Curt explains, finally looking up from the hand scale and zipping up the baggie.

"OK, well it's actually because you watched people driving for 15 and a 1/2 years and it's not quantum fucking physics. You just picked it up."

"Dude, I was 13 when I first drove a car." Curt says calmly, without any kind of a pause.

Curt is momentarily warped back to a crisp autumn day back in 1987. A carefree, simpler time when Mindy Lane's dad bought them beer, got them drunk and took them to a parking lot where he showed them how to drive a stick shift in his crappy1981 Ford Tempo and then let them drive...drunk...at 13-years-old. Later that night, by the light of the harvest moon, Curt was finger banging Mindy on the hood of her dad's Tempo while her dad watched from behind a curtain and beat off through the window of their one-room, ghetto apartment. He would later go to prison for sexually molesting a 14-and-a-half-year-old friend of hers as well as her 15-year-old sister who, by the way, happens to have a hearing impairment and developmental disabilities. It was a simpler time. He was a hero.

"Of course, you were." Dicky says, eyelids drooping. "The point is, you'll be fine. Just pay attention to the drum part when you listen to a song...and watch VH1 Classics. You should at least know the songs though, so stay in here and think about how the drums should go. Pick up those bongos and try to keep a beat."

"I don't know, Dude. It sounds risky." Curt says with no hint of irony.

"*This* sounds risky?" I ask.

Chapter XII

Out on the porch, we're sitting on our green, plastic lawn chairs, knee deep into our third case of Budweiser cans which are Luke-warm because we left them in the porch cooler overnight with no ice. It's intolerably hot and humid in a way that only St. Louis is capable of being but there are mischievous nebulas clouds rolling in from the east that are threatening to cool things down that look like conquistadors from times of old, throwing oddly shaped shade on the playground across the street. Swings are dancing in the wind, the sea-saw is masturbating back and forth, and the mini Ferris Wheel's menagerie are doing a daisy chain on each other. We go through *Best Friend's Girl* by The Cars on our guitars, Curt is keeping up on the bongos. We kill it.

"Dude, we still need a name." I say. "We're playing a practice gig at Cooper's tomorrow night, we gotta be ready."

"I know that Schultzy, we'll be ready. Trust me, we got this." Dicky says flicking a cigarette butt into the yard below.

"How about the Pink Tacos?" Curt suggests throwing me a bag of decent weed and telling me to put a wrap on one.

"No. C'mon Dude, be realistic." I say, sniffing the weed in the bag he just threw me.

"What? What Schultz, really. What is wrong with the Pink Tacos?" He's asking, convincing himself more than anyone.

"You have to think about what other people are going to think when they hear the name, and we sort of have to fit into that." I'm trying to explain. "I hate it when band names are wildly misleading. Pink Tacos sounds like a gay Mariachi band."

"It's supposed to mean, like a pone, Dude." Curt explains.

"Oh, I get it...I get it just fine. Either way, it still sucks." I say.

"Like what bands have fucked up names?" Dicky asks, stretching out his arms until they crack from every joint.

"Oh, I don't know…" I say, trying to think of examples. "Like, uh, you know, bands like; Motorhead, Metallica, Sublime, Led Zeppelin, or like, even The Doors are *good* names. They're exactly what you'd think. The name fits them perfectly."

"Dude," Curt starts, "Every band's name fits them because that's what we know them as."

"That's deep, Man. You should tattoo that on your forehead." I say, taking out a Zig-Zag rolling paper and giving it a little pep talk. Her name is Aphrodite, she is born from the sea.

"Fuck you Schultz." He says, flicking his cigarette into the yard just past Dicky's.

"There are bands that just have horrible sounding names, like The Moody Blues." I say trying to think this through.

"I kind of like The Moody Blues." Dicky says.

"Me too." I say with an appropriate hand gesture and eyebrow raise. "But I put off listening to them forever 'cause I thought they would suck because that's a pretty friggin' stupid name."

"Right," Dicky says, a glimmer of comprehension on his face. "Like the Gin Blossoms."

"Well, they're a shit band, so that sort of fits." Curt chimes in.

"So, what are we talking about then?" Dicky asks, confused, looking at both of us one at a time.

"Can we focus? I'm just saying that we need a cool name that fits our style. You know, like The Expensive Winos." I'm saying. "It doesn't really even have to be good, as long as it fits us. I don't wanna be like Iron Madden, ya know?"

"What about Iron Madden?" Curt asks defensively, leaning in a little too closely.

"Well, it's not like they suck or anything, but the name is sort of misleading." I say, trying to talk him back off the ledge. "*Iron Madden* sounds like they're a super heavy metal band but they're kind of not, ya know."

"Whoa, easy there Shela." Dicky says, his face turning red. "Iron Madden has some great songs, Motherfucker. *Fear of the Dark* bitch. Don't you ever forget that shit."

"Yeah," Curt chimes in, "but you have to admit, it's not exactly what think of when you hear the name *Iron Madden*."

"Ok," I start, trying to talk Dicky down, "think more like The Dead Milkmen for example. It sounds like a punk or heavy metal band but they're more like an indie, goofball alternative band. Not at all what you'd expect when you hear the name."

"Oh, like Suicidal Tendencies." Dicky says, finally catching on.

“Exactly! That’s a great example!” I say, snapping my fingers, pointing at things.

“So that’s like a game then: Good band/bad name.

“Yeah, but it’s also Bad band/*good* name.” Dicky says.

“Let’s just keep it simple, Alex Trebek.” I say.

“Ok, hit me with one.” Curt says.

“How about Journey?” Dicky throws out there.

“Eeeeh, that’s kind of Bad band/bad name.” I say. Not trying to shit on his first point but, unable to let that one slide and doing it anyway.

“They sing *Hot Blooded* right?” Curt asks.

“No Dude, that’s *Foreigner*.” I say.

“Dumbass.” Dicky says.

“Hey Dude, easy there.” I say, shooting up a peace sign, “Journey and Foreigner are like the exact same group. It’s like a 6 and two 3’s. They’re basically synonymous with…well, synonyms. When you want to say two things are basically the same, like say, oh I don’t know, rabbits and hares, you could just say, ‘rabbits and hares, Journey/ Foreigner.”

“Oh, I got it, how about The Yardbirds.” Dicky says, ignoring the fantastic analogy I just pulled out of thin air.

“Excuse me? What the flip is that supposed to mean?” Now *I’m* getting pissed. Maybe this was too hot a topic. I thought I knew these guys better than this. Maybe I flew to close to the sun like Icarus. Oh, maybe *Icarus* is a good name!

“Take it easy Schultzy.” Dicky says, now trying to calm *me* down. “That name doesn’t scream, *‘Kick ass rock band.’* But they were cool as fuck. Jimmy Page motherfucker.

“Yeah okay, I guess I can see that.” I say, taking a deep breath.

“Oh, what about Johnny Winter.” Dicky suggests.

“Well, that’s just his name, Dude.” Curt says, thinking he is the host of this gameshow now. “You can’t say that’s not a cool name.”

“The fuck I can’t.” Dicky says leaning back in his lawn chair.

“Yeah, that sort of put me off for a while too.” I admit, “It sounds like some old crooner, then I saw him play the guitar live and was like, ‘Dang, this white boy can play!’”

“Yeah, I hear that.” Dicky says, lone starring a beer, crushing it in his hand and then casually tossing it over the rusty patio rail into the trash can on the grass.

“O.K., I got one!” I say, excited. “How about The Grateful Dead?”

“What about them?” Dicky asks, the red mist falling. I’ve clearly struck a nerve. Have I gone too far this time? Is he gonna bite my hand…like, off?

“Well, it’s a totally misleading name.” I start nervously. “I-It sounds like they’d be a cool, rock band but…” I’m stammering.

“This motherfucker.” Dicky fumes, standing up, knocking back the lawn chair he was sitting on. It takes Curt to hold him back. “Say one more goddam thing about The Dead, Motherfucker. One. More. Motherfucking. Thing.” He warns, pointing a stern finger.

Long pause.

I take a quick look around, soak up the scenery and wipe the sweat off my brow. I take a deep breath. Visions of the Dead Farm and the concert we went to when we were kids and the “trouble” that ensued, the small part I *may* have played in that whole fiasco. I shake off my panic like

a wet dog, look at Dicky standing there, nostrils flaring, finger pointed, and I can't help but laugh.

"Dude, they're a flippin' Bluegrass band." I finally say in such a way that would make it difficult to counter.

Pause. Not a long pause, but an awkward one. Then laughter. Day-drinking, gravity bong high, visible coke residue on the nose laughter.

"That ain't what I call Rock 'n Roll." I say about to sit back down.

"You son-of-a-bitch!" Dicky lunges at me and grabs me by the collar, he holds his fist up, white knuckles, ready to clock me.

"Dude," I say, swiping his hand away casually, "can we just stop with this whole Bluegrass charade that's been going on in this city for far too long?"

"What the fuck are you talking about Schultzy baby?" He asks, clearing his throat, straightening his white Carona T-shirt, then giving my green Guinness T-shirt a wee pat down. Regaining some momentary composure.

"Come on man, seriously." I say, backing up when the patting grows firm and repetitious. "Are you honestly going to stand there and tell me that, when you were a kid, you sat alone in your bedroom for hours, learning Eric Clapton songs thinking, 'Damn, one day when I grow up, I want to get up on stage and bore the F-word out of people?'"

"Curt," Dicky says calmly. Eerily calmly. I start to perspire; it's beginning to show. "I swear to god, this moth…"

"Dude, seriously." I say, cashing a bowl from the two-foot, black ceramic bong that is somehow just sort of here now, and lighting a Marlboro. "Ever since the River City Buskers got big here, everyone thinks they're Bob Freaking Dylan.

"Hey Dude, The Buskers are fucking kick ass." They both say at the same time and it sends a panic running all the way through this crude, physical body that my soul now inhabits that cannot be expressed properly in English, only an ancient dialect of Okinawan Japanese can you find the word *kimochiwarui*, which translates to: That panic that runs through you when two men say *The River City Buskers are kick ass* simultaneously.

"Yeah, they do it right." I say, shaking that off.

Pause.

I take a drag and tell myself it'll all be alright. The truth is worth the ass whopping.

"And yeah, they make it look easy." I say, looking around cautiously. I flick my cigarette into the lawn. It goes pretty far, the second farthest in my *Fag Flicking Championship,* the game that I have going with myself and am currently, humbly winning though the competition this year is smokin'."

Then I say, "But I'm not trying to be in a freaking Bluegrass band." The tension is high, my head held low, rocking it to and fro in shame. "See, here's the thing." I say, closing my eyes, "People hear bands like Marley, Dylan, or The River City Buskers, they hear the moderate singing, the simple guitar chords that really do make it look so easy. Everyone thinks that *they* can do it too. They don't have the talent though, that certain…*je na sais quoi* that makes them stand out from all the rest of the hacks"

There's a pause, then. "I'm trying to be in a *Rock 'n Roll* band. I want to kick ass and make people want to fight, get drunk, go frickin' crazy. That's what I'm talking about. Do you feel me?"

"Schultz…" Dicky says, picking up the chair, putting it back on all fours and sitting down. The color returning to his face. "I just don't fuckin' know about you sometimes, Dude."

"Sorry Dude, but let's be realistic, Bluegrass music fucking sucks."

"Whoa there Schultz, you kiss your mother with that mouth?" Curt mocks. "You're gonna be a teacher someday, someone might hear you cuss and they'll never let you near a school again."

"Oh, screw your B-hole." I say, "I just need to get used to not swearing, I don't want to drop an F-bomb mid lesson."

Just as we're getting Dicky settled down, a crappy little blue Toyota Corolla peels around the corner on two wheels that causes us all to stop and look. It speeds down the hill by the cemetery, totally bottoming out and sending sparks flying at the bend where the cops hang out sometimes and comes to a screeching halt not quite in the middle of the street but missing the curb by a wide margin. The two nutty bitches from the other night, what's her red-headed name and her runaway, hot ass, brunette friend stumble out, laughing their asses off about something we will never know. With their arms wrapped around each other, spilling the cocktails in their hands and smoking Virginia Slim 100s from silver, plastic cigarette holders.

"These bitches again." Curt says under his breath.

"Oh boy." Dicky says, shifting uncomfortably in his chair.

"Dude, find out what their names are." I say quickly, before they reach the porch.

"What's up, Bitches?" Ginger asks, flipping her long red hair back behind her shoulder, exposing her black, tribal spiderweb tattoo that crawls up her neck. She's wearing cut off Daisy Dukes that expose her ass cheeks, a white wife beater with a black lace bra, stylishly exposed, and black leather flip-flops.

"What's up, Bitches?" I ask back. I'm squirming more than I should be, unable to regain composure.

"Look," She says flicking her half smoked, lipstick stained cigarette holder into our lawn. "we've got a bunch of pills… but ain't got no beers." She sits on my lap and kisses me hard, whiskey and stale cigarette smoke on her breath.

My eyes wide open, my legs kicking around wildly like some kind of retarded break dancer. Everyone's eyes are on me while this molestation is happening which is causing a level of anxiety that all the Xanax on the planet couldn't curb. Lolita is eyeballing us bashfully, she's wearing blue Adidas tennis shoes, matching 1970's basketball shorts and an oversized, black T-shirt that's torn to hang off the shoulder, featuring a young girl seductively sucking on a lollypop. "You see what I'm getting at." Ginger says after releasing my face.

"Well break out the pills and go get a couple cold one's, girls." Dicky says, then asks tactfully, "Hey uh, by the way, how do spell your names?" He asks with his face all squinty and his finger up unauthentically.

Ginger gives him a handful of various, unknown pills and says, "With a C." Then she goes into the house and stumbles to the fridge. She comes back out a minute later and slurs, "Hey Cunts, there's only two left."

Agonizing pause until…

Dicky turns to me, takes the fag out of his mouth and declares, "That's it, Dude!"

"What's it?" I ask, popping two of the pills.

"Our name. *2Left*. That's our name. *That's it!*" He exclaims.

"2Left huh…meeeh, it's alright." I say, shrugging my shoulders animatedly, "I'm not ready to sign off on it just yet."

"Why not 3Left? There are three of us." Curt says, posturing.

"God said that, 'There can only be two.'" Dicky quotes from some un-fact-checked source that is *not* the Bible.

"I think that's from The Highlander." I say, not wanting to sound any nerdier than I already sound.

"3Left doesn't have the same ring to it." Dicky explains. "2Left is cool man."

"Maybe." I say as the girls sit down.

Curt asks skeptically, "Dude, Highlander, really? You watch the lamest fuckin' movies."

"Like what!?" I ask, clearly offended. "What the freak, Dog?"

"Dude," He starts slowly, "You are the biggest Star Wars nerd in the galaxy, everyone knows that."

"Dude, the Star Wars stories are great! They are the most modern archetypical hero stories we have. It's frickin' Biblical, for real."

"What the fuck is he talking about?" Ginger asks, legs crossed, beer spilling.

"Well that's the thing, they aren't even close to original." I ignore her, everyone takes my queue. "Great classic *hero* stories are as old as time. They stand the test of time, that's why they keep getting retold from generation to generation in different forms. Star Wars happens to be our generation's classic *eastern* traditional tale where there is, in fact, always only two. A mentor and an apprentice. I mean, even in The Bible, those are some classic hero stories too. I mean, some of them have their obvious flaws…"

"Like what?" Curt asks, cutting me off.

"Well even the biggest story, the climax, which is the Jesus story." I say.

"What the fuck do you mean, Dude? That's the greatest story ever told." Curt says, apparently having been born again in the last 35 seconds.

"I don't know," I say, scratching my head. "I think Christianity gets a couple things wrong, that's all."

"Like what?" Curt pushes further, his tone amplifying. He's wondering if I'm going to be damned to Hell for this.

"Well, first of all," I start calmly, trying to pull things back into the realm of the civilized. "I don't think they need the whole second coming thing. The whole thing is a great story and the resurrection is a fantastic climax and ending. I think they go too far with the second coming. It doesn't add anything to the story, and it sort of leaves you hanging, feeling unsatisfied."

Pause.

"Well it means that the story isn't finished, Schultz." Curt explains. "Jesus could come back at any time. Doesn't that make it an even better story? I mean, that's pretty fucking moin, Dude! As far as stories go, it means he could come back right now."

"He's just taking his time?" Dicky asks.

"That's a fair point…" I say. I need a second, a pause to bide myself some time, then, "Dude, it's been 2,000 years. Most of us have moved on. It's like when they talk about doing the Star Wars prequels, ya know? Like, it's been 20 years already, no one's gonna care by the time they get around to making them, no one is even gonna know what Star Wars is in 10 years."

"If they ever do make them." Curt says.

"Amen to that." Says Dicky.

"Ok, well, what else." Curt asks again as if that weren't a perfectly solid answer.

"Well Curt." I say, wheels spinning. "The Devil character I guess I have a problem with. He's sort of two dimensional and boring I guess."

"What do you mean? He's the prince of fucking darkness!" Curt presses.

"Well, bringing it back to the other Holy Trinity again, it's like Darth Vader from Star Wars." I start. "He is always trying to tempt Luke to come to the dark side, only it's not really tempting at all. It's just evil for the sake of being evil and it doesn't sound like any real fun at all. It's not a convincing argument."

"The Dark Side is always cooler." Dicky says, looking at us all from behind his mirrored Aviators, not realizing that he's half right.

"I actually agree with you." I say. "The dark side should be cooler. It should be all the fun stuff in life that's bad for you only you figure out that it's actually *not* bad."

"Yeah, see? That's what I'm saying." Curt says.

"Yeah, well the problem is, that's not in the story. It should be, but it isn't. It's the same with the Bible. They don't ever get into the Devil's side of the story. I mean, we know he was God's favorite angel and he got a little cocky and then God cast him down to Hell, but I doubt that's how he would tell the story. They should get into that more. I'm not going to risk eternal damnation just to be evil for the sake of being evil. I don't think anyone really would."

I pause. I look around and am surprised to see that Curt and Dicky are still paying attention. Ginger and Chastity are smoking cigarettes and whispering about things that I'm sure are only interesting to them. I continue.

"The Jews make a much more convincing argument. The Devil, to the Jews, was much more fun. He sort of entices you to come along to the party, it's much more realistic to what real temptation is all about, you know, like in real life. Take drugs for example, you can tempt people to come along 'cause it sounds like so much fun at first. *It's the life of the party, it's cool, everyone's doing it. Come on, don't be scared, it won't kill you...* That kind of thing. In Judaism, the devil is much more convincing. He's cool, he's the life of the party, kind of a merry prankster. The kind of dude you'd like to…"

"Wait, what did you just say?" Dicky asks, cutting me off. Carefully setting down his beer on the concrete patio.

"What? I'm talking about how the devil in Jew…" I'm cut off again. This is so much more familiar than when they were paying attention to me a minute ago.

"Yeah, yeah, I heard that much." He says. Curt is now paying attention to him paying attention to me. "What did you call him?"

"Uh, the Devil?" I ask, utterly confused.

"No man, you called him a merry…something." Dicky says impatiently.

"Yeah, well, he's more of a merry prankster." I say. "Someone you could party with."

"That's it Schultzy baby." Dicky says, looking at Curt who seems to know what he's talking about.

"What's it?" I demand. "What the smurf are you two talking about, you fiends?"

"The Merry Pranksters. That's our name. The Merry fucking Pranksters." Dicky exclaims. The girls stop giggling, look up briefly, then go back to their gossips.

"The Merry Pranksters?" I ask skeptically.

"Yeah Dude," Curt chimes in. "The *Merry Pranksters* is way moin."

"Hang on." I say, hands up in a mild protest. "I think that was what Timothy Leary used to call his crew or something. There may be a book, or something already named that."

"I don't give a fuck." Dicky says decisively, "We're using it."

"Yeah Dude," Curt agrees. "We're totally using it."

"I guess I can dig it." I say, nodding. "Alright, *The Merry Pranksters* it is."

"Fucking hell." Dicky says, "Did we all just agree on something."

"Yeah Dude, don't tell Fooky." Curt says, laughing.

Chapter XIII

Around the same time every week the same-ish people stop by for ounces and pounds of weed and other drugs. A year ago, there was a lot more traffic in and out of the duplex when Curt was selling nickel bags and quarter bags, but that was bringing a lot of heat on this house so now he doesn't sell anything less than an ounce at a time and he only sells to certain people. I guess he's moving up in the drug world because at any given point you can walk in his room and his King-sized bed will just be covered with ounces of weed two feet high.

Now an ounce of weed is not a huge amount, it can fit in a single Large sized Zip-Lock bag, though that would be a snug fit, and it costs anywhere from $80 to $120 dollars, depending on the quality of the weed. Weed has gotten better recently and seems to keep getting better and more potent, not the Missouri dirt weed Stamm used to peddle out of his crappy garage. Now it all seems to be name-brand hydroponic, super skunky, purple haired nitro weed.

Curt is sort of a wholesale guy these days. He buys pounds of weed from some Irish cat that no one but Curt has ever met, and he refuses to talk about. That's quite a large amount of weed for a regular dude. There are 16 ounces in a pound. Drug dealers, by the way, are better at math and the metric system than an Asian MIT grad student. So anyway, I think Curt gets pounds for like $11 or $1,200.00. So, at, let's say $120.00 an ounce, he can make a little less than a grand per pound. I'm pretty sure he goes through like five pounds a week, give or take a couple.

When it comes to weed, it's like other produce, it's cheaper to buy in bulk. He makes about a grand by selling 16 ounces for $120.00 but if he broke it down into quarter bags for $50.00, he could more than double that but, like I said, that's just too much traffic through the crib. Plus, it takes too much time to split up the weed into little bags, things get misplaced and just getting rid of it and dealing with ten times as many shady people gets risky. Why then, don't more people just buy pounds of weed, you might ask.

Well, first of all, you don't know where to get a pound of weed. Even Stamm, back in the day would have to work for days to put that kind of a deal together. Secondly, you couldn't get rid of that much weed. Even if everyone you knew well enough to break the law with smoked weed, let's say ten people, and those ten people would only get weed from you, which is not something

that happens overnight, and they bought a quarter bag every two weeks religiously, it would still take you six months to get rid of that much weed. And last, but not least, it's best to leave these things to the professionals willing to take that kind of risk. That much weed is a felony which you can do real time for. Anything over something like 35 grams is a felony in Missouri and you can do like four years upstate for it which is not really worth the corn-holing you're going to be forced to endure in prison, just for some weed.

Now living with Curt, obviously, I get some special privileges. If, let's say, my brother or whomever he happens to be banging at the time, needs some weed, I can get them whatever small amount they want. They're just regular people, pillars of the community, they're not trying to get involved with any gangster shit. So, Curt will give me a quarter bag out of his personal stash for $35.00 and I'll give it to them for $45.00, which is a good price, and I'll pinch a joint out for myself. It's like Stamm used to say, "I'm not fucking Santa, man."

So, one day, when this dude I used to share a trailer/dorm room with my Freshman year at Lindenwood named Chad caught up to me with a strange proposition, I wasn't sure how to handle it, which angle to take. I saw him coming out of class and he was like, "Hey Brah, can you still get lots of dubage?"

Chad hasn't changed a bit, he's still clearly on the steroids. His thinning hair is thickly moussed and styled like a porn star from New Jersey. Acne scars on his face yet tanned and waxed from head to toe. He's wearing a blue satin shirt from J. Crew that is unbuttoned casually down to the fourth button, tucked into dark jeans with a black belt, both from The Buckle, and black leather loafers from L.L. Bean.

I was naturally skeptical. Most people's idea of "lots" of weed and mine are quite different so, I asked, "Like, what do you mean by *lots*?"

"Brosiph, practically no one on campus knows where to get good weed so like…a couple ounces at least." He says convincingly.

"No one on campus knows where to get good weed?" I repeat to myself.

An interesting thing I never picked up on before. Perhaps I should have taken advantage of this at least a year ago. I don't exactly have my finger on the pulse of the LU student body. I sort of think they're all a bunch of either; spoiled, rich white kids, there on Mommy and Daddy's dime or not white kids, there on an athletic scholarship. Wait, that sort of came out sounding more racist than I intended. Let me put that another way; I'm sure there are some white kids on athletic scholarships too.

Either way, earning a solid education is not the sole aim of the majority of the LU undergrads, they're not really there to learn anything. Which is unfortunate for them because obviously they weren't bright enough to get into a real University and are going to have to figure out a way to play this crappy hand of life they've been dealt without a real education. A college degree will only get your foot in the door, after that you're on your own.

The dorms at Lindenwood University are a pathetic joke too. These "dorms" are nothing more than a run-down trailer park, just off campus that the school bought, evicted all the poor, white trash living in them, and put all its undergrads in. I had to live there my Freshman year and it was the biggest s-hole I've ever lived in, and I've lived in some pretty crappy, s-holes. The trailer at LU was by far the worst. This place made Stamm's garage look like the freakin' Palace Hotel Ball Room. In the winter, me and whatever losers they stuck in there with me had to light the

stove for heat and in the summer, we had to pour ice in the bathtub and take turns getting in and out to stop from catching on fire.

You might think that those small inconveniences would be a small price to pay to get to party your ass off for four years; all the frat parties, the keg stands, sorority girls gone wild, etc.... Yeah, not so fast. The rules about drugs and alcohol on campus are stricter than sharia law under the fricking Ayatollah. They do have a fraternity and a sorority though...in the trailer park. The girls in the sorority are all chubby, even the cheerleaders. Not one of them is anywhere north of a 7 and-a-half and the Fraternity is gayer and nerdier than the Lambda Lambda Lambdas from Revenge of the Nerds, only not as intelligent or self-aware.

So, for me, this being my hometown anyway, I never really felt the need to make friends with any of these future rapists of America, already hanging with a bunch of legends anyway. Plus, I wasn't living off of my parents and they aren't paying a dime for any of this. I took out a $70,000 loan my Freshman year and I'm on the hook for that whole note whether I graduate with a degree or not. So, I'm not really there to make friends, I kind of keep my nose to the grindstone and everyone thinks I'm a big nerd there. Sitting by myself, doing the daily crossword puzzle from the newspaper in between classes probably doesn't help either but, I really don't give a smurf.

So now Chad, who is total Tri Lam, 'roid raging, rapist material is making an interesting proposition that I'm willing to entertain. I ask, "Can you get all the money beforehand? I can't like, front you anything."

"Oh yeah, Brah!" he assures me, his pecs moving up and down like a dog wagging its tail with excitement, wide grin exposing perfect teeth and chiseled jaw. "Not only can I get the money up front, I got clothes too."

Substantial pause.

"I got clothes too?" I whisper to myself at least twice before wondering, possibly out loud, "Do steroids make you retarded?" I was unaware of that specific side effect. I knew about the acne, the nad shrinking, and the man-tits but I don't think I ever heard about cognitive impairment. I'm not sure what to make of that last statement. I naturally start to walk away, thinking that this is a waste of my time when he says, "No dude, I've got like piles and piles of brand new clothes, the tags still on them from everywhere; The Gap, Abercrombie and Fitch, American Eagle, Polo, everywhere Broseph."

"You have..." Pause. "Piles of these clothes?" I ask slowly.

"Yeah Brah, I got loads of clothes." He mimics back.

"How did you score all these clothes?" I ask skeptically. Eyes squinted; head tilted to the left.

"I steal them." He says frankly, shrugging his massive shoulders.

Long pause. A lot was just said, there's a lot to unpack here.

"Show me." I finally say.

He takes me to our old trailer that he still lives in while school is in session. God what an absolute s-hole. But, there in the room we used to share, where he would bring girls, slip them roofies and then shag them while I was on my bed cry wanking myself to sleep, just like he said, are giant mountains of brand new, men's clothes from every store in Mid Rivers Mall and some stores that he had to have gone into the city to get like Gucci and Louis Vuitton. They don't have those high falutin, hard to pronounce stores anywhere in St. Charles.

"Well, this is... interesting." I say, trying to maintain a stoic poker face.

“Yeah, so I can give you money or there’s this if you want to trade.” He says, clearly proud of himself.

Pause. I thumb around a bit.

Taking a deep look at the old room, I say, “Let me talk to my guy.” and I turn to leave. Then, remembering our gig tonight, I turn back and say, “Oh yeah, we’re playing a gig tonight at Cooper’s, you should come and bring…” I say, taking one last look around at all this stuff in this crappy room that I actually used to sleep in, then waving my finger around in a general sort of way, “Ya know...people.”

Chapter XIV

I open the front door and walk through the threshold and when I hear the soles of my brown Dr. Martins hit the wooden floor, it strikes me that it's dark and empty. Our house is never empty. A curious feeling of panic mixed with endless potential runs through my veins like a shot of heroin. I wonder if it's my birthday and everyone is hiding somewhere, ready to jump out and yell, *Surprise!* Unlikely, but I take a lap around anyway just to make sure that no one is passed out or OD'd somewhere before I go looking around for the box of porn that was here when we moved in.

Looking behind the cigarette burned, brown sofa is fruitless. I search around the plywood shelf where the old Zenith television and CD player rest on to no avail. I wait for the cockroaches to scatter under the old, dusty wooden coffee table before I kneel down there to have a look. No porn. I look through my tiny bedroom closet with one old wife beater in the plastic drawer from K-Mart. I toss dirty clothes to and fro, off my cum stained mattress that lies on the floor like a prisoner. It occurs to me that Daffy probably took the porn box downstairs to his dungeon lair during one of his stints down there. I go down and have a look but it's too dusty and depressing to start rummaging around, so I walk back up the old creaky stairs, defeated.

I could still plop down on the sofa and have a nice long day wank. I turn on the T.V. to try and find something I can beat off to, maybe some scrambled porn on a cable channel that we don't get, a hip-hop video, maybe a Nair commercial but I give up all together when I see Chandra Levy's face on CNN. The tagline reads, "Levy and Conduit having affair." across the bottom of the screen.

I sit down on the couch, fish out a cigarette butt from the black, plastic ashtray and light it. When it cuts to commercial, I stamp out the cigarette and sit back on the couch, but it feels different, firmer somehow. I look around the crib and notice that everything seems slightly different now; cleaner, crisper. The Christmas lights are shining brighter, the old brown couches seem less matty, I don't see the bedsheet that used to cover them, the blinds are less dusty. Maybe Curt

gave Stephanie and Beth some weed to come and clean up, but it looks more than just straightened up. Everything looks polished, newer somehow.

Dicky and Curt were both supposed to meet me here to practice for our pre-big gig, gig at Cooper's tonight. I wonder if Valerie will be there, I wonder where she is now. I think she said that she was going to the show but it's hard to keep everything straight. I kept looking up at the clouds today and wishing she was there so I could ask her what she thought they looked like. I thought one looked like a yen/yang symbol that was spinning around eating itself, then it turned into a spider web. Another looked like a dragon. It followed me around for a while, stalking me. She would have thought they were something different, a Grateful Dead skull or maybe a Daisy with the peddles falling off one by one. She loves me, she loves me not. I pull out my phone to reread the last message she sent me. When I push the button to scroll down, I stop on a text from yesterday that reads:

Hey Baby,
I wanna C U before your show 2morrow. Call me!!
-Val
XOXO
P.S. It's always been my dream to be in yours.

Chapter XV

Valerie Montas was born Valerie Connors and grew up in St. Peters, Missouri, the youngest daughter of Walter and Carolyn Connors. Walter Connors was born Henry James Connors of Carson City, Nevada in the early 50's, the bastard son of the infamous Jay Jay Connors, who was dubbed the Robin Hood of the old west by the media for robbing at gunpoint wealthy aristocrats on their way out west and then living a lavish lifestyle while among the poor claim jumpers and preaching to them the word of Jesus and convincing them that they were the victims of class oppression.

Jay Jay was run out of town after being convicted of conspiring with the communists to overthrow the American government in 1948 after the war in Europe had been properly dealt with. After the fall of fascism in Europe, the jig was up, so to speak, in the west and the public's taste for the whole 'Robin Hood' thing had worn thin so Jay Jay moved his racket east to where the Christian spirit still held a place in their hearts for the so called, "meek" and allowed themselves to be persuaded that they should not only give, as the good book preached to give, but to pass laws that demanded, by the force of the federal government to uphold. Because, hey, if the ideas are so good, why not just make them mandatory.

So, Jay Jay went east and settled in St. Peters, Mo. He set up a church called The Church of the Triple Rock where he preached the word of God every Sunday with Gin soaked breath and "knew" well over half of the congregation, including most the girls over the age of 11-and-a-half. When his son, Walter got old enough, Jay Jay started training him to be a Charlatan, womanizing drunk like his old man, who could take over the family business when he got old enough.

America in the 1960's was a magical place and time for Walter Connors. The stars really aligned for him. It was the perfect time to be a Jesus freak hippy, quasi cult leader. There were young girls lining up that were ready to do anything he asked, there was weed, not great weed

but there was tons of it, and most of these girls had rich families that they could take for, maybe not quite everything, but a lot more than they should have gotten taken for before they knew that they were being taken.

To keep up the appearance of a good, decent, man of God, Walter knew that he would have to play the part, that meant getting married. He chose a nice girl named Carolyn, a good Christian girl from a super-rich family, obviously. They married and had two sons, Jay and Stevie and then nine years later, along came Valerie. A beautiful, angelic little girl with wild brown hair, porcelain skin and mesmerizing blue eyes. She had a magnetism that would stop people on the street dead in their tracks to gawk at her. Grown men would be brought to tears when she would enchant them with her smile. The heavens wept when she cried, and trumpets sounded when she laughed.

By that time, the Connors' were getting on in years, they were utterly corrupt and had deep ties to the American Socialist Party. They were knee deep in class warfare and every sermon was solely about inequality, equity, and the redistribution of wealth. It started with the inequity of the classes, but when The Soviet Union collapsed in the '80's, people didn't have the stomach for that anymore so by the mid-1980's, they pulled a slight of hand and shifted their ire from class warfare to race warfare. Now, white privilege had replaced the bourgeoisie and blacks and Hispanics replaced the proletariat, but the message was the same: Anyone with more than you must have stolen it, hate the man with more than you. The message quickly turned ugly when it was clear that it wasn't so much about loving the poor but hating the rich.

The problem for the Connors clan was that Walter was so drunk most of the time that his priorities became blurry. By the late 80's, when Valerie was around 10, he was so drunk and nose deep into the booger sugar, that he actually started to believe all of the nonsense he had been hustling. He became willfully blind; the shepherd became the wolf.

He started to let any Tom, Dick, and Harry off the streets come and stay with them, in their house, with his children living there and everything. Any dirty hippy, gangbanger, or runaway that passed by, Walter would scoop them up like some kind of a kennel for a bunch of stray dogs. It wasn't long before Valerie began being *mistreated* by some of these lost boys.

So, Valerie, who had always been a precocious little girl, started acting out in some disturbing new ways. She would misbehave, say age inappropriate things that were sexual in nature, and started playing with other kids in a way that became disturbing to the other parents. Carolyn became concerned. One day, she was playing with some of the runaway boys. Carolyn knew she needed to keep an eye on them because of the inappropriate behavior lately so she peeked in on them every now and again. So, after making lunch, Carolyn went to check on the children, but the bedroom door was locked from the inside. She knocked but all she heard was Valerie laughing, giggling like a small child followed by slapping noises. Carolyn knocked harder; she called their names but still there was nothing but Valerie's giggle.

"Valerie Marie Connors, open this door! Open this door this instant!" She shouted through the door.

Finally, Carolyn took a deep breath, stepped back and kicked open the door. What she found was 11-year-old Valerie bent over the lap of one of the boys. Valerie's skirt was flipped up to her back, her panties pulled down around her ankles which were crossed casually and bent up past her knees. Horror turned to an existential dread when she looked into Valerie's, once bright and

soul piercing eyes and found them hollow, lifeless orbs. She blinked and then in an instant, her eyes morphed and Valerie's expression went from a blank void to a mischievous twinkle, then, what disturbed Carolyn most of all was when the two boys, both consumed with shock mixed with panic, jumped up and ran out of the room, tossing Valerie to the hard wood floor. As Valerie looked up, Mrs. Connors was petrified as she saw Valerie's eyes once again turn to as stoned cold a gaze as she had ever seen in all of her life.

Carolyn never looked at Valerie in quite the same way ever again. There was a trial in Juvenile court. Both boys plead not guilty to rape and child endangerment charges. They even had the nerve to say that it was *Valerie's* idea. That didn't go over very well with the Judge, she sentenced them to Juvenile Detention until their 18th birthdays. But in a bizarre plot twist that no one saw coming, Mr. Connors got up and spoke on the boy's behalf. He said that with his counseling and a little help from Jesus, "All things are possible."

Carolyn couldn't believe what she was hearing. She held Valerie's head in her arms and wept silently there in the court room as the judge's gavel came down with a thud.

"Walter, how could you, after what those boys did to Valerie!" She cried.

"The boys, the boys stay." Walter explained definitively. "It's too important. It's justice. It's social justice. We deserve what we get."

"But that's our daughter. How dare you, you son of a bitch!" She pleaded before slapping his face so hard her hand stung.

"The boys stay." He said firmly, touching his cheek with his fingers. "They stay."

The Connors family went on with their lives. Carolyn kept busy around the house, cleaning, scrubbing and washing everything in sight, from top to bottom, from morning till night. She would finish scrubbing the wooden kitchen floor, the living room floor and the den, then she would move upstairs to the bedrooms. When she finished with them, if the dishes were all clean and put away and everything had been dusted twice for the day, Carolyn would go down and start scrubbing the kitchen again. It was as if she were trying to scrub away the darkness she felt on her own soul. The foul stench of betrayal had been imbedded in every dark corner of the home and Carolyn aged herself decades attempting to recapture the innocence her home had forever lost.

Walter doubled down on his attempts to rid the world of social injustice. For Walter Connors, the line between the individual and all the various intersectional groups that an individual could ascribe to had all but vanished. If an individual committed a crime, he didn't look at the individual as a person, but as a member of a group. If that group had been wronged in the past in anyway by a *dominant group*, then the responsibility for the crime didn't lie with the individual, the responsibility lied with the oppressive group who had marginalized that group.

So even when his very own, ten-year-old daughter was sexually assaulted by two boys of a "marginalized" group, he didn't blame them, he blamed himself, no matter how negatively it affected his own family. And his family was clearly falling apart. With Carolyn's cleaning, his children distancing themselves from each other, they became strangers in their own home even as the house was filling up with actual strangers that Walter was "rescuing" from off the street. He drank more than ever, but not in a social way like he always had in the past, now he drank as if he were constantly filling a bottomless glass in his soul. Even his mistresses started distancing

themselves from him. His congregation suffered as well, every Sunday, the numbers dwindled, the empty seats in the pews grew as wide as the Red Sea when Moses parted it.

The boys, Stevie and Jay were old enough to see which way the wind was blowing, and they stayed out of the house as much as possible, devoting most of their time to studying and school sports so they could get scholarships to college and move as far away as possible as soon as possible. Valerie though was a tougher safe to crack. It's hard to tell which was a consequence of which, did she become more devious and precocious because of what was going on around her or did her family falling apart all around her cause the trouble she was experiencing.

Until one night, Walter was passed out drunk on the couch watching old 700 Club re-runs and Carolyn was cleaning bathroom tiles for the third time that day, a book of matches was lit which caught Valerie's bedroom drapes on fire, which caught the rest of her room on fire which ultimately caught the whole house on fire. Though the circumstances surrounding the fire were very suspicious, the fire department determined it an accident because all the reasonable suspects had perished in the blaze. Valerie, who was deemed too young for them to suspect, managed to get out in time, Stevie and Jay were not home at the time and, tragically, Walter and Carolyn were killed in the fire.

Valerie went to live with Gene and Garret Montag, friends of Walter and Carolyn, who adopted her and raised her as their own child. Gene was also a preacher of a small, modest congregation in St. Peters, MO only he actually believed in the 10 Commandments and did not indulge in the vices that Walter did. Gene and Garret gave Valerie a loving home and put her in therapy twice a week until she manipulated her therapist into prescribing her Vicodin and Adderall, then accused the doctor of inappropriate conduct and had him arrested and his medical license revoked.

Chapter XVI

"Where in the mother of all effs are those C words?" I ask myself out loud. *Villains! Fiends!* I'm shouting as I pace back and forth in the empty living room. They better not be at Duck's or some such nonsense. I grab my acoustic guitar and go through *Alison* by Elvis Costello, *Mary* by Sublime, and *Wonderwall* by Oasis. I'm not the best singer in the world but I'll have to do the best I can, hell, another few shots of Tennessee Whiskey and I'll sound like Otis Redding. I go through the song *Chu Hi* that we just wrote but… I don't know if tonight is the night, maybe it's too soon.

It's 8:00, showtime, and there is still no sign of the boys. Dicky's guitar and amp are still here. I've been calling both their cell phones for over an hour and no answer. I'm seething. I take an Ambien, drink a glass of Popov Vodka, and take a look around at the empty house; the old brown couch with the stuffing seeping out of the cushions, the paint chipped, smoke stained walls with the cat poster and the New York skyline poster of the World Trade Center hanging with thumb tacks, the rickety shelf that the old T.V. and CD player sit on and the dusty wooden floors with cockroaches scattering about and I sigh a desperate prayer.

I decide to carry on. No matter how hopeless or pathetic things may seem, I don't really see any choice but to keep moving forward. I pack up an acoustic and an electric guitar, I bring Dicky's too, just in case. The drums are already at the bar along with one amp, so I leave mine here, jump in the Caddy and drive to Cooper's by myself.

I pull up around to the back entrance of Cooper's and can see that there are quite a few people there already. The heat is unbearable and I'm cursing myself for wearing a grey T-shirt. People are really starting to flow in as I'm setting up the acoustic and doing a mic check…alone. The bar is clean tonight, well-lit without being gaudy. It feels like home when Hiro, the owner greets me warmly.

Cooper's is painted in deep maroons and forest greens and have various versions of Guinness posters with golden frames and smoky mirrors hanging sophisticatedly along the walls with stools and tables made from dark mahogany wood. The bottles lined up along the wall of the bar create a moody aura that matches the fresh aroma of finely aged liquor and the sound of ice crackling and clanking is hypnotic. A couple of drinks and any number of magical things could happen.

"Where the holy hell are those two?" I'm swearing to myself. I half thought they would just be here drinking and waiting for me. Yeah, *probably*. The place is packed though, there are a lot of people here, but Dicky and Curt are not amongst them. I don't see Valerie or Blair either.

After waiting around for longer than I should have, having a glass of Grey Goose Vodka or four, I crush a Xanax with a lighter and a dollar bill, then roll up the dollar and snort it. Hiro tells me to break a leg and I make my way through the thick crimson curtain to the stage.

I decide to just put on my shades and get on with it, solo. I'm wearing skinny jeans, a dark grey Guns n Roses T-shirt and leather flip flops. I pull up a stool to the mic, do a quick *Lonely Stranger* intro to make sure the ole axe is tuned up and to get everyone's attention. Cooper's looks different from on the stage, it seems a lot wider, the dark wooden bar is glossy, and the stools are packed. All the bottles behind the bar look like wallpaper from here and the tables all look taller than they do from the floor. The people sitting at the tables near the stage are all dark, faceless characters with the different colored lights shining in my face. I can't see any people

walking on the sidewalk outside through the glass walls with the Cooper's name stenciled on it in Shamrock green.

I look up behind my giant mirrored shades, the crowd is distant, uninterested and clearly distracted. I clear my throat and can taste the bitterness from the Xanax in my mouth. I take another deep drink from the pint glass of straight Vodka and set it on the stool next to me and then say, "Hey everybody, thanks for coming out tonight."

I get a polite golf clap from the crowd, then I say, "We're the, uh, I mean, I'm The Merry Pranksters. The boys couldn't make it tonight. They…um…came down with something." Pause. "So, I'm just gonna carry on without them so, uh…cheers."

Small applause.

"Here we go." I say nervously and then start strumming the intro to *Wonderwall.*

Today is gonna be the day
That they're gonna throw it back to you
By now you should have somehow
Realized what you gotta do
I don't believe that anybody
Feels the way I do, about you now

A flicker of light sparks in a young girl's eyes. She blinks and the flicker ignites in someone else's eyes, then another like a menorah.

Backbeat, the word out on the street
That the fire in your heart is out
I'm sure you've heard it all before
But you never really had a doubt
I don't believe that anybody
Feels the way I do, about you now

Before I get to the chorus, most of the crowd has the fire in their eyes. No one is sure what is happening, but everyone is glowing a radiant amber.

Because maybe, you're gonna be the one that saves me
And after all, you're my wonderwall

With a little riff and a tickle of the strings, I finish the song. The crowd erupts in applause. I'm somehow not surprised by their reaction, a song they've heard a million times but are hearing it in a new way for the first time. Maybe because I can feel the fire as well, it's something that we are mutually engaged in. I'm giving it off, they are receiving it, experiencing it and then giving it back to me. It's an indescribable exchange of energy that seems to be contagious and more than a little bit magical. They loved it and applaud accordingly. People are standing up, whistling. I take a drink, light a cigarette and say, "Thanks very much."

Pause.

“Thanks very much.” I repeat, trying to make out familiar faces in the crowd but they got the heat on me. I’m blinded but I can feel that Valerie isn’t here.

I’m feeling the energy from the crowd and all the nervous energy I had seems to piss off into the ether leaving only positive vibrations. I’m feeling nothing but confidence, *Godlike*. I figure I’ll give them a little something they may be more familiar with, so I go right into *Mary* by Sublime:

Maybe one breath away,
I’ll find the words to say

The fire starts returning to the eyes of the crowd but now it’s escalating to the rest of their bodies. People start to move, rise to their feet. The magic is starting to really become tangible, really take hold. But no sooner do I get the song started, do I see a sizable group of people, belligerent and rowdy, flooding into the bar and bringing their negative vibes with them. The lights are bright. I can’t make out who these scoundrels are, but I recognize familiar voices.

I’ll sit and light the bong,
I’ll hold my hit in real long

Suddenly, I hear one of the villain's shout, *“You suck!!”* from the crowd. The fire is abruptly extinguished, replaced with an unnerving chaos.

I don’t know if I can,
Go up inside of you tonight,
Oh, Mary baby, I can do it right...

“Kill yourself Schultz, you fucking suck!” I hear someone else shout.

When we got to the pad,
Mary baby started calling me her dad
Then she gave me head
We could not find the damn bed

“Boo! Go home Jew!” More than one of those devil’s voices shout simultaneously.

I don’t know if I can,
Go so way up inside you tonight
Oh, Mary baby please don’t fuss and fight

“You’re shit! Ha ha!” More shouting. Now there is a commotion, pushing and shoving ensue. A ruckus has begun. Who are these Philistines?

...Oh, Mary baby, your daddy is coming home.

"Thank God that's over!" I hear from the crowd as the lights dim. Finally, I can put a face to the evildoers, rolling in about 10 deep, it's the usual suspects; Dicky and Curt, M. B. and Ryan Barnes, Barnes' brother Jon and Bad Bob, Josh and Derik, Conley and Mort, Martin and Daffy. Quite the Motley Crew.

"Shut up." I say as calmly as I can manage from the stage, but blood is rushing to my face turning it a crimson red. I still can't see who's doing the pushing and shoving but it's clear that there is a dust up of some kind.

"Monkey effing savages!" I'm shouting to myself. I will never forgive them for this! Screw it, the show must go on. I go into *Layla* from Eric Clapton's *Unplugged,* but I don't get past the second lead before, I hope your sitting down for this, a full out boxing match breaks out.

I hear a glass break, a whole table of shadows stands up, posturing. First everything goes silent, then more than one, "*Motherfucker!"* is shouted with bravado. It's getting kind of heavy. As tables start shifting, seemingly on their own. The whole room starts swaying like the ebbs and flows of the ocean, it's a mosh pit here at Cooper's. The lights turn on in the small bar and I'm just sitting there on my lone bar stool on the stage, guitar in hand nipping at my tall pint glass of Vodka, at first shaking my head then accepting it all. I just start to play more songs on the guitar.

"Hey pussies, just let them fight." I hear someone shout.

It seems that this is not an all-out brawl, but just between two dudes. I can tell by the way the crowd is not erupting in all out chaos but seems to just be reacting to what is happening, staying out of the way yet maneuvering to have a front row seat. But who? It could be anyone. I crush another Xanax in my fingers and snort it. There are too many people standing around to see who it is. I can't be bothered to get up and push through the mob of people to see the fight, I am on stage after all, but damn, it seems like a really good one. I can see M. B. and Martin, Curt and Dicky just standing by and watching which is odd. Why wouldn't they be in on this action? Opportunities like this only come around once every weekend or so.

A table flips over as the two dudes wrestle on the wooden floor amongst the broken glasses, the blood, and the beer. Suddenly one of the dudes flips the other one in some kind of shoulder flip and there is a break in the wall. I see who these cats are and sure enough, it's Jon Barnes and Bad Bob. Resist all urges to rationalize the situation, it's simply chaos.

The two Goliaths fall onto a table that doesn't break due to the sturdiness of the manufacturing, but it falls over sending them both sliding to the floor. Glass breaks, a small fire is ignited, and the crowd is chanting something inaudible. A small explosion shakes the bar, then they both are on their feet, they're throwing punches like an Ice Hockey brawl. Glasses break as they fall on another table, the chairs crack. I realize that I can't stay out of this for long, they'll either make it to the stage and ball up my gear or the cops are going to…Oh snap, there are the sirens in the parking lot.

Jon and Bad Bob pull themselves off of each other long enough to dust themselves off, wipe up some blood, drink more whiskey and everyone starts to head for the exits. Before everyone scatters the two make it clear that this is not over.

"Meet me at my house pussy. We're finishing this shit tonight." Barnes shouts hoarsely.

"Alright pussy. Alright pussy. I'll be there, I'll be there." Bad Bob repeats, gasping for breath and pointing a sinister forefinger.

Chapter XVII

Outside in the parking lot, Mort and Fooky are doing lines of coke off the trunk of the Caddy. They see me coming with my acoustic guitar, a bottle of Beluga Vodka Gold, and a pint glass and stand up straight, sniffing at their noses.

"Hey Bud," Mort says, eyes bulging. "that was pretty fucking moin."

"Yeah Schultz, that was fucking awesome!" Fooky says numbing his gums.

"Ya think so?" I ask pouring the pint glass full of vodka.

"Yeah, you killed it all by yourself." Fooky says, "I didn't think you had it in you."

"Well what the flip was all that crap with Curt and Dicky talking smack?" I ask, putting my guitar in the back seat gently.

"Dude, it was Barney's birthday." Fooky says with an apologetic tone. "We've been brewin' all day."

"Well, let's go to Barnes', they're gonna fucking brawl *Right now!*" Mort screeches like he has ever since that one time in Lesterville when the whole *Right now!* thing caught on.

"Alright," Fook says, "Wait, I got a bunch more coke in Martin's ride so I'm riding with them. We'll follow you."

"Alright." I say, taking the keys to the Caddy out of my pocket, wondering who I'm going to give them to.

Mort is carrying my electric guitar case and I'm carrying the amp out to the Caddy and as I'm popping the trunk. I say, "Here Mort, you drive the Caddy." Tossing him the keys.

"Uh," He says hesitantly, "Hey Dude, I'm fucking way brewed up, I probably shouldn't drive."

"Dude, you're fine." I say, "Just drive and let's get this over with. I need a drink." Getting into the passenger seat I finish my pint of vodka, wipe my lip and pour another.

We peel out of the parking lot and fishtail onto the ramp to get on highway 70, heading west, way far out west, out to Wentzville to where Barnes' trailer is, in the complete opposite direction of where I live with Mort at the helm of the Caddy.

I can tell we're going extraordinarily fast by how quickly we're flying past other cars; they look like the stars going past the Millennium Falcon when it goes into Hyper-speed. I'm drinking the pint of Beluga Vodka Gold from the bottle that I took out of the bar, trying to calm my nerves after the show. I'm wondering what I'm going to drink once this bottle is gone, I don't have anything else on me and we are speeding faster and farther away from civilization. Mort takes the Sublime CD out of the Caddy's player, tosses it out of the driver's side window and asks me if I have any Slayer.

"Oh, good band/good name." I think out loud.

"What?" He asks, swerving in and out of the fast lane.

"Uh, nothing Dude." I say, gesturing at the road.

"Put something in that doesn't suck." He says loudly, like he's wearing headphones.

I'm flipping through my CD collection, anxiety ridden though the Vodka is helping. I'm trying to find something that this crazy bastard won't throw out the window or intentionally drive this car off an exit ramp just to prove a point. I settle on Beastie Boys, *Paul's Boutique.* A modern classic. Track four, *Egg Man* starts playing.

I'm not really paying attention to Mort or the speedometer that is well past 120 mph or the trees that get bigger and fuller the farther west you get out of the city. I'm not paying attention to the cars that we're flying past or the green exit signs that are going by so fast that I can't read them. I'm starting to calm down and finally be able to enjoy this final glass of vodka and wishing I would have taken another bottle. I'm thinking about the songs I just played at Cooper's and the applause from the audience still ringing in my head. That look in their eyes that was so contagious. The adrenaline and the vodka are wrestling with each other, fighting for dominance. Round and round, the cycle, the Yen and the Yang.

I'm trying to think of other examples of good band/bad name but all I can think of are The Violent Femmes. Slayer, Mort and Martin's favorite band, fast, hard, and an underlying death wish, is a perfect name for them. I get lost in my head. I'm staring out the window, racking my brain trying to think about band names but the lyrics to *Egg Man* are sending me into a spiral. I'm spinning. Egg dripping from the ceiling. I'm not paying attention to the cars we're passing or the trees that look like a green paint brush is coloring the scenery as we go.

Mort shouts, "*Right now!*" snapping me out of my trance. I instantly notice that we are going incredibly fast. I look out of the window and see the look of sheer horror on the faces of the people in the cars we are speeding past. I look over at the speedometer and notice that the Caddy is still steady as an oak at 130 mph. It smells like the humidity of the city gas chamber. The mural that's being painted as I look out the right side of the car is nothing but Juniper Green and black with increasing intervals that include splashes of white rolling by faster than a cannon ball.

The Wentzville exit is rapidly approaching. The Caddy isn't slowing down, oblivious, laser focused. The wheel turns, the Caddy skids. We bottom out as the road starts to elevate up the exit ramp. I can see sparks fly up over the window that I'm looking out of, smoke fills the car. I look over to my left, past Mort who has a stoic expression on his face and we fly past Martin's black Caddy, a late 80's DeVille. I see Fooky looking proper horror show freaked out. "Is he in trouble?" I'm asking myself. "Why the confused look on his face?"

The red light at the top of the exit is daring us to break on through like a matador's cape, blood red and approaching fast. Mort tries to turn the steering wheel all the way to the left, off onto Wentzville Rd., he slams on the breaks and I can hear the tires screech, I can smell the burnt rubber, I can even see the smoke coming up from under the Caddy. Mort is turning the steering wheel like a sailor turns the helm of a ship, adrift at sea but we're going too fast. The Caddy just won't turn. I don't have time to brace myself, all I can do is cover my pint glass of Beluga with my hand as the Caddy screams, *"Never!"* full speed ahead. There is impact. Inertia's laws are followed to the letter. Every *i* is dotted, every *t* crossed.

Then the deafening sound of silence. Slowly, the five senses start to come around. The first is sound. I can hear a hissing coming from somewhere close. I can smell gas and burnt rubber. When a frigid breeze slaps my cheek, I realize that my head is hanging delicately out of the front windshield. I blink my eyes and the first thing I see is the cracked and twisted Cadillac hood ornament two inches from my face. An inch further is the light pole that we smashed into and on

either side of that is the hood of the Caddy, wrapped around tightly like a G-string. A melancholy wave ebbs within me before the panic sets in.

I try to move my head and feel razor-sharp glass penetrating my face and neck. I freeze but soon, the inability to move makes my instincts dictate that I shake and twist to break free. I have to resist every urge, but I can't stop the blood from pumping harder and harder. My neck is pulsating, and I can feel the veins swelling quickly, growing closer and closer to the point of puncturing from the jagged glass surrounding my face.

The taste of iron laced blood lingers in my mouth and wild visions of Valerie are flashing with every blink of my eyes which are stinging from the salty sweat. My face is piercing through the windshield at an awkward angle. I try to regulate my breathing to stop my head from swelling but I can feel the glass pressing against my face harder every moment I sit here. I stretch my arms out behind me to ensure that they are still attached, wiggle my fingers so I know that my spinal cord is not broken. I can feel skin pierced, blood dripping, a panic exploding.

Slowly I try to grab an edge of the windshield that isn't in direct contact with my skin and try to peel it away, but it's held together intentionally to avoid that very thing. I stretch my head out further so that less face and more neck is through the sharp portal and maybe I can get some slack that way, but I must be careful to protect my throat which is one swallow of thick blood away from peeling open. I slowly move my head forward, I can feel the glass tearing the flesh on my right cheek, blood streaming down my neck and skull.

Once I'm able to move my head forward and down about 3/4 of an inch, my skull is clear which finally gives me a little wiggle room. I manage to punch out the glass on my left side so I can pivot my head to the right without slicing my throat open, then I am able to punch out the right side, freeing up enough space to carefully ease my head back into the car. I fall back into a glass covered, bloodied, torn up, prickly pear of a seat, sigh a breath of relief and take a look around to assess the situation from this new perspective. I turn around to check on my guitar in the back seat, not good. She is badly beaten up, bruised and cracked. Her neck snapped at her sixth fret. The old girl didn't make it, she is dead.

"Well thith ith clearly effeth." I say to myself out loud, unable to speak properly.

I look over at Mort who is grappling with the driver's side airbag, desperately trying to deflate it and get his own head free. After he's able to get that under control, he shakes his head, touches his nose and forehead for blood and then leans back in the seat. With his eyes still closed, he leans his head forward with his hands cupping his face and says, "Dude, that fucking air bag hurt. I think my nose is broken."

"No thit." I try to say, realizing I've bitten a hole in my tongue.

He looks over at me and his expression goes from one of woe to mortal petrification instantly. "Oh shit, Dude!"

Pause.

What does he see? How bad is this? I'm touching my face and it's moist and numb, hot and unfamiliar.

He blinks hard once, twice and then asks, "Dude, are you fucking alright?"

I'm guessing by his reaction of both horror and amazement that my face looks about as good as it feels now that the pain is starting to set in.

"Yeth, iths coo, I'n coo." I slur because there is blood spewing out of my tongue which is starting to quickly feel like it's been stung by a swarm of giant African wasps, impaling my speech.

"Well look, Man," He starts, looking around at the scene that is now starting to have cars that are stopping to rubber neck. "I'm like, wanted and shit, so…I gotta get out of here."

"Iths coo, Man, do wha'ezer you golla do." I finally manage to get out.

"You sure, Man?" He asks, his hand on the door handle.

"Yeth, go." I say waving my hand.

He gets out leaving the driver's side door open and disappears into the night just as Fooky runs up to the passenger side door that is now hanging open also.

"Holy shit Schultz! Are you alright man?" He asks, heaving and rasping.

"I think tho." I lisp.

"Dude, you should be fucking dead!" He says, not exaggerating. "I saw the whole thing from Martin's car. Dude, that was fucking insane! Do you know how fast you were going? Where's Mort?"

"Iths coo Thooky, he thook oth." I say.

"He…he took an oath?" He asks, confused.

"No. He thook oth." I say doing a running motion with my hands this time. "He. Thook. Oth."

"What, he took off?! That son-of-a-bitch! How could he just leave you here to die like this?" He's shouting again.

"He thaid heth wanted." I say slowly.

"He said he's wanted?" He gasps.

"Yeth." I confirm.

"O.K., well I can see that." He concedes.

"How bad ith my thaceth?" I ask.

"Your face? Oh, uhh…Dude, you don't wanna know." He answers me honestly. The look on his face tells me all I need to know.

The cops show up with their red and blue lights flashing intimidatingly. They approach the car with caution yet with authority, flashlights beaming around. A young cop with a buzzed blond hairdo and massive biceps walks up to Fooky and shines the light in his face. Fooky puts his hands up and says dryly, "Hey man, don't shoot."

"Sir," The cop says waving his flashlight around, assessing the situation just like he learned in his rookie training at the academy. "Get the facts. Just the facts." He's repeating to himself.

"What I'm going to need you to do for me right now is to tell me what exactly happened here tonight." He says in the most professional tone he can manage, maintaining his status as an authority figure in this scenario.

"Well, this is my friend, Schultz." Fooky starts, speaking slowly like you would speak to someone who's deaf or has a learning disability. "Him," He's pointing at me. "and another guy," He pauses and offers an *I don't know* gesture. "were in this car and it smashed into that light pole." More pointing. "As you can see."

"Were you in the vehicle as well, Sir?" Junior Officer Hardass asks, trying his best to get a general assessment and timeline of the events that unfolded here.

"No Sir, I was not." Fooky replies. "I was in that black car over there, but I saw the whole thing."

"Who was driving this vehicle?" Hardass asks, licking the tip of his pen.

"I don't know, Sir." Fooky says, more or less convincingly.

"Could you tell me your name please, Sir?" Hardass asks skeptically, remembering to write all this down.

"It's Fooky. Paul Aaron Fooky." He says.

"Sorry, Faulke?" The cop asks.

"No. Fooky. F-O-O-K-Y. With an F." Fooky says as slowly and clearly as humanly possible without coming off as excessively condescending.

The cop then starts shining his light on me and all around the Caddy. At the smashed front windshield, the shattered glass scattered around, the busted guitar in the backseat, blood dripping, the jagged hole in the windshield with patches of my hair sticking out of it. I feel a chill. For a minute, when Fooky was talking to him I almost forgot that this was all about me. I think I've lost too much blood to get that nervous feeling you usually get when a cop is shining his light in your face. After giving the scene a good once over, he asks me, "Sir, whose vehicle is this?"

"Mi-ne." I say, raising my hand.

"Sir, what I need for you to do for me right now, here tonight, Sir, is for you tell me what happened here tonight?"

I really can't be bothered trying to explain this to him, so I just point to my mouth, stick out my swollen and bloodied tongue and then point to Fooky and give a thumbs up, indicating that I concur with everything he just said.

"The report I received, Sir, states that you were driving this here vehicle." Officer Hardass states, reviewing his notes.

Without lifting my head up or making any kind of eye contact, I shake my head and do an X with my arms in the negative, "No."

"But this *is* your vehicle, Sir." He starts confidently, as if that would stand up in court. "There is no one else here but you. These are the facts, Sir. Are you still going to stick with the lame story that some mystery guy was driving your car, or do you want to start telling me the truth?"

I point to the head shaped hole in the windshield. I look at him to confirm that he is keeping up with this timeline I'm laying out for him. Then I point to my bloody face. Just to drive my point home, so I don't need to repeat myself, I point to the deflated airbag coming out of the steering wheel and then point to myself once again. I can tell that the wheels are still turning in his buzz-cut head, so I offer one last point. I wave him down so his head is inside the car and I point to the blood, pieces of skull, and hair that is still stuck to the hole in the windshield and again, I point to my head and face. I stick my bleeding tongue out and let the stream of blood drip down on my battered Levis.

Defeated, he sighs heavily. A twisted smirk of confusion tweaks his facial expression exposing his vulnerability and inexperience. He finally resorts to asking, "OK, well then who was driving?" Breaking character for the first time.

"Thome dude ah met at the ba." I manage painfully.

"You let some guy you just met at the bar drive your Cadillac home?" He asks, shining his flashlight on the broken Cadillac hood ornament.

"Yeth." I confirm with a melancholy head nod. Only now realizing how stupid that must sound, but if he knew the truth, that I let *Mort* drive my Cadillac, that is exponentially stupider.

"So, you were at a bar but…wait, how old are you, Son?" He asks, calling me Son even though he's maybe five minutes older than me.

"Thwenty." I say writing the number 20 in the air with my index finger to give him a visual aid. This is no Sherlock Holmes we're dealing with tonight.

I sense Officer Hardass's confusion brimming up to a boil. He scratches his buzzed head with his pen. Will he put it back in his mouth? Oh, hell yeah, he'll put it back in his mouth. That may have been his aim all along.

"So, let me get this straight." He starts, clearing his throat, "You are only twenty years old, yet you were drinking at a bar, you have...ehem...*had* a Cadillac, and then just let some stranger drive you home in your Caddy?"

"Yeth." I say, doing a drinking gesture with my hand, followed by a, "Hey, what do you want from me." shoulder shrug.

"So, where do you live, Son?" He asks, pen in hand, tongue out...Do it!

"Sthaint Ctharleth." I say pointing behind me.

"What the fuck did he just say to me?" He asks Fooky sternly.

"He lives in St. Charles, Sir. Off First Capital." He responds as politely as he can.

"But that's…St. Charles? St. Charles is in the opposite direction from here. It's not even close!" He says, clearly overwhelmed. Mind, all the way blown.

I shrug my shoulders again and, feeling that he needs a little bit more than that, realizing how unsatisfying that must have been for him, I offer another drinking gesture before spitting out a mouthful of blood, barely missing his well-polished, black cop shoes.

"Well…I don't even know how I'm going to write this up. This doesn't make any goddam sense. Just…just get in the ambulance and get him out of here, I'll have to stay here and try to clean this mess up."

"No! No no no." I say waving my arms in a crisscross motion again. "No inthuranth. No no." I say, shaking my head emphatically.

"What, you don't have insurance?" He asks.

I do the Pictionary nose/point gesture which reminds me that my nose is busted completely open.

He looks around, confused. Then finally he pulls a mirror out of his Bat belt and holds it up to my face. "Son," he starts sincerely, "you could die right now."

"Oh thit." I say after seeing my Frankenface for the first time.

My face is effed with no Vaseline. There is a tooth sized hole in my tongue where I bit completely through. The blood is spilling out faster than I can swallow without gagging so I have to spit out a mouthful every minute or so like I'm chewing tobacco. My nose is split wide open, broken and flattened to the right. I can see the cartilage sticking out but for the most part it's a bloody mess. I notice for the first time that a piece of glass is sticking out of my head. When I go to remove it the Officer Hardass says, "Whoa, hold up there Son."

"Wha?" I ask, bracing for the pain of removing it.

"Son," He starts. "you take that piece of glass out of your skull and you won't be able to stop the blood that's gonna spray out. It's gonna look like a water fountain spraying all over the place and you'll bleed out and die before that there ambulance can get you to the hospital. You better just leave that in there right where it is."

"Allight nan, you couls hath juth thaid that latht parut." I manage to get out, thinking that was the first intelligent thing he's said all night, possibly ever.

The ambulance ride to the hospital is a wretched collision of post-adrenaline and pre-painkillers. Fooky is riding along, pocketing medical supplies as the paramedics get to work on putting my nose back together. They have me strapped down to a gurney so I can't squirm, and I think the decision to charge me with some felony is not something that is completely on or off the table at this point.

There's nothing they can really do about my tongue while we're bouncing around in the back of the ambulance like rodeo clowns, except to sop up the blood with gauze which has to be replaced every couple of minutes. It's a real horror show man. I think humans only have seven quarts of blood in their bodies, that doesn't sound like much, but it is. It's a whole frickin' lot once you see it all spilled out in front of you. There's a reason we react to the color red, our primitive brain has evolved to know that blood equals trouble but it's funny how there is no real *blood red* color. A few drops are as red as a crayon box but when there's over a pint of it in a puddle on the ground in front of you, it's more fluid than just red paint, it's dark and thick, shiny and dull at the same time. Alive.

A nameless, faceless paramedic carefully takes the piece of glass out of my head but not before a little squirt of blood sprays the guy in the face like the money shot in a porno. One little thought that won't go away and I'll probably never get an answer to is, why did Officer Hardass, who was no medical expert, not by a long shot, know what would happen when the glass was removed but not the trained, medical professional?

At the hospital, the pain starts to kick into full gear as the adrenaline has completely worn off. I'm still strapped down to the gurney like Hannibal Lector and they are being extremely miserly about pain meds here. They take me into an operating room and after about an hour of wiggling around in pain, screaming like a demented mental patient, a doctor comes in and starts poking around at my nose and asking me questions he knows that I know are rhetorical. I try to answer them anyway.

"Well, looks like you had quite a bad accident." The doctor says redundantly. I think I smell Gin on his breath.

"I gueth tho." I say with as much attitude as I can manage.

"You guess so? You're lucky to be alive." He says as he casually jabs me with random syringes.

"Ith you thay tho." I say. He's pulling my tongue out with his fingers now and that condomy taste from his gloves makes me want to bite his smug little fingers off.

"I do say so." He says as condescendingly as humanly possible.

Cunt.

"Well if ith that bad, why are you being tho thtingy with the pain medths?"

"Young man, we've given you over 100 mg of morphine already." He says, wrapping the stethoscope around his neck which is code for, *"My work is done here."*

"Dude, I could get better pain medithine at home…way better." I say.

"I don't advise doing that." He chuckles. "In fact, I'm recommending that you be held here for a day or two for observation."

"Yeah, that ain't gonna happen." I say beginning to fantasize about wrapping his stethoscope around his neck and squeezing until his eyeballs bulge out of their sockets. I bet a syringe full of pain meds would magically appear then.

"Oh, yes, it is Mr. Schultz." He says, temporarily snapping me out of that bloody fantasy.

"We'll thee about that." I say, closing my eyes. Disengaging.

They stitch up my nose and then give me a sedative and tell me to sleep. I pretend to nod off and they loosen the straps holding me down. As soon as the nurse leaves the room I get up and look for my clothes. I remember that they were all bloody and torn apart like the Incredible Hulk and I think they cut them off of me anyway.

I'm just wearing a hospital apron. This is no way to properly escape from a facility as clean and well-lit as this one, so I take my IV stroller and sneak into the room next door. There, lying asleep, is a middle aged, heavy set woman of color. She is also in an apron and her clothes are folded on the chair by the bed. I decide it doesn't matter, I just need to get out of this apron, so I quickly put on whatever clothes she has on the chair next to her and walk out to find Fooky.

I find him snoring away in the waiting room. He has his shoes off and is sprawled out across the only sofa in the room as a homeless looking woman with three kids are standing around sharing a fun-size bag of Hot Cheetos. Chandra Levy is on the television with no sound. I wake Fooky up and he shutters at the sight of me. I'm sure I look pretty ridiculous with my face all bandaged up, two black eyes and I'm all swollen. I'm also wearing a big purple afro wig, a matching one strap tank top that is baggy on me, pink spandex pants that are not that baggy on me but actually fit quite comfortably, meaning they must have been tight as hell on the lady from whom I nicked them, and I have my wallet and cell phone tucked in my bra that is bright purple.

"Schultz?" Fooky asks, rubbing his eyes and yawning broadly.

"Fook, leth geh oudda here." I say earnestly.

Trying to sneak out of a busy hospital looking like *Thing 1* from The Cat in the Hat in high heels, my entire torso terribly swollen, blood-stained and aching with a stolen IV drip is not something to be understated. Once in the parking lot, however, the thing that is hitting me the hardest is the chill in the air. Instead of the summer air, thick with humidity slapping me in the face, we're greeted with sharp, arctic air and a thin, frigid wind that is so strong it's hard to keep the IV stroller from blowing away. Getting it into Fooky's Lincoln is an entirely different kind of ball-ache.

In the passenger's seat of Fook's Lincoln, I can sense a new phobia emerging. Every time we make a turn, a panic strikes and I'm finding myself breaking into a sweat and unable to breathe. We stop by Aaron Doerhoff's crib and score a bag full of Percocets, then drop by Shop 'n Save so Fooky can steal a gallon of Smirnoff Vodka like we did in the old days, then he drops me off at my house with the ludes and the booze so I can sleep for a month or so.

Chapter XVIII

It's impossible to gauge how much time is passing as I hibernate in my bed, mummified with bloody bandages. I can no longer distinguish between reality and fiction, when I'm asleep or awake. The only thing that's real in any kind of measurable way is the pain that slithers its way into my nervous system like a serpent, reminding me that, through all the fantasies, dreams, alternate realities that are flowing around and occupying my consciousness, I have in fact been in a horrible accident, that my face and head are being held together by stitches, and that the Caddy is no more. I take a handful of pills and wash them down with vodka and then keep drinking until I'm back in some other reality that is more palatable. Heavenly, white and pure. New and elaborate.

Suddenly I feel cold. I open my eyes, blink once, twice before looking up at the ceiling and noticing for the first time the pearl Corinthian trimming contrasting the ivory white paint. While the bandages and booze are obstructing my vision, I'm seeing everything through very low resolution, I sit up slowly, wondering if I've somehow missed something. This is definitely my bedroom but there is something unfamiliar about it. I take two more Percocet's before touching around gently at my head and body to make sure everything is still attached. I pivot around on my bed to stand up and brace myself for the push up from my mattress to my feet but find that my feet are barely touching the floor. I slide off the king-sized mattress and onto the warmth of a thick purple and gold, multi-threaded Persian rug.

I stand at the foot of my bedroom door and take a blurry look back at my dark room, lit only by a small crack through the plush Armani drapes. When I carefully open my bedroom door, the bright light that floods in from the living room immediately blinds me and causes me to wince in agony. I take that first step into the light and, through the bandages, my eyes slowly begin to adjust to this new and fantastic reality.

Dicky is sitting on the black, leather couch wearing a red Cardinals jersey and gold pinky ring with his acoustic guitar and the song notebook in his lap while Curt is sitting on the opposite, matching sofa, shirtless, a leather, Harley Davidson chain wallet attached to blue jeans from The Gap, freshly shaved head, and steel-toed boots. He's playing the bongos, trying to keep a beat and not doing a horrible job, in a Meg White kind of way. Resting comfortably on a large, Polar Bear rug is a glass, Herman Miller Noguchi coffee table. On the coffee table sits a white, porcelain vase filled with fresh Daisies, a marble chess board and a Baccarat Harcourt Abysse crystal lounge ashtray.

"Schultzy, you're alive!" Dicky says, tossing the brown, leather-bound notebook on the glass coffee table.

"Dude!" Curt starts shouting at me with no regard for the hyper-stimulation that I'm experiencing like a five-year-old that just starts rattling off questions the second *Daddy* walks in the front door. "We had to go get your shit out of the Caddy the other day. It looked like a fucking accordion! That was fucked up dude." He finishes on a more somber note than he began.

"I'm glad you're alright man," Dicky says, trying to sound sincere, "really, ya' know, I'm glad you didn't fucking die, Kid." He nods at Curt who nods back in agreement. There's a pause that I feel I have to interrupt.

“Yeah well, you both can tongue my balls.” I say, feeling around at my face, unwrapping the bandages that are stiff with dried blood and pieces of skull.

“What the fuck?” Dicky asks, throwing up his hands in a gesture of genuine confusion.

“Don’t worry Dicky,” Curt says, holding a single hand out in protest. “that’s just the pain meds talking. He doesn’t know what he’s saying.”

“The hell I don’t you C-words!” I shout then tend to my throbbing head. “You both not only stood me up for the gig, I had to get up there and play all by myself and then, *and then* you all walk in and interrupt my gig, and…and then you two *f-f-fuck faces* started heckling me!”

“What?” Dicky’s imaginary pearls are clutched. “I…I don’t think” Head shaking. “…did we?” He sort of asks, his mind racing.

“I think we *maybe*, we might have said something like, ‘Hey Schultz, what up?’” Curt says, nodding, shifting around on the plush leather sofa making a crinkling noise.

“Yeah Dude, I think that’s all we said…I’m pretty sure about that Schultzy.” Dicky assures himself.

“Try,” I start, putting up air quotes, “and I quote, ‘You fucking suck. Jew. Go home you fucking Jew. Please kill yourself. You fucking Jew. Go home. Jew.’ End quote.”

“Schultz, buddy.” Dicky starts. “Here’s the thing, and Curt, I think you’ll agree with this. I don’t wanna put words in your mouth or anything Dude, but what happened there Schultz was, ya see …”

“Dude, what happened was…” Curt interrupts. “You see, we were drunk.”

Dicky thinks about it for a beat or two really hard, squints his eyes and then says, “Yeah Dude, I think that must have been what happened. Ya see, there’s really nothing anyone could have done about it.”

“Yeah Dude, there really was nothing anyone could have done Schultz.” Curt says.

“Yeah well, you both can go pull a frickin’ Daisy Chain on each other for all I care. I quit. I’m out.” I say, shaking my bottle of Percocet's then eyeballing it carefully.

“Oh, come on Schultzy Baby, don’t be like that.” Dicky pleads.

“Whatever, I’m going to take these bandages off and take a shower. Then you two fags are going to cut these stitches off my nose.”

“Alright Schultzy, love you buddy.” Dicky says lighting joint from a sterling silver, table lighter.

Chapter XIX

The mahogany Grandfather clock in our living room chimes twice, indicating that it's 2 p.m. My face is swollen and sore and my neck is starting to kink up also. Anxiety is stirring because I'm almost out of pain killers and badly in need of more. The original Jake Rosen painting titled *New York Skyline in September* contrast the velvet drapes that hang firmly down the French windows. There is a golden ice bucket on the bar by the wall to the kitchen and a bottle of E&J Brandy VSOP that is calling my name. I'm teaching Dicky *Dead Flowers* by the Stones on our respective guitars.

I'll be in my basement room
With a needle and a spoon
And a brand-new girl, to take my pain away

Take me down little Suzie, take me down
I know you think you're the queen of the underground
And you can, send me dead flowers...at my wedding
And I won't forget to put roses on your grave.

"Damn, that's a fuckin' great song." He says enthusiastically, re-energized. "We're definitely playing that one. I can't believe I've never heard that before."

"I need a brand-new girl to take my pain away." I say desperately. "Pass me that bottle."

"Dude, you're drunk." Dicky says, sliding the bottle over to me. I take it and immediately go to take a deep and intimate swig. "And get a glass and a coaster for Christ's sake! We're not in Jamaica."

"Hey fuck you, Man! What are you, The Great Gatsby or something?" I start. "I've got a fucking hole in my tongue, my nose is broken, my whole face is sore, and I've got a gash in my head the size of a hooker's privates. Not to mention the Caddy is dead, fucking totaled! Totally dead. You know I still owe money on that shit? I don't know what the fuck I'm gonna do! I'm gonna be a wandering fool, walking to and fro to work and school every day. What's your excuse ya drunk bitch?"

"Schultzy poops, that's some strong language you're using there. Let's take a minute and think about what you really want to say here." He says.

"Oh...go and...eat your...grandmother's...bum hole." I manage in short bursts.

"You gotta cheer the fuck up, Dude." Dicky says, standing up and walking casually over to the bar. He takes two glasses and sets them gently down on the wooden counter, leaning on the brown leather padding, he opens the golden ice bucket and uses the diamond studded tongs to

place three cubes in each glass then pours the E&J Brandy VSOP over them making a cracking sound that is an absolute symphony to my ears.

"I gotta get some more pain killers is what I gotta do." I say, inspecting the gold rimmed Brandy sifter curiously.

"All right Dude, just take another swig off that bottle kid." Dicky says in a Clint Eastwood voice, pointing to the Brandy sifter. "We gotta get a song written."

"Alright." I say shaking off a deep swig. "What do you want to write about?"

"Wait," Dicky says, "what did you say before?"

"Dude, I don't need any more of your crap." I say. "Let's just write this thing."

"No, I'm not giving you shit." He swears. "What did you say before, about going to work?"

"I said I'm gonna have to walk back and forth from work and school like a G.D. kid. I'll be a flippin' wandering fool." I say.

"That's it Dude, *Wandering Fool*. Give me that notebook." He says.

Dick strums some chords and whistles a little *doot do doot do dootdo* thingy and then starts writing something down when Valerie, Blair and Sarai give the door knocker a little tap before walking through the doors carrying a 12 pack of Bud Light bottles.

"Hey guys, what's up?" Blair says cheerfully, wearing white shorts and a red St. Louis Cardinal's V-neck T-shirt.

"Hey ladies, what's going on?" Dicky asks.

"Nothing, just hanging out. We wanted to come by and see how our patient is." Blair says, inspecting my face.

"Oh, fuck Schultz! I heard your face was bad but fuck me. Your face is fucked up." Sarai says sitting down, pulling the Baccarat crystal ashtray toward her and lighting a cigarette. Sarai is wearing a purple stripped tank top, a yellow golfing visor and bell bottom jeans.

"Shut up Sarai." Blair says, laughing. "It's not that bad, Dude. I mean, it'll heal. You don't look like Tom Cruise in *Vanilla Sky* or anything."

Valerie sits down next to me carefully taking all of the air in the room with her. She's glowing, her blue kaleidoscope eyes hypnotizing the rest of the room, the world out of existence. She's wearing jean cut-off shorts, a white Fruit of the Loom V-neck T shirt with her white scarf, black bra, and a red bandana holding back her wild, curly dark hair, a silver Daisy ring and brown leather flip-flops that show off her newly painted, Jet black toenails. She takes the guitar by the neck and sets it down against the black Armani couch and then gently takes my face in her hands.

Everyone and everything in the room zooms out of low-resolution focus, disappears completely. The weight of the moment suddenly becomes heavy as our hearts beat more rapidly, our pulse quickens, breathing becomes deeper. We are both looking down timidly, my lower lip begins to quiver as I'm trying to control my panting. She lifts my head up with her hands and then slowly raises her eyes to meet mine. Her eyes are clear, she is not high. She looks at me tenderly, like a fairy godmother before examining my face and head and then, with tears starting to well up in her eyes, she kisses me softly on the lips. Her hands release my face and slide behind my neck as she moves in closer until we are gelled together in embrace. She whispers in my ear, "Oh baby," Then sniffs and wipes away a tear before saying, "I thought I'd never see you again." She pauses, looks me in the eye and says, "Come on, let's go."

The shepherd and the wolf are becoming one.

She stands up slowly, with no regard for anyone else in the room, takes me by my hand and leads me to my bedroom and shuts the door quietly behind us. I'm standing in the middle of the room with my king-sized Infinity Contemporary White Platform Bed behind me, unsure what to do. I'm just sort of standing there so I put my hands in the back pockets of my Calvin's and awkwardly rock back and forth on my heels.

Valerie is still standing at the door when she finally looks up at me sheepishly with her marble blue eyes, biting her bottom lip and locks the door. Once the door is locked, the soul behind her eyes transforms into someone who's been told that she's *trouble* more than once and flicks off the light mischievously. She kicks off her flip-flop sandals, walks over to me and wraps her arms around my neck tightly, kissing my cheek gently.

I remove my hands from the pockets of my jeans and hold her firmly, first around her waist then up, under her shirt through her silky back where we stand embraced for a lifetime. She's kissing my neck and then she holds my face again and looks at me in the eyes. She whispers, "I thought I might have lost you and I…I just died."

She kisses me on the mouth deeply, she licks my lips with her tongue, inviting my tongue to Tango. We stand there on the plush Persian rug then she stops, she looks up at me and pulls her white T-shirt up over her head confidently, taking the red bandana with it, then shakes her hair out while undoing her bra from the back. As she stands in front of me holding her black satin bra up with her hands, her face once again looks embarrassed until she playfully sways her shoulders back and forth and then that naughty look returns, and she slowly lowers her hands, revealing her plump, firm breasts. She walks right up to me again, starts kissing me passionately and wraps her arms around my waist.

My hands massaging her voluptuous breasts, her hands work their way timidly around to the front of my jeans and she unbuckles my silver, Harley-Davidson belt buckle. She sinks down, kissing my chin, then around at my chest for a stint before, finally to her knees where she seductively tongues around at my stomach while releasing my belt with her hands. Her lips and tongue still driving my semi-firm abs crazy. She pulls down my C.K. jeans and allows me to step out of them one foot at a time.

With her hands, she guides my thighs towards the bed and instructs me to sit down. She looks up at me from between my legs and moves her hand up my stomach to my chest slowly, flattening me on my back. She runs her hands back down my torso and cups my dick through my Mickey Mouse boxer/briefs from H & M in her fingers and gives it a wet kiss before peeling off my underpants. The General flips up and smacks my stomach and Val lets out a giggle that says she can still be playful and isn't taking this too seriously.

She takes The General in her hands, kneels up straight and gives it a lippy smooch, then she bends down and, starting at my thigh, all the while, looking at me hard in the eyes, licks her way up the shaft to the tip. She then slowly wraps her mouth around the head of my nerd and sucks it forcefully. She goes deeper and starts to pick up momentum, bobbing her head up and down. When she starts to hum and moan, the vibration of her mouth on my penis gives a great big, flashing green light to the load that has been building up inside me since she first looked at me with those mesmerizing blue eyes back on the couch.

I pull her head off me and she gasps for breath with a thick string of saliva running from her mouth to the tip of the General. She takes two deep breaths and laughs as if she's pleasantly surprised at what is going down. I take her by her armpits and slide her up to where our faces meet and though this is usually *not* how I do business, I shove my tongue into her mouth, my hands squeezing her ass through her black satin panties. She is grinding on my rock-hard dick as we lay there kissing until she sits up, arches her back and flips her head back, holding onto my dick from the front and rocking back and forth on top of it. She starts to moan as her speed accelerates, then when her moan turns into a pant, she stops and collapses onto my chest and, deeply out of breath, she asks me, "Are you alright?"

"Yes, yes I'm alright." I say, thinking, 'Am I alright? Are you serious right now?' and then thanking God I drank enough whiskey to not turn this into an *American Pie* moment.

She sits up again, pulls her panties to the side and slowly lowers herself onto the full length of The General, letting out very satisfied gasp. Once the full length is inside of her, she sits there for a beat then begins to grind back and forth. She puts her hands on my chest and starts moving slowly up and down, then more quickly until she is bouncing on my dick. I'm gripping her white scarf with one hand and her ass cheek with the other and even let a little slap slip out causing her to yelp.

She's panting now so I start massaging her breasts while she bounces up and down on me like she's taming a stallion. Now we are both vocally peaking with her, "Oh, oh God!" and me grunting until all the whiskey in the world couldn't stop me from just exploding inside her with a full body, eye fluttering, leg twitching orgasm.

Pause.

She collapses on my chest, has a couple more goes of the old *in and out* before raising up and pulling herself off of me and falling onto her back on the king-sized bed next to me. We're both laying there on the Bone White, silk Sferra Utopia Eiderdown sheets trying to catch our breath when she suddenly sits up and says, "Let's go drink whiskey."

"I thought you'd never ask." I say, then, "You go first."

She stands up and starts to put her clothes on one piece at a time while I'm just sitting there watching like a total perv, soaking it all in.

"Hey," I say, remembering how much pain I'm in, "I just remembered how much pain I'm in, do you guys have any pain killers?"

"No," she laughs, "we've got…" she says, catching herself, "I mean um, I think Blair has something you can have. I'll ask her."

"Alright, cool." I say, starting to get up.

"Did you do something different in here?" She asks, looking around my bedroom.

"Yeah, I don't know." I say, picking up my Micky Mouse boxers with my toes.

She goes to open the door but then looks back at me and says, "Don't be too long, I'll be all alone out there." Before taking a deep breath, opening the door and walking out.

I sit there on the edge of my bed for a beat, allowing this image to solidify in my long-term memory. I can hear Dicky playing a song I've never heard before from the Living Room. I slowly stand up and put on my boxer/briefs and Calvin's, looking at my back muscles in the mirror on the wall, singing the words to Cake's *Let Me Go.*

Chapter XX

I walk into the Living Room without being acknowledged. I give the white Chateau bar stool a curious look before spinning it, take a bottle of Jamison's from the bar and sit down on the black leather couch. I pick up my guitar and start playing a blues lead to this new song Dicky's finishing. I can tell he just wrote it because the chorus goes:

'Cause I'm a wandering fool now baby,
I got everywhere to go.

Sarai takes a drink off the bottle of Jamison's, passes it to Valerie, who also takes a big swig, cringes, then looks at me and flashes me a smile that melts me from the inside out. Sarai takes out a handful of pills and hands them to me.

"Thanks." I say, taking them and popping two immediately with a whiskey chaser.

"So how are you going to get around now that the Caddy is totaled?" Sarai asks with her natural tact.

"I don't know." I say, "I guess I can walk to Lindenwood and I can walk to Steak 'n Shake so, I guess I'll just be walking everywhere."

"Damn, well if you ever need a ride, just call me." Blair says.

"Shit, you gotta take me to my probation officer." Sarai says, squinting at an imaginary watch that was never on her wrist. "I'm gonna be late again. How do my eyes look, Dude?" She asks Valerie.

"You'll be fine." Val says.

The three of them stand up and Blair says, putting on her sunglasses, "Well I hope you feel better. If I don't see you, we'll definitely be at the big show next week." She pauses, then says, "Well, I'll see you before then. Later!"

Val walks over to me, puts her hand on my face, kisses me on the lips and whispers, "I love you." in my ear, then slides her hand off my cheek and floats out the front door.

Once they're gone, I take two more of the pills, give Dicky one and then try to play along with the song he's still working the kinks out of. I go to say something, but he cuts me off instead saying, "Alright Dude, good for you. Now check this shit out. It's C, D, G to the E minor."

He starts the song over from the top, calls it *Wandering Fool* and tells me to keep up. It needs some work and maybe a kazoo which we no longer have after that whole Russian schoolgirl porn phase Curt went through a while back. Afterwards, I say, "Alright man, that's pretty good. Now let's go chip some golf balls, I've been in this house too long."

We start to get up but when I go to turn the 70-inch Sony Flat screen T.V. off, there's breaking news on CNN. They found the body of Chandra Levy in some park in New York. The police say that they are tracking down every possible lead. Wolf Blitzer reminds us all that the congressman she was working for, Gary Condit, has not been totally ruled out as a person of interest.

Maybe being in the house for a couple of days straight has given me a fresh perspective on the majesty of the natural world all around us. I think it's around the first week in September but as we step out of the front door, onto the porch and I'm able to breath in the crisp and cold autumn air for the first time, it's brisk. The park looks wiser, bigger, the trees look greener and fuller, the playground looks brighter and the cemetery looks spookier and more inviting than ever. We've got our bucket of balls that we're chipping back and forth, there is just enough breeze to feel nice but not screw up our game.

"Damn, it's nice to be out here." I say, taking another deep breath. The euphoria of the pain killers are starting to send me into a manic numbness.

"So those girls are all fucked up, huh?" Dicky asks, completely changing the subject. "You know, on heroin."

"I don't know," I say, shrugging my shoulders and squaring up to take my shot. "it's none of my business."

"Bullshit it's none of your business, Schultz, you love her. Don't try to tell me you don't love her with every cell in your blood." He says, leaning on his 9 Iron.

"What the crap are you talking about?" I ask after I chip my ball into the air. I watch it blow back and forth in the wind, left, then right, then ultimately landing just shy of the bald patch I was aiming for.

"Shut the fuck up Schultz." Dicky is saying. "She's all you think about and you know it. And not just in a back burner, *You Were Always on My Mind* kind of way, Schultz. You daydream about her all the time. I know you better than you think, Kid."

"Can we focus?" I ask.

"I bet you like, set aside time just to think about her don't you. You do, don't you. You motherfucker!" He's speculating out loud. "You want to make one of those elaborate, Rube Goldberg machines with her just to spend time with her. When you are walking around, you take the long way, you avoid the most obvious short cuts to make it last longer. I know you Schultzy, I've known your ass for a long time. Don't try to bullshit me."

"Do you have a point?" I'm begging at this point.

"Just, don't give me this, *'It's none of my business.'* bullshit. She's obviously into you too, I never seen her like she just was with you before though, shit. You guys always kept it on the down low but back there, the fucking neighbors heard that shit."

"Was it that obvious?" I ask, letting a cheeky smirk escape.

"See, look at that stupid grin on your face Schultz, oh my god, Dude. Why don't you just ask her to marry you?" He says, shaking his head.

"Is that M.B.?" I ask, pointing my 3 Iron to a red truck pulling up in front of the house.

"Yeah, put those balls in the bucket. I'm gonna go up there before they just walk in and start going through our shit." He says.

"Hey pussies!" M.B. shouts down from the street, getting out of his truck with Ryan Barnes and two cases of Budweiser cans.

We walk up the hill, cross the street and walk up the pink marble steps to our house, M.B. and Barnes are sitting on the porch, both wearing stained carpenter garb, rolling a blunt.

"Curt isn't here yet?" Barnes asks, sitting down on the Maya Teak patio duvet.

"No Dude, I guess he's still at work." Dicky says taking a beer and opening it.

"You pussies don't have any brews?" Barnes asks, "You no job having, broke ass bitches."

"Motherfucker, I do foundations. I break a sweat while your ass is still spooning this bitch in bed." Dicky says, pointing at M.B. "We stop for the day at 2."

"Yeah, and your drunk by 2:15." M.B. says.

"Shit, I'm drunk by 10:30." Dicky says, lone starring the rest of his beer.

"What's your excuse Schultz?" Barnes asks, laughing, "I'm just fucking with you. You don't look as bad as I heard it was. Fooky said you looked like Frankenstein."

"You are a dumb motherfucker, Dude." Barnes says, shaking his head, "Why the fuck would you let Mort drive your mother fucking Cadillac? What the fuck did you think was going to happen?"

"I don't know, he seemed fine in the parking lot." I say.

"And then he just took off, didn't he? That motherfucker." M.B. says, opening a beer and setting it on a coaster on the table.

"What a fuckin' dick." Barnes says. "The dude totals your Caddy and then just jets afterward. Doesn't even see if you're alright."

"No, he asked if I was alright." I say, dabbing at my skull.

"Sure, as he was running away." M.B. adds.

"And you told the cops it was him anyway." Barnes says, laughing.

"Bullcrap!" I shout, almost spitting out a mouthful of beer. "I didn't say peep."

"That's not what I heard." M.B. argues. "The cops came right?"

"Yeah." I say.

"Well what the fuck did you tell them?" M.B. asks.

"I told them it was some dude I met at the bar, I said I just met him." I insist. "Freakin' ask Fooky, he was there."

"And they believed you?" Barnes asks.

"I don't think he believed anything I said. Nothing I said was the truth except my age, and that just confused Officer Hardass more." I say. "I guess they didn't think I would be able to come up

with all these lies in the shape I was in. Then they didn't really have a choice, I clearly wasn't driving so, what the heck were they gonna do? I was sitting there bleeding out."

"That's so fucked up." Barnes says.

"Oh yeah, so who won the fight?" I ask.

"What fight?" Barnes asks.

"Well we were going out there to watch your brother and Bad Bob fight." I say, reminding him.

"Oh, they were just brewed up. All anyone talked about was your dumb asses, then everyone just went home." M.B. says laughing.

"Jesus H. Tap-dancing Christ." I say, finishing a beer and opening another one.

When Curt pulls up, we all go inside. I look at my face in the golden framed mirror on the wall. I ain't the fairest in the land. Curt, Barnes and M.B. go in his room to take care of business. They come out and smoke three giant joints, one after another then they take off just as Ginger and Lolita pull up in their shitty Honda. They're with some dude; tall, dark gay-ish looking hair, green T-shirt that is two sizes too small and a butt-chin.

Me and Dicky have resumed playing guitars and working out the details to *Wandering Fool*, Curt looks out the window and says, "Dude, those crazy bitches are here and there with some dude. The fuck?"

"The plot thickens." Dicky says, strumming and eerie E minor chord on his axe.

"Well it looks like they have beer." I say, peeking through the velvet curtains.

Chapter XXI

"What's up bitches?" Ginger, who is visibly drunk says plopping down on the couch next to me, "This is my boyfriend, Steve."

Ginger is wearing black shorts from Express, red sandals that match her hair and a white T-shirt that says, "Shut up liver, you're fine." is hiding her black, spiderweb tattoo that crawls up her neck. Lolita is wearing a Minnie Mouse T-shirt that hangs seductively over her left shoulder, her brunette hair is in pigtails and cut off jean shorts that are not quite Daisy Dukes, both are inviting rear entry.

"Hey, what's up Guys?" Steve says cheerfully, offering us all a beer.

"'Sup dude." We all kind of say out of turn, taking a beer.

"Do we not have a fridge full of brewskis?" Curt asks Dicky.

"Fuck yeah we do Man." Dicky says very matter-of-factly, "People keep coming by with brews though." He says popping one open and sucking the foam. "Roll with it kid."

"We need weed." Ginger slurs, her eyes unable to fight bobbling around in their sockets.

Curt gets up and says, "This is all you Schultz." and walks through some fancy Indian beads to his room that is now full of paisley patterned, silk throw pillows.

"How's your face?" Lolita asks me, leaning back comfortably on the Baxton Studio 'Aphrodite' grey linen Chaise Lounge, crossing her legs, then re-crossing them slowly.

"Not as bad as it looks." I say, licking my lips then stop, realizing the kind of body language I must be sending.

"What the hell happened to you Dude?" Steve asks, leaning in close, squinting at me with a dusting of PCP in his eyes.

"Long story." I say picking up my guitar and playing around with a blues lead.

"He fought a bear, Dude." Dicky says with a straight face. "Fucking thing tried to get in here the other night, Schultz had to fight it off. No shit."

"No shit?" Steve asks, uneasily shifting in his seat on the couch. His feet are causing the white Polar Bear rug to shed. I ask him politely to take his work boots off and leave them outside. He obeys.

Curt walks out of his room, shouts, "Schultz!" before walking into my room and quickly shutting the door behind him. I get up and leave the bear story to Dicky.

"Yeah dude, a fucking six-foot grizzly, must've smelled all the weed from in here. You know grizzly bears love weed. They're the fuckin' stoners of the Missouri wilderness…" Dicky is saying as I walk into my room. "That's fuckin' true shit Dude. You didn't know that…"

"What's up?" I ask walking in my room and shutting the door. Curt is throwing down a quarter bag of weed on my eggshell colored Ever Rouge Mason Manor bed comforter.

"Don't ever mention my name to any of those crazy motherfuckers." He says. "Just give me $50.00. Don't give this to that pone for anything less than $80.00, this is fucking great weed. And make him smoke a joint with you."

"Do we really want to give them a reason to hang out?" I ask, picking up the baggie.

"Ate up motherfuckers." Curt says to himself, shaking his head, checking out his back muscles in the platinum wall mirror. Then, "Well, whatever Dude, do whatever the fuck you want." He says, then, under his breath he whispers, "Did you know she had a fuckin' boyfriend?"

"I heard something about a boyfriend," I say shrugging my shoulders, "but I don't really believe anything that they've ever said. We don't really even know what their real names are. We know nothing about them."

"Whatever Dude, just don't get me involved with anything having to do with those motherfuckers. I don't want anything to do with them." He says definitively and walks out of the room.

I take a nugget out of the bag, toss it on my pine Chester drawer and then go back out into the living room where Dicky is still going on about bears…

"…Fuck yeah Dude, you didn't know that?" Dicky is still ranting. "Rats would totally be the size of bears but they live in pipes and shit so they can't grow any bigger. Those motherfuckers get as big as their environment will let them."

"So," I say cutting him off. "What'chu need?" I'm hoping to get this over with as soon as possible.

"A quarter bag." Ginger says snapping her fingers at Steve.

"Thank God." I say under my breath, tossing the bag to her. "$70 bucks."

"Here's $80.00." She says, taking the money from Steve and giving it to me. "So, what are you gonna do about a car?"

"Uh, I don't know," I sigh, having thought that this whole thing was wrapping up.

"Well you can use my car." Ginger offers quickly.

Pause.

"Um, I get up pretty early." I say, sitting up, leaning in closer.

"That's cool." She says. "Me and Steve will drop it off in the morning."

"That's uh, this is cool with you?" I feel I have to ask Steve.

What exactly am I supposed to make of this new plot twist? She's going to let me use her car, what the bloody hell is going on here? And just who in the wide world of effs is this guy? I mean, what kind of guy is this? Is this guy like the guys in Cuckold porn where he likes to watch his girl get drilled by big black dudes with giant black dude units? Is he a Cuck? What does that make me, am I the black dude? I mean, The General is nothing to be ashamed of, but is it *black dude porn* impressive? Who the in the hairy balls knows what these people are into besides day drinking, PCP and, apparently open relationships?

"Yeah Dude, it's cool." Steve the Cuck says without the slightest hint of skepticism or disbelief.

"Uh...alright cool." I say standing up and making my way to the door. "Well, Alex Keaton is supposed to be stopping by soon so, ya know…thanks for the brewskis." I say, holding the door open.

"Yeah, well thanks for the bud." Steve the Cuck says holding up the 12-pack in his hand in leu of a handshake, blessed be the Lord, and walking out the door. Ginger follows him but gives my crotch a little pat on her way out, finally, Lolita who just says, "Bye-bye." with a little wave and a smile that suggests something that I can't properly articulate.

As soon as they're gone, I shut the door behind them, take out the bag of pills Sarai gave me, toss them down on the mirrored coffee table, take out a dollar bill and a lighter that I stole. I crush up two pills with a crystal yen/yang drink coaster until they are powdery enough to snort, then cut out two lines with a platinum AmEx card. I snort one of the lines with a silver-plated straw with my initials engraved in it from the Hayneedle home bar and it burns like a firecracker. I give the other line to Dicky and then make us both a couple of Singapore Slings.

"Was that as screwed up as I thought it was?" I ask Dicky, who goes back to sitting on the black Armani leather couch, guitar in hand. "I mean, is that dude some kind of a cuck or something?"

"Hell yeah he is…wait, I mean *what*?" He says, waning confusion. "What's a…I don't know what a *cuck* is!"

"O.K. Dude, whatever." I say.

"What?" He asks, then, "Dude, I'm not worried about what that cuck, I mean, that *pone* thinks, I'm trying to get this song down. Come on, let's go through this again before someone else stops by."

"Right on, I like your focus." I say, sitting down and picking up my axe. "Alright, hit it. I'll follow you."

Wandering Fool is a good song and I'm trying to follow along but I'm having trouble fighting the nod from all the pills and drinks. I'm feeling light-headed and confused. This has been a day full of sensory overload.

"I don't know how much longer I can hold out man." I say, fighting the nod. "It's been a long day. I'm falling out."

“Alright Dude, whatever.” Dicky says.

“I gotta piss.” I say, struggling to stand up, then, halfway to my bedroom, turn around and ask, “Is it cold in here?”

“What?” He shouts from the couch.

“I said, *is it cold in here?*”

Chapter XXII

I’m standing at the foot of great mountain staring up at two paths that diverge upward. As I follow the straight, worn path with my eyes, the mountain continues to grow as high as my line of sight will allow until it disappears into some heavy and thunderous clouds above. I choose the path that is winding and overgrown without much deliberation and in no time at all, I find myself

hacking away at thick vines and massive dragon flies with a samurai sword trying to clear the path as I make my way through. I don't know where I'm going, I never think to look behind me, I can only see the jungle in front of me and my katana chopping vigorously, I just feel like I need to keep swinging and moving forward, upward and onward.

I reach the timberline and now it's a foggy hike to the peak. I sheath my sword. Only able to see an arm's length in front of me in any direction. I physically tilt my head up and simply command my legs to keep moving forward. I imagine my feet are spinning like a child's cartoon and I will them to carry on. Finally, I see the mountain top and a beam of light shines down from just above the peak and is pointing to the other side of the ridge. Though every step towards the light seems to move it forward, I persist.

When I am finally close enough to the peak of the mighty mountain, I extend my hand to grab the beam of warm light that shines down, always just out of reach. I'm crawling now, afraid, intimidated by the magnitude of the mountain I'm cowering on top of. I crawl forward and the wind begins to pick up, then a fierce hail and cold rain starts to pour down. I reach out my hand to the jagged rock and bullets of ice are pelting my arms and head but it's so close, one more push, one more rally and I'll have it.

Once I'm able to grab onto the sharp peak, I'm able to pull myself up and finally see over the rim of the mountain. A feeling of great relief washes over me as I hug the rock staked out at the peak. Suddenly it occurs to me to look down at where I started, where I came from but as soon as I turn to look, the side of the mountain erodes away into a vast expanse of nothingness. I decide to stand in the sun that is now shining down on me, it isn't easy to regain my footing but suddenly I'm looking down at a green hillside with grey boulders littering the ground like headstones in a cemetery.

Slowly the rocks begin to quake. I focus my attention on one of them and it hatches right before my eyes. A green reptile emerges from the remains and stretches its wings and jaw letting out a quaint mew. I notice all the other rocks begin to tremble and hatch as well but my focus returns to the original reptile who is now making its way toward me, growing with each clumsy step until it is a full on fire-breathing dragon running at me with a hungry look in its eyes.

I panic, freeze in fear at the sight and sheer size of this dragon which now towers over me wagging its plated tail and smashing it into the ground beside me until I remember my samurai sword. I'm hesitant to draw it at first, not wanting to upset the beast, wishing I could just cower behind a tree unnoticed. When the dragon's nostrils flare and I can sense an attack is eminent, however, I decide that it's either fight or be destroyed. Having come this far already, survival feels like a debt that I owe to a collective community of souls that seem to be supporting me from somewhere just out of the realm of my current consciousness.

There is no time to concoct any kind of plan other than to draw my sword and start defending myself against the dragon's flame. He breaths down a barrage of fire upon me and I kneel with my sword held over my head and, though it is thin, it somehow shields me from the fire which strikes down all around, singeing the grass at my feet. When the dragon gnarls his razor-sharp teeth at me, I stand up tall, shoulders out in defiance of the mighty beast. I draw back my sword and execute an overhand chop directed at its veiny green neck. I make contact leaving a sizable gash in the throat of the dragon which causes it to gasp for breath.

I see a chance and I seize it. Offensively, I swing around and slice the throat of the dragon wide open exposing an endless pit of darkness and chaos. The dragon is now jerking around violently in a fit of rage, fire spewing in all directions. I draw back my sword once more and chop the head off of the beast. I'm gasping for breath but no sooner than I can regain some composure, the dragon is back on its sharp, taloned feet with three new heads emerging from the void. Now all the dragons are three headed and they are all walking toward me with smoky flames shooting from their fierce nostrils. Once again, I draw back my sword and prepare to vanquish each one until I have slayed the heart, the source of the wickedness itself.

Suddenly a cold breeze blows, diverting my attention. The sky turns grey and the sun falls to black. I look down and my hands are covered in blood and my sword grows old and rusted before being blown away in a chilling zephyr. Valerie is kneeling on my bed, unbuckling my belt and stripping my off-brand jeans from my waist. She's not looking at me, but I can feel her laughing cynically and I notice that she is not wearing her white scarf. When she flips her hair back and finally looks up at me, I see a jagged scar, thick and pink stretching from ear to ear with white lines from where her head had been stitched on her neck running along the outside like a demon centipede.

She hisses at me exposing vampire fangs and starts going down on me with a passionate vengeance, spitting on my member like some old timey French insult. She's really gagging on it, making clogging noises with each thrust. I don't know whether to laugh or cry. She stops and starts jerking me off with her hand and tears are coming from her eyes and she asks me, "Is this what you want, is this how you like it?"

Before I can respond, her eyes become tired and her skin begins to wrinkle. Her hair greys and her cheeks sink into her face until nothing but a maggot infested skull hovers above me.

I come to with a violent convulsion. Everything I know is sucked instantly into dark corners of my mind never to be fully recovered again. Only in moments of divine inspiration will the hints of the universe I just left behind peek out and whisper a memory that I'll feel somewhere inside me but unable to quite place. I look down and realize that it's not a dream, Ginger has somehow snuck back in the house and into my room and is now having her way with me.

You really have to admire her determination. I really don't want her here but can't be bothered going through the hassle of telling her to stop. Girls don't really take that kind of rejection with much tact, being so far invested already and all. And with this bitch, who knows what she'd do, I very well may wake up with the General severed and tossed in a ditch somewhere off Bryan Rd.

I don't remember Ginger leaving but she's not there when I wake up in the morning. At 7:00 a.m. sharp, Steve the Cuck is knocking on the door. I open it and he offers a chipper, "Hey dude, what's up?"

"What's up man." I say blankly, buckling my Harley Davidson belt buckle and putting on a red T-shirt with white Chinese characters on it.

"Well, here's the keys Dude. I'll drop her off later to pick it up." He says, pointing back at the redhead in the passenger seat of his shitty Camaro, handing me the keys to Ginger's 1987 Baby Blue Honda Civic. I'm bewildered by the stupid cuck smile on his stupid cuck face. Does he really not have any clue that his chick drove over here, snuck back into the house and gave me a monumental hummer last night? Seems unlikely.

"Alright man, thanks." I say before shutting the door, then, to myself, "Ate up mother Effer."

Every time I open the door for that cuck, I get a strange feeling I'm opening up a box that cannot be closed and every time I shut it on him, I don't feel like I've achieved any closure. Like inviting a vampire into your house for the first time and herpes, no matter what you do, they're never really gone.

Chapter XXIII

I have three classes today at Lindenwood, the first one is Intro to the American Revolution. The professor is a 50-something-year-old hippy lady who looks like Steven Tyler named Professor Donaldson. Her lectures are interesting enough and she's very enthusiastic and knowledgeable about the subject matter, but she intentionally wears a lot of clanky jewelry and is always playing with her hair which is hard to ignore after 7 1/2 minutes and utterly unbearable after 25.

Today's lecture is about how, at the beginning of the Revolution, the early years, nothing was pre-determined. She is saying that, in hindsight, it's easy to assume that the revolution was inevitable. That the United States was manifest destiny or whatever, but back then it wasn't, not at all. The colonists were British citizens and most of them were proud to be British. After all, Britain was the biggest, most powerful nation in the history of the planet. A beacon of light, of liberal democracy for the world to strive toward. Anywhere you would ever possibly want to live on the planet was desirable directly because of Britain's influence. Not until right up to the end, or the beginning, did the people start talking about being *Americans*. Well maybe not Samuel Adams. But for the rest of the colonists, it must have felt like the entire world was ending.

There you have British citizens, loyal and proud citizens of this empire that dominated the globe for all of their lifetimes, their parents' lifetimes and on back for generations. They woke up every morning and went to bed every night of their lives knowing that they were part of the greatest empire the world had ever known and now, all of a sudden there is this notion brewing that a colony of that empire that you are a part of is thinking about rebelling against it. Unheard of. Those people's whole worlds were falling apart and descending into absolute chaos.

Some of them, like the Adams brothers and company were perfectly happy to spearhead this revolt against the empire. The revolution probably would never have even happened if not for those Bostonians and their rage against the machine. But then you had loyalists who weren't going anywhere. Why would they, over some taxes? Just pay it! Those people were just trying to keep food on their tables and a roof over their heads. Those people, the masses, they didn't want any trouble. Their everyday lives were as much trouble as they could deal with in life. They were trying not to starve to death or die of scurvy or some such nonsense.

Her lecture made me think about how, even the little decisions we make or don't make in our lives lead to how things end up. I start to fade out, lost in thought. It seems like every person is a train speeding down a track of life and at any point, you can get off whatever train comes through your life's station, or not. Every relationship in your life either moved forward with you in it or completely left your station with one call back or lack thereof. What else connects us? Every relationship I have, Valerie, Curt, Dicky, Josh, Martin, whomever, was a series of returned phone calls on both parts. A series of plans kept that, over time, built a friendship or relationship. How Ginger works into this is a bit of a puzzle, how has she managed to hitch her cart to my wagon? And how do I unhitch it? I hate to toss around the word *stalk* willy-nilly but if it ever applied, it would be that bitch.

But how many hundreds of people have I encountered in life where that return phone call didn't get made, on either end. Or a plan was made, and it didn't go down quite the way one or both parties expected and that sort of set each other's trains in other directions. Most of the time you never even notice. Sometimes one-party notices more than the other, that's how one-night stands go bad. One party is ready to hitch wagons and the other is ready to move on. Some trains seem to keep passing each other over and over again and there is an inevitability that can't be denied.

When me, Dicky and Curt moved in together, we didn't sit down and discuss the trajectory of where we would like our lives to go or if we were compatible enough to make those dreams manifest into a reality, I don't think a word was said. I'm sure two years from now, we won't be living together for whatever reason and I'm sure there won't be a conversation about that either. None of us, no one I know has any idea where they are going to be a year from now. We live in a continuous state of chaos.

When I was a kid, my Mom at least tried her best to provide an orderly world, she did the best she could anyway. When my Dad left, she did everything she could to show us that the sky wasn't falling even when it was. When parents' divorce, that's exactly what happens to a kid, it shatters their world. Even if it's a bad world, filled with hate and abuse and its own chaos, it's the only world a kid knows. When parents break up, that world, their world, as they know it, is over.

So, do we really have free will, or is everything already predetermined? I'm not sure that pre-determinism isn't just a fancy way to justify hindsight being 20/20. After something happens, we move on and are left with memories. Then memories of memories, which are often distorted, or all together wrong it turns out, but that certainly leads to a feeling of inevitability. To consider any alternate reality is both a fool's errand, because what's done is done, and all the resulting actions are predicated on the fact that the first event happened. It's easy to see how we rationalize the idea that everything is predetermined.

If it's not though, if we have free will to change, adapt, and evolve, well, that changes everything. If we have free will then really, if you think about it, every decision we make changes the course of human history.

So, empires rise, and empires fall. The history books explain it in concrete terms that can be measured, *King George was insane and got greedy...* but I feel like, maybe there was a collective conscious and a million decisions made by a million people that all played their roll and continue to play out a roll every day, every moment. We are all on this planet together, playing this interactive game all day, every day and every decision, every thought or action we take or don't take contributes to the game. Life is a series of moments.

Rome fell after all, same as the British empire and every other empire in the history of humanity. Maybe it's just a matter of time before these American pillars of order crumble to the ground. Ashes to ashes. As much as we humans strive for equilibrium, to even things out, and order, nothing is certain. Nothing lasts forever. We try to make sense out of it all, but really, we're all swimming, drowning, utterly emerged in madness.

Getting on heroin can put you on that trajectory real fast. That's one train you ain't gettin' off of. It's my wife, and it's my life. Heroin is one thing that breaks that rule, after one dance, you're stuck with that ball and chain till the bloody end. And it's quick too, there ain't no growing old together with that bitch. Unless you're Keith flippin' Richards or something.

I'm snapped out of my daze when someone hits my elbow walking past. I gather my books and close my notebook where a sketch of a serpent eating its tail has mysteriously emerged and my pencil is snapped in two. I get up and leave.

My next class is Psychology 102 with Professor Bloom, a cool black dude, well dressed with a clever sense of humor who reminds me of a young Redd Foxx and the kind of cat who doesn't really let his political views shine through like the rest of these hippy professors. At least I can't tell from listening to him talk, though he is a psych professor so he may know some way to slip them in subconsciously and we're all just little Manchurian Candidates waiting for his signal.

Today's lecture is about humans and our speech and language. He is telling us that all civilizations have language as a means of communication. That it is hardwired in us to communicate through speech. Even kids who are isolated and never spoken to will learn speech. There are cases of deaf children who are raised together with no adults speaking to them who will still come up with some way to communicate with each other, they will make their own signs and find a way to communicate.

The most interesting thing he said about language was when he talked about slaves from different countries who spoke totally different languages and were forced to work together would form what is called *Pidgins* where they would sort of use each other's words and form some choppy version of both of their languages merged together. But that's not the fascinating part, the really amazing thing is that these people's children, in one single generation wouldn't just build on these Pidgins, they would make their very own language complete with syntax, slang and everything else. In one generation.

My final class of the day is a General Education class with Professor Takada, a nice, older Asian lady with long salty hair and kind eyes. She is also hearing impaired and uses her lip-reading skills at baseball games, reading the lips of the pitchers when they talk to their catchers. The league is on to her however, that's why they hold their gloves up to cover their mouths when they have their mound talks.

Today's lecture is about equity. A buzz word that I've heard a lot from these education professors that sounds like *equality* and I think that they think they can slip that past us all and hope that we buy it without questioning it. What I've gathered however, is that equality is a good thing. You want to give all people an equal opportunity at life, a level playing field where everyone has an equal shot at being whatever they want to be. *Equity* however, from what I can gather, is not equality of opportunity but equality of outcomes. Let that sink in for a moment.

Someone tried to ask her what exactly she meant by equity once and she sort of brushed it off by saying, "Well, ya know, what's fair isn't always equal and what's equal isn't always fair." Which I'm not at all sure what that means but I'm pretty sure that statement is absolute horse crap. I can't help but think about the NBA. We all have an equal opportunity to be in the NBA but that doesn't mean I'll ever see the inside of a Knicks locker room. And really, I think it's probably a good idea that I let go of that dream as soon as I realize that that isn't a realistic goal for all 6 feet, 150 pounds of me, so I can go on to focus on other, more realistic things like being a legendary rock god.

Also, from what I can gather, it's not so much about adding stilts to *my* legs to give me a leg up, it's more about cutting off nine inches of other, taller people's legs and giving those to me. So many of my professors speak in this weird, sort of, double talk, this Orwellian Newspeak. Like

they are speaking in some kind of code that they are trying to get us to understand, almost subliminally. At some point around my sophomore year, I really started paying attention to the words that they were using and tried to dissect what the meaning *behind* the meaning was. I kept hearing teachers refer to Carl Marx's *Communist Manifesto,* so I decided to pick it up from the LU bookstore, where it was predominantly stocked, face out, at the front of the store and bought it.

I went home, got really high on cocaine and Quaaludes, and read it cover to cover over night. It turns out that all these teachers who have been teaching all these lectures on all this stuff; history, modern education, economics, everything. It seems like, maybe, have all been indoctrinated and worse, trying to indoctrinate all of us to this ideology in the name of some kind of warped version of fairness. Why is this like their little secret? They seem to be in this weird paradox where they preach the hell out of this book but are ashamed of it at the same time. I see where they get a lot of the language that they use. The pieces start to fall into place, the shepherd becomes the wolf.

So, in education, I think that equity means giving artificially high grades even to students who didn't work as hard as other students based on things that I thought weren't supposed to matter anymore, like race. That's fine I guess, but I feel like, at some point, doesn't it matter? Getting into college, in the real workforce? If you give someone good grades that they didn't earn, isn't that setting them up for failure at some point? I mean, surely you can't keep up this charade of giving everyone an A for doing C work when only 20% of the class actually earned an A. If there ever came a point where it really mattered, like say, in international business or anything else that lies outside of the little bubble they're in, it seems like that would be soul crushingly confusing to the person.

Imagine suddenly discovering that you really hadn't gotten the grades you thought you did, and now, you are incapable of doing the same work as the other students because when it was time to learn, you thought you were doing A work when really it was more like D+ material all along, and now that's all you are capable of doing. I would be outraged! By the way, isn't that wildly condescending? Isn't that like, what we do to people with mental disabilities? Isn't that what President Bush meant when he said, "The subtle racism of low expectations."? I mean, isn't that saying that some races of people are incapable of doing the same work as others?

Personally, I would be wildly offended if that was the way the society in which I lived perceived me. When I was 17, my front tooth got knocked out in a fight. I was living with Curt and Dicky at the time in Jackie and Melanie's duplex and trying to finish High School. I didn't have any insurance, I didn't have a pot to piss in or a window to throw it out of, and everyone told me that I qualified for Medicaid or Medicare or whatever it's called. I went along with it for about a day.

I went to the government office to apply with all the other poor people, filled out 15 pages of wildly intrusive paperwork, I stood in line to turn it in only to be told that I was in the wrong line. I stood in the other line only to be told that I was at the wrong office. I drove to the correct office, stood in line some more only to be told that they don't take these applications on Thursday. Short story long, I walked out and said to myself, "Forget all of this noise. I'll pick up some extra shifts at Steak 'n Shake and pay for this tooth myself."

I sort of try to bring this up in class, but these professors have all the answers, there's no arguing with them. All she said was something along the lines of, "Oh well, you know, at the end of the day, it's all about self-esteem anyway." Then told us that it was actually pretty racist to ask questions about it.

Um…I'm no Education professor, but I'll go ahead and call B.S. on that. I have a sneaking suspicion that self-esteem is not what makes Asian students kick our American asses in like, every subject. I doubt that self-esteem makes the top 10 on Asian's list of things to worry about in school. I think it's more like, 1 through 9: Work your ass off and kick ass at everything. But who am I? I'm just a dumb-ass college student. I never really thought about it too much. I guess I was too busy, too immersed in chaos to come up for a breath, but I know no one ever gave me anything, no one has ever given a hot crap about my feelings or my self-esteem. I was too busy turning into a wolf.

Chapter XXIV

After my classes, and after doing the New York Times Crossword puzzle on the swinging bench in the grassy common area outside of Norm Hall, watching all the hot chicks that don't want anything to do with me walk by, the happy couples holding hands and laughing, the neo-hippies tossing the frisbee, I walk down the cobblestone path that is engraved with all the names of the rich donors that could make this path possible. As I'm going over the numerous contradictions that my classes have left me with and the cognitive dissonance that is grappling with everything I thought I knew, I run into Chad, my old roommate who steals all the clothes from every store in the St. Louis metro area.

"Hey Bro!" He says, flexing his pecs up and down under his mauve colored, silk shirt in a way that makes me think twice about doing steroids. "I saw you play the other night. It was fuckin' awesome until all those crazy motherfuckers showed up! That was nuts Broseph."

"Yeah, well, it got a lot crazier." I say dully, touching at my face lightly.

"Well, hey Brah, can you still get that weed?" He asks, his tone takes a turn for the somber. "Broseph, everyone I know is jonesin'. No one knows where to get any dubage. Pills too, Ecstasy, uppers, downers, whatever. No one can get shit!"

"Yeah, I can definitely help you out." I say, sympathetically as the sound of cash registers ring in my head. "I'm just not sure how this should go down."

"Cool bro," He starts with a dusting of composure, then, changing his body language in a way that I am not at all familiar with, says, "I just got a ton of more clothes from like every store in Mid Rivers Mall, Chesterfield, The Galleria, I even went down to Union Station. Fuckin' robbed them blind bro."

There's a pause as I take a breath, take a look around the courtyard, squint at my crossword puzzle, and blink a few times before saying, "You have money too, right? This isn't like, straight up bartering. I mean, we, er…uh, I may want a shirt or two, but an ounce will be…" I say, doing the math out loud, "Like $135.00 bucks."

"Yeah, cool Brosiph." He says, nodding and smiling enthusiastically, his pecs twitching like a meth addict.

"Alright Man, let me make a call." I say, holding up a finger and dialing Curt's number on my cell phone.

"What up Schultz?" I can hear Curt say faintly into the wrong end of his cell phone.

"Dude!" I whisper sharply with my hand covering the phone, not wanting Chad to hear this exchange. "You're talking into the wrong end! Turn your G.D. phone around."

"Oh, yeah." He says more clearly. "These fucking cell phones are tricky."

"Yeah Dude. It's like a puzzle…" I say dryly. "only easier."

"Fuck off." He shouts, into the correct receiver this time.

"Anyway," I say covering my mouth for some sort of privacy, "I'm with Chad, that guy I told you about with the clothes."

"Yeah." He says.

"He wants a lot of weed, like at least a couple ounces and on a pretty regular basis." I say.

"I'm listening." He says after a pause that I'm not sure what to do with.

"I know you don't like to meet new people and everything but," I'm saying, reminding myself that he can't see my body language. There's another silent pause before I continue. "I mean, obviously it would be better for me if you two never met, he doesn't want to meet you or anything, but do you want to just meet him?"

"Schultz…" He says, unconvinced of anything.

"Dog, you gotta see all this shit, he's got more clothes than you have weed." I say.

"Schultz, this better not turn out to be some dumb shit." He warns.

"Whatever Dude." I say, doubting whether this is all worth it. "Do whatever the bleep you want…"

"It's at that shitty trailer you used to live in?" Curt asks, coming around now that I've turned the tables.

"Yeah, we're on our way there now..." I say, glancing over at Chad, then. "And yeah, it's still shitty."

"I'll come there and meet him 'cause I want to pick out the clothes." He says, then adds, "But I'm only giving the weed to you."

"OK." I say, going to hang up the phone.

"He never sees me give you the weed." Curt shouts, cutting me off from cutting him off.

"I know the drill, I'm hip." I say, then, "I'm hanging up now." Just to make sure we're clear on what's happening here. Trying to make some order out of the madness.

Twenty minutes later, I'm going through an absolute mountain of clothes in my old room of the crappy trailer I used to share with Chad. *This is not an exit!* is spray-painted in bloody red above the fold in window. I'm trying to do the math; if Curt gives me the ounce for $100.00 and I sell it to Chad for $135.00, that might get me one of these $75.00 polo shirts, depending on how much he wants for all of this stuff, Half off? 20% off? I don't know. I still have to pay off the Caddy that I no longer have so the last thing I should be spending money on is fancy new clothes. I'm sort of a jeans and a T-shirt kind of cat anyway. We all are but something about this feels like things are about to take a turn. In what direction? That's hard telling.

Curt pulls up in his red Chevy truck and walks in the trailer. He had been here plenty of times when I lived here my Freshman year and he can't help but laugh at what an S-hole it still is, sort of a scoff at how far we've come in less than couple of years. I introduce the two of them.

"What up Dog, this is Chad." I say, introducing them formally.

"Hey Bro." Chad says, his hand held out.

"What up Chad." Curt says shaking it, satisfied with the dominance his magnetism has afforded him. "Dude, how much do you pay for this place?" He asks, looking around, a shit-eating grin emerging.

"Nothin' Bra, it's free!" Chad says, extending his arms proudly.

"Yeah, well, you gotta ask yourself…" Pause. "Is it worth it?" Curt finishes with a straight face. "Let's see these clothes I've heard so much about."

"Sure Brosiph, this way." He says, leading us down the hall to the back bedroom where even Curt's short ass has to duck to avoid hitting his bald head.

Walking back into that bedroom is like walking through a time warp. The memories start flooding back; all the cry wanks, all the porno mags, all the lonely nights, the heartache. All the DNA spilt; the gym socks that could have been frozen to repopulate the planet in the event of a nuclear holocaust. The freezing winter nights, shivering myself to sleep, the sweat filled summer days I sat in this room trying to read the Romantics while Chad examined his physique in the mirror. The dry plywood peeling from the walls like ashes falling from death. The whole place screaming, *Kill me! Kill me!* Over and over again.

The bedroom we used to share is filled with clothes, like to the point that there is nowhere to sit down. Piles of clothes, three feet deep filling the piss stained twin bed, the homeless sofa rescued from the mean streets of St. Charles, and on the diarrhea colored shag carpet. All brand-new clothes, all with the tags, all men's, all regular dude sized. I would guess that he robbed some kind of truck, but if he did there would surely be women's stuff too, kids' stuff, weird out of fashion stuff, crap that's too big and too small. All this stuff looks hand-picked, intentional.

There are Polo shirts, Aloha shirts, band T-shirts, expensive button-down shirts, the latest swimming shorts, jeans, trousers, posh golf shorts, casual shorts, active wear, like nice ass track suits like Suge Knight wears, jackets, like sports jackets and leather jackets from every store around and some that I've never even heard of before and can't pronounce.

"Pretty fucking impressive Chad, I must say." Curt says hesitantly, waving a finger around aimlessly. "What are you charging for all this?"

"Well, I really gotta get rid of all this shit, ya know, Bro. I usually just say half off of the tag but if you can get the weed we need, I guess just like…" Pause. "I don't know, $10.00 for any shirt and, I don't know, $15.00 for any pants. But that's just for you two, you can buy as much as

you want, if you know people who want anything, then just charge them whatever you want, ya know, half the sticker price. How's that sound?"

Significant pause.

"Sounds good." Me and Curt finally get around to saying at more or less the same time.

"Uh, yeah, Schultz, go get my wallet out of my glove box." Curt says, indicating with his tone that the weed is in his glove box and to go get it, adding, "Both of them."

I come back into the room with two ounces of good weed. Curt has an armful of Polo T-shirts from Ralph Lauren, Nautica, and Tommy Hilfiger, a pair of boot-cut jeans from American Outfit and a pair of brown and baby blue swimming shorts from Abercrombie and Fitch.

"That's one for me," He says to me under his breath, then, "You just give me a bill for the other one."

"Well, here's this," I say to Chad handing over one of the ounces, "That's for those clothes. That's $135.00 bucks. And I'll take these two V-neck T-shirts from H & M and these Gap jeans for this." I say handing over the other ounce. "So, if you give me a hundred bucks, we'll be square."

There's a pause that lingers like smoke in a draft-less underground lair where nefarious deeds have taken place. This is one of those moments where you're in a bizarre kind of limbo. I'm working off of his math and hoping that there aren't any loopholes. This is where anything could happen, the border between chaos and order. This is where misunderstandings happen, and people get hurt but there is potential for greatness. Obviously, this seems too good to be true, and when something seems too good to be true, it usually is. Is he going to bust out the catch now? What's next?

"Cool Broseph." He finally says. "Here ya go." He whips out a wad of money and flips me out a bill. "And like I said, we can do this about once a week."

"Cool man, I'll be in touch." I say, taking note of what I'll get next time, eye-balling a brown leather jacket from Zara. I'm wondering how far this whole thing could go, there is so much supplying and demanding going on here.

Chapter XXV

Curt's phone ringing wakes me from an opiate induced nod in the wee hours of the night. I'm sliding around restlessly on my King-sized bed's silk sheets from Lord and Taylor when I hear Dicky's phone. When he doesn't answer, my phone rings. I don't recognize the number, so I assume it's Fooky because, for reasons we'll never get a straight answer to, he always seems to a have new phone number. I reluctantly pick it up, and Fooky is somber but a sense of urgency seeps through in his tone. "Schultz, wake everyone up Dude. Wake up Dicky and Curt."

I bang on Curt and Dicky's bedroom doors, tying the belt to my maroon paisley, silk robe, also from Lord & Taylor and say, "It's Fook!" They slowly come out scratching their balls through their Abercrombie & Fitch boxer/briefs and yawning. They both heard their phone ring and now this. We all know this phone call. We've all played this game before.

"What's up Fook?" I ask once we're all standing in the dark Living Room. Dicky starts putting ice in glasses and pouring us each a scotch from the bar.

"Dude," He says solemnly, "I just got off the phone with Keef, Martin's dad. Martin died earlier tonight. Dude, Martin is dead."

"Who is it, Schultz?" Curt is asking, kicking off his Royal Blue Gucci house slippers.

"It's Fooky." I say sitting down on one of the black Chateau bar stools.

"No Schultz, I mean *who is it?*" He says again with his Zippo lighter illuminating his face.

"Oh, right. It... it's Martin." I say holding my cellphone down. "Martin died."

"Shit." Dicky says sitting down heavily on the black, Armani leather couch. He looks around for a beat, then takes the last drink of scotch from his glass and crunches into an ice cube.

"What happened?" Curt demands, setting his silver Zippo down hard on the glass coffee table.

"What happened?" I ask Fook, my eyes shifting between Curt and the lighter.

"Dude." he starts, "He was with some girls that he met and would get dope for. They were just getting high, you know…" Fooky says, trailing off.

"No Fooky, I don't know!" I shout louder than I intended. "What were they doing?"

"Come on Schultz…" He starts, pauses for a beat, then says, "You know, Man."

There's a pause that everyone in the room has their own personal reaction to. For some, it's a casual pause that doesn't raise one red flag as to the severity of the topic at hand. For others, it's an eternal mind-warp that challenges everything you've ever known and causes you to question everything that you've ever learned or read. The noose is tightening.

"Yeah." I say, going through this all as logically as humanly possible. "I guess I do."

"The funeral is the day after tomorrow...blah, blah, blah..." Fooky starts overloading me with details that I'm in no condition to deal with, let alone remember. "...Blah, blah, blah... The family just wants to get it over with, just a small thing. Only close friends and family." He finally finishes.

"Alright Man." I say into the phone blankly, cutting him off.

"Alright, I'll come by in the morning." Fooky says and then hangs up the phone.

"Cool, Man." I say to a dead phone line, then. "Thanks for calling." Before killing my end.

Chapter XXVI

I'm in the bathroom shaving, with a melancholy stream of consciousness flowing down like a cascade. I'm wondering whether we actually have thoughts or if our thoughts have us. How predictable are we really? While it's shocking and heartbreaking that Martin is dead, is it really a surprise? As I'm moving the razor blade up and down my face in random strokes, I wonder if I'm not actually following the exact same shaving pattern I always follow. When I'm almost finished, I hit a zit on my right cheek. I let it bleed. It won't stop dripping its dark red splotches that contrast the pearl white marble sink. I smear the puddle with my finger and taste the irony blood. It tastes different after it's been exposed to oxygen, sourer, less bitter.

Was this in the script? Did my consciously thinking about this change the trajectory of these events? Did the very thought of my shaving somehow make it a reality then change the pattern? Was it real at all before, like a tree falling in the forest with no one around to hear it, did it even make a sound?

Fooky stayed on the couch last night so we could all go to the funeral together. I put a 5,000-thread count Louie Vuitton bedsheet down so his fat ass wouldn't stain the plush fine German leather. Fooky's wearing a black wool suit from Bill Blass, an ivory dress shirt from Tommy Hilfiger, cuff links from Colours of Bennington and black leather shoes from Calvin Klien. Curt is looking at himself in the wall mirror, he's wearing dark jeans from Old Navy, a black Harley Davidson T-shirt from The Buckle, a black J. Ferrar sports jacket and a pair of black Dr. Martins.

Dicky, who's been sitting at the bar drinking Bloody Marys since 5 a.m. is wearing a Navy-Blue suit from Haspel, a grey stripped tie from Paul Smith and brown suede Grenson lace up shoes. I walk out of my room and pour a drink from the bar. I'm wearing a black Kenneth Cole three-piece suit, white button-down shirt from Canali with a Paul Stuart pocket square and black leather Chelsea Boots from Versace Italia.

This would be as an appropriate time as ever for us to all pile in the Caddy and arrive at the funeral home in style, but for now, Fooky's Lincoln will have to suffice. We all fill our platinum plated flasks with Dal More 50-year-old Scotch and have to figure out the proper inside suit pocket to hold them in. Curt and Fooky have dugouts full of Samurai Skunk weed that is almost too sticky for a one-hitter. I'm running low on Vicodin, so I tell everyone that I don't have any more. We look each other over, acknowledge that we have all scrubbed up fairly well then head to the funeral.

Ballie's Funeral Home off of Mid Rivers Mall Dr. and Mexico Rd. has a line of cars backed up almost to Cottleville. There are a lot more people here than just close friends and family. M. B. and Ryan Barnes are there wearing modestly decent, as dark as they could find, colored clothes. M. B. is wearing kaki Dockers with black loafers, maybe from JC Pennies, and a white Versace T-shirt which he pronounces Ver*sach*, clearly a knock off but an honorable attempt with a navy sailing jacket that has gold buttons with anchors on them.

Ryan Barnes is wear wearing a beige double-breasted suit from Sears with an auburn dress shirt, off the rack, with a purple and mauve pasley clip-on tie. Chris Alexander is here and is clearly high wearing a white T-shirt that reads *SHIT HAPPENS* from where, Spencer's? This seems more than a little bit tacky, even by Curt and my own standards. Tacky may not be the right word, it's more *distasteful* than anything but the fact that he is clearly high on heroin at a funeral for a friend who just died from a heroin overdose doesn't really excuse anything.

If he were not on heroin and wore the shirt to take the piss out of the situation, or if he *is* high and the idea that wearing a T-shirt that says, *Shit Happens* to a funeral for someone who overdosed on heroin, never even crossed his mind. I don't know which would be worse.

I ask him, "Hey, have you seen Stamm?" and after he mumbles something incoherently, he manages to say that he's doing eight years in Pacific prison for possession and auto theft.

We're standing around, drinking Heinekens out of Champagne flutes and taking hits of Columbian Gold from a platinum dugout, telling Martin stories.

"Man," I start, loosening my black Gucci tie. "this must have been one of the first times we went floating in Lesterville, it was the time Fooky got his ear bit off, back in the day. This was

like the first night we were there though, everyone was passed out and it was just me and Martin, sitting around the fire, brewin' our asses off. It must've been like two or three in the morning. We reached around in one cooler, no brews, reached around in another cooler, no brewskis.

We searched every one of all of your fricking coolers and there wasn't one G.D. beer left. So, Martin tells me to grab two T-shirts and to pull my hair back in a ponytail, remember we both had long ass hair back then. We were hippie looking M.F.ers, and I'm thinking, ya' know I was like 15-years-old then, you guys, Martin included, were effin' legends to me back then."

"Who, these drunks?" Dicky laughs, pointing around with a drink in each hand.

"Yeah, *you* drunks." I say, nodding at him. "I obviously hadn't spent that much time with you all yet."

"Ouch." Daffy laughs, gripping his kidney.

"Anyway." I say, trying to get this story back on track. "I was thinking to myself, 'What the hell kind of gay ass mission is this dude trying to take me on?'

But I do what he says, I grab a T-shirt for each of us and we both pulled our hair back looking like bitches and we went out on an epic mission. A mission for brew." I pause for a laugh. "I don't know how far or long we drudged through the muck and the mire of all those Lesterville camp sites, sneaking from camp site to camp site, we almost got our heads blown off at least twice until, I think the sun was coming up, we literally stumbled across a cooler full of beers."

"No way! What'd you do then?" Josh White asks, looking for a point to shit on.

"Well we had tripped over the damned thing in the middle of this campsite where everyone was still sleeping, at least 20 minutes away from our site. We had to put all the brews and as much ice as we could pick up back in the cooler and, as quietly as we could, tiptoe the hell out of there. We carried that cooler all the way back to our campsite and got drunker than two drunk things."

"Just the two of you?" Josh asks, trying his hardest to shit on my point.

"No, actually when we got back to the site, Gus and Piper were there, they had gotten the fire going again and they were butt ass naked, drinking screwdrivers. Me and Martin plopped down the stolen cooler, dropped trau and joined them. Dicks swinging in the wind."

"That's fucking hilarious dude." Daffy laughs, wiping a tear from his cheek. Daffy and Martin have been tight since like 2nd grade and were rarely, if ever apart. He looks like he's holding up pretty well, but someone should definitely keep an eye on him. If he had any money at all, he probably would've OD'd last night.

"Yeah, you were passed out in the back of Too Brewed's truck the whole time, ya drunk." I say. "I'm sure you woke up with a dick painted on your face."

"Yeah, remember the time we were at James and Kristen Drury's wedding?" Daffy starts. "There was an open bar, but they wouldn't serve shots. Martin was at the bar and asked for five shots of Tequila and the dude said, "Uh, sorry sir, we can't pour shots."

So, Martin says, 'Alright, well give me five margaritas, no mix, no ice, no salt.' So, the dude had to give him the shots only in big ass Margarita glasses. Next thing you know, Martin is swinging from the chandelier, upside-down, drinking a bottle of Rebel Yell and screaming, *"Right now!!"*

"Dude," Dicky says, "There was one time on Christmas Eve, it must have been three or four years ago, we were getting moin at that crib I had with Dave Schwartz, the one with the Christmas Tree with nothing but Budweiser cans as ornaments."

"Yeah Dude, that was a great fucking tree!" Daffy says.

"It was late as fuck and we were just blasting away and at some point, I was like, "Dude, I gotta go to bed, my mom's picking me up at like 8 o'clock in the fucking morning to go to church."

We both stood up and Martin looked ripped as fuck, so I took this disposable camera I had and said, "Say *Merry Christmas,* Motherfucker." and snapped a picture of him.

He gave me that "Fuck you" grin and flipped me off. It's my favorite picture of him, I got it right here." He says, taking it out and showing everyone.

"That's fucking classic." Valerie says coolly. She's smoking a cigarette while hugging Blair who has been quietly sobbing for most of the morning.

"That *was* a great Christmas tree." Barnes says.

"So, I take the picture and then I'm like, 'Alright, I'm out.' and as soon as I walked in my fuckin' bedroom my goddam alarm started going off. Martin was like, "Good luck at church pone, don't get struck by lightning!"

"Ah, that's great." Blair says, allowing herself to laugh for the first time today.

"I said, 'Fuck you, Pussy, you're coming with me.'" Dicky says.

"No shit," I say. "I remember that!"

"So, he went with you?" Josh asks.

"Fuck yeah he went." Dicky says, finishing his beer and opening another one. "We took another couple blasts and my mom was out front honking the fuckin' horn. We put on giant sunglasses and left. It was the worst fucking Christmas ever!"

"Yeah Dude," Ryan Barnes starts, "One time we were down in Springfield for New Year's Eve when you all were living there." He's pointing at Blair, Sarai, and Josh. "Just after midnight, Martin told me to come with him, I don't know where the fuck to, but we took Blair's car. I didn't know you two were fighting, I just got in the car and we took off. We were fucking *hammered* driving around Springfield looking for, I don't know what the fuck we were looking for, probably coke, but we drove around for hours, lost as fuck."

"Oh yeah, you guys stole my car!" Blair says.

"We finally decided just to go back to the house but then we couldn't find that either. When we finally made it back at like 5 a.m., Blair tells us that she called the cops on us and reported her car stolen as soon as we left. We had been driving around for five fucking hours, drunk off our asses in a car that had been reported stolen in small ass Springfield, MO on New Year's Eve of all nights."

"No kidding?" I ask, laughing along with everyone else.

"No shit. Our tax dollars hard at work. The fucking cops couldn't find you with a description." Barnes says.

"Martin was such a Boug Boy." Fooky says. "He was always down for anything, always full throttle, always Martin being fuckin' Martin.

"That reminds me of an old story." I start to say. "There's a scorpion walking through the desert when he comes across a river, now the scorpion can't swim so when a frog hops by the scorpion says, 'Hey, can you give me a lift across the river?'"

"Was Martin there?" Josh asks.

"No. What? No." I'm saying, annoyed. "The frog says, "No way, you're a freakin' scorpion, you'll sting and kill me."

"So, are you the frog?" Josh asks, a point to crap on has finally been exposed. "What does this have to do with anything?"

"The scorpion says," I continue, ignoring him. "No, I won't. If I sting and kill you, you'll sink, then I'll drown and die too."

"Fair enough." Says the frog, "Hop on."

So, the scorpion crawls onto the frog's back and they start to swim across the river. Everything is going fine when, about halfway across, the scorpion whips his tail around and stings the frog. With the frog's dying breath, just before sinking under water, he asks the scorpion, "But...why?"

The scorpion replies, "Hey man, it's just who I am."

"I don't get it." M.B. says, confused. "Who's the scorpion in this story?"

"Dude, it just means that you can't change who you are." I say.

"That's deep." Daffy says.

"That's fucking dumb." Josh says.

The sermon starts and we all sit down in the viewing area where Martin's body is laying, stiff and dead in his pearl white casket. It is quite a thing, sitting there looking at the dead body of one of your best friends. We've been to dozens of these funerals and it always makes you think about mortality. I usually zone out in one of my little trances and go through the whole spectrum of emotions, from sad to happy to melancholy and everything in between. I don't necessarily feel all the emotions, I just sort of think about them. Is it sad to have this young guy laying here dead?

Yeah, sure. But if you're a religious person then you believe that he's in paradise right now, whatever *paradise* means, so you should be happy, right? Unless he's in hell, but does anyone really believe in hell anymore? I mean, really? It seems a little far-fetched that there is a place where bad folks go when they die with the Devil running around being a cunt to everyone.

It's sad that we'll never get to hang out again and I'll miss him just like I'm sure his mom will miss him, but that's kind of selfish if you think about it. Is there an afterlife, is he somewhere watching us? Is he going to Obi-wan Kenobi me sometime to tell me the meaning of life? Is he just worm food and there is nothing else to it, we're just rotting away six feet underground? Do we just get one shot at life? We all have to die, no one here gets out alive, so what the hell? What's the difference if you die at 25 or 95? I mean Martin liked getting high, *real* high, that's what he liked to do. Is it tragic to die doing something you love? If he liked skydiving, would it be tragic to die in a skydiving accident? No, not really. At least I don't think so.

I mean, I guess if you have young kids and a wife and you get hit by a car, I guess that's tragic for them. His family, his kids don't have a dad, they have to to grow up little bastards. They have a mortgage, car payments, tuition and all that, he doesn't get to see his kids grow up, never get to be cool, get married, have kids of their own or whatever. But really, it's your life, and if the thought is that you only get one, you might as well do what you want with it.

I suppose the thinking could go; Sure, Martin liked getting effed up more than anything else, but he's only 25. I guess you could argue that in a few years people's priorities change and life stops being about just getting effed up all the time and to die so young denies a person of their

real life, life past getting high non-stop. Grown up life…real, meaningful life. So, in that case, I guess it is kind of sad.

After the service, we all stand and queue up to walk past the casket. Dicky brought that picture so he could put it under his Ted Baker, London suit jacket, on his heart when he walks by. Other people brought something to leave in the casket too. Blair, who has been crying the whole time puts a Lilac in there, Fooky puts a half drunken pint of Jim Beam, Ryan Barnes puts a fat joint, Curt puts in St. Louis Rams hat, Mort puts a glass crack shooter and I saw Chris Alexander feel around and take something out.

I'm not the only one who saw that and after the viewing, Keef, Martin's dad confronts Alexander outside under the pavilion. Alexander is so stoned that he can barely keep his eyes open and after a bit of mumbling, Keef backhands him and knocks him to the ground. That kind of breaks things up and we all head back to our house for a peaceful get-together and pour out some obscenely overpriced liquor.

"Don't spill anything on the rug." I say to everyone. "That's Polar Bear."

"Not *right now!*" Daffy starts screaming, starting a *right now* chain reaction.

Chapter XXVII

Monday afternoon Curt gets home from work early, interrupting my day wank. He walks in the door more on edge than usual. He often comes home shouting about one thing or another but today he seems frantic, paranoid. He goes in his room and I hear him rummaging through things noisily, causing a ruckus then he comes out and says, “Schultz, come with me. We gotta take care of something.”

“OK, where are we going?” I ask.

“Uhh,” He starts, almost nervously, “I can’t tell you. And also, Dude...” Pause. “You uh, you can’t ever tell anyone where we’re going or what we’re about to do... like ever.”

“Alright Dog, do you have to be such a drama queen?” I ask, standing up from off the couch and trying to cover my boner.

“Schultz, you’re gonna have to trust me on this.” He says cryptically, taking a Jägermeister shot from the bar and flipping the handle on the Foosball table.

“Let’s go.” I say, putting on my new L. L. Bean brown suede Beatle Boots I have sitting next to the door. I take them off in the house now, both to protect the rugs and the tile, but also to protect the boots. The suede needs to breath.

He goes into his room again and comes out three minutes later wearing Black Docker’s with a button-down denim shirt from Polo Ralph Lauren. This makes me even more curious, what the hell kind of mission am I being dragged into this time? He’s huffing through his nose as he paces the living room, interrupting Oprah. Today’s guest is New York’s mayor, Ruddy Giuliani. He’s talking about how he thinks that Middle Eastern Islamists are plotting a terrorist attack in America. I flip to CNN and it’s saying that Giuliani is a racist and in fact, a terrorist himself for saying that all Muslims are terrorists. I flip back to Oprah to see if that is really what he said. It seems it was not. I try to point this out to Curt, but he isn't listening, just pacing ever rapidly, still breathing heavily, almost panting and zipping up a brown leather, Nautica duffle bag.

We’re driving down Highway 70 in Curt’s red Chevy F350 out to the sticks. I have no idea where we’re going and the windshield wipers brushing away the autumn rain are hypnotizingly monotonous. This is a stark reminder that 40 minutes in any direction from downtown St. Louis will get you nothing but corn rows and a vast expanse of wheat fields as far as the eye can see. The dying trees cast a dull combination of rotten banana yellows, bloody urine oranges, and baby diarrhea browns all being smeared together by the damp, cold rain that’s just speeding up the dying process and helping to pack everything back down into the earth where it can decay in some sort of conclusive peace.

Curt is still tense, wound tighter than a hand grenade. There’s a dark aura surrounding him, he’s smoking joint after joint, faster than I can roll them. After about the seventh one I have to stop. My head starts to hurt from all the weed smoke, I can feel my nose and face beginning to ache again, so I take two Percocets. Curt is sweating, eyes bloodshot, becoming a wolf. He flashes me a sinister side-eye that I’m not at all comfortable with. For some people, weed can turn into an upper like cocaine if you smoke too much of it. I’m a little out of it and Curt is still clearly amped up about something that is still unknown to me.

“You gotta get off those pills, Dude.” He says, staring at the road, white knuckling the wheel.

“What?” I ask, grappling with a migraine. “What-whatever Dog, you’re trippin’” I’m in no mood for one of his outbursts.

"Don't you know that shit is the same as heroin?" He demands.

Pause.

"I have like, a prescription for them, Man." I finally respond. I'm rubbing my temples hard, watching dead leaves fly past the windshield, some smack it and are quickly dismissed by the wipers.

"It doesn't matter." He continues ranting anyway. "What are you going to do when the prescription runs out Motherfucker. That's how everyone starts!" Now he's shouting at me. "Everyone starts that way, you know that. Next thing you know your doctor stops giving you the script and it's easier to get dope. Dude, we've seen this a hundred times. Don't be so fucking stupid!"

"I'm in serious pain here, man, my fricking…" I start but am cut off.

"Yeah, I know, you have a broken nose and a hole in your tongue, blah blah blah." He says, "I'm not going to your fucking funeral Schultz, I'll kill you myself before I let you get into that shit!" Then, changing to a more passive tone, "Just be fucking cool with those."

"Alright Dog." I say lazily, "You're still trippin' though, you know that right? I don't mean about the pills, I mean, you do know that you're trippin', right? And what the cock-n-balls is all this?" I'm gesturing at the wheat bundles along the road. "Are you gonna tell me what the flip this is all about?"

"Yeah, I know." He admits, calming down in admission. "I know what I'm doing…I think. I think something's going on and, and I-I gotta find out what the fuck is going on anyway." Is all he says, no clarification. The Boone Hills exit approaches, we pass it. We do not exit.

The Percocets I took at the beginning of this excursion are wearing off which tells me that we've been driving for far too long when my nod is interrupted by Curt finally exiting off of some road I've never heard of. Say what you will about Curt, but he isn't the kind of cat who usually gets himself or anyone else into situations that he can't get out of. There are obvious exceptions like the time he got us both arrested coming home from the East side strip bars when I was fifteen. This is starting to feel like one of those situations.

We pull up to an old cottage at the end of a long and winding, gravel driveway and get out of the truck. Curt is still edgy and he's not answering my questions. This situation is feeling more and more intense the more Curt is on edge. Very un Dog. Who in the Papa Smurf are these people, where the bald ass are we?

Curt knocks the large red door and a buff Asian dude in a tight, black and white T-shirt that he looks like he's about to *Hulk* out of, with a rooster and some Chinese characters on it and a Blackhawk Level 3 shoulder holster with a 38 Snub-nosed Special opens the door and says something in what I can only assume is Japanese.

"*Nani ga?*" Jackie Chan asks stoically.

"What up?" Curt greets him with a slight bow. "I'm here to see Iain." Curt says, seemingly understanding what the Japanese dude said. My mind is on the verge of imploding.

"*Koitsu wa dare?*" He asks, nodding at me, but not in a cool way. Not quite threatening yet not at all welcoming. I'd have to go with…disparaging.

"This is Schultz, he's uh, he's my accountant. I need him here. He's cool." Curt answers in short, staccato statements, not trying to be funny at all. Like not something my father would say to a hot waitress at T.G.I.Friday's after tasking me with calculating the tip before he took off on us when I was seven. But like he really wanted to convince Jackie Chan here that a skinny, 20-

year-old, wearing black Calvin Klien jeans, a blue themed Aloha shirt from The Gap, and $90 brown, leather flip-flops from The Buckle is his flippin' representation...like legally.

"What in the ever-loving mother of all Effs is going on up in this bi-otch?" I'm screaming to myself. After looking me up and down with utter distain, Jackie nods his head towards the inside, his body langue indicating to come in but that he isn't at all happy about what is transpiring before him. Like, culturally this offends him on some deep Asian level.

We walk through the house and it's one of those houses that looks like a medium sized cottage on the outside, surrounded by forest and gravel roads but on the inside it's all modern and outrageous. Big screen Toshiba TV, white leather couches from Penny's, shiny linoleum floors, mahogany marble kitchen, a Kimono dragon in a giant aquarium casually catches dragonflies with its reptilian tongue and eats them. An original series of paintings by Steven Walters depicting James Joyce's classic, *Ulysses.*

Two big Pitbulls come running down the hall, skidding around a corner to where we're walking and just before biting my schmeckle off, Jackie Chan says, "*Oi!*" and snaps his finger at them. They freeze. Then he snarls, "*Suware!*" and they sit down obediently.

My mind is racing, the amount of cognitive dissonance I'm standing here in this frigid house being forced to endure is staggering. I'm whispering to myself, "OK, first I learned that Curt apparently has some kind of grasp of the Japanese language. That was a pretty hard pill to swallow, but now I'm being asked to accept that these dogs speak Japanese too. Dogs don't speak Japanese, do they? Maybe an Akita or a Shih Tzu or something exotic like that, but not Pitbulls. I assumed they spoke Spanish but now I can't trust anything I thought I knew. White is black, up is down, yin is yang. I don't know what to believe!"

Jackie Chan leads us into a secret room in the back of the house that is absolutely freezing. Along the far wall, there are three 6 x 4 foot tall safes, a marble island in the middle of the room with a green study lamp, a triple beam scale, an ounce of cocaine and, standing there next to a wooden kitchen chair, weighing out grams is a tall, ginger dude, buff as Lou Ferrigno, wearing Edwin jeans and a wife beater from Uniqlo with a white apron, plastic medical gloves and a gold Rosary around his neck. Peeking out of his wife beater is a tattoo of the Virgin Mary that appears to take up his whole chest and stomach, a Shamrock on his right shoulder blade and a Celtic cross on his left. He has a reddish mohawk and beard, sort of like an Irish Mr. T. This must be Iain the Irish drug lord that we've all heard so little about.

He looks up at Curt, glances over at me, then looks at Jackie Chan and asks him in a thick Irish accent, "The fook is this cunt?"

"This is..." Curt starts.

"Was I fookin' speaking to you?" He interrupts.

"He name..." Jackie Chan struggles to produce the English. "Schultz. He say he...*nan to u-iuno"* He says under his breath, wheels spinning, then finally "accountant."

"You're this man's accountant are ya'?" Iain asks me, squinting his eyes and leaning forward, trying to read my body language.

"Uh, well..." I mumble, shifting eye contact.

"You a Jew?" He asks me, connecting with my eyes which causes an unspeakable dread.

Painfully long and awkward pause.

I stammer, clinching my fists, "I-I-I'm not sure what that has to do with anything…" I manage, then Iain interrupts…

"Aye, I'll take that as a *Yes*." Then he says, crossing his arms, accenting his well-defined biceps and nodding. "Good. If you don't have a Jew as an accountant, you're a fookin' dumb bastard."

"Alright Iain," Curt interrupts before things take a turn for the really racist. "can we just get down to business, we gotta long ride home."

Curt sets the leather duffle bag down on a wooden stool standing next to him. Iain the Irishman opens up one of the safes by spinning one of those wheel locks like they have at banks. Inside there are pounds of weed tightly wrapped in sailplane and stacks of cocaine and heroin packaged up by the kilo, along with countless unnamed pharmaceuticals. Curt and Iain the Irishman get down to business.

"I'm thinking of branching out my game." Curt says, unzipping his brown, leather Nautica bag. It's packed full of 20-dollar bills bundled into what looks like sets of $1,000.00.

"W-T-F" I'm screaming to myself, trying to remain clam.

"What'd you have in mind then?" Iain asks, standing up straight. Chest out, he cracks his neck by tilting it to one side, then the other.

"Well, it's no secret that H is blowing up around this city." Curt explains without aggression or agenda.

"Aye," He says, nodding, opening another safe. "That it is, mate. That it is." He hands Curt a small mirror with a pile of China White heroin, then walks back over to the safe.

Curt asks directly, "How pure is this shit?" Tasting it with his pinky finger like they do on T.V.

"Pure as the driven snow, Mate." He says, turning around with a kilo of coke in one hand and a silver Glock 9mm in the other.

"You sure that shit ain't cut with nothing Micky?" Curt asks with his head down, grinning almost shyly.

Pause. Those words almost freeze in the air and a shiver runs through my spine.

"The fook you callin' Micky, ya' wee cunt 'cha?" Iain demands, cocking the Glock 9 milli and pointing it straight at Curt's head.

"Look Dude, I don't want any trouble." Curt says, hands up in surrender.

Curt, hands still raised in defeat, then lets a giggle escape and, in a split second, whips out a Glock of his own from the back of his black Dockers, cocks it like he was flipping Ice Cube or something and points it right at Iain. Jackie Chan pulls a 38 snub-nosed special out of his holster and points it at Curt. Curt calls his bluff and fires a shot, knee-capping Jackie Chan. Then he points the gun back at Iain. Jackie Chan hits the floor, blood pumping from his leg like a sewage line, swearing profusely in Japanese.

There is a pause. Tables are turned. Panic erupts.

"Schultz, pick up the Gook's gun." Curt says to me with Zen-like tranquility.

There is a standoff. Words are exchanged. I'm frozen. The panic I'm experiencing is indescribable. Curt fires a shot into the heroin safe and white powder explodes in the air before slowly falling all around like a snow globe that contrasts with the dark red blood that's flooding the arctic room.

“You’re making a massive mistake Mate.” Iain says. “That’s $20,000 worth of smack you just wasted.”

Curt walks over to him with the barrel of his gun held right up to his forehead. Both of them have their guns pointed at each other’s faces.

Jackie Chan is screeching, *“Itai!”*

“Shut the fook up.” Iain demands, visibly flustered.

“You know my boy Martin?” Curt demands, not flinching a bit.

“Who?” Iain asks, genuinely confused by the question but still maintaining his composure.

Curt’s not buying it. He flips his gun around like Doc freakin’ Holiday, so the butt is faced up and upper-cuts Iain in the nose, breaking it instantly. Blood starts squirting out of his face like a fountain. *My* nose hurts after seeing that, hearing the cartilage crack. It complements his ginger hair and fair complexion. The shepherd has become the wolf.

Curt grabs the wooden chair, sweeps Iain’s legs and pins Iain down on the floor. Curt casually sits down, backwards on the wooden chair, kicks his gun away and is twirling his Glock around with his finger. Iain is squirming, Jackie Chan attempts to crawl away. I motion him back nervously, waving his own gun at him.

“I’m going to ask you one more motherfucking time.” He says calmly, pointing the gun at his forehead. “Who are the girls that Martin was with?”

“What?” He asks, starting to weep. This beautiful world he has created out here in the middle of nowhere is crumbling before him.

“You know Martin, right?” Curt barks, his gun cocked and aimed right at Iain’s forehead. “Who the fuck were the two girls he was with?”

“I swear, Mate, I have no idea.” Iain pleads.

“Nothing happens in this city without you knowing about it right?” He asks.

“Ah Mate, that’s just something I say to me clients.” He sobs.

“Well you better start answering my questions, *Mate,* or you’re never going to say anything to another living person ever again.” Curt says coldly.

“Uh… alright, alright! There was this cop a wee bit ago.” He starts, waving his hands in surrender from beneath the wooden stool. “He busted me once about two years back, but then he kept fucking with me.”

“What the fuck does that mean?” Curt demands.

“He was dirty!” He says, exacerbated. “The guy was dirty as fook. He never told me what he was up to, but he’d come around and shake me down once a month and ‘confiscate’ like a pound of coke. He was massively into PCP, a real spaz!”

“In exchange for what?” Curt asks slowly, eye squinted in curiosity.

“I guess he’d bust people that were getting in me way, you know what I mean? He never said anything about it out loud or anything, Mate! For real, but he got rid of a lot of my competition.”

“Like me?” Curt asks, the gun stops waving momentarily.

Pause. Iain pisses his trousers.

“Your name may have come up once or twice.” He admits.

“Keep going.” Curt says, waving the gun around some more.

“So yeah, last week he came over and he did have two girls with him.” Iain is saying.

“What did they look like?” Curt asks, now so engaged in the conversation that he forgets that the Glock is pointed directly at Iain’s head.

“I dunno Mate, they stayed in his shite old Camero.” He says. “But it was definitely two birds, one was hot, a ginger and the other one had dark hair. He just came in the house by himself though. The cunt was edgy as fook. He looked as if he hadn’t slept in a fortnight, all fucked up on PCP but he was going on about how he was sick of all the junkies around his city.”

“What did he mean by that?” Curt asks, redundantly, as far as I was concerned.

“I don’t know, Mate.” Iain says, almost as confused as I am.

“He just said that he was sick of all the junkies, and that he’d come back and kill me if I didn’t give him the smack.”

“Why?” Curt asks with a, *“Don’t worry, we’ll get through this together.”* look.

“I don’t know, Mate.” Iain is weeping, “I just don’t bloody know.”

“Well...” Curt says standing up from the chair and signaling me to go first out of this nightmare. “get your boy looked at.”

Driving home, somewhere just past the Wentzville exit, I ask, “So… remember when I asked you to *not* murder anyone with me around?”

There is a very intentional pause, then, “I’ll take that as a *No.*”

Chapter XXVIII

"Goddamn Dude, you fucking suck. Seriously, Dude, I like literally don't think it's possible for you to suck any more than you suck right now." Dicky rants after I tee off at White Birch, hooking The Masked Marauder into the creek. It's notably cooler today than it has been so I'm wearing a white sports jacket and matching jeans from Dolce & Gabbana, a grey Louis Vuitton button down shirt and black Paul Evans Beatle Boots with a silver, skull pinky ring from Bottega Veneta.

I tell him, "Oh, go and drop a digit on your mother." And explain to him that, A: Saying, *like literally* is a contradiction. *Like* and *Literally* negate each other, but more to your point, B: I'm trying to learn how to get better.

"Why the fuck does that make it alright, Schultz?" Dicky asks. "We have to stand around waiting for you every goddamn time we come here." He's wearing a white V-neck t-shirt from Michael Kors, blue jeans, a casual grey jacket, both from Tom Ford and a gold, David Yurman necklace.

"Because I haven't been doing this very long and…" I start to say.

"I didn't suck that bad when I first started." He says, cutting me off.

"Thanks Dicky." I say dryly, giving him a quick middle finger. "What I was about to say is, I haven't been doing this that long *and* I'm clearly not naturally talented at it either. That doesn't mean I can't improve. The point is, I'm doing what I can to get better."

"That sounds like a lame excuse, Dude." Dicky says, aiming his white, Lone Ranger disc.

"Look man, here's the thing," I start, unbuttoning my neckline down a notch. "It's alright to suck at something when you are new to it and you're trying to get better. Things take a weird turn when you don't ask for help or try to improve. The great philosopher, Bo Ideal once said, 'If you find yourself up against a new situation..."

"Who the fuck is Bo Ideal?" Curt chimes in.

"Stay with me." I assure them. *'A man of ideals will seek out the necessary skills he needs to be successful.'* Meaning, you ask for help, find a mentor, find someone who has the goods and learn from them. Someone that you admire, you admire their ability."

"Alright, well so fuckin' what?" Dicky asks, watching his disc soar across the grey, autumn sky, well into putting range.

"Can we just fucking go?" Curt shouts. He's wearing beige cargo shorts from Abercrombie & Fitch, a navy Polo shirt, brown flip-flops, and a hemp necklace that Valerie gave him for his, I don't know, 28th birthday last year.

"I'm out of my comfort zone, ya know, I know I suck, you dingleberry." I add. We're walking. "This is pushing my limits."

"Alright." He concedes, finishing the whiskey in his flask with a shiver.

"Well think about it man, what's that tattoo on your arm?" I ask him.

"It's a Yen Yang, it's fucking spiritual Dude." He says holding out his arm.

"Well what do you think it means?" I ask.

He says. "It's a fucking Asian thing Dude, it means like, the cycle of life, Man."

"Well, it's a little bit more than that. It's actually more like the struggle of life, *Man*," I'm saying. "It's the eternal struggle between chaos and order and it's right where everyone should strive to be at all times."

"What the fuck are you talking about?" He asks, taking his shot on the 3rd hole.

"It's the serpent man," I start, grabbing his wrist and pointing around at his tat that looks like it would be about par for the course in prison. "Ok, you see how the black seems to get eaten by the white, and vice versa?" I ask.

"Yeah Dude, I see it." He says pulling his arm away, shooting me a look.

"Ok, then there's a white circle in the black and a black circle in the white."

"Yeah." He agrees, looking down at it again.

"Well the black is chaos and the white is order." I'm explaining. "They move in a circle, always eating at each other."

"O.K." He says, nodding, unsure.

"So, then you have the black circle in the white, a little bit of chaos in the order. That's when you take that extra shot of Jack when you know you're already brewed up. When you push the limits, go too far. It's high stakes, high risk and high rewards. That's the snake from the Garden of Eden, Man. It's the dragon of chaos and order in their eternal struggle."

"I'm not following you Schultz." He admits.

"Dude, think about it like this, it's your imagination going wild when you hear the front door open in the middle of the night when you're supposed to be the only one home. It's like getting high or tripping or whatever, you want to get as close to the edge as you can and still be able to come back. Go too far Man, you go over the cliff, game over. That's when you OD, that's just chaos. There's nothing cool about that.

And I'm right where I should be when it comes to disk golf, right on the edge. On the edge of chaos and order man. I'm in the white, comfort, with one foot in the dark, the unknown. And the other part of me lies in the chaos, the thing that I'm not good at, with one foot in the order. That's where I see you and Curt tossing in an *orderly* way. You see what I mean?"

"No Dude," Dicky says looking up at the dark clouds rolling by. "I don't see what the fuck you mean."

"It's all about pushing yourself out of your comfort zone, challenging yourself." I'm explaining.

"Alright, so who do you *admire*?" He asks.

"Well, in this case, believe it or not, you two losers. Basically, anyone out here that's better than me, which is just about everyone except that hot chick over there. But do you notice that she's hot? That's the point, she's never going to get better; she doesn't have to. Her boyfriend just brings her out here so everyone will notice her nice tits bouncing around in that bikini. I'm watching how you throw; I'm asking for advice. Trying to improve. I come here with you, I watch you and I try to learn from you. There's nothing wrong with that. That's what you *should* do." I explain.

"Yeah?" He asks, lighting a blunt of Columbian Gold the size of a Sharpie.

"Yeah." I continue. "The problem most people have comes when they suck at something but instead of trying to get better, they try to hide it, try to cover it up. Their ego does either of two things; one, not even be able to admit that they suck at something. Think about the dumb asses we all work with here. They suck, you know that they suck, I know they suck, *everyone* knows that they suck, and deep down, they know that they suck too but they let pride keep them from asking for help.

They're scared to step into the chaos. They want to stay safely in the comforts of the white order. That kind of pride is toxic. It's like the old stereotype that men won't ask for directions, which I have never signed off on by the way, so they stay lost, because they're ashamed. It boils down to shame, shame and narcissism. Everything about most people can usually be boiled down to shame and narcissism. People get so wrapped up in their own B.S. and they never find their way. A wise man, a man of ideals like the mighty Bo, will ask for directions. You see what I mean?"

"I guess so, Dude." Dicky says, hitting the blunt a couple times, then passing it to me.

"Well, that leads to the second part. I've only been playing frisbee golf for a couple months, and no, *clearly* I am not naturally skilled at it, but I am determined to do what I have to do to get good and I'm not ashamed of that. See, again it comes down to shame, to ask for help." I say coughing out a massive series of hits, instantly stoned.

"Shame? You keep bringing up shame. What does shame have to do with anything?" Curt asks.

"Well, it has *everything* to do with everything." I say, now totally stoned, losing my train of thought. "Shame is what happens to people who have too much pride to ask for help." I'm saying. "What happens is that they try to fake it and won't admit that they need help and then so much time goes by that it would be weird for them to ask for help at that point. And that is where real shame comes in."

"Why?" Curt asks.

"Because by then, not only does everyone else know that you suck, but you know that you suck and you know that asking for help now would make you look like a huge loser because you seem childish and petty for not admitting that you sucked for so long."

"So that causes shame?" Dicky asks.

"Yeah, that's where the shame comes in and that's only the second stage." I'm explaining.

"Oh boy." Dicky says.

"Though that's where people tend to live, for a long time. You see other people succeeding at the thing that you started together at the same time, but now they're good and you still suck at. It would be really weird to ask for help at that point, so then you feel shame. Over time, you continue to do the thing that you suck at but watch everyone else continue to get better and get promoted or whatever, and you're ashamed at your incompetence. You shame yourself."

"Well Dude, it doesn't seem like all these people are walking around ashamed all the time does it?" Curt asks.

"No, that's where shame turns to rage. It's why some people in the middle east, terrorists, it's why they hate us. Or the Occupy Wall Street losers and why they're so angry. Shame leads to rage." I say.

"Dude, pass that fucking hooter!" Curt shouts. I take one more hit off of it before passing it. I'm so stoned right now, but these thoughts are stalking my conscience.

"When we were kids," I continue, blowing out the hit. "…you know, imagine walking down the street with your old man on a warm summer day, you could see some old rich guy, driving his Porsche up to his big house and your dad would say to you, 'Look at him son, he worked hard. He went out there and achieved. If you work hard, you can be successful too.' And you'd be like, 'Yeah, I sure would like to work hard and have cool stuff one day."

"Schultz…" Dicky starts.

"Hang on." I hold up a hand in protest. "These days, people, especially people our age, they look at that guy and are like, 'Hey man, why does he need such a big car or a big house? He must have stolen something from poor guys like us to get all of that stuff. Screw that guy. He stole from us, so now I'm gonna throw a brick through his window and slash his fancy-schmancy tires!"

"Dude…" Curt says firmly but I'm still rolling.

"It's a load of horse crap and it's all because of narcissistic shame. That dude got up at 5 a.m. every morning and you slept until noon. So yeah, he's successful and you're not, but he worked 100 times harder than you. He earned it. Dude, do you know what the most important verb in the English language is?" I ask.

"Fuck?" Curt suggests, eager to move on.

"Well, the F-word can be a verb, a noun, a pronoun, an article, and/or a qualifier." I explain. "Nice guess, though."

"Ok professor, what is it?" Dicky asks.

"The most important verb in the English language is *earn.*" I say, blowing even my own mind. "You don't appreciate anything that you don't earn. Inadequacy, if not properly addressed…" I'm saying, eyes closed tightly, letting this thought chain run its course. "turns to shame which, if left unchecked, leads to rage." I finish, finally satisfied.

On the 18th hole, which is at the top of a hill, if you can catch some air, your disk can soar right away, out of sight. Dicky throws his and it goes down, then up and then disappears, out of the line of sight, we don't hear chains though. Curt goes and, of course, that thing catches air and floats away, down, down over the hill, out of sight. We all stand still, listening for it. That moment of truth. The disc is out of sight but hasn't landed yet, the unknown, the hand in the dark room of chaos. Suddenly we hear it, chains! A hole in one! *Brill!*

I throw my *Masked Marauder* and it hooks into the parking lot and hits a new white Dodge Ram.

Dicky says, "Dude, you still fucking suck and you will always fucking suck."

"Whatever Dicky." I say, running down to the parking lot to assess the damage, "Tongue my B-hole."

Chapter XXIX

I feel like I need a shower to wash the shame of the Disk Golf round off of my body, my soul. A wave of depression washes over me as my Vicodin buzz fizzles to a distant memory. I hold up my prescription pill bottle, squint at it closely, give it a shake and then put it back in my pocket

deciding that I'll need these last few later on more than now. I'm sitting on the black, Armani leather sofa across from love seat that are complementing the white Polar Bear skin rug under the Orren Ellis Weatherwax glass coffee table.

Anderson Cooper is on CNN making a very strong argument that Congressman Gary Condit was having an affair with and murdered Sandra Levy. I get up to fix myself a Martini from the bar and realize that it's chillier than it should be for early September, so instead of just taking my shirt off like Curt would, I grab an off white, Abercrombie and Fitch sweater from my room.

I feel like everyone is starting to turn on me when it comes to these pain killers. On the one hand, Dicky and Curt are telling me to chill out with them and I can see that look on their faces when Morpheus' grip begins to tighten. I know what opiates do to a man's pupils and I'm well aware of what mine look like. The looks I've been getting aren't exactly *anger*, like, I don't think they're pissed at me for taking pills, 'cause at the same time, they're trying to get them off of me. It's like they won't ask for them, but they want me to offer them. It has created this weird dichotomy where they both desire what I have and yet, the look on their face is more like distain. Do they both want and loath what I'm doing at the same time?

"Is it cold in here?" I'm asking, completely zoned out.

"Dude, what's up with you and Valerie?" Dicky asks me without answering my question.

"I asked if it was cold in here?" I repeat, breathing to show that my breath is visible.

"Yeah, I heard you." Dicky says, "Then I asked you about Valerie."

"I don't know, Man." I say, unsure of where this is going. "What about her?"

"Well, look Dude, it's like this Schultzy… you love her." He says, for reasons I may never fully realize. "We all know that, so why are you fucking around with that Crazy, Ginger bitch or whatever the fuck her name is?"

"Dude, she's the one that doesn't want to put labels on us. She's not into *titles."* I say, putting up air quotes. "Formalities or whatever, ya' know?"

"Well, here's the thing dude." He starts explaining. "You love her. We all know you love her; she knows you love her, kind of, I mean, you keep doing stupid shit that makes her not know for sure, but deep down, she knows that you've always loved her."

"Well I'm not the only one doing *stupid shit*." I say in air quotes again, noting not to do that again for at least a week. "You don't live with her; you don't know what she does when she's not here."

"You think she's fucking around?" He asks.

"Dude," I start. "you know how she is, right? She's either hot or cold" I'm pouring a glass of Don Julio Tequila circa 1942 on ice, then add, "Well I'm not the only dude she's like that with." I say, handing Dicky a drink, making eye contact for emphasis.

"Shut the fuck up." He says, gulping down the drink I just gave him, then taking the bottle and pouring himself another glass. "She fucks around?"

"Dicky…" I close my eyes tightly in thought. I need this to come out right. "Dude, she's like a puzzle with...with moving parts." I say. "There are no edges, there are no male and female parts. Everything is…I don't know, *fluid* with her. She has secrets that she will take to the grave and at the same time she will open up her veins and just sit there and bleed for you. She's crazy, Man. Wild. She's crazy wild. She is…she's only what she wants us to believe she is. Or something like that, you know what I'm saying?"

"Kind of." He says, nodding along.

"She's crazy wild." I whisper to myself again. "She makes me crazy…" Pause. "She makes me wild."

"But Dude, you are so into her." He says. "Don't fucking tell me you're not. I've fucking known you since you were just a skinny ass, long haired kid, Schultz."

"Well what the fuck do you know about love, Dicky?" I ask accusingly, casually taking a drink. "I mean seriously."

"What the fuck are you saying?" He demands, slamming down his drink on the glass coffee table.

"Dude, every girlfriend that you've ever had," I start, I've actually had this speech chambered since the last time he started this *love* malarkey. "You don't love them. Did you love Christie? No. You just loved that everyone else loved her. You were in love with the image of her. And now you're fucking Jenny? Isn't she just a younger version of her? OK, she's a firecracker in the sack, fine, but think about it, all she is is a freaking accessory to you. You don't love her. You don't love anyone but your mother-grabbing self. No one even knows you. You're like some freak show enigma!"

"Hey!" He snaps, getting up and stomping over to the bar. He's throwing ice in his glass, then he throws a handful at me and starts shouting swear words.

"No, Eff you Dicky!" I say, brushing the ice off the leather sofa. "No one even knows who you really are, no one can believe anything you say because half the things you say are straight up lies and the other half are always weird twists of a part of the truth. You do that crap on purpose too. You lie so much that even when you tell the truth no one believes you. It's like you're intentionally keeping people away. Me and Curt just don't give a damn. That makes for a good poker strategy but that's your whole flipping life. Your whole life is a lie, Dude. There is no *real* you."

"You don't know what the fuck you're talking about, Schultz." He says unconvincingly.

"Really?" I ask, redundantly.

"Really." He lies, eyes shifting.

"See, you're lying right now. You always leave that little *out* so you can always say, *'Oh, I'm just fucking around, you know how I do it.'*

"I do not!" He protests.

"Dude, you don't really exist. I mean, there's a physical you, a you that plays music and writes shitty songs…"

"Hey Motherfucker!" He tries to interrupt.

"…and drinks with me every day, but there is no *real* you. I don't even think you know what the truth is. It's who you are. You're a liar, a sociopathic liar. So, don't talk to me about who I love and who I don't love."

"You motherfucker!" He says, the look on his face morphs into something I don't recognize. Something resembling sincerity. "You know what, you might be right. I might be a soulless, heartless, lying motherfucker but you know what? You're wrong about one thing Schultz, I do know love. I know it when I see it. I may not have it myself, but I sure as hell know it when I see it, Bitch. You love Valerie. I know that much Motherfucker."

"Oh, what the balls do you know?" I say.

"When you look up at a cloud," He's saying wistfully. "You imagine having conversations with her about what they are and what they represent. When they start to change, that's like, really exciting to you both and you squeeze each other a little bit tighter."

"What the flip…wait, how do you know that?" I ask, my mind racing.

"I fucking know you Schultzy. Every song you've ever written was a message to her in one way or another. She's like Wilson from that movie *Castaway*. She's this abstract object that you love but can't engage with. She seems to like you too, I guess. She lets you fuck her anyway, right?"

"Yeah, well she's a frickin' H-junkie." I say, looking down, sniffing nervously.

"Well, look Dude, be honest, you like that shit too." He says. "I've seen her when she's high and I've seen her when she's not. She's a fucking firecracker when she's high, she turns into a wolf and when she's not she's like a fucking nun."

"Well her dad *is* a preacher." I say. "Oh, and she was adopted. Her parents like, died in a fire when she was a little kid or something. She doesn't really talk about it but I think they were some kind of preachers too."

"Shut the fuck up, are you serious right now?" He asks, eyes wide.

"I am serious right now." I say.

"Holy shit." He says shaking his head, scoffing in amazement. "Dude, this is worse than I thought. This is worst-case scenario shit right here." He says soberly. "Well that's got to fuck her up right there. Look Dude, I know that you want to be the good guy here, be on the good end of this. But she's got a devil on one shoulder and an angel on the other. I know you want to be on the Angel's side but to her, you're on the Devil's side. You, me, all of us, we aren't the ones sticking a needle in her arm but to her, we're all on the same side and it ain't the fucking Angel's side, I hate to tell you. And we never will be. And, by the way, that might not be the worst thing for her, if she doesn't come out on the good side of this, that bitch, sorry Dude, is gonna end up dead. And you better hope she doesn't find out that you've been fucking around with that crazy Ginger bitch."

"Yeah well, whatever." I say finishing my drink and giving the ice a shake. "It *is* cold in here though, right?"

Chapter XXX

Dicky Sinner Jr. grew up in a small fishing town near Saginaw, Michigan on the banks of the Saginaw Bay, the penis of Lake Huron. His father, Dick Sr. was a fisherman by trade but after losing his left hand in a lobster trap one frigid February morning, had to settle for whatever work he could get as a longshoreman. As a boy he wanted to grow up to be a pirate and sail around the warm and tropical islands of the Caribbean drinking rum and scoring Booties, both monetarily and, you know, booty. After the accident though, he settled for just drinking rum on the docks of the Saginaw Bay. He was often heard dismissing Captain Morgan as not real rum, but more of a rum flavored wine cooler and thus thought it was fine to drink all day long. Sometimes first thing in the morning.

Dicky Jr.'s mother, Rhonda Baily, was a real beauty in her day, she was the youngest girl to ever win the Junior Miss Saginaw '72 beauty contest when she was just 13 years old. One of the judges that year was the Madman from the Motor City himself, Ted Nugent. After the pageant, The Nuge gave the winner and her family front row tickets to his show that night and even invited them backstage after the show. Rhonda's father joked to his wife, "Hey, I better keep an eye on you. Don't go sneaking off with Ted Nugent now, ya hear, I hear he has a way with the young ladies."

His wife and daughter laughed as they went back to the local legend's dressing room after the sold-out show. They were so excited, they wondered if they should ask him for his autograph or if that would be too tacky.

"Dad, please don't embarrass me." Rhonda said, giving him a slap to the shoulder.

"Oh, don't worry dear, I'm sure there will be hundreds of fans waiting to get their photo taken. I wouldn't get your hopes up too high, he may not even remember you. I'm sure he does this sort of thing every night." Her father, Mr. Baily said as they were led through the maze of dark corridors by a long-haired, middle-aged, chubby roadie named Noel. After her father said this, Noel the roadie turned back and gave a smirk before coming to a green and red door with a gold star on it that read: *Ted Nugent.*

The man opened the door and then stood in front of the entrance, blocking their way while he spoke in code into a walky-talky. From the hall, the family looked eagerly into the dressing room of the most famous person they had ever, and probably ever will meet. The room was empty except for a plush red sofa, a white coffee table with a giant fruit basket and a copy of Barely Legal opened to the centerfold on it, an old desk with a lightbulb filled vanity mirror to illuminate the room. The walls were peach colored and were lined with camouflage long bows, arrows and guitars of all shapes and colors.

Just as Mr. Baily was having grave and urgent second thoughts about this whole thing, The Nuge himself walked out of the bathroom wearing only a tanned, leather loin cloth and brown, leather wrist bands on both wrists. He looked like Tarzan, wild and uninhabited. His eyes were intense, he shook his head like a lion and his wild hair seemed to blow in the wind that was not

there. He stopped in the middle of the small dressing room and threw his hands up, then slowly lowered his right arm until it pointed at Rhonda. He paused for effect, then his hand made a gesturing motion for her to come. Come to him, his hand demanded. Rhonda was frozen yet she could feel her body moving toward him as if his magnetism had beckoned the universe and his gravity was pulling her toward him.

Ted motioned dismissively for Noel to shut the door and he obediently obliged. 8 1/2 minutes later the door opened again, and Mr. and Mrs. Baily were still standing, utterly petrified, exactly where they were when the door shut. They hadn't so much as blinked, breathed, or swallowed. They could not believe what was happening. They didn't even know what was happening and they couldn't believe what was happening. Noel was more than just a little uneasy as he presented some very formal and official looking papers the to the Bailys. Astonishment turned to chaotic confusion.

"What the hell is this?" Asked Mr. Baily.

"These?" Noel asked innocently, pausing briefly. "These, these are just a-a a formality." He offered dismissively.

"A formality for what?" He asked.

"For the uh, the…adoption." He said in a meek falsetto.

"Adoption? But we're her parents, why would she need to be adopted?" Mrs. Baily asked.

"Well, you see, Mr. Nugent has taken a special interest in Miss Rhonda. He'd like to work with her a little bit more closely than some of his other proteges, to help her with her career. This is really an honor; Mr. Nugent doesn't usually take this much interest in his students." Noel explained.

"His students?" Mrs. Baily asked.

"Yes, well Mr. Nugent is very involved with the youth. He loves to help children grow into their talents and has helped many young girls...er, uh *people* start their careers in show business. This is really a great honor." Noel managed, somewhat convincingly.

Pause.

"But will we be able to see her?" Mrs. Baily finally broke her silence.

"What? No, what are you crazy? This is insane! There is no way in hell…." Mr. Baily exclaimed.

"Oh sure, sure." Noel offered. "You can see her anytime you want. Just make an appointment to come by the mansion and, if it's approved, you'll be able to stop by for a closely supervised visit within the month."

"Well, if you think it's best for Rhonda?" Mr. Baily said more calmly.

"We'll send a car for her belongings. Thanks. Just sign here," Noel said, then flipped a page and then, "and here."

Rhonda spent the next three years more or less as a glorified sex slave for the Motor City Madman. She was not allowed to leave the Nugent compound under any circumstances, she was encouraged to play tennis at the tennis courts and swim in the guitar shaped pool to stay healthy. She was given good food to eat, three times a day. Ted treated her like a pet that he was fond of but would ignore and dismiss with such regularity that it caused her unimaginable psychological damage.

He would not think twice about bringing other girls, her age and younger, give or take a few months, and party with them all. Sometimes he would have Rhonda engage in three, four, or five ways with the other girls. Sometimes he would have sex with Rhonda alone, but it felt like he was just beating off to a ragdoll. After a while, he had Rhonda and 10 other girls dress in schoolgirl uniforms and stand around his bed making out while he had his 'main girl' rode him before bed.

After three years of this, at the ripe old age of 16, Rhonda went and got herself knocked-up. She was sure that the Nuge would force her to have an abortion but, being a staunch, pro-life conservative, he actually told her that he wanted her to have the baby but that he didn't want anything *personally* to do with their love child, obviously. He agreed to let her go back and live with her parents as long as she never told anyone who the father was and, on the condition that she forget about all the kinky stuff that went on there as per the clause in the contract.

Rhonda quickly and eagerly agreed and signed to the conditions and the next day a taxi dropped her off in front of her parent's house with her suitcase in her hand and Ted's bun in her oven. Of course, they embraced her with open arms, they didn't ask any questions about what had gone on there at the Nuge compound and she was happy to not have to tell. After about a week, the whole incident turned into what was treated as a family secret, the kind that gets swept under the rug for generations. A long weekend where, everyone had done things they regretted and wished they could take back but couldn't, so everyone just forgave and tried with all their might and tolerance for booze, to forget.

Back in the real-world, Rhonda ran into Dick Sinner Sr., the one-handed longshore fisherman, at the local Wal-Mart. Rhonda knew that time was of the essence, she also knew that Dick liked to have a drink or seventeen on a fairly regular basis. She chatted him up and asked him if he would buy her a drink. He said, "Yes." and they went across the parking lot to a dive bar called The Parrot's Beak. She got him drunker than he usually would have gotten by swapping her full drinks for his empty drinks and then asking for another.

He woke up later that evening in a bed at a Motel 6 with the beautiful Rhonda lying next to him rubbing her belly. He groaned, as he struggled to remember exactly what had happened. She leaned over and kissed him on the cheek and said, "Oh Dick, you were wonderful. No one has ever made me feel the way you do."

Dick wasn't sure what to say or do, he just kind of let her run with the whole thing. Two months later they were married in a small ceremony at Cypress Community Church and five months after that they welcomed little Dicky Jr. into the world. Dick Sr. was as proud as he'd ever been. He vowed to do the right thing and make a good home for Rhonda and Dicky Jr.

Dicky Jr. grew up to be a pretty tough kid. He had beady eyes, a strong back, and wild brown hair and a slight resemblance to Richard Gere. When he was just five years old, Dick Sr. took him into a pawn shop to hawk a gold ring for a few dollars and Dicky Jr. walked past a little guitar. He picked it up and started strumming it, after about two minutes of fooling around with it, he had figured out how to play Ode to Joy. By the age of seven, Dicky could play every Led Zeppelin song there was, leads and all.

Dick Sr. would sometimes look at the hook that he wore as a left hand and would wonder where Dicky Jr. got all of this talent from, but he would quickly dismiss the thought with a glass of bourbon and then safely assumed that someone on Rhonda's side of the family must be a gifted musician. He never asked her about it though, wanting to continue to believe that something great came out of him. Something that was better than him, purer than he would ever be.

Chapter XXXI

Saturday night gives way to Sunday morning but there's no telling when or how. None at all. We all may or may not have slept, I'm pretty sure I passed out after we got home from Cooper's and Dicky and I took turns doing upside-down beer bongs from our keg and Jose Cuervo Reserva de la Familia margaritas laced with cocaine in leu of salt. At some point Curt grew tired of freebasing cocaine through a straw and started rocking it up with a blowtorch. There are visions of us walking around on the black Armani couches, taking blasts like it was some Native American peyote ritual that we needed to be naked for.

How they got in was unclear, yet Crazy Ginger and Lolita showed up at some point, though I don't remember ever seeing them come through the door, they just slithered their way in. Someone must have spoken their names, whatever their names really are, out loud three times and they just manifested. It could have been me. It's hard to say.

Somewhere in between songs, after fucking Ginger on my bed but before putting it in her ass I asked her if I could tie her up to my mahogany bedposts. She got very excited. I was confused. It wasn't until the sun came up and me and the boys couldn't ignore her screaming any longer that I realized that she had misunderstood my motivation for wanting to tie her up entirely.

Either way, Sunday morning is now a reality that we all have to make our peace with whether we like it or not. Saturday night is a memory but a memory with a chain of evidence that hasn't been properly wiped clean yet. Here it is, still on fire, still bleeding. Saturday night's wounds have not had time to adequately scar over. All the sunlight does is shine a light on the debauchery that went down.

My phone starts chirping at me as I'm clinging to the crystal chandelier over the pool table, holding on for dear life, swinging around like a goddam carousel. It's M. B. calling, and once Dicky convinces me that its safe, I crawl down the maroon, velvet curtains and curl up in a ball on the sofa to take the call.

"Who in the God so loving Eff…what the finger banging hell is this all about?" I ask, cautiously, lighting a cigarette.

"You motherfuckers are ate the fuck up." The voice on the other end of the phone is shouting. "Have you slept?"

"I've uh, I've…yeah I've slept. I was just…cleaning up. Ya know, exercising. You know, drawing the curtains and the like, doing push-ups…" I say looking around the house, there is a new painting, *New York Skyline at Night*, an original Jake Rosen, hanging on the wall next to the

George Nelson, Sunflower clock. The thermometer reads 58 degrees although it feels colder than that. Dicky is sitting on the black leather sofa wearing a St. Louis Rams visor, mirrored Aviator shades from Ray-Bans, and hot pink Abercrombie and Fitch boxer/briefs, chewing on a metal coat hanger with his guitar in his lap trying to write a song but the only words on the page are *Does Dicky Do it? Dicky doesn't do it. Dicky doesn't do it.* Over and over again.

Curt is in his room, naked with a forest green and gold striped Ralph Lauren necktie knotted around his neck and tied to the ceiling fan that is on medium, attempting to beat off to the centerfold in the August addition of Samson Magazine. I walk by, closing the door telekinetically.

Lolita is curled up on the Love Seat wearing one of my black Guns 'n Roses T-shirts and pink lace and nylon panties. She is sucking her thumb and rubbing the tag of the T-shirt, the soft tag that is made of satin on her lips like a child. A morphine laced lollipop in her hand that is tapped out on the glass coffee table.

M.B. is rambling about construction work on his cell phone and I can hear Curt grunting from his room but other than that, further away, distant, I can hear a muffled moaning. Flashbacks of a wretched scene set in my bedroom begin to dawn and a paranoia starts to overwhelm me.

"Michael," I whisper into the phone. "I can't listen to this right now. Something nefarious is happening in other parts of the house."

"Take a fucking nap and then come over." He shouts. "We're BBQin' at the pool all day."

"Alright man, I'll see what I can put together." I say.

"Whatever Dude." He mocks.

"Oh, don't tell Valerie or anyone like that." I say, peeking over at Lolita and touching myself through my silk, Lord & Tayler boxer shorts.

"I don't invite junkies to my crib Dude." He says blankly.

"Well…alright then." I trail off, hanging up the phone at some point.

I go in my bedroom cautiously to see what all of the ruckus is about. I find Ginger tied up and gagged to my bed, kicking and squirming around like a hooked eel, wrinkling the satin sheets. I loosen her black, silk blindfold and she starts to give me head. Confusion doesn't begin to describe what I'm feeling. I think about Lolita and her pink panties and I cum in Ginger's mouth before I can pull out to cum on her face. I let this eat me up for, what I would consider to be a healthy amount of time before coming to grips with the reality of what just happened.

CNN is on the T.V. talking about Chandra Levy. Wolf Blitzer is now sure, and he is assuring the audience that Rep. Gary Condit was having an affair with and murdered her. I crawl into the shower to try and give myself a fighting chance of making it another day and when I emerge baptized, Fooky is beating Curt in an intense game of pool. I pop three Xanies and join Dicky at the bar for a Beefeater and tonic.

Chapter XXXII

I'm driving Ginger's shitty Honda Civic with one eye closed to cut down on the hallucinations. She is in the passenger's seat; Lolita is in the back seat with Fooky. I feel I'm the only one sober enough to drive until Fooky tells me that I'm driving backwards which causes an instant panic that I cannot be bothered to deal with in any sustainable way. I switch eyes, try to shake things off and bust an emergency break, U turn, then straighten her out just before hitting Highway 94, heading in what I pray is west.

I'm wearing faded blue jeans from American Eagle, my Harley Davidson belt with a chrome buckle, a blue tweed Vacation shirt from Zara, blue tinted aviator shades and a platinum mushroom necklace from Jarrad's that goes with my sterling silver skull, pinky ring.

"I'm thinking about my doorbell Baby, when you gonna ring it?" I ask nobody in particular.

Fooky is telling wildly racially offensive jokes from the back seat that I can't help but laugh at. He's wearing kaki cargo shorts from The Gap and a light grey Polo shirt from Kenith Cole, slim Gucci sunglasses and black and white striped, Adidas sneakers. He's smoking Durban Poison weed out of a bronze plated one-hitter that goes with a wooden, Wizzard embroidered dugout from The Smoke Shop off of Delmar Rd.

Ginger is solemnly drinking a Jack and Ice from a champagne flute that she stole from my house, that I stole from my cousin, Josiah's bar mitzvah, wearing cut off jean shorts from American Outfitters, a breezy white blouse from Abercrombie and Fitch and oversized Chanel sunglasses to cover her black eye. She's sporting matching bruises on both of her wrists and a bright red and swollen welt from where I had her gagged for the better part of last night. I give her a red scarf from Macy's and snap at her, "Cover yourself up!" Which ends up sounding way worse than I initially intended.

I notice two things that I assumed were hallucinations at first but are quickly proving to not be; one is the family of Zombies in a bronze Eddie Bauer Bronco that insists on snuggling right up in my blind spot. Try as I may to ignore this demon family of the undead, when the daughter in the baby seat, a toddler, starts eating the brains of the older boy, maybe 5 and ½, with pieces of bloody, slimy guts squirming around all over her chubby face, chewing with her mouth open, I swallow a mouthful of vomit that isn't settling well the second time.

The second thing I am no longer convinced is my imagination is Lolita throwing some serious vibes my way in the rearview mirror. Even though she's wearing large Gucci shades, I can feel

her shooting strong, direct *come on Schultz and hammer me* signals. At first, I didn't really notice, I was just looking at her 'cause she was wearing a sundress and my ripped Guns 'n Roses T-shirt and she's as sexy as an underage runaway. Her body language is screaming for the General and her pouty lips are gagging for a mouthful.

Fooky is cracking us all up with vulgar jokes but I'm distracted by the magnetism of Lolita. I'm wearing shades too, so she doesn't know I'm looking at her and I don't even know if she's looking at me but she's slithering around in a very sexy way that feels like she's vibing me. I start to think that she is *way* too young to be that good at this.

My dick gets about 3/4 hard. She licks her lips, moves her legs back and forth. *Am* I imagining all of this? What drugs have I taken? Maybe I'm sleep deprived, mad. Maybe I'm drug crazed and completely psychotic, maybe this is all a dream that I'm living through. Ginger is trying to keep my attention by massaging my thigh and Fooky is in the back hoping and praying that he'll get Lolita drunk enough to pass out so that he can pull an R. Kelly on her. I wouldn't doubt if he has a roofie chambered in a Tic-Tac case for just that kind of an opportunity.

Dazed, I think, "Wait a minute, how old is she anyway?" I don't really think anything that either of them has ever told us has been the truth. I assumed that her name was a little too ironic to be real. *Lolita.* A total stripper name, it might as well be Chastity. Like a girl named Mercedes is the least likely girl on the planet to actually drive a Mercedes. I don't really even know what Ginger's real name is. It might not even be Ginger; I think we just started calling her *Ginger* because of her scarlet hair.

I sort of assumed that Lolita was a runaway, half joking, but now I feel like this is about to get real. A ménage perhaps? Anyway, now the question presents itself in a very real way, "How old is she anyway? 18? 16? …dare I say, 14? Is this worth it? She is a runaway, right? Is that just something I made up too? Maybe not but I still get the impression that no one is like, looking for her. At least no one is going to be pressing charges, I'll not be facing a jury of my peers or anything.

Things get even more real in the mirror, as we pass Zumbehl Rd., she drops down her shades to show me that, yes, she is in fact looking at me with hunger in her eyes. She crosses then uncrosses her legs and shows me her panties. Pink lace and nylon from Victoria's Secret, then bends down to get something off the floor and shows me her tits, nips and all. I almost crash Ginger's car into the median and everyone trips out on me but Lolita just giggles. Now I know that she knows that I know that she knows what's going on, which is technically referred to as *common knowledge* by the way.

We pull up to M.B. and Ryan Barnes' apartment complex and park by the pool. There's about 20 people there already doing some brewin' and Q'n. They just moved here not too long ago, and this is the first time I've been to this common area. I'm impressed at how nice it is, there are two swimming pools, brand-new stainless-steel grills from Broil King, a full gym and white sand volleyball courts.

It looks like a Budweiser commercial come to life. It's open to everyone in the complex so there are lots of people at the pool, playing sand volleyball, BBQing and sunbathing despite it being quite chilly out. There are no kids, everyone is young and good looking. The pool is crisp and shiny, the BBQ pits all look brand new and the sand volleyball court looks like a great place to take a nap or have some kind of hedonistic human sacrifice.

I sit down across from Fooky under a Corona umbrella, set down my blue Ray-Ban aviator shades on the white plastic table and squeeze a lime wedge into a frosty beer.

"Dude, this girl was a 10. A perfect 10." Fooky is saying to the table.

"Dude, there is no perfect 10." I'm trying to explain to Fooky how the female hotness scale is widely misunderstood by our generation.

"Schultz, I'm telling you, this girl was a 10." He stubbornly insists.

"Fooky, you're making a complete mockery of the whole point system as an institution." I say.

"Schultz, you didn't see this girl." He's pleading.

"Fook, you're not hearing me." I say, speaking very slowly. "There *is* no 10. It doesn't exist, it's a hypothetical scenario. It's a rainbow-colored unicorn, it's unattainable, not to mention, the whole thing completely subjective."

"There has to be a 10 out there somewhere, Schultz." Fooky says.

"Dude." I start. "She would have to speak English with just a hint of a French accent yet be fluent in Japanese. She would have to be able to write a song that could make a grown man cry. She would have to write Haikus about me and leave them on Post-it notes around the house. She would have to be an absolute angel in the kitchen and a nasty devil in the bedroom. And it's different for everyone, a 10 for you may be only a 6 and ½ for me, you see what I'm saying? Am I getting through to you at all?"

"Alright, whatever Dude. You know who you kind of remind me of, Howard Stern. Annoyingly Jewy but kind of funny. Like, he's funny on the radio but I think I'd hate him in real life." Fooky finally concedes, popping open two beers and handing me one then asks, "Do you have anyone like that?"

"Like what?" I ask, taking the beer.

"Who's someone famous that you're sure you'd hate in real life?"

"What do you mean?" I ask.

"What the fuck are you nerds arguing about now?" Ryan Barnes asks, pulling up a lawn chair and emptying a gram of coke onto a small, hand mirror.

"Well, like an actor that you like in the movies, like you think they're a good actor but in real life you think he's a dick." He explains.

"You mean like Michael Jackson or something?" Barnes asks.

"Uh, yeah, sure. If you like Michael Jackson's songs and shit but think he's a little boy fucker in real life then yeah, like Michael Jackson." Fooky says.

"Alright, well that was a dumb fucking question then." Barnes says cutting out four fat lines on the mirror.

"Well, M.J. is kind of a bad example because, while he's super talented, you wouldn't go buy his CD or anything." Fooky says, snorting a rail. "He's sort of turned into just a bad guy. I'm talking about someone you really like as far as their acting or music or whatever but then in real life, you hate."

"Well then like who the fuck are you thinking of, Motherfucker?" Barnes asks, "Why'd you bring this up?"

"Uh…O.K.," Fooky says, wheels spinning. "Like Sean Penn. I really like the movies he's in but not just the movies he's in but his characters, he's a really good actor but in real life, he's a huge douche bag."

"Sean Penn?" I ask, throwing up my arms, beer spilling on my Aloha shirt and gold mushroom necklace. "What the fuck did he ever do to you?"

"Oh, ya'know, he's just a world class dickhead." He says, wheels still spinning, trying desperately to make a coherent argument. "He just has no sense of humor; he pals around the world with murderous dictators and makes them out to be heroes and shit like that. On the other hand, his movies are awesome! He was fucking great in Fast Times at Ridgemout High, Carlito's Way, I am Sam, Mystic River, Mystic River was fucking great! Did you see that?"

"Heck yeah!" I say, leaning forward, snorting half a line, sniffing it all in, burning, then snorting the other half. "We watched that together at your Mom's house back in the day. Yeah, that was a classic."

"So, if he wasn't so good, you would have let his off-screen shit get in the way of his movies. Is that what you're saying?" Barnes attempts to clarify.

"Exactly." Fook says. "I want nothing more than to hate his guts but his roles in movies are so goddam good! I can't help but like him."

"Oh, *Oliver Stone!"* I shout, raising my hand.

"O.K. I feel you." Fooky says, "I think I know where you're going with this Schultz."

"What?!" Barnes demands, "What the fuck are you nerds talking about?"

"Oh, Oliver Stone is a complete knob." I step in, "He's a freak."

"And he's a pervert, isn't he?" Fook says.

"What?" I ask. Barnes asks too, then, "Whatever."

"So, who do you got?" I ask.

"Alright…I got it". Fooky says, eyes wide. "Eddie Murphy!"

"Eddie Murphy? He's a funny motherfucker." Barnes says with visible signs of aggression and coke residue. "What did he ever do that wasn't cool."

"Well maybe this is sort of a different category, but think about it, we all know he's funny as hell, right?" Fooky says.

"Yeah, so what the hell are you talking about?" Barnes asks for the third time.

"Well yeah, he's hell'a funny, but can you imagine him like," Fooky is asking, "not being able to *take* a joke? You see what I'm saying?"

"Oh yeah, kind of. Like he's the funniest dude alive, but if you had him on America's Greatest Home Videos getting totally punked, he'd throw a massive fit, right?" I ask licking the salt off my Macho Margarita.

"Exactly!" Fooky says swinging his index finger, which is sporting a solid gold, index finger ring with a pentagram on its face.

"Ok, like Oasis." I say enthusiastically.

"Oh my fucking God, Dude, here you go again about Oasis." Fooky pouts.

"No Dude, Eff you, by the way! They're one of the greatest bands of our generation." I say, giving him my best Liam duck face slash British middle finger, which is just a backward peace sign. "Liam," I continue. "the younger brother seems like he's funny, and he is, but he wouldn't be cool to be like 'in on the joke' where Noel, the older brother doesn't seem as funny but would totally go along with the joke. Whatever that joke was. He's actually way funnier."

Ryan Barnes sits for a minute in a contemplative frown, scratching at the peach fuzz on his chin. Then does a 180-degree shift, taking us all by surprise, "Schultz, is that fucking crazy ass redhead your bitch now or what?" He asks me tactlessly.

"Uh, I don't know. Ask Dicky, I think he knows her." I'm slurring.

"Shut the fuck up." He says, laughing. "I don't give a fuck what you do, you know that shit motherfucker. But the last three times I've seen your skinny, Jewish ass, that crazy red headed bitch has been there wishing I wasn't there so she could be sucking your dick." He says, sitting back in his thrown. "That's a motherfucking fact. You tellin' me that she ain't your bitch?"

"Dude, I don't really even know who she is. I don't really even know her real name. Dicky, am I lying?" I ask Dicky who is walking by, double fisted with margaritas.

"No Dude, I don't fuck around with that shit anymore." Dicky slurs, not slowing down a beat.

"See what I'm saying, we don't even know who they are." I say, posing a grander position.

"Whoa, hold up there Schultz," Dicky says, balking, walking back to clarify. "That don't mean you don't know who they are. They ain't no fucking stowaways. You've been fucking the shit outta that bitch for at least two weeks." He says stumbling a bit, unable to find his footing. "I'm just being real. I know we don't know they're real names and shit, that shit might be true, but you know the fuck out of that bitch. In the biblical sense, you know what I'm saying?" He asks rhetorically. "You know her like Adam knew Eve motherfucker."

Tim Foreman is trying to get a sand volleyball game started and is going about it very diplomatically. He's wearing jean shorts, no shirt-good build and tan, frosted tips in his hair and a brown leather necklace with a pentagon medallion. He makes himself and M.B. captains and they alternate picking people for their teams. Me and Fooky aren't picked so we pretend to hate volleyball.

Ginger and Lolita are stumbling around, mingling with Rosie and the other girls and actually not making complete fools of themselves and not being too clingy either.

"Mother Effing Lord and savior, hear my plea; No one better be making friends with these bitches." I think, definitely out loud.

Fooky agrees. We're sitting under a Corona umbrella drinking cold Red Stripe beers from frosted mugs and packing one hits of *Loud Dream* weed from a platinum coated one hitter out of a gold-plated weed dugout.

"Alright," Fooky starts, "I got one for you. Two guys meet in the street, one guy swears that he's a liar, the other guy swears that he never lies." He pauses for effect, then, "Who is telling the truth?"

"OK, well…" I start but am cut off.

"'Cause you see," He starts, contemptuously, "if the one guy is really a liar…"

"Oh, I get it Fooky baby." I laugh, sarcastically. "I get it."

There's a brief pause.

"Well right?" He asks redundantly, shrugging his shoulders.

"Ok," I say, starting to work this out. "so, if the guy who says he always lies is lying about lying, that doesn't mean that he's telling the truth. And the guy who says he never lies…wait, does one of them *have* to be a liar? I mean, is that in the riddle somewhere?"

"Shit I don't know." He says just as I'm getting a text on my cellphone. It's Valerie asking if her and Blair can stop by later. I flip it shut and shove it deep into my jean's pocket. My hands

are sweating suddenly, I wipe them restlessly on the thighs of my jeans, teeth clenched, sweat beginning to bead and drip from my forehead.

"Who was that?" Fook asks me, eager to change topics.

"Uh, just this bird I met."

"What's her name?"

"What, are you writing a book? Her name's Nunya." I answer dryly.

"Ha ha, Nerd."

My phone starts buzzing again from inside my pocket. "These little bastards are seriously intrusive." I say.

"Cellphones are cool though; they definitely make meeting up for Mardi Gras way easier. Remember back in the day, like last year, we'd have to all agree three days in advance on a place and time to meet up. Then it would change 15 times and then we'd all end up meeting at Maggie O'Brian's anyway. Now all we have to do is call each other on the way there."

"Just call me." I sing.

"What a great invention." Josh White says, pulling up a lawn chair and looking at his Motorola flip-phone.

"Oh, alright, here's a great question, What's the most important invention ever?" Fooky asks all of us.

"Ever, ever?" I ask.

"Yeah, in history. What's the most important invention in history?" Fooky clarifies.

"That's a good question." Josh says, thinking, sipping at his margarita "The *ultranet* I guess?"

"You mean the *inter*net?" I ask, laughing. I take some salt from my margarita in my pinky and snort it. Not bad, it stings a little.

"I know what the fuck it's called, Dork." He says slurping his margarita loudly like Elwood sips champagne at the Che Paul.

"Yeah," I say, leaning in. "that's a pretty big invention, you know there's a place, a website I guess, called Guitar Tabs.com where you can find the guitar tabs for any song. For real, any song at all. You just type in the song and the band and it gives you all the tabs, solos and all."

"Yeah, that's pretty cool." He says ignoring me, eyeing a young blond in an American Flag bikini. Maybe 13, nice cans, poor judgment. Not bad.

"The atomic bomb was a huge invention. Talk about changing the world, has anything changed the world like the atomic bomb has?" Josh asks.

"It did for sure but that's nothing compared to electricity though. We wouldn't have any of those things without electricity." I say. "I think I'd have to go with that. It totally changed not only the political world but the way we live our everyday lives."

"Oh, yeah. I guess that makes sense." He says, wanting to crap on my point but unsure how to go about it just yet.

"Dude," I start. "electricity totally changed the way we do everything. It changed the way we freaking sleep, did you know that?"

"No, it didn't." Josh smells a chink in my argument and is ready to pounce.

"Dude, people used to sleep and wake up with the sun man, there were no other lights except fire and candles and whatever. Some people were studying how people lived back in the day and, in reading these old books and journals and stuff, they kept coming across something over and

over that they didn't know what it was. They kept reading about this thing that they were calling 'first sleep' and 'second sleep'. They didn't think much of it at first but then they kept seeing it and finally someone was like, 'What the hell is this *first sleep* and *second sleep* business about?'

So they looked into it and found that, before there was electricity, people got up when the sun came up and went to sleep when the sun went down because that was the only real light there was so our bodies were programed to go to sleep when it got dark and wake up when it got light. Evolution, right? But sometimes in the year, there is more daytime than nighttime. So, when there was more nighttime than people needed, they would go to sleep when the sun went down, that was the first sleep. But then, at like 1 or 2 in the morning, they would wake up and stay awake for a couple hours, they would read or bang their wives or do whatever, then they would go back to sleep for the second sleep. Then they would get up for good when the sun came up and start their days. Those were simpler times."

"Damn, that does seem like a simpler time. I'd like to have lived back then." Fooky says.

"Well, hang on there Biggie, think about the crazy stuff they had to deal with." I say. "They had to be way more reliant on themselves for everything. They had to grow anything they ever wanted to eat, if they had a bad year, if it was too cold, too hot, not enough rain, whatever, they were effed with a capital F. If someone got sick, they probably died. It's why we say, 'Bless you.' when you sneeze."

"What?" Josh asks skeptically, "Why?"

"Oh, there are a couple different theories." I'm saying. "One is that if you got sick back in the day, and sneezed, you were probably going to die."

"Yeah, well, no shit." He says as if he knew that, but it was so simple it wasn't worth bringing up.

"Think about the dust bowl and the stock market crash of 1929, and that was after electricity, people were starting to have a somewhat high standard of living. Then one day in 1929 I think, the stock market crashed, and, in an instant, billions of dollars just vanished into thin air. That same year, in the southwest especially, the summer was brutal, and it didn't rain as much as it should have for a few years. People were screwed.

The crazy part was, back then, people didn't even know how or why they were screwed they just knew that they were screwed. They didn't watch the news to tell them that the stock market crashed, and that people had lost everything they had in an instant. Dudes were jumping out of windows and stuff, they didn't know how to go home and tell their families that they just lost everything they ever had, everything they had been working for.

Think about even a couple years ago, and not having a cell phone, like you were just saying, back then, in the '20's, I read about these hobos who used to be able to just walk up to a house and ask for food and people would straight up give them food, it was a thing back then, people were much more generous when everything was local. Then all of a sudden, they were being turned away because the flippin' people were cooking their dogs and cats to eat, no one had any food, and nobody knew why. Those hobos didn't read the newspaper or watch the news, they just knew that all of a sudden, no one had jack crap. It was complete chaos."

Josh White comes back from the bathroom wiping his nose and immediately starts arguing. "Dude, what are you guys even talking about?" His tone is more than just a little bit accusatory.

"Josh, we're just talking about the stock market crash of 1929 and how badly it screwed the country." I say calmly.

"You don't have any evidence for that. If you can't cite the study…"

"Josh, read a book. Like *a* book, seriously, any book. Please." I plead.

Ginger walks by, sipping on a fruity drink, still wearing the red scarf and dark sunglasses. Rosie is walking by about a yard behind her and fake whispers to me with her hand on one side of her mouth, "Get that girl some conditioner."

"Oh my god, Dude, did you just see that?" I ask Fooky.

"Yeah Dude." He says shrugging his shoulders, "She gives love a bad name?"

"Hey!" I snap.

"What? I can quote shitty song lyrics too." He says, laughing.

"Gosh damn Dude, she is such a B-word." I say, somewhat flabbergasted.

"Yeah Dude, I hear you." He says, dismissively.

"No Dude, I don't think you understand." I say, setting down my beer next to my margarita.

"What then Dude, what the fuck?" He asks.

"Dude." I start, "She is such a ball twisting, hair bending, boner killing, cock churning B-word that words cannot properly describe. I remember going on quite a rant about another girl who I considered…oh, let's say was left to center on the B-word-o-meter."

"Yeah man, I really don't dig her either." He says.

"Fooky, I don't think you are hearing me correctly." I say, holding up a hand, then another.

"Sorry Schultz, I'm trying to work on my buzz here." He says, waving a dismissive arm. "I'm not trying to hear a sermon right now, or whatever they call it in Jew."

"All I'm saying is that this brand of B-word runs deep. Still water runs deep man. This is not just your average, everyday nagging broad. Do you know anything about her, like, before she got together with Spearman?" I ask, bringing the heat.

"Dude, I really don't give a fuck." He says, finishing his drink.

"Fook, I really think I might know what's going on there." I say.

"Schultz, you took two psychology classes and you think you're fucking Sigmund Freud?" Josh says.

"Hear me out." I say, holding up an index finger to estow an authority which I think I've earned. "And piss off, by the way, but here is my analysis: She's dangerous." I start, which is met with immediate negative feedback.

"Dude, chill out." Josh interrupts.

"Schultz, she's fucking hot." Fook argues as if that is some kind of excuse for being a wretched human being.

"Hey!" I say, holding up a stern hand. "What she is doing right now, what she has been up to for like…a long time now, is not good, Man. It ain't no good. Did she used to be really chubby or something?"

"Yeah Schultzy, I heard you the first time." Fooky says, cutting out a fat line of coke for himself and snorting it loudly.

"She's messed up." I continue, shaking my head. "It sounds like a typical fat girl syndrome to me. I think she was not only a mere fat girl amongst other fat girls. No. She was *the* fat girl. She was singled out and horribly ostracized by her peers. Her High School years must have been ab-

solute torture, riddled with bullying of the highest order followed by some kind of climax, a tipping point where she decided that she would take no more. She must have gone completely militant in her training to shed the fat girl skin, like something out of *Terminator 2* when Sarah Connor was doing one armed pull-ups in her cell. She didn't go to school with us, did she?"

"No Dude, she went to North." Fook says, annoyed.

"O.K., well, there you go then." I say. "That's what I'm saying, Dude. I think she's fighting this battle with herself, this battle that's going on inside her head, Man, it's biblically fierce! This battle will end in nothing but carnage for those she sees as her enemies."

"Well, who are her enemies?" Barnes asks, grabbing his crotch and sniffing, shuffling in his seat.

"All of us. All of humankind!" I say, thinking about how to make that statement more presentable. "She is mad at anyone who wasn't *that* kid. Though we've all been *that* kid at some point. She takes it ultra-personal, and we all have to pay. She has an emptiness in her soul that can't be filled, it's insatiable. Just like her hunger for Ho-Ho's was as a child, she's traded one addiction for another. Her appetite for revenge is all that drives her now. For real Dude."

"Schultz, you're fuckin' tripping, Dude." Josh says.

"Am I?" I ask no one in particular, though I'm throwing vibes in Fooky's direction. "She is trying to make order out of chaos." I say, taking a drag off a Marlboro and blowing it out, then setting my fag down in the ashtray while I focus on my drink and which direction I should steer this conversation. "That's her way of working through this, some girls cut themselves, others sleep around with dudes that Daddy wouldn't approve of. What Rosie is doing now is far more destructive, more sinister…" I'm saying to everyone, anyone.

"Like what, Dude?" Barnes asks, unconvinced.

"I think her resentment now, her anger towards the entire human race runs so deep that she's like Cain from the Bible, like Cain and Abel. She's mad at humanity, mad at God. She's become a wolf, man."

"Why?" Josh asks.

"She's mad at God for the sin of being." I say, my hands shaking. "She's ready to strike down anyone who she deems guilty of being one of the *Beautiful People*."

"Dude, I know what you're saying Schultz," Fooky is saying, setting his fizzy drink down. "I've been with you all along. We've been talking about what a bitch Rosie is for as long as you've had pubes. I guess what I'm asking now is, what do you have to look forward to on the Rosie horizon, what do you see in her future for?"

"Well that's a great question, Fook." I say, stirring my Dandelion and Burdock with my forefinger. "First of all, she's all hot now. She's infiltrated the enemy line, so now she's out for blood. The future? Well, there is zero chance that she won't become one of *those moms.*" I say, sitting up straight, posturing. Making sure everyone is on board with the, *those moms'* bit.

"What would hell be like for her?" Fooky asks, taking this deeper than I was going to go.

"Oh, well it starts with her finding some poor schlub to marry and subsequently murder by means of a 40-year, slow strangulation." I start. "She'll marry a dude who has money but is fat and ugly, they'll have kids that look just like him. She'll be ashamed of them, especially the daughter." I'm saying, "Then, due to the lack of love, the daughter will end up being all Goth and

do everything she can to piss her off; she'll cut, date black dudes, act out sexually, strip, get into drugs, freebase, prey on younger kids, that kind of thing…"

"Jesus Schultz," Josh interrupts. "You think about this shit too much."

"The husband will become emotionally unavailable the more successful he becomes." I continue.

"What makes you think the husband will be successful if he's such a schlub?" Josh asks. "He sounds like he'd be a loser."

"Good question Joshy poops." I say, "Thanks for trying your hardest to crap on my point though, Cunt. But to answer your question, he'll be successful because he never wants to leave work and go home to his miserable family, so he'll spend 80 hours a week busting his ass on his career because it's nothing compared to what awaits him at home."

"Fair enough." Josh admits with just a dusting of distain.

"He won't care one way or another what a bitch she is, he'll be so completely tuned out; emotionally, sexually, physically, he'll drink too much, probably in secret because she will surely not allow anyone under the influence to be around her precious children."

"Alright Dude, now you're just being a dick." Fook says.

"Oh, I'm not finished." I continue. "So, she'll act out in a million different ways to try to get his attention; she'll fake pregnancies, she'll drink all day long in her white silk bathrobe, take loads of pills, she'll try some lame suicide attempts, desperate cries for help. You know the routine."

"Schultz…" Fooky tries to cut in.

"The husband will eventually figure things out and get his stuff together. He'll stash away some money, start hitting the gym, buy a new suit, a used Porsche 944, probably an automatic, and then leave her for someone younger, hotter, and *way* less of a pain in the ass. By then, she'll be an old 40, worn and haggard. Puffy and pasty from her kidneys starting to shut down. She'll have money. She'll have the most expensive vibrator on the planet, but only then will it begin to dawn on her, it will be the biggest epiphany that Quaaludes ever forgot; That money can't buy happiness."

"Dude…" I hear someone say. I'm oblivious.

"She may try to write in a pathetic attempt to stay relevant. She'll write un-readable romance novels projecting what she doesn't have and will never have. Passion. Love. She's known that for years, but it's all she has now. She'll no doubt drown one day in the shallow end of a backyard, above ground swimming pool that she is also ashamed of. No one will attend her funeral. Not one person. Not her kids, not the ex-husband, not any of the lads she hooked up with at the Corner bar on random weeknights. No one.

The preacher will say, "Here lies Rosie. She surely had a mother, one who no doubt felt something for her at some point along the way if not very early on. She was once a shepherd, no more. She will be missed…" He'll say, removing his bifocals, "I suppose we should pray."

Chapter XXXIII

We leave the BBQ and now Fooky's driving Ginger's car, she's in the front seat and I'm in the back with Lolita. There has been some, let's call it tension, going on all day but now that we've had a bit to drink and the sunlight has had its way with us, we are sort of blatantly fooling around. It's like Ginger isn't even here. Lolita starts by touching my leg, then she walks her fingers over and touches my hand and by the time we get to 1st Capital, we're holding hands like some old married couple and I don't think either of us really care what it looks like.

Fooky looks in the rearview mirror and says, "Jesus you two, get a room."

I laugh that off and Lolita leans over and kisses me on the cheek, intentionally making a loud smooching noise but then licks my cheek before sitting back down. I look at Ginger who is looking at me out of the corner of her eye, shooting fire balls at me. I'm thinking, "Hey, this is *your* friend." Shifting the blame onto her. "This could still be innocent right?" My deflection continues as we blow through a red light.

When we pull up to the house and pile out of the car, Steve the Cuck is sitting on the patio drinking a bottle of water. He stands up as we stumble up the hill to the door and he snaps at Ginger, "Get back in the car Bitch. We're out of here!"

"Ha ha, what's the matter?" Fooky shouts as they peel away. "You don't like your bitch getting fucked by a Jew, you fucking *cuck!*"

We're laughing as we walk up the stairs to the house, me and Lolita are propping each other up while spilling the cocktails from our brandy sifters. She's still wearing my Ray-Ban aviator shades and before we walk through the door she slurs, "Don't worry about her, we're invisible, remember." She pushes me up against the porch rail, licks my face again and grabs my crotch.

I've already forgotten about Ginger and her cuck boyfriend. If Ginger wants to mess around with me right in front of her goofy boyfriend and her hot runaway bestie, who is dying to suck on the General. Whatever. What am I supposed to do here, care?

When we finally make it inside, Curt, Fook, and Dicky are already sitting on the leather couches cutting up lines of coke nine inches long and snorting them through a platinum straw from Things Remembered on the glass Sequoia Coffee Table.

"Dude, did you know that Steve the Cuck was out there?" I ask, causing Lolita to giggle.

"Yeah, he was sitting out there when we got here like 15 minutes ago." Dicky says.

"He looked pissed, Dude." Fooky says with his face in the mirror.

I don't care but now I'm curious, so I ask, "Well did he say anything?"

"Yeah, he said he'd been sitting there for hours waiting for Ginger. I guess she was supposed to pick him up hours ago." Curt explains after doing a monster line.

"So, you just left him out there?" I ask.

"Naw, Curt asked him if he wanted to come in. He said he was cool though." Dicky says.

"No, I didn't." Curt says. "I said, it was cool to wait. I didn't tell him to come in."

"Oh, I guess we didn't." Dicky says, shrugging his shoulders and numbing his gums.

I laugh but a passing thought breezes by that gives me a chill and hints to me that Steve the Cuck has got to be flaming pissed about all of this. Unless he actually is some kind of a legit cuck. I was joking before, but for Eff sake...any red-blooded dude would be frogging pissed about all of this. Even if you only knew half of what was going on, if this doesn't send shock waves through your veins, I don't know, maybe he has his own thing going on on the side and he can't be bothered about his crazy ass bitch. That doesn't seem to be the case though. What does he think is going on? Does he have any clue?

Lolita is sitting next to me, rubbing my leg while Dicky and I are going over some songs for the big gig at Cooper's this weekend. Curt is sitting on a bar stool keeping a decent beat on the bongos wearing steel toed boots, blue jeans from The Gap and a leather necklace with a shark tooth medallion.

"Dude, we've only got a few days." Dicky says after I screw up the lead to *Santeria* by Sublime. "We still gotta write one more song."

"Right!" I say, pushing Lolita's hand off my lap, really trying to focus. "So, what do we have?"

Dicky lights a cigarette and holds up the notebook with all our songs in it and says, "Well, let's see, we got; *Alison*, Schultz, you gotta play lead on that, I'll sing. *Wonderwall*, that's an acoustic special for both of us. Curt, the drums are easy on that one, just keep a beat. *Wandering Fool*, we need to seriously work on that Schultz, for real, Dude. *Dead Flowers* is ready..." He's flipping the page in the notebook, cigarette still between his lips, smoke filling his eyes causing him to squint. "So...it looks like we just need one more."

"Chu Hi." I say. "That song I wrote the other day. It's solid."

"Meh, that song always sounds good in the moment but sounds like shit if we're not drunk." Dicky says.

While we're going through *Don't Look Back in Anger,* Lolita's hand slides up my thigh and she starts rubbing The General. Dicky just laughs and keeps playing. She leans over and starts sucking on my ear lobe and licking my cheek making it impossible to focus. She's breathing heavily in my ear and it's really effing hot. Finally, she whispers, "I want you to fuck me. I need to feel you inside me." She's looking at me with hungry eyes that go from naughty to innocent and back again with every blink, showing me her menu.

She stands up, grabs my hand and leads me into my bedroom. "I just gotta piss really quick." I shout back into the living room. "I'll be right ba..."

As soon as she shuts the bedroom door behind us, she pushes me up against the wall and slams into me, shoving her tongue deep in my mouth. She's already moaning and pressing her body against me aggressively. My hands quickly move down her back and grope her ass which is tight as hell as she's grinding her pone against my crotch. I pull up her sundress and caress her ass cheeks through her pink, nylon panties.

She rips my blue Aloha shirt off by the buttons and starts flicking my nipples with her tongue, she takes my hand and moves it from her firm ass around to the front where her pone is already

dripping wet. I use my whole hand to rub between her legs as she lifts her left leg and, with no regard for the noises we're making, stomps the wall with her foot repeatedly.

"Oh God!" She shouts, grinding her pussy against my hand before dropping to her knees. Panting wildly, she's almost growling. She looks up at me with devil eyes and a wide-open mouth. She undoes my Harley belt and pulls my Colores of Bennington jeans down around my ankles. When she sees the General bulging out of my hot pink boxer/briefs from H & M, she looks at it and then looks up at me again and gives out a mischievous laugh.

"Oh my God." She says, stroking the full length of my dick like the toys that she never got for Christmas. She's gagging as she tries to take in as much as she can. I'm holding her hair back and moving along with her bobbing head. She comes up for breath and saliva strings still connect her lips to my cock, she's not breaking eye contact like we're engaged in a staring contest that I have no problem losing.

She is really good at this, a very talented young lady. I never really thought about why they call it a *hummer* before, but now I get it. I'm rubbing her tits and she is moaning to the point of orgasm with my dick sliding in and out of her mouth until she takes a short pause to pull her sundress up over her head. She shakes her hair out and then gets back to sucking, bobbing her head back and forth like some kind of retarded pigeon.

"Oh yeah." She's saying as she uses both hands to stroke my cock like a flippin' Solo Flex machine, that is so wet from her spit that there is no friction. The look in her eyes are screaming that she wants this more than she has ever wanted anything in her short little, unloved and abandoned life. She stands up and turns around, pressing her ass and body against me urgently. Through her pink nylon panties, she is grinding on my dick with her arms wrapped around my neck, my hands massaging her tight ass, little titties. *Oh, Oh, Oh...* She is shouting in short, staccato bursts. My dick is as hard as Mandarin Chinese grammar and it's getting slippery rubbing against her pussy that is bleeding through her panties.

She starts to urge my thighs backward towards the bed, so I pull up my pink boxer/briefs, so I don't trip over them. Then, pushing me down on my firm, king-sized bed and crawling on top of me, Lolita is grinding her pussy against my rock-solid dork through my underwear. She's kissing me passionately on the mouth when she takes her right breast and releases it from her lace tank top. I tear my mouth away from her mouth and start to suck on her nipple, flicking my tongue at it slowly, driving her crazy. She's alternating between tongue kisses and nipple sucks. I move my hands down to her ass and give her bare cheeks a quick smack that will definitely leave a substantial mark.

She cuts me off and licks her way slowly down to my chin, then my chest, hitting both nipples along the way, onto my belly-button where she spends a considerable amount of time tickling me with her wet tongue before finally biting at the leather strap of my leather Harley belt and pulling my jeans down to my ankles with her teeth, snarling like a rabid dog. She pulls my jeans all the way off with a mischievous grin until I'm down to my pink boxer-briefs and she's kissing The General seductively through them as I hold her hair back so I can see her face while she's playing the role of *horny girl next door* to perfection.

She peels back my underwear, unleashing the General once again and she immediately grabs hold of it and licks the shaft from the base up slowly to the head where she starts kissing it passionately. She's looking at me hard in the eyes while she takes short pops on the head and then

takes deep breaths, all the while, caressing my cock and balls with her hand. She goes down to the jewels and, after a quick licking which almost makes me cum, she takes my right ball into her mouth and hums eagerly. She does the same to the left and I'm going crazy.

She flips her hair back and then starts going to town on my dick again, this time taking it all in, harder and faster this time. I give her a subtle nudge to sit up and she does, giving her breasts a brief massage and I pinch her nipples hard enough to cause her to squeal. I sit up and move my hand up and down her thigh as she maneuvers to straddle me. We kiss passionately for a minute while I rub her firm tits. She pushes me down on the bed and starts grinding on top of me through her pink satin panties which are still on. She takes my hands and moves them up to her breasts and I start massaging them while she moves back and forth on top of me, her head tilted back all the way, speaking in tongues.

My hands are on her hips, keeping up with her pace as she grinds on my cock. I can feel her panties getting soaking wet as she goes faster, harder. Leveraging her hands on my shoulders. She leans back and starts rubbing my dick with her hand while she's rocking back and forth with her dripping pussy. She moves her panties to the side and is now rubbing her raw pussy lips against my dick. I stick my right thumb in her vagina, and she starts panting heavily.

After a small climax, she stops, stands up over me and takes off her pink panties and then sits on my face. I shove my tongue into her tight, nicely trimmed pussy and start humming the ABC's. Her thigh muscles are flexing and un-flexing around my neck and she's bucking like an unbroken horse. She stops, rolls off of my face, and positions herself over The General. She flips her hair back again and gives me a naughty lip bite/ pouty face combination before easing herself down the shaft of my cock with a relieved sigh. She starts off strong -bouncing- giving quite the performance, then she leans back and is holding my ankles, grinding my cock around inside of her.

I'm rubbing her tits and going through all 50 states and their capitals in my head to keep from cumming too soon but almost nut anyway when I get stuck on *Montpelier*. Lolita is biting her lip trying not to scream and frothing at the mouth while bouncing up and down on my cock. This can't possibly last much longer. I reach around and put my middle finger in her ass hole causing her to seize violently. She does the same and is now shaking on top of me while shouting the filthiest profanities that overrides the slapping sound of her ass coming down on my lap.

My legs start to shiver, and I give her ass a tight pinch that signals to her that I'm about to blow this load, so she gets up off of me, kneels down and, with her mouth and hand, starts jerking me off. I grab her by the pig tails and am slamming her head into my cock until I start to cum and I release her head and just as she comes up for breath, with tears in her eyes, she's gagging, I cum in her mouth and then on her face, topping off on her eyes because, for some reason I felt like it.

Chapter XXXIV

I wake up to my alarm shouting something about it being 9:00. I look around and when I see that Lolita is still lying on my king-sized bed sucking her thumb and rubbing her lip with her forefinger that I assume she refers to as her *pointer finger*, all the memories come rushing back. As late as I'm going to be, I can't just leave her there with her ass looking the way it does so I start rubbing my nerd on her ass then start fucking her through her pink underwear and finish by beating off and nutting on her satin panties.

I have classes today that I would love to skip but I can't. Since the Caddy got totaled, Ginger and Steve the Cuck have been dropping off her car so I can use it all day but after last night, that's probably not going to happen. I untie Lolita from my nightstand and call her a cab. As I'm shutting the door behind me, she turns around from the backseat of the taxi and gives an innocent wave. Her eyes are telling a sad story that doesn't have a happy ending.

Today I have 3 classes, the first class is about Russia and the few times that we as a nation, and as a world really, were moments away from nuclear holocaust because of those crazy fuckers. I swear, the more I learn about the Russians the more I'm convinced that they are the craziest *white* people on the planet. The first time was during the Cold War when both sides were posturing our nuclear weapons towards each other.

We both had our hands on the button but more specifically, we each had a single guy, respectively with their hands on the button. Both guys, one in the U. S., one in Russia, sat in a room and waited for the *GO* order. In Russia's case at least, this guy had direct orders to push that button, no questions asked, if the order came down. This was communist Russia, you did not defy an order, no matter what. So, one day, the order comes down, "Go." or however you say *go* in Russian.

This guy knew what that meant, this is what he must have sat in his little Russian room and thought about all day, every day. That if the order came, he was going to have to push that button and that the world as we know it would never be the same again. He knew what mutually assured destruction, *MAD*, meant. But when the order came, he balked, he didn't push the button right away. Now he knew that this would mean certain death for him, there was no doubt about that, but he balked anyway. Those seconds must have seemed like hours as he sat there with his fingertips shaking above the button, absolute chaos, but something must have told him to at least wait, give it a second. Sure enough, about a minute later, he got a second order, "False alarm. Don't push the button." Oh God, that guy must have gone home that night and just drowned himself in Vodka.

Another time was the Cuban missile crisis. That was when Kennedy had spy planes fly over Cuba, who were in bed with the Russians, and took pictures of Russian missiles stocked up there, 90 miles from Florida. Things got tense when one of the spy planes was shot down and the pilot was killed. This was the red line that Kennedy told the blood thirsty Generals he would not let Russia cross. Now it happened. They accused us of spying and flying where we weren't supposed to be, and we accused them of having the missiles that they said didn't exist. Well, one thing led to another and the next thing you know, Russia has war ships full of nuclear missiles headed for Cuba and a freaking Mexican stand-off starts.

Kennedy, this young Democrat, whose Generals were all itching for a good war with the Ruskies anyway, had to keep them from starting crap just because that's what they did, but without looking weak to the Russians because he's straight up telling them, ordering them to turn the ships around and head back to Moscow. Things went from tense to utterly insane the closer the Russians ships got to Cuba. Absolute chaos in the hearts and minds of all Americans, Russian's too, most likely. And even more likely, the whole world. So, the Russian ships are full steam ahead towards Cuba, Kennedy is ordering them to turn around and go home. They're like, "Screw you, what are you going to do?" and then, at the last minute, the last frickin' second, kids are doing nuke drills where they got under their desks at school, the Ruskies turn around. That was so close, one wrong move on anyone's part, anyone, one little mistake and the course of human history would have been changed forever.

The last one was one that I'd never even heard of, and that was the day President Reagan was shot. That day, Russia was actually planning on invading Poland but after hearing the news about Reagan, they, by the early eighties, I suppose had enough sense to realize that the U.S. would

have thought that that was too much of a coincidence and blame Russia. They pushed the pause button on that invasion even though it had nothing to do with them, it had to do with John Hinkley Jr.'s insane obsession with Jodi Foster. So, a crazy celebrity stalker inadvertently stopped an international nuclear war.

We are moshing around this planet on ice thin enough to cut out lines of coke on. Try as we may to add a bit of order to our lives, in our world, but we are always either the white dot in the black serpent of chaos in the Yen and Yang symbol, that thin sheet of order among the chaos. Either that or we are the black dot in the white, pushing things to the limits, taking that next step into the unknown. Reaching into the darkness of an empty room and flipping the switch.

It's 2001 now, it's been 55 years since we dropped the Atomic bomb on Japan that leveled two cities. The haunting scene of a nuclear blast so strong that human shadows were imprinted on the sidewalks after the victims were completely eviscerated from existence. A brother carries his sister on his back to safety, her skin melting from her bones, her eyeball falls out of its socket. The brother tries to put it back in but the orbital socket in the skull is so warped that repair is impossible. The sister dies on his back, her flesh melted onto his clothing. Her name was Tomoko.

Since then other countries have gotten atomic capabilities, more are to come. If even one fraction of an atomic bomb were to go off anywhere near a large city like say, New York it would be devastating. More lives could be lost in minutes than in all the wars we've fought combined. Nothing would be the same after that, life would go on, but it would be a different world than the one we know, unrecognizable.

My next class is Psychology 301. Morality. Professor Patterson, a southern gentleman of African descent, a dry sense of humor and a voice like Kermit the Frog is explaining that feeling a sense of morality, moral feeling, who we care about depends on a few seemingly arbitrary factors. Of course, we care more about our own kids than other random kids. Slightly less obviously though, we favor our own group over other groups. The thing is, we are all a member of many groups; man, woman, student, teacher, black, white, whatever.

Showing favor towards people in your group is a human thing and defining who is in your group can be extremely random, it can literally be as easy as flipping a coin. If you take 100 people and everyone flips a coin and you separate the heads from the tails, the heads will identify and sympathize with the heads and the tails will sympathize with the tails. The heads will even start to think more favorably towards other heads over tails.

Taken to an even further extreme, there was the social experiment called the *Robber's Cave* where there was a camp of young boys, all middle class, whiteish, same age boys. They separated the boys into two cabins, and they assigned leaders. The Eagles and the Rattlers. They developed their own unique cultures, in competition, the in-group intensity grew. They cared about their own group way more than the other group and started assigning random, negative stereotypes to the opposite camp. Cultures began to emerge. The Eagles were clean cut and didn't swear, they saw the Rattlers as rugged and tough, dirty. And vice versa.

Things took a turn for the violent though when, in competition, they would fight, burn each other's flags and swear at each other. They created two different warring cultures so the guy running the experiment had to figure out how to make peace, how to make them friends again. They held peace talks, two reps from each team talked. That failed. The two boys were ostracized as treasonous. Instead of group competition, they would compete as individuals. That also failed.

Shared meals turned into food fights. Shared movies, fights. Fireworks, miserable fail. The guy brought a priest in to talk about brotherly love. Interestingly enough, the boys took away, "Yes, I should love my neighbor…my fellow *Eagle*!" All attempts at peace failed.

Finally, the guy told the kids that the water line to the camp was cut and they all had to defend the camp. He introduced a goal everyone had to share, a common enemy. Finally, the boys put aside their group think and worked *together*. The moral of this tale is, in order to bring together all the people fighting in the country or the world, to stop all the; religious, political, racial, class warfare is to be attacked by an outside force.

Obviously, that's not likely having the giant military that we have here in the U.S. and god forbid, something that grave would fall upon us, the bright side would be that it could bring us together. Similarly, the only way to bring together all the warring countries and religions of this planet, is an Alien attack. An attack from an outside force, from abroad. We haven't had an attack on U.S. soil since the civil war. I wonder what that would even look like. Is it even possible?

My third class is another Psychology class about when things go wrong: Mental Illness. Dr. Shapiro talked about schizophrenia and how it can be genetic. I started tripping because my older brother, Ryan is paranoid schizophrenic. He started talking about how if you have a twin sibling that has schizophrenia that you have a 50% chance of being crazy yourself. That put my mind about half at ease because that suggests that it is a 50/50 split between nature vs. nurture. If it was all nature, then a twin's chance of becoming nuts if your twin is schizo would be 100%. Before I was finished wiping that voice of optimism from my head, he took another turn when he said that an early childhood trauma could spark the illness.

Was the early childhood trauma of our dad leaving us when I was 7 and he was 13 enough to trigger schizophrenia in him? Was it the scene when my 13-year-old brother begged our dad to not leave us and our poor mother and two younger brothers and sisters? Begged and pleaded, sobbing, tugging at his packed suitcase to not leave the family forever. Not leave for a plush apartment in the city off of Delmar and Washington, not jet off across the country and move to Florida with the rest of the deadbeat dads, no his bags were packed and there was a one way ticket to Brazil where he was off to start a new family that he wasn't going to be there for.

Was that enough to set off the schizophrenia in my brother? Perhaps. Fast forward to a year later, I remember him telling me the story of when he was about 14-years-old in a car full of friends and, when they got pulled over by the cops with a sheet full of acid, he offered to fall on that grenade and swallow the whole 100 hits to keep his friends out of trouble. He told me on more than one occasion that he has never come down from that trip.

"Little brother," He'd say with that bat-shit crazy look in his eye, "I've been tripping for five years straight." Then he would tell me how bad-ass Bruce Lee was and how he could punch me within a 1/2 inch in front of my face without making contact like, three times in a row. Also, he'd ask me how a match could burn twice…then he'd light a match, count that as once, then blow it out, look at me for a reaction, when he was satisfied with my seven-year-old confusion, he would touch the match to my forearm. As my confusion turned to disbelief, turned to torture, he would exclaim proudly, "See, it burned twice."

Good one you psychopath. That could be the trauma that sent me over the edge to being the chaotic mess that I am today, why I do the things I do. Something that was never lost on me when we used to eat acid for breakfast and alternate between hallucinogenic drugs day to day to

avoid the tolerance build up that is inevitable when you live your life skipping from trip to trip like we used to do back in the day. Somewhere floating around in my twisted little mind was always the fear that I would never come down from this.

Then Dr. Shapiro started talking about a bizarre case that took place in France back in the early 20th century called *The Crimes of the Papin Sisters* that blew my ever-loving mind.

In the French city of Le Mans back in 1933, two peasant sisters named Christine, 27 and Lea, 21 Papin were working as maids for a rich family named Lancelin. They had worked at the Lancelin manner for six years. Everything was going smoothly until one evening on February 2nd when Mr. Lancelin came home and the door was locked. He knocked on the door, no one answered. He saw a light on from inside so he called the police. The police became alarmed and sent three officers to go check it out. They pushed the door open. Silence.

Their flashlights revealed a very nice house, expensive furniture, etc.... They climbed the dark staircase lit only by their flashlights and at the top of the staircase saw a round object. They bent down to get a closer look and were horrified to find an *eyeball*. Terror! They inspected the rest of the house and found two bodies, faces plumaged, lacerations on the legs. Eyes gouged out. They thought that the killer may still be in the house.

They called for the Sergent and he told the two young cops to stay back. They moved carefully from room to room. The attic was empty, the Iron was left on the ironing board, there was work left undone. They searched the entire house until there was only one room left. They knocked on the door, nothing. They tried to open it; it was locked. The question arose, where were the maids?

"They might be all dead in there." The first cop said.

"We need a locksmith right away." Said the second cop.

They waited there with their ears glued to the door, there was no sound. Hours passed until the locksmith came. When the lock was finally picked, they barged into the small bedroom where horror gave way to incomprehension. There were the two maids cuddling together on the bed in their night robes. It was the Pepin sisters. *What?!*

"We were expecting you." Christine, the older sister said.

Next to the bed was a candle, a bloody sledgehammer with bits of hair stuck to it, and a blood-stained knife.

"It was self-defense." Christine declared.

"Get up!" Said the sergeant.

"Fuck off, I'll get up if I want to." Said Christine.

The sergeant went to question Lea but with one glance from Christine, her older sister she shut down and declared, "I am deaf and dumb."

"Take them away." The sergeant demanded.

The crime went down like this; The Mom's body was found face down, her right arm extended, her right hand covered in blood. Some of her hair was glued to it. Deep wounds could be seen on the gluteus and her calves were severely lacerated. The daughter was on her back, legs spread apart. Only her right foot had a shoe on. The right side of her face and skull were completely smashed in. The eyes removed; the mouth was no longer recognizable. Teeth were projected all around the room. The detached eye found at the top of the staircase, away from the body. Another found beneath the mother's body after it was removed from the orbital socket. Both women

had their dresses lifted up over their waists and their knickers pulled down. Blood splattered all over the room, on the walls and on the ceiling.

The confession went like this: The sisters said, quote: "The iron had broken, twice. When Mrs. and Ms. Lancelin saw this, they approached us and attacked us. She smacked me on the cheek. I jumped on her and tore her eyes out. My sister did the same. I went downstairs to the kitchen to get the hammer and the knife. When I went back upstairs, the two ladies were still squirming around on the floor, screaming and crying though they had no eyes. I came back in the room and smashed their heads in with the hammer and pot. Me and my sister swapped instruments several times. We cut the legs, pulled their dresses up and pulled their underpants down and shoved the hammer into their vaginas. When they were dead, we washed our hands to get the blood off and then took the hammer and knife into the bedroom and locked the door to wait for the police to come." End quote.

The Papin sisters came from a troubled family in Le Mans, France. Their mother was Clemence Derre and their father was Gustave Papin. Although rumors were going around town that Clemence was having an affair with her boss, Gustave loved her. In October 1901, when Clemence became pregnant Gustave married her even though his parents strongly opposed the wedding and accused Clemence of being a "scheming woman".

After the wedding, Clemence gave birth to Annabelle, her first daughter. Clemente was distant and cold to her daughter and husband and Gustave could never be sure if the child was actually his. He tried to catch Clemence and her boss together by surprising the two, but he failed to get solid evidence so instead he took a job in another town and moved the family away. Clemente put up a fight and threatened to kill herself and the baby but ultimately moved away with her husband and baby daughter. She got pregnant again and tried to divorce but realized that no one else would want a pregnant, married woman so she gave up. She had Christine but was still miserable and often complained that she hated taking care of children.

She gave Christine to her sister who took care of her for seven happy years. Then Clemence had Lea and went back to being more miserable than ever. Gustave couldn't take it anymore and started drinking heavily so all three girls were sent to live in an orphanage. The oldest, Annebelle became a nun and the two younger sisters, Christine and Lea became…crazy.

The two sisters started working for the Lanceline family and were model employees for six years though the Lancelines were very strict. They put gloves on to check for dust. They only gave the sisters a two hour break a day but instead of going out and enjoying the day, they went in their rooms and closed the door.

After being evaluated by every doctor in France, the trial began, and it was a media frenzy. Everyone expected the sisters to be monsters but when they came in the court room, they were timid and silent. They admitted to everything but just before sentencing, Dr. Doom took the stand. He said that he knew the guilty person's identity, and everyone went crazy. Who was it?

On the stand, Dr. Doom revealed his theory. Everyone was waiting with bated breath. Finally, he came out with his proposal that the guilty party was not Christine, and it was not Lea. The guilty party was a 3rd party! Silence fell on the courtroom; all eyes were on Dr. Doom. The 3rd culprit was the couple formed by Christine and Lea. *Twin Delirium.* He concluded by saying, "I cannot say that they acted in a fit of madness. When the sisters were together, their chemistry made them manic, when apart, they simply went mad."

The legal experts could not proclaim that they were normal. They were both sentenced to prison to be served separately. The bond between them broke and they both went crazy without each other. Christine was finally moved to a mental hospital where she refused to eat or drink anything and attempted suicide several times but, in a fit of madness she called for a Judge where she offered a shocking second confession.

Quote: "I haven't told you the whole truth. She had not provoked me. I was overcome by a nervous fit. She walked in on us…together. I first knocked her down with the pitcher. Then her daughter came in and I knocked her out too. I knocked her down and tore her eyes out. My sister walked in and saw what was happening. The daughter was about to get up and Lea threw herself onto her. I told her to tear her eyes out. Then I gave her the pitcher to smash her head with. Then I went down to get a knife and a hammer to slaughter them with." End quote.

After that, the judge started asking her questions, but she only answered with one sentence. One sentence that she repeated over and over again until she finally starved herself to death in a dark, insect infested padded room. That sentence was quote, "No one on this Earth will ever know me like my sister." End quote.

Chapter XXXV

My mind keeps playing that story over and over in my head as I walk past the old brick and cobblestone buildings of Lindenwood University with ivy growing up the sides, along the newly paved, tar pathways with the names of all the alumni and donors engraved into them. The sun is shining brightly on giant oak trees with all their shade and security looming over like a protective guardian and their giant autumn leaves of yellow and gold that swirl down in the frosty breeze from high above landing peacefully along the pristinely landscaped lawns where undergraduates toss frisbees back and forth and subtly discuss the deconstruction of western civilization as the squirrels that inhabit the grounds idly scamper with the arrogance of a Middle Eastern Imam, casually ambling their acorns to and fro with no sense of urgency or danger. The green grasses, all landscaped to perfection of Lindenwood University to where the pathway ends. Then I stand at the foot of 1st Capital Dr. and watch the cars speed past.

A hot blond wearing dark sunglasses and a green tank-top with a tattoo sleeve, decent face, drives past in a newly waxed Mazda Maida T-top listening to *The Sign* by Ace of Base at a high volume. A rusty haired man with a graying goat-T wearing a denim cut off work shirt, stained with oil and automobile semen putters by in a baby blue Ford pick-up truck that has long since past its prime, held together with chewing tobacco and electrical tape.

When the sea parts, I cross 1st Capital into my neighborhood. I'm wearing Army green cotton trousers from Canali with a matching belt from Rag & Bone, grey ankle high socks from Uniqlo and beige suede loafers from Johnston & Murphy. My denim button down shirt from Tommy Hilfiger is untucked and my sleeves are unbuttoned but not rolled up. It's unseasonably cold so

I'm also wearing a brown suede jacket from J. Crew. I take my Ray-Ban tortious shell sunglasses out of my brown leather Alexander Olch shoulder bag and put them on before I step foot onto Pal-Terris St.

As I walk up the dark, pot-hole filled street, past all the run down duplexes, the wild children running the streets, the dilapidated houses with plywood boarding up the windows, the spray paint, the graffiti, the cars on cinderblocks, the broken 40's, the trash, the people out making the best of it all. The smell of rust in the air, the sound of shitty music coming from the shitty radios of shitty cars and shitty babies crying all around.

The lesson about The Palin Sisters still haunts me with visions of Twin Delirium, lesbian incest, eyeballs rolling around a French bourgeoisie mansion, love, while Pink Floyd's *Thin Ice* is just starting to play in my head as clear as if it were playing on the radio.

Momma loves her baby,
Daddy loves you too
The sea may look warm to you baby,
The sky may look blue
but...
Don't be surprised when a crack in the ice
Appears under your feet
You slip out of your depth and out of your mind
With your fear flowing out behind you
As you crawl for thin ice

We really are just all walking around this life on thin ice with giant sea creatures circling just below the surface waiting to devour us. It's a tale as old as time, Jesus spoke about it when he told the parable of the foolish man who built his house of straw and the wise man who built his house out of stone. More psychological than theological. When the storm comes, it will be the man who built his house upon the rock that will not perish or whatever. He didn't say *if* the storm comes, but *when* the storm comes. It's the same as The Three Little Pigs story, the wolf, the dragon of chaos comes for all of us. The question is, how prepared will we be when the wolf comes a knockin'?

It's just like that chick, Chandra Levy. She was doing all the right things, making all the right moves, moving up the ladder, probably sleeping her way to the top, not judging, just a theory, and she ends up dead. The storm is coming for us, all we can do is be prepared for when it comes and pray it doesn't kill us.

Just as I'm wrapping up this train of thought I walk up the stairs to our front porch, put my key in the lock to open my front door, I pause and turn around to look at the park and sniff the BBQ that is coming from all around. I push the door open and...what in the ever-loving mother of all effing goddamn fucks is this? What in the absolute fuck is this motherfucking shit right here that I'm supposed to be fucking looking at right now? My house, what the stinky ass-fuck happened to my house. It's trashed!!

The marble and mirror coffee table is flipped over, the pillows are all cut up and cotton is everywhere like Christmas tinsel. My guitar, I almost have a heart attack when I see my guitar,

it's broken in half. Half of it is smashed into the 60-inch, flat screen TV and the other half is smashed into my Fender amp. The green felt pool table is completely stripped and torn up and the original Jake Rosen painting, *The World Trade Center at Night* was set on fire and is a heap of ashes on the floor behind the bar. *Fuck you!* is written on the mirror in blood red lipstick, the Baccarat Harcourt Abysse crystal ashtray is smashed into a thousand pieces, and our black leather, Armani couches are torn to shreds, fine Italian cotton is scattered all around.

What devil, what scoundrel is responsible for this villainy? One of Curt's disgruntled drug customers? Iain the Irish drug lord come to get his revenge? Someone trying to steal Curt's stash. I'm dizzy, I put my hand on my head, turn around and my question is answered when I see, in dripping red spray paint, graffitied on our wall reads, in all capital letters, *DON'T STICK YOUR DICK IN MY FRIENDS!!* Two exclamation marks with a smiley under the two dots.

Oh, shit. Ginger! What did that little runaway do, go right over and tell her? Maybe she just assumed. Maybe she tortured the poor girl with a blow torch and rusty pliers until she spilled every last detail. Who knows these things?

I'm pacing the floor when Dicky gets home and is like "Whoa!! What in the fuck Schultz?!"

Then Curt gets home and completely loses his shit, not utilizing his anger management skills even a little bit. "Dude, what the fuck did I tell you!?" He's shouting, level 11 ½. "That bitch is fucking nuts. I've been saying it this whole fucking time, have I not? Schultz, and you too Dicky, I fucking told both you motherfuckers to stay away from all of those crazy fuckers and now look, our fucking house is trashed and all our stuff is fucked!"

The boy's sort of look at me and I'm like, "What dude, like you two pones wouldn't have hit that last night."

"Fair enough." Curt concedes.

Then Dicky says, "Well what the fuck are we going to do, we got our gig coming up?"

"Balls, I don't know." I say, I'm rubbing my face with both hands.

"Damn, what the fuck are we going to do?" He repeats.

"I don't know, Man. We can't give up; I know that much. When the going gets tough, the tough get going." I'm saying with as much confidence as I can muster.

Dicky says, "No Dude, I mean what can we do right now? What is our move right here, right now?"

"I don't know Dude, let's clean this place up." Curt says.

I fill a trash bag with cut up satin pillows and cotton and take it out to the back. When I walk back into the living room, Valerie and Blair are standing in the living room soaking in everything. A panic oozes its way through me that is utterly indescribable.

Dicky is talking to them with a straight face, which is never good, "Yeah, this chick I met... Her name was uh, Thel...Thelma. Yeah, Thelma was her name. Yeah, we hooked up a couple times, ya' know. And she had this friend, her name was uh… Louise and, you know how I do it. I hooked up with Thelma and then I went out with Louise and I hooked up with her too. I know I shouldn't have, I just...I just did it anyway. I'm a real fuckin' ass hole. I'm ashamed. Girls, I'm really ashamed of myself. I think I'm gonna see someone about this, like a therapist or something. I need a drink, girls, can I get you one? How 'bout some coke?"

I can see they're not buying it. Valerie isn't buying it. Blair sits down in the tan Lazy Boy, but Valerie is just standing there, her eyes welling up with tears. Staring at the writing on the wall, *"Don't stick your dick in my friends!!"*

Pause.

"Who is she?" Valerie asks me blankly, void of emotion. "Who are they?"

Another pause.

"Uh, well…". I'm stammering. "Dicky, what did you say their names were, Thelma and uh… Louise?" I try but can't pull off. I don't have it.

"I'm uh," She sniffs, wiping away a solitary tear. "I actually am trying to have a conversation with you." She does one of those laughs that means the opposite of a laugh. "I'm trying to see if you are capable of having a human conversation about what is really going on here. I'm trying to gauge how much humanity is still left in you." She's saying, wearing an orange sundress from The Buckle, faded blue jean shorts from the Goodwill, her white scarf and a stainless steel, Daisy pinky ring. "Are you even capable of leveling with me or are you so far gone that you can't even admit to yourself how far gone you are."

"Baby, look…" I say.

"Don't fucking *Baby* me." She says, half crying, half laughing. "I am *not* your Baby." She states firmly. "How dare you. You're not just fucking someone else, but your cheating on her too!" Then the rapid-fire questioning begins. "How many other girls are you fucking, and cheating on? Does she, the first one, does she even know about me? Oh my god, are you really married and have a family somewhere? Am I the other woman too? Are you cheating on her with me? Is that what I am to you? Don't just fucking stand there, what am I to you?"

"Babe…Val..." I start to say, then she continues.

"Because right now, I have no idea. This is absolutely crazy!" She says shaking her head back and forth. "I don't know what to believe and right now, you are just lying to me. You are all lying to me!" She's looking around. "You too Dicky, the way that you just spoke up and assumed responsibility like that shows that you all know, you're all in on it."

"Well…" Dicky starts to say.

"You think you can just go and fuck anybody you want and that it won't have any consequences? What are we all to you? I trusted you, I *loved* you. Do you even know what that means?"

"Yeah, well…" I try.

"Love is like...an ocean and your love is like a goddamn puddle of piss." She's rolling, frantic. "What is wrong with you? You...you are too easy. Does nothing mean anything to you, is nothing sacred to you?"

"Alright, take it easy." I finally cut in, waving my hands. "Let's get a little perspective here. Are you going to stand here and lecture me about how easy *I am*? You never fucked anyone else? The whole time you weren't fucking me. I was a fucking laughingstock. We've been "together" for a *long time*, meanwhile, you were fucking everyone *but* me. How do you think that made me feel?"

"No, no." She says, shaking her head again, adding a stern finger wave that I'm not at all comfortable with. "No, that's what your problem is. That's what your problem has always been, I was always just an ego boost to you. You never gave a shit about me, you just wanted to have some-

thing, someone. That's why I could never sleep with you. I knew you would just turn me into another one of your hos. So yeah, I fucked Martin, I fucked some other people too. And guess what, it didn't mean *shit* to me. I loved you. I loved you so much I waited."

"You fucked my boyfriend?" Blair asks calmly. "You fucked Martin?"

"Oh, come on Blair, you knew what was going on." Valerie says dismissively.

"Well if we're all going to lay all of our cards on the table…" Blair starts to say slowly.

"Holy Smurf. No, don't do it Blair!" I'm screaming to myself, hands beginning to tremble. "No, no, no. Shit, shit, shit, shit, fuck me…Balls, balls, balls in heaven Blair, don't fucking do this. Not now!"

"Then, I fucked Schultz too." Blair admits.

Blair, you are dead to me. I feel the Earth shaking beneath me, the walls start trembling, vases fall from the shelf. The noose is tightening, the bridge to escape is crumbling. My hands are clinched in fists of panic fueled rage. The floor begins to crack and split; everything falls into the empty black abyss.

Dicky starts laughing and says, "Oh shit." in a high-pitched falsetto.

"Well I wish that I was surprised." Val says soberly. "This is, this is just too much. Too much insanity. I don't think this is how people are supposed to live. Like, this is just too much craziness. People can't live like this; I can't live like this. This isn't supposed to be how life works." Pause. "And you…you're …you're too easy." She finally says before breaking down in tears.

Blair puts her hand on Valerie's shoulder, but she shrugs her off, pivots and walks out the front door. Blair gives me a look of disappointment and follows after her, shutting the front door softly behind her.

"Well this is fucked." I say, tossing a broken 9 iron on the floor. "Everything is fucked."

"Yeah, fuck this." Curt says dropping the trash bag he's holding. "I'm gonna call Beth and Stephanie and give them a quarter bag to clean all this shit up and paint the walls. Let's go chip some golf balls."

"Dude, you alright?" Dicky asks me.

I'm unable to catch a decent breath, my hands are trembling. Dicky hands me a drink and I wave it off, my bloodshot eyes answer for me.

Chapter XXXVI

Across the street at the park, the sun is shining, and an arctic breeze is blowing. I ask Curt after chipping a ball, "What in the blue balls are we going to do about the gig? I don't have a guitar or an amp...I got nothing." I say hooking a Wilson with a bent 3 iron into the playground, almost hitting a young mother, not un-hot, and her baby who should have a warmer blanket covering it because it's freezing out.

"You know what you're gonna to have to do?" Curt asks, leaning on his 7 Iron, deep in thought.

"What?" I ask. Not really in the mood for one of his stupid jokes.

"Dude...you gotta rob the pawn shop." Pause. As he speaks these words, they manifest in the freezing September air then, one by one, shatter and fall to the ground.

"Who, me?" I ask looking around, shivering. "Motherf...Curtis, I'm not robbing the G.D. pawn shop!"

"No Dude," Dicky chimes in, "you totally could."

"Shut the hell up Dicky." I say, pointing my 3 Iron at him, then turn to Curt, "Curt, you shut the crap up too.

"Schultz, I don't think you have a choice." Curt says matter-of-factly.

"Dude, if you don't, we'll have to call Hiro at Cooper's and cancel the gig." Dicky adds. "He'll be disappointed, ya know, it fuckin' sucks kid, but, ya know, whatever. I'd just hate to do that to him, ya' know?

Hiro Takada was born in a small farming village called Houfu in the Japanese countryside. His parents, Yoshimasa and Michiko were rice farmers and also owned an izakaya bar, simple folk, very traditional in their ways. They raised Hiro and his younger sister Hinako, the most beautiful 17-year-old girl in all of Houfu, to be very traditional as well. They taught them the traditional art of archery, the tea ceremony, calligraphy and singing bad English songs at Karaoke.

They were not so simple, however, that they could not see which way the wind blew in international affairs and realized, if they wanted their children to be successful that they would need to learn the language of the round eyes; English or *Eigo* as they call it, better than they would learn it from the Japanese public-school system. Houfu is what you might call a "one horse town", it has one restaurant called Joyful, one bar called Avanti, one internet cafe called The Internet Cafe, and one giant shopping mall called Saty. Located on the fourth floor of Saty is Houfu's one and only English school called Nova.

Nova had one foreigner who taught a great number of Houfu's citizens English, a Canadian named Greg. Back in Canada, Greg was a schlub. Not particularly handsome, not particularly cool, not particularly funny, and generally, just not a particularly interesting human being. But there in the small town of Houfu, Greg was elevated to an otherwise unnatural, god-like status of a cool, handsome, funny and interesting guy.

Like the yellow sun of Earth that gave Superman his superhuman powers, so the yellow skin of the Japanese gave Greg quasi-superhuman "powers" in a small farming village of Japan. Greg utilized this to the absolute maximum, but his sights were set on the ultimate prize. He looked at all girls as a prize and he thought that they saw themselves as something to be won as well. He thought that by winning a lot of small victories that he would one day be entitled to have a shot at the ultimate trophy: Hinako.

Hiro and Hinako took English lessons from Greg at Nova but were able to see through his sleezy routines of playing under-the-table grab-ass with the housewives and schoolgirls and just go through the motions and learn 'the English'. Life was great for Greg until one day, news started to spread of a new foreigner who had come to Houfu to teach English at Nova, a young Irishman named Liam McGuinness. Unlike Greg, Liam McGuinness actually was very handsome, hilarious, and a pretty fascinating human being to be around.

Liam McGuinness was an instant sensation in the village of Houfu. Everyone wanted to learn about him, hang out with him, and most importantly, take his English lessons. Greg could only pretend that he was happy for the newcomer for so long, after about a month or so, it was clear that Liam no longer needed the guidance and wisdom of Greg's experience in the land of the rising sun. After Liam started making secret dates and friends of his own, he no longer had any need for Greg and Greg knew it better than anyone, although everyone knew it.

When Hinako started taking only Liam's lessons at Nova and she had that awe-struck twinkle in her eye, that was the last straw for Greg. He could take no more, so he concocted a plan. He bought a one-way plane ticket back to Canada, secretly cleaned out his bank account and tossed out everything in his apartment that couldn't fit into one suitcase. The day of his flight, he called in sick to work but went to Saty anyway. He knew that Hinako had a lesson at Nova with Liam that ended at 4:30. Greg went to the game center adjacent to the 4th floor Nova, slid behind the photo booth where the schoolgirls go to take their *'kawaii'* pictures with peace signs and emojis and he waited.

When Hinako and her best friend, Mayu giggled through the crimson red curtain of the photo booth they had one thing on their minds, *kawaii* cuteness. So, as the two chose the Hello Kitty background of the photoshoot they were about to take, they had a plethora of cuteness to choose from that was unthinkable in the outside, western world. They could write messages across the picture, put cute hearts on the eyes and create pigtails where they hadn't existed before. The girls innocently bent far over to copy and paste a fictional image of themselves that was of course, a half-truth. It's their story, however, let the wee lasses tell it like they wished as far as modern, turn of the century technology would allow them to play around with.

Greg, of course was waiting to take that all away from the two girls. Just as he had taken the hearts and souls out of every girl he ever came into contact with, Greg was waiting around the back side of the photobooth with an ether rag and a jigsaw knife ready to end anything good or decent the girls, the world had ever accomplished.

Greg slithered into the photobooth like a serpent straight from the underworld. As he stood upon them, he held the ether rag like a knife. The girls giggled when they first saw him which sent him into a rage that caused him to pause. As the girls slowly began to realize that Greg's intentions were more than just to be a perv and it began to dawn on them that they should actually be afraid, that also caused them to giggle. This was more than Greg could bear, he was standing there with a jigsaw knife and an ether rag with madness in his eyes and vengeance in his heart and these girls *still* couldn't keep a straight face, couldn't take him seriously.

This was a new level of humiliation, even for Greg whose entire life was a series of pathetic and humiliating endeavors occurring one right after another. His green eyes blazed as he raised his right arm holding the ether rag but then he paused again, realizing that the way in which he imagined this scenario going down was simply not going to be possible now. He could not just smother the girls with the ether rag and have them pass out cold and then have his lustful way with their unconscious bodies, white cotton schoolgirl panties pulled to the side and then anally penetrated and what not. No, he needed this to be what it was, revenge. And if true revenge is to be achieved, both the victimizer and the victim must be fully conscious and aware of exactly what is happening and why.

Greg didn't have all day to sit and contemplate this new philosophy however, so he did what he always did in these tantrums of masculine stripping fits of moral humiliation, and, as per usual, there was more than one helpless girl there that had found herself in an unimaginably horrid position and was beginning to make a real fuss that even the polite perverts and timid schoolgirls at the shopping mall game center would soon be unable to ignore over all the blows and whistles of the attractions.

Greg had stunned them for the moment and was holding them both by the mouths with both hands, but their survival instincts began to kick in and the squirming and squealing really started to distract from Greg's loathsome train of thought. When Hinako opened up her mouth and bit his hand, a demon of blathering mischief arose and Greg's inner monster, Greg, took over. A red mist fell over him, chills ran down his spine and through his nervous system, his eyelids began to twitch and the theme from *Grease* began playing in his head and everything became a dream-like trance.

He used his brute strength to knock their heads together causing both girls to lose instant consciousness and slump to the ground like ragdolls beneath his black, JC Penny's loafers. This gave

quer. He took a moment and looked around the small photo booth; the blood splattered on the white walls, the two girls, half-conscious, bloody and ravaged.

He knew he couldn't leave them alive now, they would surely accuse him alone of the deeds, so he bent down and tapped both of their mouths with his cock, then zipped up and slit both of the young girls' throats with the jigsaw knife and left them both there on the floor of the game center's photo booth to bleed out and die with their panties crumpled around their ankles and semen running down their faces. Greg wiped his hands off on Hinako's skirt, buckled his black belt and stepped out of the photo booth, headed down to the ground floor of Saty and left for the airport, never to step foot in Japan again.

Hiro vowed to hunt down Greg if it took him to the ends of the Earth to avenge Hinako's murder and his families honor. The closest he could get to Canada on a student visa, however, was St. Charles, MO.

While a student at Lindenwold University in St. Charles, MO, Hiro studied hard, became fluent in English and made some great friends. He fell in love with American culture; the music, the food, fashion, capitalism, and way of life. He vowed to return one day when he finished with school and open an Irish Pub here in St. Charles.

In a few days, he is having a Grand Opening celebration and Hiro asked us to play a four or five song set. Which we of course agreed to, even though we were very, very, very, very, very, very, *VERY,* very drunk at the time.

Chapter XXXVII

"Dude, I'm not robbing the mother F'ing pawn shop!" I'm shouting. "We don't do that kind of thing anymore. And I *never* did that kind of thing."

"Because we usually don't need to." Dicky says. "We need to now. Drastic times call for drastic measures, Dude."

"Oh, now it's *we*?" I ask.

"Yeah, well, you know…" Dicky starts to say.

"Dude," Curt cuts him off. "We ain't letting you do this by yourself, Jesus Christ."

"Schultz, you would fuck this up so royally." Dicky adds.

"Dude, no flipping way I or *we* or anyone else is robbing the mother grabbin' pawn shop." I say, trying to keep things grounded in some kind of reality. "Why don't you front me some weed?"

"Dude, you can't get rid of that much weed." Curt says shutting down that idea on the spot, "*I* can't get rid of that much weed. I just got three more pounds and can't get rid of it by tomorrow night or I would and just give you the money. How much do you need anyway?"

"Well I guess I can get a decent guitar for like $750 and an amp for about $500 so I guess about $1,200 bucks. Something like that."

"We gotta rob the Pawn Shop." Curt concludes.

"Alright, alright, alright..." Pause. "What do you propose, what's the plan?" I ask rubbing my forehead.

"Dude," Dicky starts, "I got it! We can start a fucking fire and then…"

"*No!*" Me and Curt say at the same time.

Then Curt starts to hatch a plan. "Alright Dude check this out, we could break in at night. We wear masks, clip the locks on the front door, go in, take a guitar and amp and we get the fuck out."

"That's your plan?" I ask sincerely. "That's literally the *worst* plan I've ever heard. Seriously Dude, of all the plans that have ever been plotted in the history of plans, of all the horrible plans that the future holds, not one of them will be an imbecilic as that dumb ass plan you just suggested."

"Well what the fuck is your plan?" Curt shouts.

"Well, I guess we could..." I say, thinking. "shit I don't know. I don't have a mind for this kind of thing."

"Yeah, no shit you don't." Dicky says just as Alan Hudson comes by in his meat truck that he drives around, slanging slabs of meat to people all day in.

He has mushrooms that he wants to trade for weed. It would be wildly out of character for him to not at least try to sell us some meat. That's just who he is, who he always has been and who he will more than likely, unless acted upon by an outside force, always will be. Somehow, he Jedi mind tricks Curt into trading a half a cow of T-bones for two Tommy Hilfiger shirts and a black leather jacket from The Gap. We toss the steaks on the BBQ pit under the park's pavilion and fire it up. I haven't eaten mushrooms in years, but we all eat a couple grams and then the plans for the great Pawn Shop heist of 2001 start to get very interesting.

"What are those chicks doing in there?" Hudson asks, nodding up towards our house.

"They're cleaning and painting." Curt says.

"Some chick that Schultz is fucking trashed the place today." Dicky offers. I look down at my hand and can see the veins pulsating and there is a radiation effect going on that doesn't end with my hand or my body. The impression I'm getting is that it runs through all of us, through everything and everyone all the time and throughout infinity.

"What, why!?" Hudson asks.

"'Cause he fucked her best friend last night." Dicky explains.

"No way! Was she hot?" Hudson asks.

"Yeah, she's fucking smoking hot." Curt answers.

"So, you're not fucking around with Valerie anymore?" He asks.

"He never was." Dicky answers for me.

"Eat a schmeckle." I say.

"Hey man..." Dicky says to me, "Am I lying? If I'm lyin' I'm dyin' Kid."

"Not anymore." I answer Hudson. "She came over today and saw what the crazy bitch spray painted on our wall so I think that ship may have sailed."

"Are you guys fucking with me?" He asks in amazement. "What did she spray paint on your wall?"

"Don't stick your dick in my friends!" Curt says, igniting a two-minute fit of laughter.

"Shut the fuck up!" He says. "Get the fuck outta here."

"For real Dude." Dicky says.

"Shut up Dicky. Schultz, does it really say that?" He asks me.

"Yeah Dude, no kidding." I say as a tiny spaceship rocks up, hovers for a beat, then zips off without making a sound.

"Right now, in that house," He says pointing at our house. "'*Don't stick your dick in my friends'* is spray painted on the wall.

"Yeah." Curt laughs. "In blood red spray paint."

"I gotta see this. Wait, what did Valerie say?" He asks.

"She was pissed man." I say, telling this story for the first time, the severity is starting to sink in. "I don't know if she'll ever talk to me again."

"Can I hit it?" Hudson asks.

"Too soon man, too soon." I say.

"Well who are these other bitches?" He asks.

"These two crazy bitches we met at a bar a couple weeks ago. The one girl, Ginger or whatever, has sort of been stalking me." I say.

"Yeah, and she has a boyfriend who's so pussy whipped, he doesn't even care that Schultz bangs her all the time." Curt says, then adds, "He even drops her car off for Schultz to use every morning. The dude's a real Cuck."

"No shit? I mean, wait a *what*?" He says, then. "What the hell? I need to start hanging out here more often."

The steaks are ready just as the 'shrooms start to peak which turns the park into a magical kingdom where the cardinals are in a massive turf war with the sparrows, the evening sunset casts all kinds of twisted and complex characters on the mighty elm and oak trees. Our golf clubs quickly morph into great weapons of battle, our only protection against the chaos all around us that is growing ever more unstable.

Chapter XXXVIII

"I can't believe we used to do this all the time." I say, breaking an epic pause. "It's so crazy. When you smoke weed or do coke, even take pills, you more or less know what you're going to get but with these 'shrooms man, anything can happen. It's nuts." I finish, possibly to myself but even the silent thought seems to reverberate throughout the park.

"Yeah…man." Dicky gets around to saying at some point.

Curt is ranting about something I can't be bothered with. His mouth is running like a piston and noises are coming out but what he could possibly be talking about is anyone's guess.

"Hey man, I gotta tell you something." I start hesitantly. "There's something I feel like I have to say, I've been thinking about this, or it's been sort of swirling around in my head for a while and I haven't really thought it through, but now I feel like I have to get it off my chest." I'm nervous though I'm not sure why. I can almost feel myself being watched, like the trees themselves are watching, listening…spying.

"You're gay, Schultz." Dicky says. "We know. We've always known."

Pause.

"No Man like at school, at Lindenwood, it feels...like something is off. There's like a whole weird feeling I get that there is like a secret cult or something going on, Man. Only it's not secret, it's not even unspoken, it's just kind of an attitude. I don't really know how to explain it or, I haven't really thought it through all the way but it's kind of like..."

"Schultz, what the fuck are you talking about?" Curt snaps.

"Alright so," I'm gathering my thoughts, my courage. "You know how when we were in Elementary school, we were taught that America was the greatest country in the history of the world and everything that America does is right and just and good?"

"Yeah, I'm following you so far." Curt says.

"High school didn't really scratch the surface that much further; they just added a few more details, right?" I say.

"Still with you." Dicky says.

"Well then you get to college and all that changes, right from the beginning. They shatter that whole image and they start to tell you the *real* truth. It's like they peel the onion back a layer that no one has peeled back before."

"Like what?" Curt asks, his face melting partially off.

"Oh, stuff like, that all the founding fathers were a bunch of slave owners, or that we stole the land from the Native Americans and then stole half of Mexico from the Mexicans, that the whole system is set up by rich, white men in order to keep everyone else down and keep rich whitey rich, crap like that. George Bush, our president, well he's a fake president. He stole the 2000 election from Al Gore. Al Gore, he's all environmental and everything. He's the only one who is going to save the planet from the greedy capitalists that are just out to make a buck and don't care who they hurt or how dirty our air and water is. You follow?"

"You lost me, Dude." Dicky says.

"Yeah, Dude, what the fuck are you talking about?" Curt piggybacks.

"O.K., look, first you have the Republicans." I start, eyes tightly shut. "The Republicans, they're on the right, they hate poor people, so they don't want to help them at all. They want to take away the food stamps and welfare from poor families who are just trying to put food on the table and clothes on the backs of their kids. They have been keeping the black man down, the brown man down the whole time, oppressing them with the help of the fat cats in Washington, their corporate buddies, Wall St., all those A-holes. America is a racist, horrible place that turns everything it touches to balls."

"Alright, so the Republicans are ass holes. Got it." Hudson confirms.

"So, then you have the Democrats, they're on the left like Clinton and Al Gore, see they're the good guys. They want to help the poor people, the working man, by giving them the assistance that they need, to give them the food and the money that they need to support their families. To take from those greedy capitalists who don't pay their fair share of taxes and give to the hard-working people who are just trying to make ends meet. To save the planet from corporations who are polluting the planet just to make a couple million dollars. And health care. Remember Bill Clinton's wife, what's her name, Hilary, tried to get health care for all Americans, it didn't work but she tried. Why didn't it work? The damn Republicans don't care if people die with no health care, they just don't want to pay for it because they are greedy capitalist pigs."

"Yeah!!" Curt shouts.

"Just look at the news, they agree. They talk about it all the time, every night they are talking about it just like at Lindenwood. It's not just one or two teachers, it's *all* the teachers. All the teachers, who teach *all* the students say that what we have grown up to believe about God, and

America, and our parents, and rich whitey, it's all bullcrap. They opened all of our eyes to what is really going on in the world."

"Yeah, so what's the problem?" Curt asks.

"The problem is…" I whisper, looking around to make sure no one else is listening. I'm shivering but it may be from the frigid cold. "The problem is…" I'm leaning in. Whispering. "The problem is Man... that I think it just might all be bullshit."

"What?!" Curt shouts.

"Shh! Keep your voice down, they'll hear us!" I say, completely paranoid.

"What the fuck do you mean?" Dicky asks.

"All of it." I repeat.

"What do you mean?" Curt asks again.

"Alright, stay with me here." I start, clearing my throat. "So, when we were kids there was an onion called America and everything that we learned was peeling back one layer of that onion. Then you get to college and all the things I just described to you, that's peeling back another layer of the onion. Only now that I've been in school for three years and have had time to sort of look into this a little, I've realized that that's where they stop. They stop peeling back the onion after that second layer, they don't go any further."

"You're losing me Schultz." Dicky says.

"I started to notice things not really adding up a little while ago. Little things like, I don't know, like; slavery for example. They tell us that America is a horrible place because we founded the country on slavery. So, is all that true? Well yes, of course that's true. We all know that but it's not the whole story. You have to peel back the onion further. So yes, we had slavery in the United States and that was a really *really* bad thing. No one argues that, but if you think about it, everywhere had slaves. Every civilization or country in the history of the world had slaves. White people had other white slaves. The Irish were basically slaves, hell, even Africans had African slaves.

But when they talk about America, you'd think we were the only people to ever have slavery, like we invented it or something. So, the question really shouldn't be who *had* slaves, because the answer is everyone. The question should really be; Who *ended* slavery?"

Pause.

"The answer is, we did. We fought a war against our own people to end slavery that killed more Americans than any other war, which is kind of a *no shit* point if you think about it. But anyway, it wasn't even the slaves who stood up and revolted, it was the regular people that did that. The people decided that it was bad, and we ended it."

"Yeah Dude, but we still did really shitty things to a lot of people. What about the Indians, sorry, the Native Americans?"

"O.K. well think about that, God didn't create the universe and on the seventh day said, 'Let North America belong to the Native Americans and Mexico and its borders belong to the Mexicans.' did he? No. Native Americans fought over territory and a million other things for centuries way before the Europeans ever got here. Mexico fought wars and claimed territory in the same way every other country on the planet has ever become a country.

So why is the narrative, the story they tell, that the white man came and stole it? Because we have it now? Think about that, that doesn't make any kind of sense. What happened was, we

fought a war with Mexico, we won that war and then *paid* Mexico for the land we won. When have you ever heard of a country winning a war over land and then paying the loser for it? We didn't have to do that, but we did."

"Yeah but Dude, really, we killed like, all of the indigenous people living here. It was a genocide." Hudson chimes in.

"That's true. That is totally true and really crappy but to be fair, and to be truly intellectually honest, the world was a brutal place back then." I'm uncomfortable saying this out loud for the first time. It feels so dirty, so ugly but I feel like it needs to be said so I continue. "Do you have any idea what things were like back then? Without going down that rabbit hole too far, you really can't retroactively go back and judge history through the morality of today. The world was a completely different place back then, and it was effing brutal."

"I don't know about all that, Dude." Dicky says, unimpressed.

"You have to peel back the onion a little further to get to a fuller picture, to realize that all of these arguments that they are constantly spewing, they're all kind of nonsense. You don't have to dig that much deeper to see that all these arguments are pretty much horse crap."

There's a pause while I catch my breath. Dicky sticks his finger in the air and finally asks, "Well, what about the welfare and the inner cities and all the poor people just trying to make ends meet and all that shit?"

"Good question." I continue. "The Democrats, that's the Clintons and the Gores of the world, they like to think that they are the compassionate ones because they want to help the poor people in the inner-cities, but think about it, how do you really help people? You know the saying, 'Give a man a fish and he eats for a day but *teach* a man to fish and he eats for a lifetime.' Well that's what the Democrats are doing, they're just giving people fish without teaching them *how* to fish. We're meant to work man, we're beasts of burden. If you take away our need to work, our drive, you take away our whole reason for existing. We're supposed to take on our responsibility head on, not farm it out to the government."

"That's harsh, Dude." Dicky says, shaking his head slightly.

"Is it?" I ask. "They make it seem like it's all or nothing. There's a huge difference between helping people get started, giving them a leg up and completely enabling them. We as a country do a lot for poor people, but at some point, you stop helping and you start hurting them, crippling them to the point that they don't know how to take care of themselves, even if they wanted to.

O.K., here's another example. What about when you go to a pond and the sign says, 'Don't feed the ducks. They will become dependent on humans and not learn how to feed themselves.' That's what they're doing. It's like they want to people to be the ducks and be reliant on the government for everything."

"They wouldn't do that, why would they do that?" Hudson asks.

"Well, in a word, *Power* I guess, and some warped sense of fairness."

"Damn." Curt says.

"Think about all their causes; racism, global cooling, inequality, and all that stuff. These are all boogeyman issues that are impossible to solve especially by the federal government. You solve these problems locally, in people's hearts and minds. In the family, in the community, not by the federal government holding a gun to your head. Even if it were the government's job to tackle all of those things, which it is not and never has been in this country...at all, the only way to do that

would be for the government to take over everything and control it like the communists did in Russia and China in the 20th century."

"Why?" Dicky asks.

"Well, for one, because there's no way to pay for it! Whenever you hear about the government paying for something or doing anything, you have to remember, the government doesn't make anything, they don't sell anything. All they do is spend taxpayer money. That's the money that *we* earn, and they take and spend. The problem with a big government is that they run out of other people's money, *our* money to spend."

"Fuckin' hell, Dude." Hudson says, rubbing his temples.

"I'm all for helping people. I want everyone to be able to live their lives in peace, prosperity, have clean air to breathe and everything else, I just think that the government is the last place I would look to for solutions for anything. And by the way, isn't that wildly condescending and more than just a little bit racist to imply that certain groups in our society are incapable of taking care of themselves and need to be treated differently than other groups, like children? I mean, you and I don't get money from the government and I wouldn't want it.

You know, when I first moved out of my mom's house when I was 16-and-a-half, I was working at Steak n' Shake right. I didn't have any insurance at all and then my front tooth got knocked out, remember that?"

"Yeah Schultz, I was there." Curt reminds me.

"It was $200 bucks. Everyone told me to get on Medicaid or Medicare and I could get a tooth for free, so I went to the government place which is the most depressing place on earth and filled out a thousand forms and it was a huge pain in the ass. Then they told me I had to go to another place and wait, and then another place and before too long I decided, 'You know what, screw this. I'll pull a couple extra shifts and pay for this tooth myself.' And that's what I did. You see what I mean, it's almost like the Democrats want people to not get their crap together so they stay dependent on them and keep voting for them, so they stay in power."

Pause.

"Dude get the fuck outta here. That's crazy!" Dicky laughs, thinking that I'm fucking with everyone the way he fucks with people.

"Is it?" I say again. "Look at every big city in the country, look at St. Louis or Goodfellow and Duck's neighborhood, they have all been run by Democrats since at least the late 60's, now it's 2001, are they any better off? Not a Republican in sight and they are all still S-holes and not getting any better. Look at Duck's freaking 'hood. And they blame the Republicans and call *them* racist?"

"So, what, are you a Republican now?" Dicky asks.

"No man," I say shaking my head. "I don't like teams, I'm not a team player. I can't get behind all the social nonsense like religion, the war on drugs, and censorship. I'm not down with the man telling people what to do. Whoever is telling people what to do, what to think, what they can or can't say, and what to do with their time and money, I'm not down with that."

"So, what are you then?" Curt asks.

"Well since I've had a total of 28 minutes to think this through, I guess I'd say I'm pretty libertarian on most things."

"What the fuck is that?" Curt asks.

"Well, basically, it means liberty. You're free to do whatever you want...as long as you can pay for it. It's all about personal liberty, not these collective groups that they try to put us in to divide us: victim vs. victimizer, oppressor vs. oppressed. That's straight out of The Communist Manifesto. The hard truth is that the world is never going to be equal. People don't put in equal effort for one, but even trees and animals are unequal, there really is no other way to do it without stealing one person's stuff to give it to another person. Nothing is free, man. Mice die in traps because they don't understand why the cheese is free."

"Yeah Dude, the hood has been the hood for a long time. That shit's true." Curt says.

"Well isn't it fucked up that the rich people don't pay their fair share of taxes?" Dicky asks.

"Dude, when they talk about rich people and companies not paying their "fair share" of taxes, well that's complete bullcrap." I go on to explain further.

"Dude, rich people don't pay taxes. We all know that." Hudson says confidently.

"No man, sorry but that is simply not even close to being true." I'm explaining. "The wealthy not only pay their fair share; they pay almost everyone's share. They're not the problem, they're the ones paying for everything. Do you know that the top 10% of wage earners, the richest 10% in this country pay 85% of the taxes? The top 25% pay for 90% of the taxes. The bottom 30% don't pay taxes at all."

"Is that true?" Curt asks.

"Eff yeah it's true! Look it up on the internet." I'm shouting.

"The what?" Hudson asks.

"Oh, you know, on a computer." I say. "That place where you can watch Pamela Anderson giving Tommy Lee a hummer."

"Oh yeah. That's just for nerds and pervs isn't it?" Hudson asks.

"Maybe, but there is all the information in the history of the planet there, so... Anyway, we went to war for our independence back in the day because Britain was taxing us without us being represented, remember "Taxation without Representation." Well what we have now is "Representation without Taxation." It's completely ass backwards. You have people who have a vested interest in one party over the other because they have been conditioned to depend on them for *everything*, without contributing anything."

"You know who are the biggest people pushing this? It's the rich white kids and professors and Democratic politicians. But these rich, white kids, who have grown up with *all* the privileges that our free market, capitalist society has to offer, they are the quickest ones to tell others that they should give their stuff away. They want all the privilege as well as all the virtue of being poor, as if being poor or a victim is virtuous by itself. They're not willing to give up *their* money, no no, or their seat at this prestigious University to people less fortunate, but they sure want everyone else to do it. It's wealth distribution, Man! It's stealing. It's a friggin' legal, Mafia style shakedown. Taxation is theft, Dude."

"I don't know, Schultz. That all seems like pretty crazy." Dicky says.

"You know, think about it this way, why is sex with your girlfriend not rape? Consent, right? What makes going to work not slavery? Consent. So, what makes taxes not theft?" I pause for effect. "Flippin' crickets' man. It's a mystery! That's taxes."

"Alright Dude, well, you know more about this shit than I do so, whatever." Curt says.

"Dude, I can't believe it took a mushroom trip for me to see things so clearly. I gotta tell people about this!" I finally finish, taking a deep breath.

"Yeah, good luck with that Schultz." Dicky says as we all gather our thoughts and head up the hill back to our house.

"Well Dude," Curt starts, "It's fucking hard to take something away from people once you've started giving it to them."

"That's a good point, Dog." I say walking through our front door for the first time since the disaster.

"Damn Dude, Beth and Stephanie did a fucking great job." Dicky says.

"Wait a second, is this real? This doesn't seem real." I say, taking a good look around.

"No shit, the place looks as good as new." Dicky says.

"Did you always have a pool table and a bar in here?" Hudson asks.

"I don't know. I don't know what I know." I say out loud. "Everything is suspect."

"See, I know bitches who straighten shit out." Curt says accusingly. "You two only seem to find bitches who fuck shit up."

Chapter XXXIX

It's just after midnight when my phone starts ringing and by the *Love is a Laserquest* ringtone, I know straight away that it's Valerie. I'm overwhelmed with an unknown dread that is mixed with the slightest dusting of relief. I just want to talk to her, hear her voice and explain that, I don't know, I just want to do whatever I have to do or say so that she'll talk to me. The emotional separation is killing me, it's hell. It's hell on Earth.

I balk until after the first chorus to pick it up anyway, then sheepishly say, "Hey," Pause. "I'm so glad you called."

"Um, excuse me, is this Schultz?" An older woman's voice quietly asks on the other line.

"Uh, yes. Who is this?" I ask politely in my best *mom* voice that we all have chambered.

"This is Margret, Valerie's mother." The voice says.

"Um, hello Mrs. Montas." I say, clearing my throat, anxiety bubbling, trembling.

"Schultz," she says as matter-of-factly as she can though I can feel that there is something more on the way. "this is the last number that Valerie dialed on her phone and…I recognized your name. I-I knew that the two of you were close."

"Yeah, listen Mrs. Montas…is there any way that I could just, I mean, with all due respect ma'am, could you just put Valerie on the ph…"

"Schultz," She cuts me off. "Valerie is in the hospital. We...we're at the hospital now."

My heart immediately sinks down an animated portal like some Bahamian waterslide into the pits of hell. The hell that resides in all of us, where our deepest, darkest fears come true. Where our worlds end, where we don't know up from down, dark from light, the snake, the serpent that chases the slayer, the chaos that chases the order, constantly nipping at each other's heels. The shepherd has become the wolf and the wolf has become the shepherd.

The phone drops to the frosty marbled floor that is so cold that when my phone hits it, it just slides across the room. I see a cockroach try to scatter but is snatched up by an unknown tongue, a long, slithering red tongue that goes from 0 to 120 in a nanosecond from under the couch. I'm

stricken with a terror that is as indescribable as it is unbearable. Did she just say what I think she just said? "Valerie is in the hospital." She didn't say why or how this happened, but I know. I know that I know, though I need to hear it out loud, but I'm petrified, frozen. I start to tremble; I can feel my body but I'm not in control of its functions. I'm incapable of picking up the cell phone on the floor to make her say the words.

I can see Curt and Dicky saying things at me but I'm without consciousness. Try as I may, I can't move, the room is spinning out of control. They walk over to me and grab me as I lose my physical composure and now they're propping me up and then helping me sit down on the black leather love seat. I feel a slap on my face that feels cold and hot at the same time. Dicky picks up the phone and is speaking to Valerie's mom on the other end.

All I know is that I cannot let this happen. I try to shout *No!* But words do not come out. Whatever he says will be the polar opposite of what should be said. I grab around for the phone but I'm not really in control of my actions. I feel like a toddler with no sense of perspective, trying to grasp at a rattle. I realize that this is not the way that I want to be portrayed to her mom, but words are not coming out the way I want them to. I'm incapable of proper speech right now and drool is spewing from my mouth. I can't catch my breath, sweat is beaded and bleeding, my tell-tale heart is thumping so loudly that it adds to my paranoia.

Oh my god, I can't breathe! I'm engulfed in a full panic attack. I see Dicky hang up the phone. This adds a layer of relief. I'm sitting on the couch now, gasping at deep breaths. I can hear Curt and Dicky's voices now saying, "Schultz, Schultz, come on Buddy. Snap out of it."

Finally, the fog begins to lift. I blink once, twice then stretch my fingers. I reach around for a bottle and Dicky puts a chilled 1976 Dom Perignon in my hands and I nurse it like an infant, inconsolable.

"What did…what did you say to her?" I gasp once I'm able to form words again.

"I just told her you were sort of panicking and couldn't talk. She said that it was alright, but that Valerie is in the hospital, she really didn't say anything else." He says.

"Did he say some dumb shit?" I ask Curt.

"No Dude, he was cool. It's cool." He assures me.

"Well I have to call her back." I'm demanding. "I have to see how she is. She's in the hospital, we have to go see her. Dude, where are my boots?"

"Uh, yeah Man, call her back. It's not like they're sleeping. They're at the hospital with her." Dicky says handing me back my phone.

I call Valerie's phone back but after six rings it goes to voicemail. I leave a brief message. I wait 10 minutes, drink to calm my shaking hands, then call back and after four rings, her mom picks up. "Hello Schultz," she says, sniffling.

"Hello Mrs. Montas. I'm sorry about before…" I start saying. "I'm so sorry about..." I'm weeping. "Wh-what hospital are you at? If it's alright with you, I'd like to come there and see her. I know we never really met but me and Valerie are actually pretty close and…"

"I know." She interrupts. "Valerie always told me more than you might think. She was always honest with me..." Pause. "Of all the things she did that we disapproved of, she always told me the truth in the end. I know that you were a good guy and loved her very much…" She starts to trail off in silent sobs. Sniffs, then, "I read a letter that you wrote to her one time. It was very sweet."

"Thanks, so uh, about the hospital, is it St. John's then?" I ask.

"We found her unconscious in her bedroom about two hours ago." She continues, still not answering my question. "We saw the drugs Schultz; we saw the needle and the marks on her arm." Sobbing. "She looked peaceful." She manages before breaking down.

"Mrs. Montas," I politely interrupt. "you're speaking about her in the past tense. If it's alright with you, I really would like to come there to be with her."

"Schultz, I'm sorry. After you hung up the first time, the Doctors...they pronounced her dead. Valerie is...she's dead." She manages to say before breaking down and hanging up the phone.

"She's dead?" I ask no one, hanging up the phone myself. "She's dead."

"Fuck Dude, I'm sorry Schultz." Curt says, wrapping his arms around me firmly.

"Damn Man," I say. "she left here pissed at me, went home and fucking ODed. This is my fault." I say, then repeat, "This is all my fault."

"No dude, you didn't put that needle in her arm." Curt says, hugging me tightly. "Only she did that."

"I just talked to her mom, she said that she tells her everything. Do you think they know about today, the wall? I mean, she said that she knew I was a good guy so…" I say, trying to work this out in my head.

"Well, no Dude." Curt says. "I don't think she would have gone home, told her mom what happened and then went to her room and shot up. She may have mentioned it days from now."

"Fuck, what if they find out though." I say. "They'll blame me for sure. They'll press charges. I'll be charged with...I don't know, some weird crime like adultery or being a whore like Frank Sinatra!"

"Well, really only Blair would have known about it." Dicky says. "Think about it, if anyone were to say something, it'd be Blair."

Chapter XL

I'm shivering in the back seat of Dicky's '95 Durango even though I'm wearing a wool V-neck sweater from Banana Republic, new skinny jeans from American Eagle and the windows are rolled up with the heat blasting in my face. My last two suggestions for robbing the Pawn Shop, whose parking lot we are idling in, were quickly dismissed but now that I've had few pulls off my sterling silver flask I think I can make the case for blasting in with blow torches and pipe bombs and burning the place down a little bit more palatable to the boys.

Curt is sitting in the front seat sniffing cocaine from a Bubbleyum gum wrapper wearing a red flannel lumberjack from Eddie Bauer and a platinum, pentagram pinky ring talking about the dudes he works with as if me and Dicky have any idea who they are. Dicky is drinking from a Jim Beam bottle like he used to in high school while scoping out the Pawn Shop with binoculars from Sports Authority giving us the low down on the inner workings of the store. It's Sunday morning, the day before the big gig at Cooper's.

"Dude, pass me those binoculars." Curt is snapping from shotgun.

"It looks like there are two dudes working in there, one handling the jewelry half of the store and the other dude is on instrument duty." Dicky is saying. "The windows are barred and so is the glass door. They got a chain with a pad lock on the door." He concludes.

"Yeah, I think there's a dude in the back too. The back door leads to an ally and just has a regular deadbolt lock." Says Curt.

"That looks like our best bet." Dicky says.

"What about through the roof?" I say, half joking. Then I hear something, a faint whisper floating on an autumn zephyr from far away that sounds warm and familiar.

"That's actually not a bad idea Schultz." Curt says. "If we could pry that AC unit up without tripping an alarm we could probably get in that way."

"O.K., but what about getting out with a guitar and an amp?" Dicky asks, bringing up a prudent point.

"Shit." Curt starts. "Well, we'd just need some rope, electrical tape, a pair of gloves, snips, a crowbar and a tarp or something."

“Yeah MacGyver, and Tom Cruise wearing a tin foil hat with piano wire wrapped around his balls hanging from the AC duct.” I say dryly.

“Well, I’ll give it to you Schultzy, this might be harder than we thought.” Dicky says.

“Yeah, well there’s a reason you don’t hear about these kinds of places getting robbed more often.” I say, half distracted by this gentle ringing in my ear like someone far away is talking about me. “If it were easy, they’d be getting robbed all the time.”

Curt asks, “What are some movies or books where they pull off a great heist? We should just steal a plan from one of those.”

“What about *Heat*? Remember that shit?” Dicky is suggesting. “We could do it like that, we just need a couple of Uzi machine guns. I think Lavista can hook us up with those.”

“Oh yeah, remember those dudes copied that movie robbing a bank right afterwards.” Curt answers.

“Dude they all got killed.” I say.

“In the movie or in the copycat one?” Dicky asks.

“Both!” I shout.

“I don’t think they all got killed.” Curt chimes in.

“The fuck they didn’t.” I say, swearing unintentionally.

“Those movies are all bullshit.” Curt starts ranting. “Even if they weren’t bullshit, after they came out, that makes them all the more impossible because now all the cops know about the movie.”

“We don’t have guns anyway.” Dicky says.

“Curt does.” I say, looking up from the binoculars.

“That’s true, I do.” He admits.

“How many?” Dicky asks.

“One. I got a glock 45.” Curt says.

“Well this place has a whole arsenal.” I say, putting down the binoculars.

“Not loaded.” Dicky says.

“You don’t think they keep the best stuff behind the counter, cocked and loaded like a small militia?” I ask redundantly.

“Dude, you may have a point.” Curt says.

“This is insane!” I’m kind of pouting, “I don’t want anyone to get hurt, or killed over this. I can't have this become part of my story.”

“No one ever wants anyone to get hurt, it still happens.” Curt says, “Anything can happen in a robbery.”

“I can’t do this, not armed robbery. No way.” I say, shaking my head in protest.

“Well, we’ll have to cancel the gig.” Dicky says, instigating a massive pause.

It’s so cold that the windshield keeps frosting over and Dicky has to keep turning the defrost up. The wind blowing through the cracked backseat window sends an eerie chill down my skinny jeans and I can tell that my balls are like a couple of raisins down there. Once again, I sense the faintest whisper that feels like a soft kiss. I look into the direction of the sound and see a brownish-red Cardinal bird perched on the hood ornament of a Cadillac fluttering in the cold. I follow it to where there is a small tornado of trash and dust circling around in the parking lot and wonder if I’m not hallucinating.

Suddenly, out of the chaos of the tornado, a fresh-looking daisy emerges and floats ever so gently to the ground. I follow it with my eyes while it dances along the car park. It makes its way to an early '90's, black Pontiac Grand Prix with a *River City Buskers* bumper sticker. That gets my mind going down a series of complicated rabbit holes. All the times we used to see *The Buskers* live, the riot of the Battle of the Bands of '96. Then a brown leather Backgammon set slowly makes its way to the forefront of my mind's eye. A plan begins to hatch.

"Wait a minute." I say, snapping us out of our collective daze. "Wait just a cotton-picking minute here." I say. "Remember that time, way back in the day when we were at a bar with Paul Lorenz, watching *The Buskers* and they had a nice Backgammon set? We were playing it for a while and at the end of the night, Paully pulled a total Jedi mind trick and just casually walked the hell out of the door with the fancy looking leather case, just like it was his, like he was supposed to be walking out with it? No one questioned it."

"Yeah, I remember that shit." Dicky says. "That was pretty dope."

"Yeah, that was a fucking Jedi mind trick, level 8.5 at least." Curt says. "Dude, that guy was a real legend."

"And then remember when we were at that bar in Columbia and you saw that poster of Clint Eastwood above the pool table and you were talking about how much Doug Garrett would've like it?" I ask.

"Yeah." Dicky says turning up the defrost again.

"So, I told you to do the same thing." I say starting to make dramatic hand gestures.

"Oh yeah, I totally forgot about that." Dicky says.

"Yeah, remember I told you that you have to believe that it's yours. That's what Pauly told me when I asked him about the Backgammon set, it's all about you believing that its really yours, believe that Doug, rest in peace, was there and wanted you to have it for him, take it in his honor." I say.

"Yeah, that was pretty bad ass." Dicky says.

"Well, why don't we just try that?" I say.

"Dude, that might work for a game and a poster on the wall of a bar but a fucking guitar and an amp? No fucking way." Curt is saying, blood pressure elevating.

"Bullcrap." I say. "You just have to believe. Remember in *Empire* when Luke didn't believe that Yoda could lift his ship out of the swamp?"

"Schultz…" Curt starts.

"No man, think about it." I'm saying, "What does Yoda tell him. Size matters not. Try not. Do or do not. There is no try."

"I guess it's worth a shot." Curt says.

"I think it might be our only shot." I say.

"Alright, we have to believe..." I start ranting. "In the name of everything that is holy and in the name of this gig, let's just walk into the pawn shop, ask to play a guitar and hook it up to a kick ass, Fender amp, play it for a couple minutes, then do the greatest Jedi mind trick in the history of Jedi mind tricks and simply pack up and walk out of the door. We have to be confident about it though. It all depends on our collective confidence."

"We should drink something first." Curt says.

"Oh, we're going to need a *lot* of Vodka." Dicky says.

"Oh, fuck yeah." Curt says.

We drive to Shooter's off of 1st Capital and park in the back-parking lot. We walk in and sit down at a table for four, maybe five. Melanie, our waitress is wearing Khaki shorts from The Gap and a navy Polo shirt with the collar popped. Dicky orders Corona's and three shots of Vodka and is mildly polite about it.

"You want shots of straight Vodka?" Melanie asks us in a somewhat snarky tone.

"Isn't that what the definition of a shot is?" Dicky asks back, stone cold stoic expression.

"Yeah, well…" She starts to say, deflating.

"Yeah well," Dicky says confidently, "just bring the shot glasses and leave the bottle Sugar, there'll be an extra $20 in it for you...make it a $40 in case I get drunk and call you a bitch later."

"We can't drink too much." I say, checking out Melanie's ass as she walks away, and I have one thought- Not bad. "For real, we have serious business to take care of. If this thing we're about to do doesn't go down today, the whole thing is effed. The gig is effed. Everything is effed, royally effed."

"Alright man, we have to stay positive." Dicky says, sniffing deeply. "We got this, we totally got this."

"Right, we gotta do this. Do this for all that is good. Do it for the gig, do it for the Pranksters. Do it for Valerie, for Martin, for Doug, for everyone who can't be here with us today. We only have this one life and god knows tomorrow is never promised." Curt says, holding up his shot glass for a toast.

"Yeah man, take your passion and make it happen." I say, holding up mine.

"Let's do it!!" Dicky says, already pouring another round of shots.

"*Kompai!*" We shout before we all take our shots, cringing.

Chapter XLI

We step out of Dicky's Durango and are baptized by the frigid autumn air. I take a deep breath, exhale a drag off my Marlboro and flick the butt into the parking lot of the pawn shop, crack my neck and shake off a mauve colored, paisley dream. I take a look around and notice that I'm now wearing a blue Rhinestone buttoned shirt from The Buckle, Boot-cut jeans from American Outfitters and brown leather Chelsea Boots from J. Crew, large mirrored aviator shades from Oliver Goldsmith and a silver Keith Richards skull ring.

The sky is a hazy shade of purple and the world around me is moving in slow motion. Dicky is wearing black leather pants from Dolce & Gabbana, a white cotton button down shirt from Saturdays NYC, black Ray-Ban sunglasses and maroon ostrich skin Tony Llama cowboy boots. We're not so much walking as we are floating and there is an aura surrounding us that can only be described as *God-like*. Curt is wearing a green Guinness T-shirt from where, Target? Faded jeans from The Gap, black Sliver sunglasses and black Dr. Martin's.

Dicky brings in his Starburst colored Fender Telecaster from the car and he walks up to the counter to give his speech to Lazlo, the Hungarian pawn shop owner.

"Hey Dude," He starts, "is it cool if I try out some amps?"

"Yes, my friend." Lazlo says tapping his diamond studded, gold pinky ring on the glass counter.

"Thanks Bro. My wife just left me for my little fuckin' brother and the bitch took my amp. You believe that shit? I fucking raised that kid when Dad ran off with *his* brother's girl almost 15 years ago. The cycle continues Man, you hear me. The fucking never ending cycle, Bro, the yen and the motherfucking yang." Dicky is saying, sticking his tattoo in the Eastern European owner's face. "If we don't fucking study history, we're damned to defeat it, ya' know. No one wants to be defeated."

Lazlo finally says, "Yes my friend, I know the woman people all too well." Grinning widely, exposing a sparkling gold tooth.

Dicky plugs into a Marshall mini stack and starts playing some little blues riffs. I give the lineup of guitars hanging on the wall behind the counter a look over, there are some beautiful axes up there. There's a Gibson SG like Angus Young from AC/DC plays. I've never been a huge fan; the neck is too wide. There is a pearl colored Fender Strat which is cool but Strats tend to have the action set too high and the strings are too high off the neck. Then something catches my eye. I see it glowing up there on the smoke-stained wall, a Jet-Black Gibson Les Paul with a St. Louis Cardinals pick guard that is practically winking at me.

I ask to play it and Lazlo takes it down for me, grabs me a chord and says, "Yes, yes. Good choice my friend."

Curt sits down at a drum set and starts to keep a beat that gets the attention of some of the customers, mostly crack-heads and heroin junkies trying to pawn stolen electronics and jewelry for dope money. I grab a mic and give it a test, plug in the guitar to a Fender amp that Curt could easily walk out with and give it a quick tuning then join in the little jam that Curt and Dicky have started. A simple blues riff that is not unlike *One Way Out* by the Allman Brothers.

Slowly we work our way into a little jazzy improv that, after we've gotten everyone's attention turns into *White Orchid*, a modern classic by the White Stripes. Me and Dicky take turns with the leads and Curt doesn't miss a beat. The other customers there have all stopped their shoplifting and schemes to watch and get in on the vibe. Even people walking by on the sidewalk come in to check out what all the racket is about and join in. By the time we wrap it up, the place is packed and erupts in applause like when the Blues Brothers are at Ray's Music Exchange.

I look at Dicky and Curt, we can't take our eyes off of the mission we're on. We never got around to discussing what songs we were going to play and now we need to keep this going or else things are going to fall apart faster than a cannonball. Suddenly it hits me. I shout into the microphone, *"All aboard!! Ha ha ha!!"* Dicky immediately starts doing the intro to *Crazy Train* that Randy Rhodes would do in concert.

I join in doing the bass and chords, Curt comes in right on time with the drums. The place goes nuts! We never really even practiced this song but somehow, we all know how to play it. The microphone is in front of me, so I start with the vocals:

Crazy, but that's how it goes.
Millions of people living as foes
Maybe it's not too late
To learn how to love and forget how to hate

The crowd becomes mesmerized. Their eyes seem to glaze over, that energy I felt at the last gig is returning and everyone is nodding their heads in unison. I can feel a familiar buzzing running through me and it seems to be contagious. I can feel it, almost see it spreading through the crowd. Everyone is catching the fever, the contact high.

Mental wounds not healing
Driving me insane

I'm going off the rails on the Crazy Train

After the lead, I give the boys a look and I do a thing with the guitar that lets Dicky and Curt know that we're wrapping this up. We end with a bang. All couple of dozen or so people cramped in this Pawn Shop go crazy. We flippin' *rocked it!* I shoot Dicky a look that says to keep going on his own with a nod and a smile then shoot Curt a look that is stern and full of urgency, saying, "Let's do this."

Dicky turns all of the dials on the amp up to 1o and then starts in with *Eruption* by Eddie Van Halen which keeps the crowd occupied while Curt picks up the amp. The crowd and the owners are still high from the songs we just played; the energy is still coursing through their veins. I put the black Les Paul in its case and position them to get carried away. We give Dicky the, "We're out." look and he prepares to wrap it up. Just as everyone is cheering again Dicky says into the microphone, "Thanks very much. We're *The Merry Pranksters*. Check us out tomorrow night at Coopers on Main St.!"

Dicky keeps it going by playing the intro to *Seek and Destroy* to maintain the vibe. While a crowd surrounds Dicky like a pack of zombies, wanting him to sign some autographs and a couple of titties, possibly an ass cheek while Curt and I posture to execute our plan. With a nice crowd still engulfing Dicky, me and Curt pack up Dicky's guitar, my new Les Paul and both amps and, imagining that we're invisible, we stealthily, casually walk out the front door then amble to Dicky's red Durango and throw everything in the trunk.

Me and Curt get in the car and start it up. We both start to shiver while waiting for Dicky to get out here. The moments tick by painfully as our minds race to catch up with the energy we just harnessed and projected to the crackheads and Eastern Europeans at the Pawn Shop. Dicky is taking way too long. We're getting anxious and consider leaving him here, but he finally jogs out smiling, plops down leisurely in the passenger seat and lets out an impoverished sigh.

"What the fuck took you so long!?" Curt barks as we peel out of the gravel parking lot.

"What dude, I was signing autographs." He says. "You gotta leave the fans happy, Curtis."

"No *Richard*, you always leave them wanting more." Curt says impatiently. I'm nodding along in agreement. "You could have fucked up this whole thing."

"Dude, chill the fuck out." Dicky says reaching around at the floorboard for the bottle of Jim Beam. "We fuckin' killed it in there."

"He did eff it up." I say, lighting a Marlboro Red and cracking the window, letting the frigid air rush in.

"What, why?" Dicky asks, finally pulling up the bottle of Beam, swigging and then passing it around. "Why the fuck do you always have to be such a downer, Schultz? Goddamn Dude."

"You said our *fucking* name Genius." I say, leaning up from the back seat.

"No, I didn't." He dismisses.

"The hell you didn't." I say, "You said, "Thanks, we're The Merry Pranksters." Then you told them where we would be tomorrow night."

"Well..." Pause. "Fuck it Man, ya' know," He says. "Let's drop this shit off at the crib and go play frisbee golf."

Chapter XLII

Monday, September 10th, 2001.

Valerie's passing is weighing heavily on my mind, on everyone's mind. Though I feel utterly defeated, like the dragon of chaos came up from the pits of hell and devoured me alive and it's my fault is devastating. I feel like everything is dead, everything worth anything is dead. God is dead. Nothing good is left on this wretched Earth. And oddly, just when I feel that the bells of sorrow have tolled and I can't go on, the feeling kind of ebbs and I can feel her here with me. Feel her here with every breath of the frosty wind, I can feel that she wants us to carry on and it gives me the strength to go the distance.

Guitars in hand, Dicky and I are sitting in the living room drinking 75-year-old scotch on the rocks and wishing we had some cocaine. I have my new jet black 1976 Les Paul from Gibson that I've named Val, Dicky has a 1982 Sunburst Fender Strat and we're going over our set list for our big gig tonight at Cooper's. This is the gig we've been honing up for weeks. An S-load of people are going to be there and we gotta get this right.

I'm trying to write a song about Val, and I want it to be really heart felt and express everything I'm feeling about her. I want to say everything I never said to her in person, really pour my heart out and tell her that she is not dead to me. She will somehow never be really dead to me. Every version of her still exists in my memory somewhere. The crying, the laughing, the good the bad. No part of her is dead in my heart, my memory.

I need to say something that Paul McCartney would be able to articulate perfectly but the best I'm able to pull off is coming across like:

Cross my heart and hope to die
Fill that rig up, stick it in my eye
Double down, heat it up and then
Fly, fly, fly

She was my funky junky mama
But I lied, lied, lied
Go crazy, fuck around
and she'll cry, cry, cry
Break her dopey little heart
and she'll die, die, die
She was my funky junky mama...
and she died.

It's not exactly coming out the way I wanted it to, but songs tend to take on a life of their own. You just have to roll with it. When you sit down to write a song, you're staring at a blank white page and a dream. I start to fade in and out of consciousness. The page is empty, the glass is full, and you have to just start emptying one and filling up the other. It's chaos. It's the epitome of chaos; nothing but emptiness and potential.

As you write, you just start to try to put some order to it. You strum some chords and hope that they blend well together and pray to god that it doesn't come out sounding like another song. You hum along to try to form some kind of a melody and if you're lucky, you have an idea for a chorus that doesn't suck. But after that, that's all you can really do. You stick your antenna up and hope that it connects with the right wavelength that's on the same frequency that you are.

It's like that stupid country song, *Jesus Take the Wheel,* which is not any kind of advice that I would give to someone behind the wheel of a car like the song suggests by the way, but when you're diving into an artistic endeavor, man, that's about the best advice I could give. That's when you wake up in the morning, spooning your guitar and you've got 10 pages written, you don't know how it got there but it's fricking brilliant. The mysterious unknown where chaos meets order. That's what I'm trying to tap into.

"Hey, Schultz!" I faintly hear Dicky shouting, trying to snap me out of my daze.

I shake my head, pause and take a look around the Living Room. There is a new black and white, porcelain vase with fresh Daisies on the ebony marble coffee table. The chandelier is dimmed to a dull glow, but its reflections are dazzling. I see a snake slither under the east end of the ivory colored, leather Hartwell U-shaped sofa from Ethan Allen that Dicky is sitting on the south end of and the original Steve Walters painting *The Daisy* is in need of a dusting.

An unnamed aura makes itself at home that fills an emptiness in my soul. The silver framed painting of New York Skyline above the bar is a stunning contrast between light and dark the way the city lights of the George Washington bridge and the World Trade Center illuminates the pitch-black night sky. The Gobelins pool table is positioned according to Feng Shui, the Chinese art of decorating, so it's easy to maneuver around to get to the Ashley Heights black stain home bar that looks like it's been recently stocked and it's so cold in the house that the ice isn't even melting.

After a substantial pause, I finally look at Dicky and ask, "How the hell are we still sitting here?"

"Huh? Dude, what do you mean?" He asks, not engaged at all.

"I mean, how the hell are we still here, sitting in this living room? How are we really still here trying to write songs for this gig with all the shit that's been going on all around us?"

"You just gotta keep on keepin' on, Man." He says, shrugging his shoulders and setting down his cigarette in the Baccarat Harcourt crystal ashtray.

"Dude, I'm serious." I say. "Look around. I mean, are we insane? Is it just me or like, are we actually like, legitimately insane or something?"

"Yeah Dude, I know what you mean." He says blankly.

"No, Man." I say, attempting to make eye contact. "Like, take this in the spirit in which it's intended or whatever, but I don't think you do."

"Yeah, Schultz, I think I do get it." He says genuinely, finally connecting visually. "I just think it has to do with not thinking too much about things."

There is a pause here where I have to decide how offended I feel like being.

"What the hell does that mean?" I finally ask, deciding that a six/six-and-a-half is appropriate. "Like we don't care enough? Like *I* don't care enough?"

"No man," he starts, setting down his glass gently. "I don't mean we don't care. I said not *think* about things. And I don't mean like, we don't choose to think about things either. It's like, Dude, think about it, there is so much shit going on right now, so much craziness that we don't have time to think about things."

I'm wondering how seriously I should be taking all of this when he continues, "Like if you're in a war or something, or if you're getting chased by a bear, you don't have time to be depressed or think about shit. You see what I mean?"

There's a pause that I'm not at all sure how to deal with.

"Dude, are you fucking with me right now?" I ask, thinking to myself that what he just said is actually not the dumbest thing I've ever heard and wondering if it's not just some old song lyric that I'm not familiar with.

"No Dude, seriously." He continues. "I think that maybe later, maybe tomorrow at Valerie's funeral or maybe years from now, I don't fucking know, all this shit that we're dealing with now, all the death and violence and mind numbing shit we swallow or put up our nose, the crazy parties and the chaos is going to catch up with us and we'll probably either have a real life mental melt down or we will just keep boozing it up to mask the pain and avoid having to really sit down and like, work this all out. But for now, Man, we're smack dab in the thick of all of this shit and all we can do is survive. We're in survival mode brother, all of us, every single one of us, ya know."

He winks at me and then stands up and walks to the bar to make us the world's best Bloody Mary. He's wearing a maroon, silk robe that is loosely tied and Little Dicky and the Lads are shriveled up like a marshmallow that got dropped in the campfire because of the cold.

After forcing myself to look away, I'm able to ask something like, "So it's not like we don't care?"

"No, it's not that we don't care." He says cutting up the lime and oranges. "It's our lizard, primitive mind that can only deal with so much shit at one time. We compartmentalize, or whatever, it all and now, right now man, we're still fucking running, just running away from it all, you feel me?"

"Believe it or not, I just might feel you." I say, still not sure that I'm not just crazy, like legit insane like my brother and completely imagining all of this.

"We're still just trying to make it through the fucking woods with all the trees and shadows and the roots and we're just running to stay alive, not trip over them and not look back. We're in that arc where we're being chased by the dragon man, the dragon of chaos that you're always talking about, and we're chasing the dragon too." He says stirring a pitcher of the world's greatest Bloody Mary and pouring two glasses topped with; olives, orange slices, pineapple wedges and celery.

There's a brief pause. There's a lot to take in here. Then Dicky continues.

"This is our time, Buddy. Our time on the edge, the edge of chaos and order. We're walking a tightrope, you know. We wouldn't be here if we weren't, you know, we're out here, trying to slay the dragon without him slaying us, and look around man, look at all of us who haven't made it. Martin, Valerie, and that's just this week. Not all of us are going to make it, but we have to just keep fighting, we have to just keep swinging these axes." He says holding up his guitar, "These are our axes, and this is our message." He says holding up the song notebook. "This is our rebel yell; our war cry. Say what you got to say, Motherfucker, and say it now, 'cause it ain't ever gonna get any easier to say it."

"Yeah, I hear you." I say, slurping my Bloody Mary.

"You think 20 years from now, you or me are going to be sitting around thinking about this shit? If we even make it that long, God willing, you think we're going to give a single fuck about us? Give a single thought about all these dead motherfuckers? Fuck no! If we ever make it out of here alive, it ain't going to be about keeping it real. Fuck that shit, it's going to be about shedding skin. Life is about shedding your fucking skin and moving on, Dude. No one here gets out alive.

You know, if a snake, a dragon, tries to hold on to his skin too long, you know what would happen?"

"Well actually…" I start.

"It would fucking suffocate him." He continues, cutting me off. "And you, motherfuckin' college boy, and I don't mean that in a bad way, but the truth is, I'm pouring concrete foundations for a living. I'm gonna be pouring foundations for the rest of my life. If I make it out of this dumb-ass Boug Boy shit without killing myself first, I'm still going to be on the job for the rest of my fuckin' life. If you have any chance, and you do, you fucking bitch, you go do your thing and don't ever look back at this shit. Remember the story about Sodom and Gomorrah from the Bible?" He asks.

"Yes, I do. Why, do you?" I ask, more than a little puzzled.

"Sure." He shrugs off. "What's his fucking name was jetting the place, but his bitch wanted to look back and what happened to her? She turned into a block of salt."

"What the fuck does that mean?" I ask. "And why do you suddenly know all of this? Where the bleep is all of this coming from?"

"I don't know, Man." He says, ignoring my question. "But I think that it has something to do with not having good thoughts about a shitty past. Not having nostalgia for the past. Don't look back man. Don't look back in anger."

"Dicky, I swear to God..."

"You know, Schultzy, people have a crazy ability to balance themselves out, to find some kind of an equilibrium when they have to. Not even just one person but like, a whole group of people, a whole country can fight through some crazy hard times together and somehow get through it.

Remember the other day when you were talking about the Great Depression, you were saying that they didn't have TVs or radios back then. People didn't even know what was going on, they just knew that one day everyone had money and food and shit, and practically overnight, there was nothing.

Well think about it, people weren't walking around thinking about their own mortality, being depressed, even though it was called the *Depression*, but they were just focused on survival, right? They were in straight up survival mode. And that was like our Grandparents too, no wonder they call us spoiled. We aren't going overseas to fight in a war, we aren't starving to death. We're killing *ourselves,* overdosing on drugs and parting too much. You know, we think forest fires are a horrible thing, but the fact is, if there isn't a fire for a long time, the underbrush gets so thick that nothing can grow."

"Forest fires?" I ask skeptically, wondering where I've heard all of this before.

"Stay with me, Curt was telling me about this shit." He assures me. "So without a fire, shit grows too thick, then when the fire *does* come, and the fire always comes, all the underbrush, the fat, is so thick and settled that the fire burns down to the top soil and scorches it all away, nothing can grow for a long time. Eventually it will grow back, but not without a lot of pain and suffering. So, it's good to burn down every so often so the forest, so *we,"* He looks at me for emphasis. "can rebuild ourselves without too much suffering.

God forbid we have another national tragedy like the Depression or a World War or worse, something that brings our country, our society to its knees, but sometimes that's just what we need to keep us in our primal, animal element. When we as humans, or any animal or anything, when things are too good, we don't get happy because, oh, finally, we've gotten what we've been struggling for. That's cool for like a long weekend but after any more than that, a depression starts to set in. And that depression turns to a sort of uneasiness which leads to a sort of disgust which leads to rage.

It's like doing push-ups on the moon. What I mean by that is, when astronauts go to space, there's no gravity."

"No gravity?" I ask.

"Well, there is *some* gravity, but not enough for our muscles to get a workout and so they atrophy, they shrink and turn to flab. We need to be pushed so we don't go to total shit. Think about when it's winter and I don't work for weeks at a time. How long does it take for me to turn into a complete degenerate drunk?"

"By like Tuesday morning?" I ask, not sure of anything anymore.

"Right! We're built for struggle, Schultzy. We like to bitch about having to get up and go to work but the alternative, even if we had plenty of money is fucking scary man, you don't want to be that dude or around that dude for any amount of time. It's chaos. Self-inflicted chaos. We function much better as people in society when we're working toward something, striving toward something. Fighting something."

"But Dicky..." I'm saying with my head in my hands.

"That's the double-edged sword of life, Schultzy. You work so hard to achieve your goals, you sacrifice, you go without so many things, you live like we're living now, busting our ass and the dream is to have that cushy job where you can just kick up your feet on the desk in the office with a bad-ass view of the St. Louis Arch and you think, 'Well, if I get there, I'll finally be happy

and I can relax and enjoy my life.' But that ain't the way we're wired Man, not even a little bit. You bought the ticket, you gotta learn to enjoy the ride, Brother."

Pause.

"That's deep, Man." I say, "I don't know where the hell that came from but thanks."

"Life is but a dream, Dude. That's all this life is, a fucking dream." He says.

"I hear that, Dicky." I say gazing casually at the pool table, the bar, the chandelier and the polar bear rug decorating the living room.

"Shaboom." He says, winking at me and slurping the last of his Bloody Mary through a swirly straw.

I finish my drink then say, "Alright." but I'm not really referring to anything in particular. I'm letting all of this sink in, I look at Dicky more than once skeptically, then finally shake it off and pour us two more Bloody Mary's from the pitcher.

"Alright Man, are we ready for this thing?" Dicky asks.

"I think so. I'm a little nervous." I admit.

"Me too." Dicky says. "Let's score some coke and chip some golf balls."

Chapter XLIII

"Dude, what are you going to wear?" I shout from my room. I'm standing in front of my mirrored sliding glass closet flipping through hangers of clothes. I grab two shirts and walk out to the living room where Dicky is sitting leisurely at the bar stirring a glass of scotch with his finger.

"Schultz," He says without looking up from his drink. "I've heard you say a lot of gay shit over the years. I've known you for a long time, Kid, since you were a skinny ass fucking hippy, scamming motherfuckers for crack money in Stamm's shitty garage. But that is head and shoulders beyond the gayest thing I have ever heard you or any other motherfucker say in my entire life."

"So…" I start, holding both shirts up to my neck, alternating back and forth between the two. "Which one, the Louis Vuitton polo or the Navy Boglioli button down?"

"Get the fuck outta here with that shit Schultzy, you're too caught up in all that bullshit." He says, pouring himself and me another drink from the bar now that we're back on the scotch. "It's all in your head, Man. You know, that right? All this shit…" He slurs, pointing around in a general sort of way, spilling his scotch on the polar bear rug. "All this shit is just in your fuckin' head, Man."

"I'll take that as a vote for the *Louie*." I say, putting on the shirt, taking the drink he poured me, drinking it all and handing the glass back to him, shaking the ice suggestively. "Is that what you're wearing?" I ask looking him up and down. He's wearing flip-flops from Wal-Mart, stained

blue jeans, a faded black and gold Mizzu T-shirt though he never went there and mirrored Aviator shades from Ray-Ban. He pours me another drink, hands it to me graciously, then tells me to *Fuck off.*

"Where are we on the coke?" I ask, though I'm distracted by the lack of definition in my Deltoids I'm inspecting in the gold-plated mirror in the living room. "And where the hell is Curt?"

"He said he had it taken care of." He says without looking up.

"Well where the mother F-word is he?" I ask, pacing the living room.

"He said he'd meet us there." Dicky says, tossing a Xanax into the air and catching it in his mouth.

"Wait, when did you talk to him?" I ask skeptically. Grabbing the cue ball from the pool table and tossing it casually into the air and catching it.

"He just fuckin' called, Dude." He says calmly. "Chill the fuck out."

"Can we crush some of those Xanax and snort a whole bunch of them?" I ask, setting the white cue ball down on the table less than gently.

"No Dude." He says dryly, finally looking at me from behind his mirrored shades.

"Then can we get the blow torch and start smoking them?" I demand, aggressively rolling the cue ball into the black 8 ball, missing the corner pocket.

"Dude, you need to chill the fuck out." He says, tossing me a Xanax which I also catch in my mouth like a dog.

"That's what I'm trying to do." I say, holding my hands out in front of me to show how bad the shaking is. Dicky is sitting on the bar stool, swiveling idly back and forth with his foot. Suddenly something hits me, and I ask, "Wait, he told you over the phone that he could; get coke, meet us at the gig, and be ready to pull this all off by 7 o'clock?" I ask, then digging in further, "When?"

"Dude, Schultz, I just got off the fuckin' phone with him." He says, holding up his cell phone, as if that offers any kind of assurance.

"Goddamn it, Richard!" I shout. "He's not that good at these things. He doesn't know...*the things!* Details get rearranged, misunderstandings all you see!"

"Chill out Dude, he'll be there. Let's pack this shit up and head out. Put a fucking T-shirt on and let's go you fuckin' queer." He says tossing a handful of ice cubes at me.

Chapter XLIV

The redial button on my phone is frozen solid. I give up trying to call Curt when we finally pull into Cooper's back parking that's already filled with cars and start to unpack our gear. With guitars in hand, we look up and see our name on the Marque: *The Merry Pranksters.* Biblical!

We enter through the back door and walk onto the dark stage to set up behind a thick velvet, maroon curtain. There's an S-load of people out there. All the boys are out there representing. Chad from Lindenwood and a massive amount of people I kind of recognize from school are here too. After getting everything set up, we grab a bottle of Courvoisier from the bar and go into the green room. Dicky is now sharing in my concern over Curt's absence.

Curt finally ambles through the door of the small room where me and Dicky are sitting on stools, tuning our guitars. Though it's freezing, he's shirtless, wearing a silver necklace with a skull medallion, a chain wallet connected to faded Lee jeans, one-armed shades and no coke.

"Oh, my fucking God, Dude." I'm saying as I pace back and forth of the little back room that passes for a backstage. There's a plush purple loveseat and a small glass table with two barstools

and a mirror on the table where the cocaine *isn't*. "I knew this was going to happen. Did I not say that this was going to happen?"

"Chill out Schultz." Curt says relatively calmly, not sure who to yell at yet.

"I did say that this was going to happen right?" I'm saying at Dicky. "Like, I *literally* said the words out loud."

"You said that *you* had it!" Curt is screaming now. "Why the fuck would I have it? I've been at work all day. You two Motherfuckers had nothing to do but get ready and get some fucking cocaine!"

"Alright, alright, alright, Dude." Dicky says, interrupting our respective melt downs. "We have some options, what are they? We just gotta think this through."

"Right, OK." Curt says after taking ten deep breaths and twirling his drumsticks. "M.B. said that no one has any, he's been trying to get some all day. That's why we're in this mess."

"Dog, you could haul ass to Duck's and get some stones." Dicky suggests.

I take a deep breath before saying to no one, "Some stones, really?"

"Yeah, or *you* could haul ass to Duck's to get some stones." Curt retorts, ignoring me all together.

"Your plan is to smoke crack before the gig, before *this* gig?" I'm shouting. Schvitzing.

"What's your brilliant plan college boy?" Curt asks me in a snarky tone.

Pause. I hear a commotion coming from the bar and I flash a glance towards the curtain suspiciously. Dicky and Curt notice it too but continue shouting at each other.

I shake it off then humbly offer, "Well, I guess we could just go out there and play without doing coke first."

"Schultz!" Dicky snaps, head down, unable to make eye contact. "This motherfucker, Dog. I swear to fucking God." He says looking at Curt but pointing at me, shaking his head.

"Be fuckin' realistic Schultz." Curt says calmly, almost begging.

We hear the noise again coming from the bar and the three of us peek behind the curtain to see what the hell is going on. The lights are shining in our eyes, but we can make out Barnes walking in the bar and trying to find a seat only he's being stalked by what looks like a red Cardinal following him in. He's trying to be cool, but this bird is not letting up and R.B. is walking through the bar shouting, "Get this motherfuckin' bird off of me!"

Dicky and Curt seem to settle on some kind of plan, but I can't take my eyes off of that bird. After R.B. makes it halfway in the bar, it floats gracefully up to the painting of a Daisy and a Shamrock intertwined, hanging above the bar and perches itself comfortably atop the golden frame.

Dicky pulls me by the collar out on to the stage. I'm wearing faded Levis, a black Johnny Cash T-shirt and flip-flops, I sit down at the drums. Dicky is wearing corduroy bell-bottoms, black Chuck Taylor's and an off brand, white button-down shirt casually undone. He picks up his axe and gives it a quick tune. Without saying anything to the crowd, I start playing *Fucking in the Bushes*, the song Oasis starts every show with. Dicky starts in with the guitar riff. This gets the crowd's attention but can't go on forever.

Curt goes out the back door and then comes back in through the front door, walks through the bar and slaps R.B. on the shoulder. He says something in his ear and they get up and walk out the front door. R.B. comes back in five minutes later and Curt finally peeks his head through the cur-

tain. Me and Dicky wrap up the song and Dicky says, "Hey everybody, thanks for coming out. We're The Merry Pranksters and uh...we'll be right back."

Applause.

We go in the back room and Curt already has six fatties broken out. We each do one, do a numby, take a drink from the bottle of Armand de Brignac, then do the other line. We take a deep breath then Curt stands up and says, "Alright boys, you ready to do this?"

"Fuck yeah, let's do this." Dicky says with a deep sniff.

We walk through the thick maroon, velvet curtain out onto the stage. I strap on my new axe, Valerie and adjust the tone. I'm wearing brown leather trousers with a silver and turquoise belt, snakeskin boots, a blue jean, rhinestone shirt with only two buttons done, my silver Keith skull ring and a silver necklace with dark Ray-Ban sunglasses. Dicky plugs in his axe and flips all the nobs on the amp up to 10. He's wearing a black suede cowboy hat, black leather pants, a ripped Union Jack T-shirt under a black, leather jacket, a diamond studded pinky ring and giant mirrored, aviator shades. Curt sits down at the drums wearing white, skinny jeans with black leather suspenders, no shirt, no accessories accept his one-armed shades.

Silence spreads across the bar like a black death. We don't say a word but when I notice that there is a tension building, I look at the crowd and hold out my arms and the crowd erupts. We go directly into *(What's the Story) Morning Glory.* Dicky starts with the guitar intro, then I start singing:

All your dreams are made
When you're chained to a mirror and a razor blade
Today's the day that all the world will see

The crowd is into it, I can feel it, everyone can feel it. The energy is returning; the pulse, the chills, it's all rushing back like a tsunami. They start to sway in unison. That leads to bobbing which gives way to bouncing up and down in a massive wave.

Need a little time to wake up
Need a little time to rest your mind
You know you should so I guess you might as well
What's the story morning glory

It's impossible to make out anyone's face in the crowd but everyone is on their feet cheering and shouting at us. The thick cigarette smoke mixing with the lights shining in our face makes this look like an 80's rock video. The only thing I can clearly make out is the red Cardinal perched upon the Daisy painting. The song ends, the vibe lives on.

"What's next boys?" Curt asks, wiping the sweat from his forehead.

I look at Dicky and ask, *"Best Friend's Girl?"*

"Why not." He shrugs.

Dicky starts in with the F, B#, C and starts singing:

You're always dancing down the street

With your suede blue eyes
And every new boy that you meet
He doesn't know the real surprise

Then I come in with the back lead and vocals, Curt comes in on the drums. As we're going through the chords and the singing, a oneness starts to engulf everyone in the room, the Pranksters included. It's an out of body experience that breaks everything down to an almost molecular level. It's out of our hands, it's a pulse, a heartbeat, a great awakening that we're all simultaneously affecting and being affected by. It's like being at a spiritual revival. We're being baptized by the force of it and it's absolutely brilliant.

Here she comes again
When she's dancing 'neath the starry skies
Ooh, she'll make you flip
Here she comes again
I kinda like the way she dips

'Cause she's my best friend's girl
She's my best friend's girl
But she used to be mine...

As the crowd erupts in applause, the heavens open, the stars align and are speaking to us, almost telling us what to say and what to play.

"Thanks for coming out tonight everybody." I start, "As some of you may know, we've lost a lot of people recently to drugs..." Pause. "Well not just any drugs, heroin mostly. Now, it's no secret that The Pranksters have been known to catch a good buzz every now and again and I would never preach to you, it's just, ya' know, you gotta live if you wanna catch that next buzz. I lost someone pretty close to me the other night, this one's for you Val. The boys are going to go get a drink and I'm gonna take this one by myself. Save me a *drink* boys." I say touching my thumb to my nose. "If I screw it up, just start clapping louder if you don't mind. It's called *Alison.*"

Oh, it's so funny to be seeing you after so long girl
And with the way you look I understand
That you are not impressed
But I heard you let that little friend of mine
Take off your party dress

The spotlight is on me and the room is silent but there is no anxiety, the stool I'm sitting on, the faceless crowd, the energy. It's all coming together.

I'm not gonna get too sentimental like those other sticker Valentines
'Cause I don't know if you've been loving somebody

I only know it isn't mine

Alison, I know this world is killing you
Oh, Alison, my aim is true...

When the lights go down and faces emerge, I see that there isn't a dry eye in the house.

"Thanks very much." I say as the crowd starts cheering vibrantly. The boys come back out and take up their axes.

"How 'bout we do an old favorite?" Dicky says into the microphone. "What'd ya say boys, *Martian*?"

Then he asks the crowd, "Any *Misfits* fans out there tonight?"

The audience gives a modest applause.

"Well this one's for you." He says.

I start in with classic the A E D intro that stabs you through the gut with a machete.

Possession of the mind is a terrible thing
It's a transformation with an urge to kill
Not the body of a man from Earth,
Not the face of a one you love 'cause

When I turned into a Martian
(Oh Oh Oh)
Well I can't even recall my name
(Oh Oh Oh)
Times I never hardly sleep at night
(Oh Oh Oh)
When I turned into a Martian today.

The feeling in the room is electric.

Dicky says, "Thanks for coming out tonight. We're The Merry Pranksters. This is a song, it's about two days old. Schultz just taught it to me this morning. You know who you are all you Funky Junkie Mammas!!! Let's Go!"

The vibe in the room is pure flowing energy. The crowd is acting like one entity, they're all moving together. Dicky does a stage dive and they all pick him up and pass him around, touching him like a god. Like a swarm of bees, they all somehow know what to do, are subconsciously working toward the same goal though no one is aware of what that is in the moment, but everyone knows that it is somehow exactly what they should be doing. Biblical.

I took my girl, I took her down...took her downtown
We scored a boulder, then we flipped it around...around a pound

Cross my heart and hope to die
Fill that rig up, stick it in my eye

Double down, heat it up and then
Fly, fly, fly

She was my funky junky mama
But I lied, lied, lied
Go crazy, fuck around
and she'll cry, cry, cry
Break her dopey little heart
and she'll die, die, die
She was my funky junky mama...
and she died.

Halfway through the song we see about five cops come in and they do not look like they're here to enjoy the show. They start pushing and shoving their way in the door and through the crowd. They must have seen our name on the marque and did the pawn shop math. This could blow the encore, how the fudgesicles are we going to get out of this? Dicky looks at me, I'm looking at him, we look back at Curt and he looks out to the crowd for M.B. and Ryan Barnes. I look at M.B. and motion with my eyes to the cops. He sees them and knows just what to do. We start playing *I Predict a Riot*. The crowd reacts and instinctively works to help us out. Mother nature working in our favor.

M.B. stands up, gives us a nod, then takes a chair and flings it across the room. The chair explodes against the wall opposite them and shatters into a thousand pieces like box of toothpicks. Everyone turns to look at the ruckus which offers M.B. the diversion needed to really set this thing off. He then takes a bottle of Grolsh and smashes it on the head of an LU football player by the name of Pete "The Beast" Hollenbrook.

The bottle breaks over his head, but this does nothing except aggravate The Beast. He shakes off the broken glass, the fine German beer, and the blood that is pouring from the temple of his head from the gash of the bottle and postures to clobber M.B. Before he can raise a fist however, M.B. lands a shin kick slash two finger eye gouge combo that blinds The Beast long enough for M.B. to hit him square in the nose, M.B.'s signature knock-out punch that rarely needs to be repeated.

Ryan Barnes steps up and completely flips over the table they were sitting at, beer bottles, black, plastic ashtrays and all onto the Lambda Lambda Lambdas. They respond as you would imagine a table full of Fraternity brothers would respond, they stand up and are steaming. Once they shake off the beer that was spilt on them, they are absolutely livid. The first guy comes at Barnes but instead of punching him, Barnes tries to implement a bigger strategy, one that will deal with six big dudes at once.

Barnes takes the first dude, an LU linebacker named Trenton, by the head and smashes his face into the glass window of Cooper's, causing the glass to shatter but only slightly, the way the windshield of the Caddy did not. There's a little bit of blood in the meager dent that the dude's face put in the glass wall but as Barnes pulls the guy's face back by his hair, he sees that his nose is not broken, just a steady blood stream. So, Barnes smashes his face in the glass once more in the same spot and pulls his head back again.

Of course, the guy is squirming around and trying to cup his hands at his nose which is no doubt in a great deal of pain, yet not quite broken. Ryan goes for round three, annoyed that this is taking longer than it should, even harder this time. *Bam!* Face right back into the glass but when he pulls the guy's head back this time, blood is squirting from his nose which has finally broken.

Just in the nick of time because the rest of the Tri Lambdas are now positioned to attack, so Ryan holds Trenton's head by the hair with his right hand and, holding his left arm with Ryan's left hand behind Trenton's back, is able to leverage his head and spray the Lambdas with enough Frat boy blood to hold them off until they are not only covered and blinded by all the blood squirting like a fire hose, covering their faces and the floor but also slipping around in it, unable to gain any kind of footing needed to participate in a fight in any kind of realistic way.

All the Lindenwood nerds there have no idea what kind of chaos they're inviting into their lives, a brawl immediately ensues. Bottles are flying, chairs are breaking, blood is flowing, teeth are scattered everywhere. An eyeball flies across the room and lands on the stage by my suede Chelsea Boots. The cops are immediately distracted and are shouting for order. They start beating people with their batons and calling for back-up but it's too loud and violent. The police are incapable of maintaining any kind of order out of this chaos and they don't know what to do about it. One of them starts crying and shouting, "We will have order. We will have order!" until he gets knocked out by a flying beer mug. M.B. and Ryan Barnes are behind the bar now, watching their handywork playout, pouring glasses of Tequila and drinking them, cheers-ing each other along the way.

Me and the Pranksters have already started taking apart our gear and stealing anything we can fit in the car. This place is going to be trashed after this so we might as well take what we can. What the hell, Hiro has insurance. Not the drum set or anything, but guitar chords and mics and stuff. We make two trips to the car, fill it up and then peel the hell out of the parking lot.

As we drive away, I look back at Coopers from the back seat of Dicky's Durango and see plumes of smoke beginning to obscure the marquee that read, The Merry Pranksters. I turn back around, facing the future and say, "Well boys, that was as close to God as we're ever likely to ascend."

Chapter XLV

In case the cops figure out where we live, we stash the newly stolen guitar and amps in a damp and dreary corner of the basement, past the washer and dryer that no one uses and then stash about 30 ounces of weed from Curt's room, his gun, and the Jack Daniels drug box in the clean part of the basement that is set up like a living room for when Daffy cycles back around and stays with us.

Back upstairs, we each take a hippopotamus tranquilizer to take the edge off, then I make a pitcher of Martinis from the bar and pour each of us a stiff drink. Curt empties out a mountain of coke on the mirror coffee table and cuts out gigantic lines that are the size of snow piles on the side of the road after a blizzard. Dicky goes out the back door and cuts about a foot-long piece off the garden hose to use as a straw. The idea of rocking some of it up to blast is tossed around but ultimately discarded as a waste of time because people, and more than likely, the cops, will surely be coming by soon.

We're on our third pitcher of Beefeater Gin martinis and Nelly is on the Moon Audio's Dark Star Opulence stereo singing Country Grammar when M.B. and Ryan Barnes walk in the house without knocking carrying a case of Heineken Bottles and two bottles of Tanqueray with the bar nozzles taken off that they stole from Cooper's and two smoking hot girls that I recognize from Lindenwood, wearing hip hugger jeans from Abercrombie and Fitch, and tank tops.

The brunette, who may or may not be an Eskimo, has a *Rachel* haircut and is chewing gum and blowing little bubbles when she is not laughing at what Barnes is saying. The blond is not ugly per se, she just unfortunately has a striking resemblance to an anorexic Cabbage Patch doll with braces. Decent body, no back acne or anything. I'm sure she's pretty good from far, but far from good.

"What's up girls?" I say looking up from my martini.

"Hey, you guys were like, so fucking amazing!" The blond says. I think her name is Amanda.

"Yeah, that was awesome!" The dark-haired Eskimo says, her name could be Amy, could be Quin, but I could be totally wrong about both of those. She's batting her eyes at Dicky then says, "Has anyone ever told you that you look like Richard Gere?"

"No, I've never heard that before." Dicky lies.

They go into his bedroom and all I hear is, *ZZZZIIIIP.*

"You guys fucking missed it." Barnes and M.B. both sort of say at the same time, sitting down on the leather sofas and dumping another mountain of cocaine on the table.

"What?" We ask, passing the garden hose around.

"You guys already jetted, but that brawl got way moin." M.B. is explaining. "After everyone started fighting, me and Barnes just hopped behind the bar and started brewin'. Those Lindenwold pussies fight like little bitches, Dude. They kept tossing drinks and flipping over tables instead of throwing punches. So, I guess all the candles that were on the tables all fell on the floor when the tables got knocked over and all the alcohol that was covering the place started to catch on fire!"

"Yeah Dude," Barnes takes over the story. "So, the floor is catching on fire like it was nothing but gasoline, like in a fucking movie, then some of the tables started to catch on fire and then this dude's fucking arm caught on fire!" He ends dramatically.

"No fucking way!" Curt says.

"Fuck yeah, Dude! That got everyone's attention and everyone kind of chilled out and stopped fighting. People tried to splash water on it, but it must have been a glass of vodka or something because it just spread to his face. His hair caught on fire and then he started freaking out and ended up running into the glass."

"Did he crash through like you did with that dude's face?" Curt asks.

"Not the first time." Barnes laughs.

"What? Get the fuck outta here." Dicky says.

"No Dude," Barnes says, "he ran into the glass the first time, I think he was looking for the door but ended up running into it again and one of the cops tried to put the fire out on the dude and they both ended up crashing through the glass wall and out onto the sidewalk."

"No flippin' way!" I say.

"Yeah, the fucking cop was on fire too. He had to take his belt off and throw it so his glock didn't start going off and killing people. Just then the other cop found the fire extinguisher and hosed them off, but someone had stolen his belt." MB says.

"Fuck no!?" Curt says.

"Yeah, I think it was Mort." M.B. says.

"Was it you?" I ask them both in my most earnest tone.

"Fuck no," He says. "we were behind the bar brewin' the whole time."

"Dude," Curt shouts, "if the fuckin' cops somehow track us down and there is a stolen cop belt anywhere near here, we'd all be royally fucked."

"It wasn't us, chill the fuck out." Barnes says.

"Well what happened then?" Fook asks. "Did anyone get sketted?"

"Maybe, no one we knew." Barnes says. "When the fire trucks started showing up, we all took off."

"Yeah, there weren't enough cops there to start arresting anyone. It was a fucking free for all." M.B. says.

"Fucking hell." Fooky says.

"Well it was nice diversion anyway." Curt says holding up his Martini glass for everyone to cheers.

"Yeah, no shit. *Cheers!*" We all say, smashing our glasses together.

Chapter XLVI

It's so cold in the house that even Curt is wearing a navy-blue pull-over from Tommy Hilfiger. It sounds like Barnes is beating M.B. in a heated Foosball match, but I can't bring myself to care. Elvis Costello is on the stereo singing *Less Than Zero* and CNN is now incessantly coving the murder of Chandra Levy. A black snake just slithered around the bar and left it's shed skin under

the Polar Bear rug, and I can't stop thinking about Valerie. I can almost feel her with me everywhere I've gone since she died.

It's hard to believe that it was just two nights ago that her mom called and told me the news, a lot has gone down since then. Cabbage Patch Amanda and Quin the Eskimo are sitting on the bar stools drinking Heineken beers from the tap and shots of Jägermeister as fast as Fooky can pour them. He's trying to show them a magic trick with a deck of cards but keeps balling it up, possibly just biding time before the roofies that he more than likely slipped them kick in.

Curt is sitting on the leather sofa trying to light a joint that is slightly bigger than a California sushi roll but the cold breeze in the house keeps blowing out his golden Zippo lighter until a blow torch is introduced. Dicky is sitting next to me on the couch snorting bumps out of a platinum ladle from the kitchen. After a significant pause, he sits up straight and says, "Schultz…" He's pinching his nose and sniffing deeply.

"What?" I ask, posturing for a massive line of cocaine.

"Dude, did you know that at the same time Van Halen was coming up in L. A., Randy Rhodes was coming up at the same time?"

"Yeah, I kind of did know that." I say, inhaling a gram of coke then taking one, two, eight bumps. "Why?" I ask letting a drop of water drip off of my finger into my nose and snorting until I can feel it all rushing down my throat, numbing everything on its way through my digestive system.

"Isn't that fucked up?" He asks. "I mean that two of the arguably greatest guitar players of the eighties came up at the same time and place. Isn't that like... a huge fuckin' coincidence?"

"Yeah, there can only be two." I say, sinking back into the sofa. Distracted. "We were just talking about this the other day, remember?"

"What the fuck does that mean?" Fooky asks from behind the bar, across the room.

"Well, it's just like in Star Wars…" I start to say.

"Oh, here we fucking go again." M.B. says after slamming his foosball strikers so hard that the table scuffs the marble tile floor, scoring on Barnes.

"Well there's a reason that Star Wars always has two heroes, a master and an apprentice. It's an ancient archetype. All the European hero stories have the same dynamic." I say.

"Yeah, but that's fiction. Eddie Van Halen and Randy Rhodes are real people." Fooky argues.

"Were you not here when we talked about this?" I ask.

"Well I don't know what the fuck you're talking about so no, I guess I wasn't Schultz." He answers with a snark to out-snark all snarks.

"Yeah, well, the fictional stories we know, the good ones, the ones that stand the test of time come from the real world around us. Think about other examples of exactly the same thing: Bob Marley and Peter Tosh, Malcolm X and Martin Luther King Jr., even that Yen/Yang tattooed on your arm. It's the dark and the light. Bob Marley was the light, the positive vs. the darker side of Peter Tosh. Same with Malcolm X, he was the negative, violent Yang to MLK's peaceful Yen. You can't have light without dark, night without day. In all chaos there is a cosmos, in all disorder, a secret order."

"Who said that?" Fooky asks.

"Carl Jung." I say, guessing. "The point is, there's a reason you read about, or see in movies the same story played out over and over again; the hero and the villain, the master and the apprentice, it's because that's what is played out in life over and over again, throughout history."

"Yeah, that is pretty fucked up how real it is." Curt says mixing cocaine with water and dripping it in his eye.

"It is." I say. "The fact that it keeps coming up, I don't know how exactly it keeps coming up over and over, but it does. It's like, which came first, the chicken or the egg, you know what I mean?"

"No Dude, what do you mean?" Fook asks.

"Well, maybe if it weren't for Bob Marley being so positive, Peter Tosh wouldn't have gone so extreme in the other direction. Or maybe it was the other way around."

"I heard Peter Tosh was pissed because the American record company wanted to make The Wailers, *Bob Marley* and The Wailers because he was light skinned and that would help record sales in the States." Dicky says.

"That's probably true, whatever the reason, they started out more or less equal and then as time went on, after spinning around and round, they became more and more polarized. I mean, look at God and Satan. Satan was God's favorite angel, but that's not the way humans work, they could never just continue as good buddies, it's human nature to split and evolve. When one goes further one way, the other goes further the opposite way. It's the same with politics today."

"But God and Satan aren't human." Fook redundantly points out.

"It's all a metaphor for human behavior, it's the ultimate in human experiences." I'm saying. "That's why it's called a meta-story. Because it's runs so deep in our DNA, our human, our animal DNA that it comes out in every good story throughout history."

"That's deep Dude." Fook says, freebasing a ladle full of cocaine through a platinum straw that has *The Beast* engraved on it.

Chapter XLVII

As the grandfather clock chimes two, the adrenaline has worn off. The booze, the coke, the unnamed divine energy from above have extinguished like a menorah after Chanukah. I struggle to my feet as the room spins out of any means of control and limp clumsily towards my bedroom.

"Schultz, where the hell are you going? We're just about to break out the nitrous tank!" Curt shouts at me.

"I gotta see a cat about a dog." I say, stumbling and gripping at the wall.

"What?" I can hear someone shout from the living room.

“I gotta piss.” I shout back. I slip into my bedroom, flop down on my king-sized bed and slide away into the welcoming arms of Morpheus. I allow my thoughts to drift. I wish Valerie could have seen us tonight. I think she would have been proud of us, of me. The notion that I will never see her glowing aura again, never smell the faint whiffs of patchouli coming from her bronze skin again, never know anyone like her ever again for the rest of my life. Suddenly a loneliness seeps in as that train of thought works its way around me, surrounds me, wraps me up and spins me into a sleep-like trance, one for the ages.

Visions of snow falling upwards, serpents outsmarting dragons, angels and dragon slayers, rats and flooded bedrooms in familiar dwellings create a biblical narrative until suddenly, my trance is shattered. I’m awoken by Ginger, who has slipped into my room, wanting some of the General. My silk boxers from Lord & Taylor are around my ankles and Ginger is deep throating my nerd, gagging on it. I gently take hold of her red hair and ease her mouth off the General.

“Whoa, whoa, whoa. Hang on.” I say, jabbing her mouth one last time.

“What the fuck?” She says, wiping her mouth with her thumb.

“Hey.” I say sitting up and covering myself modestly. “I don’t think we should do this anymore. I-I can’t do this anymore. It’s not right.” I say, covering my nerd with my down comforter so she can’t bite it off or something.

“What?” She snaps, her eyes catching on fire.

“Look… C’mon. You have to see how messed up this is.” I’m pleading. “You know I’m like, in love with someone else and that Steve guy seems to love you. If you're going to screw around, you should break up with him. It’s the only thing to do, it’s the right thing to do.”

“You have to be fucking joking me.” She says with an evil cackle.

A magma of terror explodes like a premonition of flying machines crashing into buildings. To avenge her scorn, there are no depths to which this creature will not delve. Her face is aglow with rage as I lose whatever composure I once had like Adam when he became conscience that Eve had just doomed humanity for all eternity. When sparks begin to fly from her fingertips, this whole dream is vanquished when I hear a loud banging from the living room that was not supposed to there.

Bam! Bam!

“Shit.” I say, kind of pushing her off of me, my composure returning. “I think the cops might be here.”

“Why would the cops be here?” She asks, blowing the smoke away from her fingernails.

“Long story.” I say, trying to pull up my silk L & Ts up with my toes.

The commotion continues curiously from the Living Room, then a familiar voice demands, “Where is she? Where the fuck is that bitch?!”

“Is that your fucking boyfriend?” I ask, an air of confusion blows in the room, across the bed, blowing pillows over and sending chills down my spine.

“Oh, who cares about him.” She slurs, snapping her black, lace bra back in place.

“He’s standing ten yards away for fuck sake, he’s just on the other side of that door!” I’m thinking to myself, then say as much out loud. At least I can take some sort of comfort in the notion that there is zero chance that cuck is getting past *that* room full of *those* boug boys. Then I hear…

“Oh yeah man, she’s in there with Schultz.” Dicky says followed bellows of drunken laughter. Thanks, you smarmy pricks.

Before I can get my silk boxers up all the way, Ginger still fumbling awkwardly with her bra, Steve the Cuck kicks in my bedroom door. His silhouette huffing against the noise and light flooding my dark bedroom from the living room. He stands there, a black shadow in my doorway for a beat before sobbing, “You bitch! You fucking bitch!”

“Alright, take it easy Dude.” I say, unsure of who I’m trying to convince.

“Get the fuck out of here!” Ginger says in a bitchy tone that I was unaware was in her repertoire until now.

I’m standing by my bed now, casually grabbing at my Calvin Kline jeans from off the floor in the same way I would during any other one of our exchanges in the history of our exchanges, only I’m not putting them on. Something is telling me that this is not like any of our other exchanges, something is telling me that I should not open myself up to the vulnerable position of putting my jeans on while this guy is standing in front of me trembling while his girlfriend is lying half-naked on my bed. I try to look past him to see what the boys are waiting for, why is this cuck not an unconscious cuck heap in my doorway right now? Is this what PCP looks like?

His silhouette shifts slightly, I can see Dicky standing next to Curt signing something silently with his hands. He points to Steve the Cuck’s waistband as Ryan Barnes holds M. B. back clumsily, knocking over a bottle of Grey Goose Vodka from the bar and sending it crashing to the floor. In a panic, Steve the Cuck reaches behind his back and pulls out a black Smith and Wesson pistol from his waist, steps into my room and points it at me, then at Ginger, then back at me.

Instantly, the sky falls from the heavens. Nothing is the same. This is not the same house it was a moment ago. I’m suddenly hyper aware of everything, every movement, every breath, every heartbeat, every bead of sweat. Everyone’s position is now a strategic 3-D chess move. Steve the Cuck is now standing on the inside of my bedroom door, a wall now between him and the boys who are standing just outside the door.

Ginger, still sitting on my bed looking bored, says dryly, “Put that thing away.”

“You fucking bitch!” He shouts, somewhere in-between a plea and a sob. “I fucking loved you, I gave you everything!”

“Oh, don’t be such a cry-baby, you didn’t give me shit.” She says dismissively, doing nothing to deescalate the situation.

“But you're my wife! What about us, what about our family, our daughter?” He sobs, holding the gun to his own head now. The shepherd has become the wolf, the wolf has become the shepherd.

Did he just say *wife*? As that word bounces around in my head for a Mississippi or two, I hear it echoed by the boys on the other side of the wall. The word *daughter* is sort of buried by the whole *wife* bombshell but is still tiptoeing around on the sidelines of my mind, waiting to be acknowledged which, come to think of it, sounds like an accurate description of this daughter’s whole existence. Poor kid, god knows what she was born addicted to or what kind of neglect she’s exposed to on the reg.

Steve the Cuck is pacing back and forth now with little to no regard for the gun in his hand or where or whom it’s pointed at. He’s in such a panic now, weeping and trembling, drooling and seething from his mouth. His eyes are on fire and he’s tearing his greasy hair out by the fistful.

This is extremely painful to have to sit through, watching him turn from a grown man, as pathetic a cuck of a man he is, a man none the less, rocking himself back and forth across my bedroom floor repeating, *You whore! You filthy whore!* with a gun waving around every other minute or so is spiraling out of control into a nerve twisting crescendo that I'm in no condition to handle with any kind of wits about me.

I can see the boys plotting something from the living room. All I'm able to make out are their shadows moving around on the wall, but the crystal margarita pitcher is missing from the table and the 7 iron is out of its sheath from the rack by the corner of the front door. It occurs to me that Curt may be planning to employ his glock before I remember that we just stashed it in the basement.

Steve the Cuck's face is a pulsating dickhead purple now, his head looks like he just underwent a third round of chemo, his greasy hair scampered around my floor like an Italian barber shop, he's growling like a rabid dog. Ginger has even done away with that bitchy smirk on her face and is now staring at him with a queer expression that I have no idea how to read. Almost careful not to add one more strand to this tangled web she's weaved. She's woven it just perfectly and now she is just observing him, curious as to just how far he's going to take this whole thing. Marveling in awe at the chaos she's created and is now unfolding before us all.

As Steve the Cuck's breakdown is at its peak, his patterns become predictable. A subconscious attempt to reenact some kind of order to this whole mess. This gives the boys a chance to intervene. The shadows on the wall have stopped moving and are now in a sedimentary, Charlie's Angels position on my opened bedroom door. I'm standing, cornered against my bed and the back wall with my Calvin's in my hand. I have managed to slip my Harley Davidson belt out of its loops and wrapped it around my right hand with the silver buckle loose, ready to strike if the opportunity presents itself.

With pristine timing, when Steve the Cuck's march approaches the bedroom door, Dicky reaches around from the other side and smashes the Margarita pitcher on his temple with a mighty crash. It shatters against his head instantly sending glass flying in all directions, he stumbles back against the wall, bloody with the gun still in his hand. I take a step forward and whip him in the head with my belt buckle just as M. B. steps around from outside the door, grabs his right hand and slams it up over his head, against the wall in an attempt to knock the gun out of his hand. The gun goes off with a deafening explosion as smoke fills the room and pieces of drywall and ceiling fall to the floor like ashen soot.

In a PCP induced rage, Steve the Cuck frees his hand, fires the gun into the floor and, despite several otherwise knockout blows from M. B., Curt and Ryan Barnes, he manages to scramble his way out of my bedroom, through the living room, spraying blood all over the Polar Bear rug and leather sofas before he is forced out of the front door with blows and kicks. Once the door is able to fasten shut, Curt turns the deadlock and leaves Steve the Cuck banging on it from the outside with the butt of the gun and screaming from the front porch.

He's raging on from the freezing night. "How could you do this to me? How could you fucking do this!? What about our daughter, what about our home, our family? Blah, blah, blah...You fucking bitch. You fucking whore! Blah, blah..."

I walk back into my bedroom where Ginger is still sitting on my bed with her eyes glazed over, mesmerized and tell her to stay put while I finally put on my jeans then go out to the living

room, look around at the boys, the blood and the broken glass and manage to say, "What in the absolute, arctic monkey fucking hell?"

No one is laughing as we all stand around and sort of survey the house, looking at it for the first time in this new way, this new light. This is not the same house it was eleven and-a-half minutes ago. Nothing is the same. Of all the crazy shit that has gone down amongst these four walls, all the mind-bending realities that have shaped the way we all perceive this place, nothing has done anything to shatter the reality of this house like what has just transpired. No one invited this snake into the garden, yet we are all responsible for letting it in. Neither God nor man can keep the dragon of chaos from entering the walled garden.

No one is under the delusion that this is over either, Steve the Cuck is still banging on the front door with a vengeance that only a PCP high can account for. He's screaming, "Bitch, get out here. Let me in you motherfuckers! You fucking whore. I'll kill you!!"

"Somebody's gonna call the fucking cops, Dude." Dicky says, finishing a glass of Wild Turkey and ice.

"They probably already have." I say, grabbing a bottle of Jack Daniels from the bar and taking a deep swig. Unable to stand the banging anymore, I foolishly open the front door and try to explain this to Steve the Cuck but all that I can manage to verbalize is, "Hey, fuck right off ya cunt!"

As soon as I open the door, however, Steve the Cuck knocks me in the face with the butt of his faggy little gun through the door like a little bitch. I slam it quickly, grip my nose and cup my lip which are both bleeding and wonder how I'm going to snort anything with this amount of blockage. "That mothercucker." I say, shaking my head, my hand cupping my face, so no more blood gets on our furniture, the Polar Bear rug, or my suede boots.

This has gone on long enough. The boys and I are fed up and, without counseling each other, collectively we all decide to end this right here and now. Curt walks over and grabs the 7 Iron that is lying by the door and heads out the back-door growling, "This motherfucker, I knew these motherfuckers were trouble since the first time I saw them!"

I'm right behind him and everyone else is right behind me, out the back door, around the side of the house and on to the front where Steve the Cuck is still banging and shouting at the top of his lungs. The air is sharp and frigid, the dark night illuminated by the full moon shining down. The dead, frozen leaves crunching beneath our feet as we approach the front of the house.

"Hey!" Curt barks as he approaches the Cuck and before Steve can fully turn around, *BAM!!* Curt whacks him across the face with the 7 Iron.

Pause.

Suddenly everything stops. There is no sound, no wind, no time, no motion. Then a pulse. A single heartbeat before the play button is pressed and the heavy breathing resumes. Curt is standing there in front of him, 7 iron in hand. He snarls. "I told you to shut the fuck up you pathetic cuck."

Steve the Cuck wobbles, holding his face, he stumbles one foot at a time, no two steps are in the same direction. He manages to maintain his footing down the hill and into the road where the streetlights and the moon above capture his dark silhouette and blood pouring through his shaking fingers. I walk up to square off with him, ready for whatever is to come. Each breath from

my mouth comes out in a frosty cloud that hangs lazily in the dark night before escaping into the darkness. I'm shivering.

Curt goes to hit him again, to finish him off. I stop him.

He's holding the left side of his face with both hands, dark blood dripping down, it's a real horror show. He's bent down but then stands up straight, seemingly gaining some sort of composure. We're all standing there waiting to see what he's going to do. The light is shining down on him and finally, he slowly lowers his hands from his face.

A bitter wind blows, a terrifying gasp escapes his lips. It takes a moment to comprehend what exactly we're looking at but when things come into focus, I realize that his mother fucking eyeball is pulsing inside of his cupped hands. The left side of his face is completely shattered and sunken in. His eyeball, no more, just a black, empty socket steaming as his soul slides away into the frigid autumn air.

He gasps for breath, but the air is obstructed by something, so it comes out a coughing kind of a gag. He spits out a mouthful of thick blood and only once the blood hits the street do I notice his teeth are mixed in there like an adolescent nightmare.

The harvest moon peeks from behind a dark nebulous cloud, shining down from the sky, illuminating the park, the street, Steve the Cuck and his smashed in face. He's still holding his eyeball in his cupped hands, looking at it, or is it looking at him. Nerves, or possibly the loss of blood finally overcome him, and his legs become feeble. He sinks down to his knees and begins to sob. I can't help but wonder where the tears are coming out but I don't dare grab him by the hair to hold his head up so my question can be answered. This will surely haunt me for the rest of my days.

I don't take any enjoyment in what I'm seeing before me. I never had any ill feelings toward Steve, as big of a cuck as he was. I felt sorry for the poor bastard, and I feel bad for him now. The same way you feel bad for a conquistador that has the tables turned on him and ends up with a bull's horn sticking out of his ass. You feel bad enough but can't help but think that there's a reason for the saying, "If you fuck with a bull, you get the horn."

In the same way, you don't blame the bull. It's what bulls do. It's like the scorpion and the frog story, it's just in the scorpion's nature. We don't call Curt *The Dog* for nothing after all.

In the distance we can hear sirens nearing, red and blue lights begin to strobe around the perimeters of the park. Curt doesn't even bother trying to hide anywhere. We all kind of gather to confirm what we all know; That dude barged in our house; we were just defending the crib, the rug.

The sirens are fast approaching. Fooky goes inside and stashes everything illegal, sneaks Ginger out the back and drives her to an unknown location in the Lincoln. Someone probably called the cops 25 minutes ago when Steve the Cuck fired two shots in the house or while he was pounding on the door and screaming that he was going to kill us all. Too bad they didn't get here in time to save this poor twat. It is worth mentioning to Steve the Cuck that he brought this whole mess on himself and he should think very carefully before he considers making this out to be something that it isn't.

Ryan Barnes takes it upon himself to walk over and explains with as much tact as he can muster, "Hey Motherfucker, your ass is lucky that you're sitting here with your eyeball in your motherfucking hands. You broke into my boy's house and started waving a gun around and

throwing punches, your ass is lucky you're still fucking breathing. Next time you won't be so lucky, don't even think about trying to twist this around on us." Then he takes the gun from his hand and empties the bullets, wipes it clean for fingerprints then shoves it back in Steve the Cuck's Wrangler jeans. "Everyone on this street heard you banging on their door and screaming that you were going to kill all of us. That's why the cops are on the way now. Remember that shit you fucking cuck ass bitch."

With Steve the Cuck sobbing unconsolably on his knees in the middle of the dark street, the cops pull up and me and the boys are all standing on the sidewalk, leaning against the wall to our yard. I light a Marlboro Red. The cops get out of their patrol cars and immediately call for an ambulance. Two cops, Sanchez and his rookie partner Johnson, walk up and look us up and down with their flashlights. Sanchez gives his thick mustache a wipe before landing his flashlight on Curt and asks, "You want to tell me what went on here tonight?"

"Uh, well, that dude broke into our house with a gun and tried to kill us all, so I had to hit him." Curt explains calmly.

"So, what you're telling me right now is that you hit him?" Sanchez asks, smacking on a piece of Nicorette gum.

"Yeah." Curt answers.

"Just you? It looks like you all beat the crap out of him." Johnson, the heavy-set rookie chimes in.

"No sir. I just hit him once." Curt says.

"Well, I hit him in the house with a Martini pitcher." Dicky admits.

"I see. And you, you hit him with what?" Sanchez asks, flipping to a fresh page in his notebook.

"A 7 iron." Curt says, trying his hardest not to let a smirk escape him.

"Where is it?" Sanchez digs deeper, writing this all down.

"I tossed it into the park. Over there." He says pointing into the darkness.

Pause.

"So, he has a gun?" Johnson finally asks, nodding toward Steve the one-eyed Cuck.

"Yeah." I answer for Curt.

"Where is the gun now?" Sanchez asks.

"I think it's still on him." Barnes says.

"Why was he trying to break into your house?" Sanchez asks, squinting and unconvinced.

"Uh, he thought his girlfriend was in there uh…partying." Dicky says, flirting with the truth.

"Partying?" Johnson questions.

"He thought that she was with me." I admit.

"Was she?" He asks.

"No, she wasn't." Curt jumps in, sticking to the story. "He was drunk or on PCP or something. He was pounding on our door and screaming. At one point he got in and threatened to kill us all. He was waving the gun around and screaming like a fucking lunatic. That's when he hit him." He finishes, gesturing at my bleeding nose.

"Who, him?" He asks, writing all of this down, eyeballing me suspiciously. "What's Cyclopes' name?"

Long pause. No one says anything. Looks are exchanged, shoulders are shrugged.

“What?” Sanchez asks smacking loudly at his Nicorette gum, pen in hand. “Who is he, what’s his name?” He demands.

“Uh, I don’t know.” Dicky finally says.

“Yeah man, I don’t know.” Curt says. “We don’t know.”

“I mean, we called him Steve the Cuck I guess, but we really didn’t know him.” I offer.

“Steve the what?” Sanchez asks.

“The Cuck. Steve the Cuck. You know what a cuck is?” Curt is saying.

“Uh, yeah! I mean, wait…what?” Sanchez asks in faux confusion.

“Yeah, he came over here like twice but none of us really knew who he was.” I say.

“Well what about the girl?” He asks, eager to get to the bottom of this, prepared to finally write a name down, he licks the tip of his pen. “Who was she?”

“Uh…I really don’t know.” Curt says again shattering all of Officer Johnson’s hopes and dreams like he shattered Steve the Cuck’s face.

“Well what about you Loverboy?” He asks, shining the flashlight in my face. “It sounds like you knew her pretty damn well, who was she?”

“Honestly?” I start hesitantly, realizing how wildly unsatisfying this must sound to a cop. “Again, we called her Ginger, but I don’t really know who she was. I don’t even know her real name. I don’t know who she was.”

“So, she was just some girl that you all partied with and that lump of bones over there is her boyfriend but none of you know who the hell they are?” He asks, his patience running thin.

“Actually, I think they’re married.” Curt says as a crisp autumn breeze blows by, sending a chain reaction of chills through us all.

“Oh yeah, no shit.” Dicky laughs.

“For real Sir, we really never knew who they were.” Curt says.

“Yeah Dude, you can give us a lie detector test.” Dicky says. “We never really knew them at all.”

“Yeah, we really don’t know anything about them.” I add.

“Alright, you boys stay put while we try to figure this mess out.” Sanchez says. He motions for Johnson to follow him. They’re clearly annoyed and in need of some closure.

What an absolute buzz kill. I light another cigarette and look around, no one speaks a word, there really is nothing to say. I look out at the park and though the moon has ducked behind a dark and luminous cloud, through the darkness, all is made clear. I can make out every swing and slide at the playground, every spot that I ever hit a golf ball, every BBQ grill around the pavilion. I don’t even have to turn around to know what every brick looks like on our house, exactly where the chairs are on the porch, what everything looks like through the window. Everything I know is right around me and I’m forced to entertain the thought that this very well may be the last time I ever see any of this.

A light snow begins to fall, and I can’t help thinking that, whatever happens from now is unknown, unknowable. As chaotic as my life, all of our lives, have been for as long as I can remember, compared to now, that all made sense, that was order. We are all about to step into a vast bottomless pit of chaos. Even if we don’t all go to jail for this, somehow, this place will never be the same again. Maybe one day I’ll come back here, maybe tomorrow morning, maybe ten

years from now but either way, it will be different. Tainted and bloody. It will never be like this again. This house, this street, this town, hell, maybe even this country.

Maybe it's like that fire that burned down St. Louis back in the day. I remember Dicky repeating what I had told Curt, that it was a good thing for the fires to burn the forest. That it clears the brush and the undergrowth and allows the forest to grow back, rise from the ashes.

Maybe that's us. Maybe we have to die to be reborn, maybe we have to destroy everything in order to start new, start fresh. For there to be growth, we have to let go of the past. We don't want to do it, no one ever wants to do it. Letting go of even the most bitter poison is painful, so we don't consciously do it but somewhere within all seven of us here tonight, including Steve the Cuck, we do it. Maybe whatever force brought us all here tonight was so that we could collectively burn this mother fucker down so we can all start over, be reborn, and rise from the ashes.

As we're leaning against the brick wall, silently looking out into the vast emptiness of the night, a little red Cardinal bird flutters by. Ryan Barnes sees it and says, "Is that that motherfucking bird from the bar. I'd kill that little bitch if the cops weren't here."

After getting my attention, the bird flirts around on the street, flies up to the streetlight and pivots around before flying off again, playfully dancing with the lightly falling snow, across the street, down into the park where it rests on a swing. In the silence of the night, the sweet song she sings carries all the way back to my ears and warms my soul with a familiar tune. She stops, looks back at me, and whistles one more verse of love. The swing rocks gently back and then forth as the snow begins to settle on her crimson feathers.

After a ball-twistingly long pause, Officer Sanchez comes back and says, "Yeah, he's not talking. I don't think he *can* talk; hell, he may never talk again. You really bashed the hell out of that guy. On the bright side, a couple of your neighbors corroborated your story that he was pounding on your door and screaming about killing people and that they heard the shots from in the house. We also found the gun on him; it was unloaded though; did you know that? On the not so bright side, he's going to look like the bad Terminator from T2 for the rest of his life. Someone has to go to jail for that, if nothing else to get an official statement and to get this all on the books. Here's a hint; If you're going to beat someone half to death for breaking and entering your house, make sure you do it inside the house."

"The rug though." I say. "It's Polar Bear."

"Hey Sanchez!" Johnson shouts from the street where Steve the one-eyed Cuck is still kneeling in a pathetic ball. "This is gonna be a code 999."

"What's that, say again?" Sanchez shouts back, then continues explaining to us what is going to happen. "So, he's going to the hospital. They'll see what they can do about his face and eyeball...."

"Hey Boss..." Johnson is bent over catching his breath after running up from the street. "Boss..." He's panting. "That's gonna be a Code 999."

"A 999?" Sanchez asks skeptically. "You sure about that?"

"What the bleep is a 999?" I ask Curt out of the side of my mouth.

"I don't know, I thought it meant *officer down* but I guess..." He starts.

"Yeah Boss, we got an officer down." Johnson says, finally catching his breath.

"Who, Cyclopes?" Sanchez asks, squinting and pointing.

"Yes Sir. That bag of bones over there is Hovey, Sir." Johnson the Rookie says.

"Hovey? I thought he was dead." Says Sanchez.

"Yes Sir. Me too, Sir. We all did when we lost track of him after he went undercover and then... well, you know."

"Jesus." Sanchez says, closing his notepad and giving the ole 'tash a good rubbing. After a beat he turns to us and says, "Well boys, it looks like there's good news and bad news."

"What's the good news?" Curt asks for both of us.

"The good news is, you boys just found the missing link. Officer Hovey over there was the dirtiest cop this city has seen in two generations. He went deep cover a few years back, too deep, and got mixed up with the international drug cartels. He went off the radar in '98 after bodies of his mob boss, Iain O'Leary, started piling up and it looked like Hovey was good for the hits. No one's heard from him since then. You boys are lucky to be alive; he's thought to have murdered at least eight people in cold blood.

"Uh, well...you're welcome?" Curt asks shyly.

"Well, then there's the bad news." Sanchez is reminded after that trip down crooked cop memory lane. "As dirty as he was, *is* I guess, he is still technically a cop so..."

"You two, turn around. I gotta cuff you." Johnson says taking out his handcuffs.

Sitting in the back seat of the patrol car, handcuffed behind my back with Curt, a couple things I wish needn't be said become relevant. After a substantial pause, I turn to Curt and say, "So, remember when I asked you, pretty nicely, a few times at least, if you could please, and I'm fairly certain I said please, if you could just not get us arrested. Do you remember that at all, ringing any bells, Curtis?"

"Schultz." He starts calmly, employing his anger management strategies, "Do you remember when I told you that those fucking people were nothing but trouble and to please, now Schultz, I don't know if I said please or not but I'm pretty sure I made myself crystal fucking clear, to please keep those crazy motherfuckers the mother fuck away from me? Ringing any fucking Chanukah bells?"

"Fair enough, Curtis, fair enough." I say, trying to scratch my nose with my knee. "So, what...are we even then?"

"Let's just call it a push." He says, then, "I hope that broad was worth it, Schultz."

With an involuntary eyebrow raise and a sigh, I say, "I've done worse."

The End

Made in the USA
Middletown, DE
02 February 2020

84079790R00137